AFORETHOUGHT

Colin Butler

ISBN: 9781724024930

AmazonKDP

For the good times in Toronto.

Thanks, guys!

ALSO BY COLIN BUTLER

IN THE WATER AND FIRE TRILOGY

Death by Drowning

Dangerous Knowledge

Table of Contents

Chapter 1

A death in August

"I've really enjoyed talking to you, Mr van Piet. Here, let me give you my card."

Geoffrey Slade – tall, wavy grey-white hair, bespoke suit and elegant hand-made shoes – opened his cardholder with practised ease. Willem van Piet – shorter and not easily noticed - slipped the card into his summer-weight overcoat.

"My pleasure, Mr Slade. Get home safely."

It was a Tuesday afternoon in August, and the airport was London Stansted. Time was moving on. Van Piet was thinking about a taxi, when he caught sight of a familiar figure in a baggy tweed suit.

"Hullo, Eddie. What brings you here?"

Eddie Snape was Chief Constable of Essex Police. But part of him had stayed CID, so if the right case came along, he wasn't above putting his name on it.

"Just keeping my eyes open." He glanced up at an Arrivals monitor. "What about you? What took you to Lisbon?"

"A bankers' conference. Not much fun, but they go with the job."

Willem van Piet was the British-born son of Joost van Piet, the owner of a private bank in Amsterdam called Van Piet Banking. The bank's publicity said Willem was on the advisory board, but it kept quiet about his second job, which was with the UK's Serious Risks Office – a tight-lipped Crown agency headquartered in London.

Snape looked at his watch.

"I was thinking it was time I was going," he said. "I'll run you home if you like."

"Is that legal?"

"We don't pay you, but you're on our books, so I'll say yes. You can update me on money crime as we go."

Snape had come in an unmarked Volvo estate. It belonged to Road Policing, but they weren't using it, so Snape had booked it out.

"Was that one of your banker friends came through the barrier with you?" he asked as he reversed out of a bay marked 'Essex Police'. Slade had headed for the shuttle to the Mid Stay car park.

"He's not a banker, he's a fixer, and he's not a friend either. But yes, he was in Lisbon with us. He's a middleman for tax havens. You know, off-shores."

"Not posh enough for you, then."

"Too risky more like, but he seems to be doing all right. He was like a dog with two tails about his brand new Maserati. He had several thousand pictures on his smartphone, and I got the lot."

Snape asked what his name was.

"Geoffrey Slade."

"Doesn't ring a bell. Does he live around here?"

"Near Pleshey, and there's a Mrs Slade as well. That's all I know, and all I wanted to. It took me all my time fending off dinner with them."

Snape was going back to Police HQ in Chelmsford, Essex's county town. Van Piet lived by the Blackwater estuary a bit further on, so it was no big deal to drop him off.

"We'll take the Roman road," Snape decided. "With any luck it'll be empty. It usually is."

The Roman road was a B road. It had a very long straight section, then a tight right-hander followed by another long straight. If the Romans didn't build it, they should have. As Snape had surmised, it was empty. Bone dry, too. It had been a rain-and-shine summer, but it hadn't rained in Essex for the last two or three days. Edging up to the speed limit, Snape asked van Piet how his family was doing. Van Piet said they were both in France.

"Célestine's seeing her parents, and Jackie's on school holidays, so she's gone with her. I've got some leave from the SRO, but what with Lisbon and some jobs to do at the Hall, I opted not to go with them. I wish I hadn't now."

The Hall was Gorris Hall, a fifteenth century manor house and the van Piets' pride and joy.

"So you're on your own in that great place of yours, are you?"

"Not quite. You'll remember Stafford and Celia Tyler. They've moved into the guest wing to keep me company."

"Célestine's orders?"

"Something like that."

Célestine van Piet, a retired showjumper, had opened a riding school for children in the grounds of the Hall. The Tylers helped her run it.

But Snape wasn't listening.

"Someone's feeling frisky," he muttered and checked his cameras were on as the silver Maserati he'd seen in his mirror caught them up and swept past them. "That was your Mr Slade, Willem. I hope his brakes work. He's pushing 90 already, and he's got that bend coming up."

Snape moved to put his blue lights on, then he thought better of it - some drivers like to race when they see who's behind them. But as he changed his mind, the Maserati accelerated and kept on accelerating.

Snape and van Piet both knew the bend well – the red-rimmed warning sign, the order to reduce speed, and the oversize white-on-black arrows on the bend itself. Behind the arrows were a straggly hedge, a rising stretch of scrubland, and an elongated disused gravel pit that was always full of water. The spoil had been cleared away from the end behind the arrows. In time the rest would go, and a community water sports centre would move nearer to completion.

They could see what would happen, then it did. Instead of decelerating, the Maserati powered straight on, smashed through the arrows and the hedge, and tore across the scrubland towards the gravel pit. The water caught the front wheels, the car flipped over twice with two almighty slams, then ploughed below the surface in a maelstrom of whitish bubbles. According to Snape's front camera, it had hit the arrows at 138 mph. He closed up at speed and jammed on his brakes. The blue lights were on now, and they stayed on. So did the hazard lights.

"Run through and take a look while I get some help!" he rapped to van Piet. "But stay clear of the tyre tracks!"

He called in an ambulance, Fire and Rescue, and the Major Traffic Incident Unit.

"Seal the Roman road off, nil traffic in both directions. And keep the media out. We'll talk to them when we've got something to say."

He jumped out and ran towards the gravel pit, hoping the Maserati was still afloat. But when he got there, he had to accept it had sunk and taken its driver with it.

"He could still be in an air bubble," he panted, badly out of breath. "I'll get the MRU in."

He whipped out his smartphone and called the Marine Rescue Unit at Harwich International Port.

"They're on their way," he told van Piet when he'd done. "Remotely Operated Vehicles, underwater scanners, the works - a Chinook's bringing them in. They're talking to Fire and Rescue on the way. If he's alive, they'll get him out between them."

He took a last look at the water, which was returning to cold indifference. They'd better get back to the road, he said, he didn't want any ghouls trampling over the tyre tracks. As they cleared the hedge, a Renault saloon was coming to a halt. Snape showed his ID and sent it on his way, but more vehicles might arrive before the road could be sealed off, so he took a traffic baton from the Volvo, switched it on and gave it to van Piet, while he stepped back to do more phoning. When he'd finished, he and van Piet dug in to wait. They had just two more cars and a van to move on, then they heard the sirens.

"Stay here, Willem. I've got people to talk to."

Van Piet switched off the baton and retreated into the Volvo. Snape joined him as soon as he could and reversed out of the way.

"I want to take another look at what we saw," he said, blue lights from outside reflecting on his face. He played the crash through once, then again, slowing it down here and there and freeze-framing parts of it. When he was finished, he switched on the interior light. The light outside was beginning to fade.

"That kind of car can brake on a sixpence," he mused, keeping his eye on who was doing what through his windows, "yet this one was doing nearly 140 when it left the road. Its brake lights didn't come on either, and there were no signs of braking in the tracks it left." He made up his mind. "This one's mine, Willem. I don't understand it yet, but I will. I'll phone my deputy right now."

When he'd finished, he recalled van Piet had said he was on leave.

"Tax havens and off-shores, they're just words to me. Can you get a secondment to lend me a hand with them? You've swung it before."

Van Piet had seen it happen too, and unlike Snape, he was sure Slade was dead. A heavy-duty crane lumbered past, followed by a flat-top recovery vehicle. He had no choice.

"I'll ask. I'll call Ashell House, Mr Benjamin might still be there. If not, I'll try his mobile."

Ashell House was the SRO's headquarters, and Luke Benjamin was the Director General. Mr Benjamin was busy right now, he heard, but he'd call back in fifteen minutes. While he was waiting, van Piet called Celia Tyler to let her know he'd be getting home late. Sorry, he couldn't say when. He'd find something for himself when he got back. As Snape was finishing his own call home, there was a knock on the side window, and he let down the glass. The badge said Fire and Rescue. 'Pollard' was on the name tag.

"Hullo, Wendy. What do you want to tell me?"

"The Chinook should be here any time now, Sir. We're standing by to assist once the Maserati's on dry land."

"I want that car kept as intact as possible. How will they get it out?"

"If it's in one piece and not buried in sludge, they'll work cradles underneath it and use the Chinook to pull it up. If it's smashed up, they'll do the same thing with the big pieces and let the ROVs do the rest."

"Do you think the driver's got a chance?"

He wanted her to say yes, but he knew she wouldn't.

"I don't see it, Sir. If the car sank straight away, it must have filled with water. In your place, I'd send for a hearse."

She looked up and said she had to go, the Chinook was manoeuvring in. Its lights were beaming down, and it had a full load slung underneath it. The noise and the downdraught were immense. Once it was landed, Snape bit the bullet and rang an undertaker's in Bishop's Stortford. It had a twenty-four hour number, and it was listed to take on police work.

"What about Mrs Slade?" van Piet asked him when he'd terminated.

"I haven't forgotten her, but if a death's violent, unnatural, sudden or unexplained, the coroner has to be told, and this death's all four of them. So I'll move things on with the coroner first, then I'll see to Mrs Slade."

Hettie Tait, the district coroner, was in her living room lengthening a dress for her granddaughter when the call came through. She answered after the third ring, and Snape turned up his smartphone so van Piet could hear what she said.

"I'll get a forensic pathologist out to you," she said in her usual practical way. "If he gets a move on, he can oversee the body's recovery, that's always a plus. And the post mortem can go ahead as soon as it's been identified."

"Sounds good."

"I haven't finished yet. If it helps the relatives, tell them I can release the body to the undertaker's straight after the post mortem, if the cause of death is clear, since the fp's report will be all I'll need for the inquest." She paused, and her tone of voice changed. "Death can bring a lot of pain, Eddie. It's something we have to be careful about."

Snape agreed – they'd both been there before.

After he'd terminated, he took a deep breath and asked van Piet whether Slade had mentioned his wife's first name. Van Piet replied it was Verity, and Esklivia Investments was the company he worked for. He reached over to the back seat, pulled Slade's card out of his overcoat pocket and handed it to Snape, who said,

"I'll get her located and send a couple of trained colleagues to her. I'll tell them what they can't say as well as what they can, and they can slip in about identifying the body as soon as they get the chance. With any luck she'll agree to make it soon."

The Maserati was raised at eighteen minutes past midnight. The frame was badly wrung, especially at the front, the bonnet was rammed back against where the windscreen had been, the doors were forced open and the side windows were gone, but it was essentially still in one piece. It was allowed to drain, then it was painstakingly photographed before Slade's mangled body was freed and his death confirmed by the fp. By that time two police officers – one male, one female – had called on Verity Slade to prepare her for the worst. Straight away, Verity had called her daughter, Laura Slade, who lived a few miles away in Bishop's Green. Laura had hurried an overnight bag together and driven over fast.

Benjamin called van Piet back after fifteen minutes precisely and OK-ed his secondment without too much fuss, since van Piet was on leave anyway. Van Piet then called his secretary, Tom Garry, who was at home in Barnet mending a neighbour's lawnmower. He told him to go back to Ashell House and set up a secure link with Snape's office in Chelmsford. Garry had no problem with that. It was something he'd done before.

"Copy all the pics to Tom," van Piet told Snape as they finally left the crash site, "including the ones from your Volvo. I'll get an SRO mobile couriered to you, and if a Dr Penny Warrener asks to visit the crash site, say yes. Crashes are something she's good at."

Chapter 2

The man who sold the Maserati

At 7.22 the next morning van Piet was in his study starting his report on Lisbon when his mobile buzzed. It was Snape calling from Police HQ. He'd stayed there overnight and snatched what sleep he could.

"The SRO mobile's arrived, as you can hear, and the secure link's looking good," he said. "Mrs Slade was distraught when she heard the bad news, and so was her daughter, but they've agreed to identify the body today, if someone can take them to the mortuary. I've asked the colleagues who broke the news, since the Slades know them already, and they can ask Mrs Slade whether we can speak to her soon while they're with her. If she says no, I'll have to put pressure on her, and I don't want to do that.

"That's by way of background, but for right now what I want to say is this. The dealership Slade bought his car from was on his number plates. It's called Rufus For Maseratis, and it's on the Clacton road. It's owned and managed by a man called Derek

Rufus, and we're booked in for 11.00. I say 'we', because I took it you'd want to come."

Van Piet looked wistfully at his computer screen. Writing reports was something he hated like the plague. For that reason, once he started one, he didn't like to stop till he'd got it out of the way. Even so...

"You're right, I do. How are we getting there?"

He stifled a yawn. He hadn't had much sleep himself.

"You come here first, I want a witness statement from you about last night. Then we'll take one of our cars, it'll give you a bit more standing."

Snape terminated, and feeling more than a little aggrieved, van Piet saved what he'd written for another day.

Tyler was out in the lanes getting a new pony used to traffic. Van Piet called him to tell him he had to go out, and he could be gone for some while.

"What about tea?" he heard back.

"Apologies to Celia, I'll give her a call when I know."

Snape parked outside Rufus For Maseratis at 10.58, and Rufus was openly grateful they hadn't come in a marked car. No offence, he explained, but police on the forecourt would give the place a bad name. Rufus was wiry, conspicuously fit, and looked to be in his forties. He projected success, and so did his office. Framed Maserati certificates decorated the walls, and an East Essex Triathlonners shield was prominent on his desk. No, he had no objection to Mr van Piet being present, he was always glad to help the law. And, honestly, he hadn't in the least minded Snape's early morning phone call, he'd actually been waking up already. He served Blue Mountain coffee in bone china cups and said how sorry he was to hear about Mr Slade.

"I went back to his file just before you arrived. What can I tell you about him?"

"I'm not sure what we're looking for yet," Snape began, wanting to keep things low-key. "Let's start with how long Mr Slade had had his Maserati before he lost his life."

"He took possession on 21st July, a Friday. That makes it – let me check my diary - two weeks and four days exactly. He'd already paid in full on the day he signed the deal, less his trade-in. That was 28th June, and he'd paid by cheque. If money was a problem, it didn't show."

"I thought Maseratis were taking longer than that to come through. Something about a strike somewhere. What moved him up the queue?"

"It was a cancelled order. He snapped it up."

Snape made notes as he went. Van Piet listened in.

"Tell me about this car," Snape went on. "It was fast, that's for sure."

"0-60 in 4·5 seconds. 190 flat out."

"What about stopping?"

"From 60 to zero in 100 feet. It was a very safe car."

"And Mr Slade was a safe driver, was he?"

Rufus brought his fingertips together and touched his necktie with his thumbs.

"Normally I wouldn't answer that question, but in the circumstances… The truth is, he'd told his wife he was coming to us, and she rang me up – she was in something of a state, I might add – to ask me not to sell it to him. This was on the 26th June – a Monday. We stay open late on Mondays to give the week a good start. I felt Mr Slade should take his own decisions and politely said as much, but I also said I'd recommend our New Owner's course to him, if he could come to the phone. Which I did, and he said he'd think about it."

This New Owner's course, what was that all about?

"Most drivers need help with their first fast car, and we have an arrangement with a training facility near Frinton – Ferrari and Lamborghini use it as well. Mr Slade phoned back the next day to say he'd take the course and, as I've said, he bought the car on the 28th. He turned out to have two areas of weakness, and Frinton will have them on file. Acceleration was one – the car kept getting away from him – and cornering was the other. He went back to Frinton twice more, and by his last visit he was definitely better. I know because he rang me up to tell me."

"All credit to his instructors. What about on his own?"

"He'd done the course, Mr Snape. That's really all I can say."

Snape looked at van Piet. Did he want to ask anything? Van Piet put his cup down and asked whether the car had a named mechanic to look after it.

"Absolutely, it's a major part of our policy, and if you'll forgive me, Sir, we call them engineers. Unfortunately, we had to replace Mr Slade's engineer, since he left us a week ago last Friday. We informed Mr Slade in advance, and he was happy with the change."

Van Piet asked about the engineer who'd left.

"His name was Matteo Pachini, Sir. He came to us from Italy four, could be five years ago, I'd have to re-check that. He'd been trained at Modena no less, and he turned out to be just what we needed. His parents own a hotel and restaurant in Parma, and he'd been talking off and on about going back to join them in the business. Then he came in one day and said he'd definitely be going, so he worked out his notice, and we gave him a send-off to remember us by."

Snape asked to see Pachini's file and a copy of Slade's bill of sale.

"I'll have them fetched. Can I offer you more coffee?"

They shook their heads, so he pressed a button in his designer console and asked his secretary to bring him both items. He didn't have to wait long, and van Piet wondered if she'd been told to have them ready. Like Snape, he memorised the name on her ID badge. It was Stephanie Hayward. It would go into Snape's notebook later.

Snape moved his chair so van Piet could see the file and the bill. The file's top page carried a passport-size photo of a slim-faced young man with black curly hair, naturally dark skin and soft brown eyes. His name was given as Matteo Alessandro Pachini, and his English address, which had been updated once, was 32, Walsingham Close, Clacton-on-Sea. Snape made more notes, thought for a moment, added the address of Pachini's parents and asked whether he could take a picture of the photo with his smartphone. Rufus said he could save Snape the trouble. He pressed the same button as before and this time asked for one of the spare photos of Matteo Pachini from the set marked Meet The Team.

"We all have our photos taken by a photographer from London, including people behind the scenes," he explained. "Then they're labelled, framed and put on display in our showroom. Our customers like to know who they're dealing with."

His secretary brought in a 2½" x 3½" portrait. He handed it to Snape, who looked at it, showed it to van Piet, and put it into the envelope it came with. While Snape was handing the file back, van Piet asked whether Pachini owned or rented where he lived.

"He rented. It's a buy-to-let house, and the landlady lives next door. Miss Davis is her name, and her number is 34. She owns quite a few buy-to-lets in Clacton. If any of our staff want more space or whatever, she's the one we send them to."

There was a pause. Then, still van Piet,

"You mentioned a trade-in. You must get quite a few of them. What do you do with them?"

"If they're Maseratis, we spruce them up and sell them from here. If they're any other make, I've got a used car place and body shop in Colchester. My wife's in charge there – her name's Anita, Mr Snape - and a manager takes care of the day-to-day stuff for her. I worked myself up by repairing and selling used cars, so you can't call me a snob, but I don't want other makes taking the shine off this place. I'm sure you'd say the same."

Van Piet said he probably would, and when Rufus added he made his staff park out of sight round the back, van Piet saw the sense of that as well. Snape skimmed through the bill of sale. He couldn't see anything wrong with it.

"I see Mr Slade bought an anti-theft package," he noted as he gave it back.

"He certainly did. It was part of the original order, but I'd have pushed it anyway. It's light years ahead of the standard one, and top cars attract thieves, I'm sorry to say. You must know all about that."

Snape said he did, they lived in a wicked world. He asked Rufus how long he'd known Slade. Rufus didn't blink.

"Oh, it must be fifteen years. I got to know him on a flight home from Bologna. The used car business in Colchester was doing well, but I wanted a Maserati franchise to fill a gap in the market I'd spotted, so I'd been to Modena to talk things over. Money was the problem, as you'd expect, but anyway, I found myself sitting next to Mr Slade on the way back. He'd been to Bologna on a conference, and I told him where I'd been and why. He was interested enough to invite me and Mrs Rufus to his house in Theydon Bois, and he and Mrs Slade went through my business plan. They liked it, and to cut a long story short, they offered to loan us the money against our used car business at 1% less than the banks were asking."

"And you said yes."

"No question, and it's paid off in spades."

Van Piet wondered whether he and Mrs Rufus had invested in any of Esklivia's off-shore deals.

"Very much so. We've done well out of them, and so has the taxman. Mr Snape can go through our accounts any time he likes, everything's there in black and white. Confidentiality respected, of course."

Snape nodded his appreciation and changed tack.

"Can you tell us where you were between 5.00 and 9.00 last night?" he asked.

Rufus leaned forward with a smile and tapped the triathlonners' shield.

"I was in the swimming pool in Clacton Leisure Centre. So was Mrs Rufus. It was club night for Essex Swimmers, so there were plenty of people with us. They'll vouch for us, if you ask them."

Snape finished his notes and thanked Rufus for his time. Rufus said he was only too eager to help. He'd be going for a training run shortly - he liked to run during his lunchtimes - but if there was anything else he could tell them, he'd be there all afternoon.

When Snape and van Piet were outside, Snape looked at his watch.

"There's a transport café down the road from here," he said. "We'll get something to eat there, then we'll take a look at where Pachini used to live. Something's not right, Willem, I'm sure of it. We'll see if this Miss Davis can make things any clearer."

Chapter 3

The landlady

Walsingham Close was a quiet, middle-class street with 1960s three-bedroom houses on either side. They were all well maintained and all detached. Number 32 looked empty, and the For Rent sign made it look emptier still. When Snape rang 34's doorbell, there were quick sounds of footsteps in the hall, then a friendly-looking, fair-haired woman in her middle to late forties was standing in the doorway. Snape showed his ID, explained he'd come from Rufus For Maseratis and said he was making enquiries about a recent tenant of hers, a Mr Matteo Pachini. He didn't say why, and he noticed she didn't ask. She simply stood there smiling and waited for him to go on. He asked whether she could show him round Number 32, and she said, of course, it was no trouble at all. She'd bring the rent book too, she was sure he'd want to see it, and no, she didn't mind in the least van Piet not being a policeman.

"Give me a minute," she twittered amiably, "I need to close a programme down. I work at home, I'm pleased to say. I'm a freelance translator."

When she re-emerged, she had the rent book clasped against her handbag and a set of keys on a ring.

"You're lucky to catch me in," she chirruped as she walked them briskly from her own front gate to next door's. "I've been staying with friends in Bristol – Linda and Gregory Hales their names are, since I'm sure you'll want to know - and I didn't get back till midday today. It's a *very* long drive, I have to say – I hardly stopped at all, and it still took me well over four hours. But stay in touch is my motto and always has been. It's paid off over the years, I can tell you, and none of us is getting any younger."

Snape asked her when she'd driven over there.

"Last Sunday morning first thing. I thought there'd be less traffic on a Sunday, but I couldn't have been more wrong. August holidays, of course, but they'd completely slipped my mind. I'll write Linda and Gregory's address down for you before you go, I expect you like everything just so, being in the police. I know how it is, I'm exactly the same."

They started upstairs and progressed methodically downwards. The rooms were all furnished, and though they'd been cleaned, Snape thought they could do with re-decorating. As they were sitting in the living room, he asked whether Pachini had left anything behind.

"Nothing at all. Once he'd handed in his notice, he started to get rid of his things till a suitcase was all he needed. He was very well organised."

"What about his car? I take it he drove to work."

27

"Yes, he did. He sold it to one of his workmates, and it changed hands on his last day there. His workmate brought him home and drove off with it, I saw him drop him off."

"So when did he actually move out?"

She checked the rent book.

"July 28th, that's a week ago last Friday. That's when he finished at Mr Rufus's place. Mr Rufus laid on a farewell party, and he left the same evening."

Snape asked her to take him through how it had happened.

"When he left, you mean? Well, his workmate dropped him off at seven fifteen or so, and about twenty minutes later, he came round mine to say goodbye. Apparently a friend was picking him up, and he'd be staying with this friend till he caught his plane. Don't ask me where his friend lived, because I simply don't know, but Mr Pachini's idea was to stay in England for a tiny bit longer so he could visit all the people he'd got to know. I thought it was a lovely idea, and I said so as soon as he told me. Anyway, after he'd said goodbye, he went next door again, and at about a quarter to nine another car pulled up. I went to my window to give him a wave, he put his keys through the letter box exactly as I'd told him to, and then he was gone. I don't mind telling you, Mr Snape, I shall miss him. I thought he was sweet."

There was a pause while Snape checked his notes.

"Had he bought his flight ticket, do you know?"

"There you have me, I don't think he ever mentioned it. No, I'm sure he didn't, it's the sort of thing I'd remember."

Van Piet looked up from the rent book, which he'd picked up following a nod from Davis to say he could.

"I see he paid quarterly in advance."

"That's right, and this time he paid to the end of September. In cash it was, on the nail, as they say. I returned his deposit on the day before he left, less a deduction for the utilities and a smaller one for wear and tear. That was in cash again, as you can see. It was what he wanted, and who was I to argue? I expect he was between banks."

"That could be. Do you know which bank he used?"

"Lloyds in Clacton."

Snape wanted to know what kind of car he'd left in.

"Just an ordinary family saloon. It was white, if that helps."

Would she recognise the driver if she saw him again? Or her?

"Oh dear, I have to say no to that, Mr Snape. Now you mention it, it could well have been a woman, I never gave it a thought. The streetlamps had come on by then, but they make the insides of cars even darker, don't they, and whoever was driving had one of these tracksuit tops on with the hood up. I saw that much when the interior light came on, but to tell you the truth, I was far too busy waving to Mr Pachini to notice who else was in the car."

Snape kept her talking a bit longer, and then it was time to go. He gave her a sheet of paper from his notebook, lent her a pen and waited patiently while she wrote down the Hales's names and address. When she'd finished, van Piet asked her for one of her business cards. Looking flattered, she opened her handbag and placed one in his hand. It gave her first name as Barbara, plus her e-mail address and phone numbers, and it said her languages were English, German and Spanish.

"You must be fluent in all three languages if you can earn your living from them," van Piet said as he added her house address. "That's quite an achievement."

"Not really, though I'm glad you think so. I grew up in Hampstead, but my father was German and my mother was Spanish, so I have three first languages. Davis isn't a German name I grant you, but when I was ten, my parents became British citizens, and we all became Davises shortly after that. My parents were textile experts in the Victoria and Albert Museum, that's how they met in fact. They felt very British working there, they were more British than the British in some ways, so what with one thing and another, they decided to go the whole hog and become British nationals. But I must add, that wasn't the reason they changed our name, if that's what you're thinking. They changed it because I was being teased at school, or so they said at the time. My father's surname was Winckler, so I was called Winkle, and I hated it. But my parents felt they were more Davis than Winckler, so perhaps they'd have changed it anyway."

Van Piet said it was a nice story, and Davis was opening the front door for them when Snape asked her whether she knew a Geoffrey or a Verity Slade. The smile disappeared, she closed the door, and she said she knew both of them well. Mr Slade's death had shocked her dreadfully, she'd heard about it on her car radio as she'd been driving home, and Mrs

Slade must be in a terrible state. She was going to ring her during the afternoon, but she was still plucking up the courage to do it. But to answer Snape's question more fully, she'd got to know Mr Rufus first, because when he was setting up as a Maserati dealer, he'd contacted her about a couple of buy-to-lets for two of his new staff. He'd seen one of her adverts and given her a call.

"After that, we became close," she went on. "Not personally, you understand, he's a married man, and I don't interfere in things like that, but professionally, if you get my meaning. I've met Mrs Rufus several times in fact, and we couldn't get on better, I shouldn't want you to get the wrong impression. Now, where was I? Ah, yes, Mr Rufus told me the owner of a company called Esklivia was helping him with his financing – that was Mrs Slade – and a bit later he said Esklivia was putting some very nice investments his way and was I interested? Well, I was doing very nicely, thank you very much, but you can always do with a pound or two more, so I said I could be, and that's how I got to know the Slades, because they came round to see me."

"And you're still investing through Esklivia, are you?"

"I'd be a fool not to, Mr Snape, the returns are so good, even with the tax taken off, which I'm very particular about, unlike some people you read about. I could have had a cheap loan as well, but I didn't need it, so I said thank you, but no thank you to that. I've hung on to the investments, though, and I don't mind admitting it. It's nice to go to bed richer than when you got up without having to do anything for it."

The smile was back and she was still chirruping when they reached the gate. She gave them a big wave as they closed the car doors.

"Clacton Leisure Centre and now Bristol," Snape grumbled as he and van Piet motored back to Chelmsford. "I'll have them both checked, but if these people need alibis, they're coming up with some good ones. Then there's Pachini. Did he know more than he should have? Is that why he's disappeared?"

Snape kept his mind on the road after that, so van Piet called Celia Tyler to say when he thought he might be back. He felt guilty he couldn't be sure, but she said not to worry, she'd leave him something he could heat up. With his conscience halfway eased, he sent an encrypted text to Garry asking him to find out about Davis's buy-to-lets, and another one to Joost van Piet asking him to run the rule over Esklivia Investments. Everything was vague at the moment, he told his father, but that could alter, and he'd be in touch if it did. After another two or three miles, he sent a second text to Garry asking him to research Davis's background. She'd given two reasons for her name change. Was that to mask a third?

They were on the outskirts of Chelmsford when a call reached Snape from Police HQ, and he pulled over to take it. Mrs and Miss Slade had identified Geoffrey Slade's body at 1.10 pm, and the forensic pathologist had begun his post mortem shortly afterwards – grizzling mightily about being rushed, by all accounts. Mrs Slade had said Snape and van Piet could come to her house at 10.00 the next morning, and Miss Slade would be there too. Snape was reminded the colleagues who'd taken the Slades to the mortuary had come in before shift to do it. He replied August was tricky with people going away, but he'd see them right when he could. That went into his notebook too.

He terminated and re-started the car.

"Mrs Slade lives in a village called Lower Mindle," he said to van Piet, who'd been sharing the message. "Do you know it?"

"Only by name. I don't think I've ever been there."

"You haven't missed much, it's just a few upmarket houses with a lot of land round them. Mrs Slade's is called The Lodge, and County Planning says it stands in eight and a half acres, so it's not as big as your place, but mine would disappear in it. I'll get someone to pick you up at 9.00."

Snape was feeling nervy. Interviewing upset people was something he'd never enjoyed.

"I know I've been pushing things," he went on, glad to be able to share how he felt, "but if I could avoid seeing them this soon, I would. I just hope we get something out of it."

Chapter 4

Inside The Lodge

Access to The Lodge was between two lofty
wrought-iron gates made of vertical spiked
rods held together by horizontal bands. They
were bolted to red-brick rectangular towers that
looked as if they'd been copied from a fortress, and
the high curtain walls that led off them were made of
the same red brick. They were meant to look
forbidding, and they did. They screened The Lodge's
grounds from the road, they were topped with razor
wire, and they carried regular warnings the entire
estate was guarded by cctv. Van Piet noticed the
cameras were wireless.

The Lodge itself didn't come into view until
the evergreens lining most of its drive had been
passed through. When it did, the bricks it was made
of were visibly older and warmer.   Its spacious
forecourt, like the drive, was made of fine-grained
granite setts, and an ornate fountain burbled idly in
the middle of it. To the right was a block of garages
with a black Range Rover parked outside one of
them, and to the left was a still, broad lake

surrounded by a large and immaculate lawn that swept away to a distant line of poplars. On the lakeshore nearest the house was a dark-tiled hut built of fashionable Cotswold stone. Some deck chairs and a picnic table with matching benches stood on a wooden sundeck, and a landing stage jutted out into the lake. A rowing boat was moored against it. Like everything else, it was in mint condition.

Snape eased to a halt outside the front door, and as he did so, a woman with expensively styled dark brown hair came out to meet them. She looked to be about thirty, and while at first she seemed delicately built, from close up she looked strong, as if she played racquet sports a lot. The sun had been veiled by clouds all morning, and she was wearing a light cardigan over her frock. But what really caught Snape's and van Piet's attention was her face: It was unnaturally white, and her eyes were red and puffy.

"Hullo," she said, looking firmly at them. "I'm Laura Slade, Geoffrey Slade's daughter. It was me you talked to from the gate."

She dabbed her eyes with a handkerchief she was gripping in her hand.

"I'm sorry, I don't seem able to stop crying," she added quickly and not nearly so firmly. "It's been such an awful shock. But please, come in. My mother is expecting you."

She led them into a sumptuously furnished drawing room in the back of the house. The ceiling was stuccoed and gilded, and a vast fireplace promised warmth and cheer for the dark months of the year. Tall windows gave onto a knot garden framed by Portland stone walkways along all four sides. Beyond the garden was a brick wall with a weather-beaten oak door in it, and outhouses formed a terrace along one of the garden's shorter sides. The garden wall and the outhouses were built with the same warm bricks as the house, except for the furthest outhouse. Its bricks were identical to those in the gate towers and the curtain walls.

Verity Slade was sitting in an armchair by the fireplace, her hands resting limply in her lap. As Snape and van Piet came in, she stood up slowly, and a dutiful smile covered her exhausted features. She was twenty-four years older than her daughter, but time had treated her well. Her hair was still more auburn than grey, her face was largely free of lines, and her figure had stayed trim. Like her daughter, she was wearing a cardigan against the weather.

As soon as she could, she said, as if she was determined to get it in first,

"When my father died before his time, I cried and cried, it hurt so much. And when my mother died two years later because she couldn't live without him, I cried and cried again. Since then, I've always believed I could manage grief if it came my way yet again, but now I know I can't. I'm telling you this, Mr Snape and you, too, Mr van Piet, in case I have to break off while you're here. For the moment, however, I feel I can cope. Laura has made tea and coffee for you, it's on the sideboard behind you. Please help yourselves, and then I'll answer your questions."

Self-consciously they fetched some coffee. Laura dabbed her eyes once more and discreetly blew her nose.

"We're trying to understand how your husband met his death," Snape began, trying not to sound too official. "It could have been an accident, but it was witnessed, and there are certain things we have to account for. Tell me, did Mr Slade suffer from depression?"

"Depression? Ah, I see. No, never. He was the happiest of men, always looking on the bright side. That's right, isn't it, Laura?"

Laura nodded, her hand against her mouth.

"And he had no money worries?"

"None at all, he was very wealthy. I can say that categorically, because we held most of our funds jointly. We always have done."

Van Piet remembered Slade had paid for his Maserati by cheque.

"Could you have blocked Mr Slade's spending at any time?" he asked.

"Good heavens, no. He could always prove which money was his, if he had to, and any court of law would back him up."

Snape consulted at his notes.

"His money came," he said, "from Esklivia Investments. Was Esklivia jointly owned as well?"

"No, Geoffrey owned no part of it. He could have done, but he didn't want the responsibility. He liked travelling, meeting clients and doing deals, but that's where it stopped. I founded Esklivia with a bequest from my father when Geoffrey and I were working for Barclays Bank in London. We were already married by then, but from the start I paid him a salary plus commissions – they were both incredibly tiny - because that was what he wanted. We kept to the same arrangement as things improved, and it suited us both perfectly."

Snape wondered whether there were any stresses in the business that might have got to Mr Slade.

"No, none at all. Esklivia now has prime office space in Lombard Street, and we – I - have this lovely country house, which we also owned jointly, till my husband was taken from me. Laura works for Esklivia, she's Head of Compliance, and a bright young computer expert we poached from J.P. Morgan is both our Head of IT and Laura's partner. So, we're a family firm in the best sense of the phrase, and in case your next question is how Laura and her partner are paid, they're both salaried and taxed at source. Esklivia is an honest company, Mr Snape. We make a lot of money, but we pay every penny we owe."

She paused to gather herself, so Snape turned to Laura and asked her what her partner's name was.

"Millicent.   Millicent Cottrell," she replied. "We all call her Millie."

Snape wrote it all down, making sure of the spellings, since his own spelling could be unconventional.

Van Piet returned to Verity. He wondered how long she'd lived in The Lodge.   She counted up mentally.

"Twelve years, I make it. Geoffrey and I both started out in rooms, and we continued to rent after we were married till we could afford a house in Theydon Bois we liked very much. Five years later we bought this house on a twenty year mortgage, and we've added to it till it was exactly as we wanted it. We were also able to move Esklivia out of much smaller premises in Gracechurch Street to where it is now."

She stopped short.

"And now Geoffrey's gone," she resumed falteringly, "but his things are still all here... I know he's dead because I had to see him yesterday, but - "

Her control ran out and she subsided into sobbing. Laura, struggling with tears herself, looked anxiously at Snape for guidance.

"If it was up to me, Miss Slade," he said, feeling discomforted but still a policeman, "I'd stop right now. But I must ask three more questions, then we'll leave you in peace."

"Can I can answer them for you? My mother will hear what I say."

"I need to know about the Maserati your father was killed in. Do you know how he came to buy it?"

"He'd talked about it off and on for I don't know how long. It was a vanity project really, and if you ask me, it should have stayed that way. But he had the money, so he made up his mind. He knew the dealer, you see, they had a longstanding business relationship. My mother was frightened for him because he'd had one or two scrapes in the past – to tell you the truth, he'd reached the point where his insurer was making difficulties - and when he said he was definitely going ahead, she rang the dealer and tried to prevent the sale."

"Were you told that or were you present?"

"I was in this room, sitting in this chair. My mother and I had spent most of the day in Lombard Street, but there were still some legal matters we had to discuss, so I'd come back with her for dinner. It happened to be a day the dealer stayed open late, so she caught him while he was there. He said he'd suggest my father take some lessons, presumably because he didn't want to lose the sale. As you can imagine, my mother was less than convinced, but she gave in because she didn't have any choice. So, *very* unwillingly – that's right, isn't it, Mum? – she handed the phone to my father. She told me later she secretly hoped the lessons would teach him the hard way he had to get rid of the car, but unfortunately they didn't. And now this. I can't put into words how terrible it is."

Snape turned back to Verity, who was drying her eyes. How would she replace her husband at Esklivia?

"He had his assistants," she answered. "I'll promote one of them to take the routine work over, and the more sensitive commissions will come to me until I can get a handle on things. It shouldn't be too difficult, I've always looked over his shoulder. Now, what's your third question?"

"One you'll appreciate I have to ask. Can you tell me where you were between 5.00 and 9.00 Tuesday evening?"

"I was here all the time."

"And you, Miss Slade. Where were you?"

"I was at home in Bishop's Green."

"All the time?"

"All the time, Mr Snape. I didn't leave the house till my mother phoned me. That was after your colleagues had been to see her."

Snape closed his notebook and thanked them for answering his questions. Verity asked Laura to show their guests to the door. Van Piet and Snape had already stepped outside and were turning to say goodbye when Laura spoke with such pent-up passion, it was like a furnace door swinging open.

"I didn't want to say this in front of my mother, gentlemen, but I want you to know this. I loved my father more than any other person on this earth, he was the sun, moon and stars of my life. If anyone has harmed him, and I appreciate there's an 'if', I want that person destroyed."

Snape, startled by her vehemence, assured her everything would be done to find out the truth - he didn't know what else to say. Laura reined herself in.

"I'm sorry," she said, all politeness again. "I didn't mean to put you under pressure, and I'm sure you'll do your best." She blinked and gave him a sociable smile. "I'll open the gate from here as you go, then you won't have to wait when you reach the road."

"I'm glad that's over," Snape grunted as they left The Lodge's grounds. "They were both suffering all right, there was no acting there. Did you get anything?"

"The house is four hundred years old at a guess, but these walls and the gateposts are new, and so is one of the outhouses. So I'm wondering why the Slades had a complete extra outhouse constructed when they already had a set of them. Can you find out who the builder was?"

Snape cleared some spots of rain from the windscreen.

"The new outhouse is called the boulting house, County Planning told me. That's boulting with a 'u'. I suppose you know what that is, but I had to ask."

"It's where flour is sifted through sackcloth to get rid of the bran. The others would have been a bake house, a brew house, a dairy, and probably a stable. But what about the builder? Can you trace him?"

"I might be able to. When the builders move in, the complaints never stop, and we write them all down, so you're in with a chance. I'll ask Records and let you know."

He decided to head for Pleshey. There was a cafeteria near the castle that served home-made stew and dumplings. While they were letting theirs cool, he said out of nowhere,

"Slade's trade-in was a Lexus GS, we know that from Driver and Vehicle Licensing. If the deal had been blocked and he'd kept it, he might be alive today."

"And?"

"Don't ask me. I've thought about it three times and come up with three different answers. That's what happens when you're out of facts."

Later that evening, with the rain coming down steadily, van Piet's mobile buzzed. It was Snape. The name of the Slades' builder was Neville Thurston. He did the boulting house, the gateposts and the walls as a single job, and he came from Leicestershire to do it. He owned a granite quarry near Mountsorrel, and he laid the drive and forecourt as well.

"He's still in business," Snape continued. "You can check his website under Thurston's Quarry and Building Services, but one other thing before you do. I've had a fax of the fp's report. Slade died from catastrophic cerebral trauma, which means his brain shut down so fast, he didn't have time to die of anything else. There were no traces of alcohol and no traces of drugs, so we can forget about those. The coroner's happy to release the body, and when I told Mrs Slade, she said her Chelmsford solicitor had recommended an undertaker's she could trust. It turned out to be Chatsley and Sons - you might have seen their place when you've come into town. They've been in Chelmsford for donkey's years."

Snape terminated, and van Piet went into Thurston's website. It showed a robust-looking man in squeaky clean denim dungarees smiling full-face at the camera from next to a glistening Range Rover - presumably a pitch to the upper end of the market. His greying hair and the lines round his eyes made him look much the same age as Verity Slade, and when van Piet clicked into About Thurston's Quarry, he read it went back four generations before Neville Thurston, who'd been the first Thurston to branch out into building. Included under Contact was a private address, and van Piet noted it down. The Range Rover's registration he already knew. He'd seen it that morning outside The Lodge.

Chapter 5

An ominous find

It was Friday morning, and Laura had decided to stay with her mother for a little while longer, leaving Cottrell to commute between Bishop's Green and Lombard Street on her own. According to Cottrell, Esklivia was running itself, but Verity thought she was saying that to stop her worrying, so over breakfast she told Laura she'd phone Esklivia herself when she got back from seeing Mr Chatsley senior. She'd be taking a taxi both ways. Parking in Chelmsford was always a problem, and it looked as if it might rain again.

"Are you sure you don't want me to come with you?" Laura asked.

Her mother was still looking very upset.

"I told you last night, my sweet, I want to be alone with your father for one last time. I've got to manage without him now, so memories will be all I have. You'll understand better when you go this afternoon. You won't want anyone else there either."

There was a prickly silence after that. As Laura was pouring herself more tea, she heard the distant sound of drilling. It was coming from the boulting house, and Verity said it was Neville Thurston working on a job.

"Oh, really!" Laura snapped. "Must he be here right now? He was here yesterday morning as well. You should have asked him to stay away till all this is over."

Verity stiffened, and her knuckles showed white.

"If you talked to Mr Thurston when he was here," she responded angrily, "you'd know more about what he was doing. But you've never liked him, and since your father passed away, you've been like the walking dead yourself, mooning about the house from room to room all day. I arranged for Mr Thurston to come before your father died, and the appointment is standing because I need it to. If I let things slide now, I'll let them slide for the rest of my life, and I'm not prepared to do that. It's not just Mr Thurston either. The gardeners will come this afternoon, and after I've spent time with your father, I shall go to the bank. Please don't treat me like a child, Laura, it's unbecoming for both of us."

Laura reached across the breakfast table and squeezed her mother's hand. Not for the first time, she noticed how bony it was. It was one of the few give-aways the years were getting to Verity, and it made Laura feel extra loving towards her.

"My fault," she said softly. "I didn't think. Sorry." Then, wanting to make things seem like normal again, she asked matter-of-factly, "What's Mr Thurston up to anyway?"

"We're getting damp in the boulting house, and he's drilling holes in the walls to put chemicals in. You say he was here yesterday morning, and so he

45

was, but what you didn't know was that he'd driven from Leicestershire the evening before and stayed in a hotel in Chelmsford just to start here on time. He was doing his assessing and measuring when you saw him yesterday, then he drove back to Leicestershire to get what he needed, and he came back last night to be ready for this morning. I pay him well for his trouble, but I still think very few tradesmen would go to such lengths. I'm grateful to him for it."

She was winding herself up again, and Laura felt she was misusing her grief so as not to be contradicted. It made her scratchy again.

"But he was here just a fortnight ago," she came back. "A fortnight ago yesterday. I remember quite clearly saying hullo to him. What was he doing that time?"

"He was checking the drive, the forecourt, and the pointing in the walls he built. It's all in his maintenance contract, which you've read, and he was gone the next day. I wish I'd noticed the damp before he left, but I hadn't, so I gave him a call and asked him to do something about it, because the last thing I want is mould setting in. And now if you'll excuse me, I really must get myself ready. My taxi must be half way here by now."

But she didn't get up straight away. Instead, she stopped short, compressed her lips and looked down at the table. When she spoke again, her tone was completely different.

"Now it's my turn to say sorry, poppet, I shouldn't have reacted like that. Don't worry about clearing up. I'll do it when I get back."

She kissed Laura on the forehead and went out, leaving Laura dismayed with herself. She'd seen how edgy her mother had been, but she'd still had to argue with her. Why hadn't she just shut up?

When the taxi arrived and the front door was finally shut, Laura stood in the hallway feeling completely depressed. But after a little while the intermittent drilling, which she could still faintly hear, pulled her out of herself. She realised she was completely alone in the house itself, and a feeling she knew from her teens welled up unbidden inside her. Later than some adolescents, she'd been curious enough about her parents' private lives to poke and pry when they were out of the house to see what she could find out. There was always the danger of getting caught, of course, but that only sent the erotic charge higher up the scale. She wanted to do much the same thing now, not out of left-over prurience, but because she might learn more about her father's death. Laura and her Daddy, that's how it had always been, and the fact the police were asking questions had introduced something so jagged into her mourning, she had to do something about it. She glanced at the hall clock and calculated her mother would be out for two hours at least – probably longer, if she went to the bank, which she'd definitely do now she'd said she would. Suddenly deciding, Laura cleared the breakfast things away to make her feel in charge of herself again. Then she started the dishwasher and made for the main staircase.

Her parents had slept in the same bedroom since they'd all moved into The Lodge from Theydon Bois. It was at the back of the house, and it had a panoramic view through either of its windows over the Essex countryside. They'd never locked their door and it wasn't locked now, as Laura depressed the ornate brass handle. She felt tense and, despite herself, she also felt grubby. If she'd known anyone was trespassing in the bedroom she shared with Millie, she'd have been outraged. But she still went in.

The room had the heaviness of other people's secrets, and it smelled intimately of bed linen. The carpet was so thick, her feet sank into it, and her father's bedside table still had some of his things on it – a small earthenware bowl for keys and coins, a life of Donald Campbell with a book-mark in it, a box of tissues, a photo of Verity taken on a windy day in Cornwall, and another one of Laura with the Eiffel Tower in the background. They were so poignant, she half-wished she hadn't seen them. Her mother's side of the bed had been slept in and re-made, but when she looked for the photo of her father which normally stood on her bedside table, she saw it had disappeared. That made sense, she reasoned, it must be too painful for her mother to see it there now. She opted to go through the cupboards first, then the walk-in wardrobes, and finally the two chests of drawers. They formed a matching pair on either side of the room.

The cupboards had spare linen in them, extra boxes of tissues, shoes - the usual things - and if there were any secrets in the wardrobes, she didn't find them. That left the chests of drawers. She went through her father's first, fighting hard not to rush as her nerves began to fray. There were shirts, handkerchiefs, several bow ties, a black cummerbund, a paisley one, underwear, pullovers and cardigans. But that was all, even though she felt right to the backs of the drawers. Then she went to her mother's. First came a drawer full of underwear, which she felt acutely embarrassed to go through. Then came blouses and tops, followed by pullovers, cardigans and lightweight scarfs. It had never occurred to her before how many changes of clothes her mother had, and she was already concluding she was wasting her time when she pulled open the bottom drawer. On the left hand side were shawls - mostly cashmere, though some were made of silk - and on the right were silk, satin and cashmere wraps. They looked totally innocent, just lying there in neatly folded piles, but there were a lot of them, and just the quantity could be useful for hiding something. So, doing her best not to disturb anything, she worked her hand in layer by layer and pressed gently down as well. It was under the very last layer of shawls and right at the back that she felt something hard. Gingerly, she pulled it out, her hand trembling. It was the missing photo of her father, and it was still in its frame. It must have been taken out from behind its glazing and then put back, because two thick black lines ran diagonally across it in the form of an X. They'd been made with a marker pen, and they crossed her father out. They looked recent too, and they terrified her.

"They must be for closure," she compelled herself to think. "They can't be for anything else. They're Mum's way of accepting Daddy is dead."

She held the photo for a long while. It was obviously posed, but as she looked at it, her father's sense of humour, his quirkiness, and his endless capacity for love came alive again. It was too much for her. Tears forced their way into her eyes, and all she wanted to do was let them flow. But she was afraid they might run onto the glazing, so she laid the photo on top of the drawers till she'd fought them back. Then she placed it back under the shawls, taking immense care to leave everything, so far as she could tell, exactly as she'd found it.

She closed the drawer and looked at her watch. She felt she had plenty of time yet so, with her mind still on her father, she moved unthinkingly near one of the windows to take in the room as a whole just as Thurston, who was covered in dust, was making his way along the back of the knot garden towards the oak door. He was fetching a flask of tea from his van, which he was using instead of his Range Rover and which he'd parked out of sight behind the wall. Perhaps because Laura was moving, he glanced up, but she retreated instantly into the room, and she was sure he hadn't noticed her, because he didn't let his eyes settle on her. Anyway, there was rain on the window panes, so he couldn't have possibly seen in. It must have come on during the last little while, and she wondered why she hadn't noticed it.

Once she was downstairs again, she was at a loss what to do next. She sat around for a while, but she didn't fancy reading any of the magazines that leaned side by side in their polished fruitwood rack, so she settled for making a fresh cup of tea. In the kitchen, her mind kept returning to the photo she'd found, but it was only when she was pouring hot water into the pot that it occurred to her that her mother might have crossed out the photo *before* her father had died. Instantly she told herself not to be so silly, but the thought wouldn't go away, so she let the tea draw while she compulsively tidied up. Then she filled her cup up and took it into a small drawing room overlooking the forecourt. It was a room she liked to think of as hers, and it was far enough away to screen out any drilling, though on reflection she thought it might have stopped. The tea tasted good, she gradually relaxed, and the foolish idea she'd had about the photo faded away as she stared at the rainy window panes. She let her thoughts drift wherever they wanted to. She'd slept badly the night before, and now it was catching up with her. She began to doze off.

The doorbell made her come to with a start, and she was still dragging her eyes open as she made for the front door. Thurston was standing outside, and he'd clearly cleaned himself up. The gardeners used a converted barn for storing things in, and they could wash and change in there as well when they'd finished their work, though they tended not to. Thurston must have a key to it. Rain was still sprinkling down, but he made no attempt to come in.

"Sorry if I disturbed you, Miss," he said affably. "I just wanted to say I'm off now, and I'd be grateful if you'd open the gates for me. I've tidied up as much as I can, but there's still a lot of dust where I've been drilling, so I've left the dust sheets where they were."

"Are they yours or ours?"

"They're mine, but I can pick them up another time. I've filled in where I've gone into the walls, and when I come back, I'll make the whole thing good so nobody will know I've been here."

"Thank you, it's very kind of you," was all Laura could manage.

She asked about locking the boulting house up.

"It's already done, Miss. I called Mrs Slade on her smartphone when I finished, and she's locked it up remotely."

Simply and straightforwardly, she wanted him to go away. She was worried he might say something about her father, how sorry he was or something like that, and she didn't want to hear it just then. On top of that, if he'd been speaking to her mother, he might have said something about seeing her upstairs, if in fact he had seen her and – it dawned on her - if he knew whose room she'd been in. But why should he know that?

"Let me give you this key back," he finished with. "It's for the barn the gardeners use. Mrs Slade let me have it this morning."

"I can open every door in this house except the one to the boulting house," she thought resentfully as she took the key from him. "I've never been in there either. That's something I ought to change."

After Thurston had gone, she felt fear steal over her. She was alone in a house that wasn't hers, and her father's photo seemed threatening again. She still felt afraid when her mother came back. The cremation would take place on August 24th, a Thursday, Verity informed her with a mixture of exasperation and defiance. That meant a lot had to be done in very little time, but it was better than waiting till 29th September, which was the next nearest date on offer. It wasn't until Laura left for the undertaker's herself that her fear dwindled into the background. August 24th – she ran through the dates in her head – that was in a fortnight's time, less a day. By then, she had to know what had really happened to her father, or she'd never feel he and she were at rest.

Chapter 6

"That would make it murder"

While Laura Slade had been falling out with her mother, Snape and van Piet had been driving to Brunel University in west London. It was named after Isambard Kingdom Brunel, one of Britain's greatest engineers, and it had a reputation to go with the name. They'd had rain on and off all the way, but Snape was in upbeat mood because according to van Piet, who'd arranged the meeting, he'd learn exactly what had happened to Geoffrey Slade's car.

"If I hadn't gone into banking, I'd have been an engineer," van Piet mentioned casually as they finally drove down Kingston Lane. "Tried to be, anyway."

"It's no good thinking like that, Willem. It only makes you dissatisfied."

Being a policeman was everything to Snape, he couldn't imagine any other life.

"Would you like to say who Penny Warrener is now?" he went on. "I know the name, I've let her onto the crash site, and now I'm going to meet her, but I still don't know who she is."

"She's a kinetic physicist. She analyses how things move and why."

"What things?"

"Bullets, aeroplanes, you name it – if they move, she's the expert. She works for Brunel, but she also works for the SRO, and I didn't want you to know that until you had to. Now you do, I'll ask you to keep it to yourself."

Van Piet collected his entry permit from the Eastern Gateway Building, signed Snape in, and Snape was quick to grab a space on the Visitors' crowded car park as someone else drove off. They were near enough to the newly-opened Newton-Dirac research complex for them not to get too wet, and Warrener was waiting for them in the foyer. A brightly-lit corridor led to a door marked Kinetic Physics, and she opened it with an iris scanner and a palm reader. The blinds in her office were lowered, and the equipment she needed was set up on standby.

"The percolator's bubbling nicely," she said as she showed them where to sit. But they could hear and smell it anyway, and after she'd handed the coffee round, she got straight to the point. "Willem's told me why you've come, Mr Snape, and Tom Garry's sent me the pics. I'll run through the ones from your Volvo first, if you'd look at this screen. This one is from your rear-view camera. It's got a good long reach, and you can see the Maserati in the distance. Now it's catching up with you, and as it overtakes you, your rear-view camera loses it. Does anything strike you so far?"

Snape said it was exceeding the speed limit.

"That's right. It was doing 78·9 mph on a road restricted to 60 as it reached you. But you'll notice its acceleration was fairly gradual for a car of its class."

"Novice driver. He hadn't had it long."

"That could be. Now watch this – it's from your front-view camera this time, and again the long reach is helpful. Here he is passing your bonnet, and as he moves back into your lane, his speed is 89·4 mph, so he's building it up, though not nearly as aggressively as he could. But now, out of nowhere, he's accelerating hard, and he slams into the arrows at 138mph. So let me ask you: Why should all that be?"

"He said on Facebook he'd give his new car some welly. He'd do it on a long straight road near where he lived."

"All right, but you'd think, if he'd wanted to gun the engine, he'd have started sooner so he could slow down into the bend. Let's take another look. I'll run it a bit faster to help you."

They watched again, and this time Snape saw it.

"There's a wobble just before he goes for it."

"I saw it too, so I went through all the other pics Tom sent me. They turned out to be so interesting, I drove over to the Roman road yesterday with a couple of colleagues, and we took a good look round despite the rain. We took some readings with a theodolite, then we put a drone up and took some pics from the air. I'll bring them up now."

She showed the long first straight of the Roman road, the bend on its own and the crash site from the arrows onwards so Snape and van Piet could get their bearings. Then, on a composite of all three with their respective scales unified, she drew a line from where the wobble ended, through where the Maserati had suddenly speeded up, and on again through the arrows to the gravel pit. It was dead straight.

"So the wobble was a course correction, is that what you're saying?" Snape asked.

"Well, we couldn't rule it out, so we took a closer look at the crash site – without disturbing anything, I'd better add, I don't want you getting nervous. The hedge was so skimpy, it might as well not have been there, and the arrows were showing their age. Their bolts were corroded, and the soil where the stanchions were fixed into their base blocks was pretty much washed away. When we got back here, we did the maths, ran all the possible models through, and established that if the Maserati hit the arrows at 138 full frontal, it wouldn't be deflected, it would plough straight through them and keep on going."

"And the wobble set that up?"

"That's what it looks like."

"And beyond the arrows was the gravel pit – straight ahead and full of water."

"Correct. And I gather from Willem there were no brake marks at any point."

She poured more coffee and asked whether Snape's technicians had found anything wrong with the brakes, including the lights.

"There's a lot of damage, but the short answer is no, and they don't think they will. And we have it from two sources the driver wasn't suicidal. So where does that leave us?"

"We think the car was hacked, most likely from where it wobbled, because up to that point, it was being driven with a certain amount of care. Once it was lined up, however, the brakes were shut off, the steering was locked and the speed was ramped up hard. Let me tell you something else while I'm at it."

"I'm listening."

56

She screened a sequence of shots showing the Maserati's engine compartment. The cabling, the tubing and the reservoirs had all been ripped out. The front of the motor had moved upwards and out of alignment, twisting the frame and wrenching its mountings loose. There was a gap round the cylinder head too.

"Water can be as hard as concrete," she said when she was through. "If you've ever done a belly flop, you'll know that for yourself. And if you force it into a confined space, the damage can beggar belief. Both of those things happened here. The car took some almighty bangs and water was forced into every crack and orifice. The pressures must have been enormous."

"And?"

"The car didn't have to be doing 138 to finish up in the gravel pit – anything over 110 would have produced the same result. We think it was made to go a lot faster than that so any traces of interference would be wiped out. Whoever dreamed this one up thought it through from start to finish."

"That would make it murder. It's the only explanation."

"That's for you to say."

Snape took his time to respond.

"I might think it," he said at last, "but I'm not going to say it out loud again. Officially the death is unexplained, and I'll have less trouble with the people I have to talk to if I keep it that way. I'll ask you to respect that, please."

"You don't have to. That you're talking to me at all is a state secret."

A silence developed, then van Piet asked if Warrener knew how the hacking was done. Even a guess would be better than nothing.

"A guess could be entirely wrong," she replied, "but if it helps, I'd suggest a laptop and some very careful planning. Could the hacker have been watching from the roadside? If they were, we found a good place for it."

She brought up a sequence of pics from the drone.

"This is the Roman road near where you were when the Maserati passed you. You'll see there's a sort of embankment running parallel to the road, with trees and bushes in clumps on it, plus a footpath. It's part of a web of footpaths and bridleways, they run through the fields between the embankment and a B road which – see, right here – has several places a car could park without being noticed. It'd be easy for someone to put a laptop in a rucksack, take up position in one of these clumps and do the necessary. They'd need the basic software and a bit of practice, but the software's easy enough to get on the dark net. You pay using a cryptocurrency, and no one knows you've got it unless you go around telling people. I emphasise, though, this is a guess. I've got no evidence at all."

"You'd erase the software afterwards, would you?" Snape asked.

She shook her head.

"No, I'd smash the laptop and lose the pieces. It's the only way to be sure."

It was time to get back to Essex. Van Piet was adamant Warrener wasn't to testify in any kind of court, and Snape changed the subject by moaning about the rain, which had come on yet again, saying it'd wash away any clues there might have been on the footpaths and the B road. Then he came back to Pachini.

"Pachini knew Slade's Maserati inside out. We've now got reason to believe it's been hacked, and suddenly he's vanished. He could be staying with this friend of his, he could be kidnapped, he could be dead – take your pick, Willem, they're all the same price."

"Missing Persons? Would that help?"

A lorry in front braked sharply, forcing Snape to do the same. The driver behind had been motoring too close and nearly crashed into Snape's boot. Snape got his number and radioed it in. He had a thing about tail-gating.

"It's been done," he replied once he was cruising again, "but don't hold your breath. The National Crime Agency is the stop for missing persons, and they get a thousand enquiries a day, near enough. I've put Lloyds Bank in the frame as well, and I've asked Border Force to let me know as soon as any Matteo Alessandro Pachini books a flight or a ferry to anywhere, if he hasn't done it already. Will that do?"

"What about his parents? You've got their details."

"Not so easy. If I ring them up, I might get an honest answer, or they might cover up for him and warn him I'm looking for him. I could always go to the Italian police, but that could cause its own problems."

"Too right it could. They'll want to know why you're asking, and I don't want that to happen till I know where this is leading. Let me have a go."

As Snape passed a milk tanker, van Piet took out his smartphone and selected a number for Verona, Italy, where, on a picture-book hillside and with the outside temperature touching 35°C, a grey-haired nun called Sister Agnese was busy in the cool room of the Convent of Hope for Grace. The convent dated back to the time of St Benedict, but the cool room was twenty-first century, and Sister Agnese was turning shelf after shelf of goat's cheeses. Every so often she'd push a cheese trier into one to see how mature it was, and if she was pleased with the result, as she usually was, she was also relieved. The convent was into an expanding market, and demand was outstripping supply. She and van Piet were old friends. Van Piet Banking had steered the convent through the global financial collapse. Now it was helping it build its future.

"They're in Parma, you say?" van Piet heard in effortless English. Sister Agnese had a Master's in Biochemistry from the University of Vancouver, and van Piet had told her Snape was listening in. "That's less than two hours' drive from here. I'll have to seek permission to leave the convent, and that could mean a delay. And I mustn't alarm *Signore e Signora Pachini*, just ask them if they've heard from Matteo lately and how people in England can get in touch with him. Give me a day or two. I'll see what I can do."

As Snape was approaching Chelmsford, Laura Slade was driving back to Lower Mindle. Her mother had been right, she'd wanted very much to be on her own, so she hadn't even taken a taxi. That meant she'd got wet twice between the car park and the undertaker's, but it had been worth it - she felt more tranquil now she'd seen her father in repose. She'd also promised him solemnly she'd get to the truth about his death. Nothing, but nothing would stop her.

When she let herself into The Lodge, her mother didn't seem to be around. That suited Laura, who wanted to change out of the black two piece she was wearing and simply sit quietly for ten minutes. If the gardeners were still about, she couldn't hear them. But as she was approaching her bedroom, her mother came out from her own bedroom looking fundamentally distressed.

"I thought I heard you come in!" she exclaimed. "Come and give me a hug. I desperately need one from my lovely, lovely girl. We're all we've got left now your father's gone."

They clasped each other tightly and felt each other's warmth as their tears flowed. But when they stepped apart, they sniffled and smiled embarrassedly, as if they'd done something improper. Verity let Laura go on to her room, then quickening her step, she went downstairs to start the dinner, still sniffling and wiping her face with a handkerchief. When Laura eventually came down, not feeling the least bit hungry, she found Verity determinedly beating eggs for an omelette.

"I phoned Esklivia this afternoon," Verity said, avoiding eye contact by keeping her gaze on the egg whisk. "Apparently the Financial Conduct Authority has sent in a large pile of new regulations, and it's on your desk right now. I want you to go in first thing tomorrow, read everything through carefully and report back to me. Off-shores are out of favour at the moment. Any slips could cost us dear."

Laura could see that, but she felt something was going unsaid.

"What about you?" she asked, not wanting to resist directly again. "Are you sure you want to be on your own?"

"Thank you, my precious, but I shan't be on my own. Millie is coming over to help me with the boulting house. I know it's mucky in there, but there are some jobs I want her to do now Mr Thurston is out of the way. I'll be asking her about new codes for the door and the windows while she's here. It's an outhouse after all, so we have to be doubly careful. Your father would agree with that, if he were still alive, and I'm sure you agree as well."

Chapter 7

A woman scorned

The sky was clearing by Saturday, and Snape drove into Police HQ early to organise a search along the footpaths and the B road Warrener had flagged up. When he was done, he saw a chance to slip out to the shops. His wife's birthday was coming up, and he wanted some flowers to be delivered on the day. Anyway, he liked walking about in Chelmsford on a Saturday. He'd been doing it most of his life.

He found a parking space near the High Chelmer Shopping Centre. There was only a trickle of customers in the florist's, so he soon had a mixed bouquet sorted out, complete with a hand-written message. The florist knew him too well to suggest altering the spelling. As he was leaving, he caught sight of someone he thought he recognised. It was Stephanie Hayward, Derek Rufus's secretary. She'd replaced the would-be sophisticated one-piece she wore at Rufus For Maseratis with raspberry corduroys and a well-worn poplin jacket, and she was wearing her hair long; but he was certain who it was.

She was heading for a nearby Starbucks, and she might just be meeting someone he ought to know about, so he went in himself and joined the queue a little way behind her. But she didn't seem to be expecting anyone, so while she was carrying an iced caffè latte towards an empty table, he paid for his espresso and moved in the same direction. Maybe he could get her to talk about Rufus. She'd already sat down as he got nearer. She glanced up, took a longer look, and gave him a little wave.

"It's Mr Snape, isn't it?" she said with a guileless big smile. "Please, be my guest. I'm off duty now, so you can call me Steph if you like. I've driven over to do my weekly shop."

Snape wondered how much of what he said would get back to Rufus - it was something he had to watch. He didn't have endless time either, so he took a chance and pitched straight in.

"You've got a good head for names, Steph, but as I expect you know, I was seeing Mr Rufus about a car accident. One of your customers had gone off the road and lost his life."

"That was Mr Slade, and Mr Rufus wasn't happy about it. He thought our sales might take a knock."

She sipped at her caffè latte while Snape started his espresso. Mr Rufus had a point, he said. Sometimes it was the driver who was the problem, not the car, but the car still got the blame. Had she heard Mr Slade had had to take special lessons?

"Of course. A lot of our customers have to, and as a rule they're for it. But Mr Rufus told me Mr Slade had to be persuaded, and that did surprise me. He must have known a Maserati could be a handful."

"He'd owned one before, had he?"

"I've no idea, he's not someone I knew out of hours. But we don't just sell Maseratis, we hire them out, as you may or may not know from our website, and Mr Slade hired one from the first Saturday in June for a week. He was definitely thinking of buying one – at least, that's what he told me when I was taking him through the agreement - but he wanted to get the feel of one before he finally made up his mind. He seemed a nice man – not all mouth and money like some of the types we get. As soon as you met him, you sort of warmed to him."

Snape asked whether Slade's agreement stated he had to keep the car in a secure place.

"They all do that, and you can see why, but in his case it wasn't a problem. He said he didn't want his family to know he was trying out a Maserati in case they made a fuss, so we let him use one of the lock-ups we've got behind our showroom."

"Meaning he'd drive over to your place and take the Maserati out whenever he had the time. Did he ever say where he was going?"

"Not to me, but then I didn't see him to speak to that often. You'd have to ask Mr Rufus that."

"What about passengers? Was he insured for them under the deal?"

"Yes, it's what we normally offer. Mr Rufus went with him at least once, I know that for certain, because he usually tells me when he's going somewhere, and he knows all the best routes for test-driving our cars. I wouldn't know about anyone else going with him, but if they did, they probably got out and walked after five minutes, since he definitely had his problems. One afternoon he came back with a gouge all along the passenger side. Mr Rufus was very angry about that, but he touched it up overnight and let him hang on to the car. He said he'd get it fixed properly later. Then the day before the hire period was up, Mr Slade phoned in late afternoon to say he'd gone into a ditch."

"On a bend?"

"Yes."

"On the Roman road?"

"No, near Wivenhoe. We had to send a breakdown lorry out, and Mr Rufus had had enough. He wouldn't let him have a replacement car, he gave him his money back instead. All of it."

"And the date was?"

"8th June. A Thursday."

Snape finished his espresso and looked straight across at her.

"Why are you telling me all this, Steph?

She held his gaze.

"What's that supposed to mean?"

"I've spent a lot of my life asking questions, and when the answers flow like yours, I tend to wonder whether they've been worked out in advance. That would mean, of course, that you'd either hoped or guessed I'd be here round about now, and that I'd recognise you if I saw you."

She held her hands up briefly, as if she was surrendering.

"It's a fair cop," she laughed, "and actually, it was easier than you think. You're often on TV or in the papers, and I usually come in here when I'm shopping in Chelmsford, so I've seen you about the place, and I've known who you are as well. This time I hoped you'd know who *I* was, even if I wasn't dressed up to please Mr Rufus, and I figured, if I came in here for a coffee, you might follow me in and see what you could find out. Which you did."

So she'd caught him out. Well, he could live with that.

"Point to you, Steph," he acknowledged. "But you still haven't told me why."

"Try spite, Mr Snape." She wasn't laughing now. "Mr Rufus and I have had a very close personal relationship, but over the summer he's been crawling back to his wife, and I don't like it. I've been waiting to do something about it, and now I can."

He asked whether Mrs Rufus knew what was going on.

"I'm sure she does, or as good as. She's not whiter than white either, I know that for a fact, but it's one rule for her and another for Mr Rufus. She's got this terrible temper, and she always has to have her own way. She gets insanely jealous too, you can virtually see her go green. I've heard her say some very bad things to Mr Rufus when she didn't know I was listening."

"And you want me to say some bad things to him as well, do you?"

"I resent what he's doing, even if he is under her thumb, so yes, that's exactly what I want. I've told you what he ought to have told you himself about Mr Slade, and I want you to make him pay for keeping his mouth shut."

Snape was wondering how old she was. He'd guessed in her mid-twenties, but when her face hardened, she looked nearer thirty. Naïve with it, though, and completely mixed up in what she wanted. Had she any other reason than spite, he asked. She took her time draining her cup, then she said,

"Protection from the police. From you, if you like. I should've thought you could work that out for yourself."

"And if I can't?"

She sighed impatiently. The games people play!

"All right, Mr Snape, have it your way. When Mr Slade picked up that gouge, Mr Rufus let him keep the car, which wasn't like him at all. In fact the whole car had to finish up in a ditch before he called it in. But what struck me as even more odd, he didn't activate the insurance for the gouge or any of the other damage, even though he could have done. It was one of those deals where Mr Rufus could claim from his own insurance, and they'd get their money back from the customer's."

"So what did he do instead?"

"He put the jobs through our body shop with nothing written down, and he removed all trace of the agreement Mr Slade had signed. I know, because I see all the paperwork in Rufus For Maseratis, and when I made a point of looking, that's what I turned up. Until now, I haven't said anything to anyone, and Mr Rufus hasn't either, so far as I know. But you're going to find things out, it's what you're paid for, and I don't want you doing me for holding back information. Now can you see what I mean by protection from the police?"

Snape said he got the idea, then he asked her whether she was holding anything back about Matteo Pachini.

"So far as I'm aware, everything Mr Rufus told you was true, and I know what he said, because I was listening. Mr Rufus doesn't know it, but his intercom's defective. I have to press a button at my end for it to switch off, and I don't always do it."

"And you don't know where Mr Pachini is now?"

"Not a clue, I didn't even know he was missing till you turned up. Now one last thing before I get on with my shopping, which I was telling the truth about, though I don't suppose you believe me. I want you to crack down hard on Mr Rufus, but he mustn't know I've told you anything. Can you give me your word on that?"

Snape said it was in his interest to, there might be more things she'd want to tell him further down the line. But she didn't take the hint, and Snape let it go. He felt anxious about her, she was meddling in what was looking like a murder hunt – two, even, counting in Pachini - and that could be fatal for her. He took out his notebook and wrote down a phone number.

"If you see or hear anything suspicious, don't tell anyone else, just call this number on the quiet. It's mine, and if anyone else answers, you can trust them to speak to, or they'll get me to call you back, if that suits you better."

"What if I do tell someone else? Not the police, I mean."

"That's your risk, but I'll say it again – don't do it. It could come with a cost you wouldn't like."

He tore the page out and handed it over. As he did so, he saw scorn in her eyes. Scorn and contempt.

"I might have to contact you myself," he added, sliding his pen and notebook towards her. "If you give me your address and a number, I won't have to chase them up."

In a confident, spacious hand she wrote 'Nightingale Cottage, Five Willows'. After a moment's hesitation with the pen poised in the air, she added a landline number and a mobile one.

"Do you know where Five Willows is?" she asked, making it sound like a challenge.

He said he did, and she looked disappointed. She pushed back her chair and got to her feet.

"Time's up," she said with a flick of her hair. "We'll see what happens next."

Back in Police HQ, Snape had to wait till late afternoon before he could speak to van Piet, who'd gone over to Ashell House and wasn't taking calls. Snape took him through the conversation he'd had with Hayward.

"Do you think she was telling the truth?" van Piet asked.

"That's what I have to find out, but I'd bet my pension she was keeping something back. I think she wants Rufus frightened enough to go back to her for comfort, and if it doesn't work this time round, she's got something a whole lot bigger to hit him with. I told her not to do anything without speaking to me first. I hope it sunk in, but I doubt it."

Van Piet had some news of his own. Davis had eleven buy-to-lets in Clacton, but they weren't the usual deal. They belonged to a registered company called CampionForresterStiles of Clacton, of which Davis was the only director, and all the profits went to her. So far, so legal, even if the company wasn't mentioned in Pachini's rent book. But CampionForresterStiles of Clacton was owned by CampionForresterStiles International, which was a letterbox firm in Samoa. It had bought the buy-to-lets outright, then transferred them to CampionForresterStiles of Clacton, so effectively they were Davis's. But she'd been spared the capital costs, presumably because they'd been beyond her declared income.

"So why brighten her life with eleven little earners, and who's behind it all, Eddie? When we know those two things, we'll be a lot further forward."

Chapter 8

An attaché case mystery

Laura Slade was also pleased the sky was clearing as she drove from The Lodge to Theydon Bois underground station, all set to take the Central Line to Bank. She wasn't pleased about too much else, though – especially the pile of paper from the FCA. Was it really worth a trip to London on a Saturday morning? More likely she was being kept out of the boulting house, because that was how it had always been. She'd never been shown round, she'd never been given the code to get in with, and its fake-antique shutters were always closed. Her parents said it was where they worked on deals that had nothing to do with Esklivia, and Cottrell, who was in and out there a lot, always backed them up.

The underground was half empty as it left Theydon Bois, and Laura hoped it would stay that way as she dug in for the thirteen station ride. She pulled some Law Society circulars out of her briefcase, but she couldn't focus on them, so she put them away and took out an easy-reading account of Pompeii. She'd been there with Millie, so the memories were good, but she couldn't focus on that either, so it followed the circulars back into her briefcase.

"Why revamp the security on the boulting house right now?"

The question wouldn't leave her, and she didn't like the answer she kept coming up with – Thurston had seen her in her parents' bedroom and told her mother about it. It had to be spin-off from that. But did he really know it was her parents' bedroom? And what was it to do with him anyway? She reminded herself her parents could keep her out of the boulting house if they liked, it was their property, and that was that. But the police asking questions, and her father's photo with the big cross through it - they impacted on her directly.

At Mile End station a lot more people got on than got off, and at Liverpool Street half of London seemed to pile in. She brightened up once it had happened, people were glad it was Saturday, and their unencumbered mood took her out of herself. But when she got out at Bank, bad temper and puzzlement came seeping back. A hint of fear as well.

Esklivia Investments was housed in a five-storey building not far from the Gresham Grasshopper. The stainless steel nameplate said Esklivia House, and just seeing it normally gave Laura a lift. But the magic didn't work this time round, things had changed too much.

A security camera stared at her from over the black wooden outside door, but she took no notice, because she knew it was off. Only the fire doors at the back of the building had cameras trained on them that were switched on all the while. Office hours were officially 9.00 – 5.00 Monday to Friday, but with London being global, clients often asked to come in outside of those hours, so senior managers worked flexi-time to suit them. And since the last thing most clients wanted was to be recorded, the cctv only went on between 10.15 at night and 7.15 in the morning, weekends included. Effectively that turned 10.00 pm into a curfew, and senior managers stuck to it rigidly. There were – or had been - three exceptions to that, though. One was Verity Slade. If she was seeing someone late, she could shut the cctv off with a zapper while she was still outside and off-camera. Laura had a similar zapper, since she, too, saw image-shy clients at all hours - in her case to help them stay legal or become legal again. Geoffrey Slade had made up the trio. Apart from being useful, the zappers were status symbols. In Verity's view, only a Slade should have one, so that was the way it was.

Security at the outside door was a punched-in code, a card in a scanner and an old-fashioned Chubb key turned in the lock. Laura could go through it in her sleep.

"Good morning, Miss," she heard as she pushed the door to and re-locked it. "A welcome change in the weather, if I may say so."

It was Arthur, one of the porters who manned the front entrance when the cctv wasn't on. All of Esklivia's porters were male, although the policy was never admitted, and they had to wear dark suits with white shirts and sombre neckties. Verity thought they gave Esklivia class.

Laura returned the greeting and asked whether anyone else was in.

"Not today, Miss. You've got the place to yourself at the moment."

"Long may it last. I don't want to take any calls while I'm here, so please don't put any through, and you may hear me moving around from time to time. I'll have some checking to do."

"Yes, Miss." He hesitated for a moment. "We were sorry to hear about Mr Slade," he went on. "He always had time for the support staff."

Laura felt her eyes prickle. She'd been caught off guard.

"Thank you, Arthur," she said, fumbling a tissue out of her handbag. "I know he did. He was good to everyone." She managed to add, "I'm grateful for your kind words," before she hurried to the lift. She was afraid of breaking down in front of him.

Her office led off a landing on the first floor, as did Cottrell's. Her mother's and her father's were a storey higher. All the landing's colours were light, the carpeting looked as if it had just been laid, and the small tables placed against the walls had fresh bright flowers on them. The message was clear and deliberate: Esklivia was clean, it had nothing to hide. On Laura's desk were two sets of papers in separate trays. One set was correspondence, pre-opened by her secretary and date-stamped. The other was the FCA consignment. Her mother had said it was a lot, and she'd been right.

With zero enthusiasm Laura went through the correspondence, making brief notes in the margins with a red felt-tip. She'd dictate the replies on Monday. Then she slid the FCA's words of wisdom towards her, checked they were in the right order, and began reading steadily. This time she made notes on her laptop. She'd write them up when she got back to Bishop's Green.

After an hour or so, she felt she deserved a break. She'd been gradually becoming thirsty, and she needed to look at some charts that were in her mother's filing cabinet. It would be locked, but she had a duplicate key. She decided to walk up a floor to stretch her legs, then treat herself to some coffee when she got back. She'd brought a small flask with her in her briefcase.

She'd often been in the building when no one else was around except for the duty porter. It had an atmosphere she could cosy into – no comings and goings, no phones, just her and whatever she wanted to get on with. It was like that this time, and as a result, the demons she'd arrived with were losing their bite. When she reached her father's office, she had half a mind to go in, but then she couldn't bear to, so she walked determinedly past it and unlocked the door to her mother's.

It clearly belonged to the boss. It was the biggest office in the building, and its grandiose desk on the one hand, and on the other, the deep easy chairs, the drinks cabinet and the elegant low-level coffee table meant that Verity could switch from handing out orders to pampering top clients just by changing where she sat. A designer set of international clocks dominated one wall, the wallpaper was its own price-tag, and the top-of-the-range eco windows with their anti-wireless inlay were disguised as quaintly old-fashioned sash ones. There were two side doors, one leading into the office of Verity's private secretary, the other into Verity's personal ensuite. In a corner was a three-seater settee Verity could fold down into a bed if she worked late, which she often did. Laura had a two-seater one in her smaller office and it, too, earned its keep.

With the exception of the clocks, everything in the office seemed frozen in time. A row of files was laid out on the desk, the memo pad had a pen in it to mark a fresh page, and Verity's tan attaché case was standing by her chair. The attaché case looked new because it was. Slade had been a hobby historian like Laura, and in an idle hour he'd dreamed up the custom of annually presenting Verity with a brand new attaché case to mark Esklivia's foundation. It was entirely a fun thing, distantly modelled on Elizabeth I's Accession Day celebrations, and the staff liked it because they got a free lunch in the garden at the back plus the rest of the day off. After dessert and with the aroma of coffee hanging in the air, Verity's outgoing attaché case would be auctioned off for charity. Since Verity was watching, it always fetched a good price.

"Good old Daddy," Laura whispered as she unlocked her mother's filing cabinet. "You always cheered things up."

She found the charts she was looking for, confirmed she'd remembered them right, and locked them away again. She was about to return to her own office when, out of nowhere, she felt she had to pick up the attaché case. The room was empty, all the surveillance had to be off, and just touching it would bring back a flood of happy memories. She felt the handle first, then she raised the whole case up and held it out to admire the craftsmanship. It felt empty, but she wouldn't have opened it anyway, even if she knew the combination. It was beautifully made, and if it were hers, she'd be permanently scared of standing it down in case she marked it - unlike her mother, who had produced a longish scratch when, early in June, she'd stood it down on Theydon Bois station and someone had caught it with his foot. She must have stood the case on the only sharp stone big enough to reach past the studs in the bottom, and Laura knew about it because Verity, dismayed in case her father saw the damage, had asked her whether she could get it out with shoe polish. Laura had assured her she'd never get a colour match, but no one would see the scratch unless they were looking for it. So between them, they'd let it be their secret. Smiling fondly, Laura turned the case upside down to see the scratch again. It wasn't there.

It made no sense, it had to be there, unless her mother had hidden it after all. She ran a fingertip over the leather and held the case at different angles, but there was absolutely no sign of it. So it had to be a different case, but an exactly similar one. That would be easy enough to get hold of - the make, the code number and the colour would be enough. But it wasn't likely Verity had actually done that, since they'd agreed between them, if anything affected their secret, they'd let the other person know. That way they wouldn't say the wrong thing when her father was around.

Suddenly Verity's office felt menacing. Laura was a trained lawyer, and as she saw it, the most obvious reason for two identical cases was that they could be exchanged without anyone noticing. On a train, perhaps, where you could pretend you didn't know the person who sat down opposite you and who put a case like yours under the table. Or somewhere private, where no one would see the handover, but when one or both parties might afterwards need to be seen carrying what looked like the case they'd arrived with. 'Somewhere private' could be anywhere – a hotel room, or someone's house or flat. Or right here in this office, especially after 10.15 at night. Her nerves tightening, Laura scrabbled her zapper from her handbag to check whether the surveillance in her mother's office was really off. She pressed Camera 1/Check, and the zapper's mini-screen stayed blank, so yes, it was off all right. Her hand was unsteady as she put the zapper back in her handbag. But she had to keep going now.

So when did her mother work late, and was there a pattern to it? If Laura had been living in The Lodge, it would have been easy to come up with some answers, but working flexi-time and living in Bishop's Green meant she couldn't even guess. Scanning the office but not sure what she was looking for, she caught sight of Verity's appointments diary mostly hidden by one of the files. There was nothing secret in it - if Laura needed to consult it, she didn't even have to ask. In fact it had a digital counterpart she and Verity could access remotely, so in that sense it was redundant. But Verity knew the value of solemnly entering a further appointment by hand when she had a rich client sitting in front of her.

Carefully Laura slid the diary out and paged slowly through it, but the entries seemed too random to tell her anything. Afraid she'd been suspiciously long in her mother's office, she glanced at the clocks to see what the London one was showing, and that gave her an idea. Verity did a lot of phoning to off-shores like the Cayman Islands, Panama City and the British Virgin Islands, and the time differences between them and the UK made it natural for her to do it in the evening, British time. She'd normally set these calls up in advance, and being stealthy by nature, she'd simply enter a time plus 'eppc' - meaning encrypted, person-to-person and confidential - instead of writing in who the call was to. Laura combed through the diary again, and now she noticed the third Tuesday of every calendar month finished with an eppc that was after 10.15. That could be it. The third Tuesday in August was coming up – it would be after the weekend - and the eppc was down for 10.45. Nerving herself, she put the diary back exactly where she'd found it. When the third Tuesday came round, she knew where she had to be.

Chapter 9

A village with a past

On Sunday morning, while Snape was setting out the breakfast things, he was thinking he'd drive out to Five Willows to refresh his memory of the place. He'd take Sal Gulliver with him. She was the Head of Essex Police's Armed Support Unit. He might need her shooting skills before long, so he'd phase her in now.

He wanted to speak to Anita Rufus as well, so he went into Colchester's official website, and under Businesses he found the Rufuses' used car outlet. It was called The Rufus Car Mart, and its website was stuffed full of oversize lettering, colours from outer space, and exclamation marks like bombs going off. Musing whether any stolen vehicles finished up there, he clicked on Meet The Team, and first off he found a robust, open face, wide hazel eyes, blonde hair that looked natural and very white teeth. The caption read simply, 'Anita', as if that said it all. In her late thirties, Snape guessed, so some ten years older than Hayward. Was that why Hayward had been getting the attention? He wrote the opening times and the phone number in his notebook. If he couldn't reach her at work, he'd try the Rufuses' home number. He had that already.

That left van Piet.

"Are you still in Ashell House?" Snape asked after he'd reached him on his mobile.

"No, I'm at home now. What's on your mind?"

Snape told him he was going to see where Hayward lived. Did he want to come along?

"Sounds as if I ought to. Expect me by 9.30."

That gave Snape time to eat some toast, clear his things away, and take his wife's tea up. They'd been married thirty-seven years, and she'd never grouched about the hours he worked. He'd been lucky there, and he knew it. Stress at work and aggro at home had seen a lot of his colleagues out of the force. The trouble was, the aggro was usually justified – unsocial hours, never being at home for the children, no friends outside the force. He knew the list.

From Chelmsford to Five Willows took over an hour, and they went in an unmarked car. The traffic on the A roads was light, but when they hit the country lanes they had to slow right up. They were narrow and twisty, and one oncoming car could be one too many. Snape was driving and talking at the same time. He wanted the geography fixed in people's heads.

"The next junction's a sort of grassy island with a signpost in the middle," he said as he completed a blind corner. "We turn right there, keep straight on where the road divides, and then we're in Five Willows. At the crossroads and on the right again is a newsagent's and general store. We'll park there and do the rest on foot."

"What if Hayward sees us?" asked Gulliver.

"That's a chance we take, we're here for her benefit, not ours. She might even see it that way, though I doubt it."

The car park was small, but three or four spaces were empty, and Snape took the nearest one. Van Piet thought they wouldn't be so obvious if he went in to buy a newspaper. While he was gone, Gulliver compared the lanes they'd just come through with the maps on her tablet, and Snape tried Anita's work number.

"The Rufus Car Mart, Jason speaking," he heard. "How can I help you?"

Snape asked for Mrs Rufus, and after more of *The Four Seasons* than he really wanted to hear, there was an abrupt clunk. Anita was on the line, and he said his piece.

"Make it three o'clock, we'll both be there," she said without any fuss. "Have you got our address?"

He said he had and asked whether anyone else would be in the house apart from herself and Mr Rufus.

"No, just us. Oliver – that's our son - would normally be about, but he's in New Zealand with one of his uncles and aunts. He won't be back till into September."

Did Hayward have anything to do with that, like by poisoning the atmosphere at home? It would be useful to know. Snape thanked her, terminated, and opened a message from Police HQ that had come in while he'd been speaking. Out of the corner of his eye, he saw van Piet coming back with a newspaper in his hand.

"Good and bad news, Willem," he told him quietly through his open window. "The good news is, the Rufuses will see us at three in their house. The bad news is, Forensics can't find anything on the footpaths and the B road Penny Warrener picked out for us."

"So you don't know whether the rain washed out something that was there, or there was nothing to find in the first place."

"Right first time. We've simply got no idea."

Snape locked the car, and they crossed the road they'd come in on – it was called the High Street while it was in the village. Soon they were on a rising footpath behind the cluster of buildings that made up the village centre. Gulliver was in civvies, but her uniform was folded in the boot, since she'd be doing a door-to-door in Walsingham Close later. Snape and van Piet were in suits and ties, ready to call on the Rufuses, so they were grateful the sky was overcast and the sea was only a few miles away, even if they couldn't see it. A mild sea breeze was keeping the temperature down.

"This will do," said Snape after they'd gained some height. "You can get an idea of the whole village from here, and if you're wondering where the five willows are, Oliver Cromwell's men used them for firewood during the Civil War. I won't point in case anyone's watching, but if you look from right to left, the building on the far side of the road with the corrugated roof is the village hall. The pub by the crossroads is called The Brace of Pheasants – it's the only pub in the village – and a bit further along, the half-timbered house set back from the road is the doctor's surgery. There's no school, no church, and there are no street lights either. Beyond the last house to your left, the grey-looking one with the privet hedge, you'll see a turn-off to the right, and if you track it past the field with the horses in it, you'll see a two-storey white-walled cottage with a slate roof covered in moss. That's where Hayward lives, and the electoral roll says she lives on her own. Any thoughts, Sal?"

Gulliver pulled a face.

"It's a death trap, no question. It looks pretty-pretty right now, but she's got no neighbours, just fields, and it must be pitch dark at night. What on earth made her buy it?"

"It's not far from her work, and her parents are close - they own a toy shop near Clacton pier. I'd guess it didn't cost much either. Property here's bargain basement."

"How come you know so much about this place?" van Piet asked. "I'd never even heard of it till you told me about it."

Snape frowned.

"There was a murder here six years ago, and we turned the whole village over. We never solved it, though. It wasn't my case, but I helped out where I could. You never forget an unsolved murder."

"So who was killed?"

"A vet named Ashley Johnson. He was twenty-eight years old, and he was about to marry the young lady he was living with. He'd had a gap year in South Africa after his school exams, then he'd qualified in London and spent a couple of years spaying cats and worming dogs in Bermondsey. But his big ambition was to treat farm animals, so he kept an eye on the *Veterinary Times*, saw an article about this area being hard up for vets, and decided to do something about it. He bought a house here, had a brass plate made and screwed it to his front wall by the door. He also spent two or three evenings a week in The Brace of Pheasants. A lot of farmers drink in there, and some of them come from a fair way off, so it was a good way to get his name known. When the landlord called time, he'd take his torch, walk along the High Street almost to the last house to your left – the one with the privet hedge – and cross over to the detached house opposite. That's where he and his fiancée lived. You can see the roof from here, it's the one with the weather vane fixed to the chimney.

"One November evening, he was shot and killed between his garden gate and his front door with a silenced Walther PPK ·380 ACP. He took three bullets in all – one into the back from the garden gate, we think, and two from close range into the head from a standing position sideways on. Whoever shot him wanted to be certain he was dead. We never found the gun or the torch he had with him. According to his fiancée, it was a heavy-duty rubberised one he used for his call-outs. We think the murderer removed it, but that's speculation.

"In her statement, which I witnessed, his fiancée said she discovered his body when she went out to look for him because he was late. She used the light switch by the front door, she saw him on the ground, and his shattered head told her there was no hope for him. He never wore a hat, she said, not even in winter, and other people we spoke to said the same. To this day, we don't know who did it or why. They might be dead themselves by now, or moved away. Or we might have passed them in the village this morning."

Gulliver asked whether Hayward might know there could be a murderer loose in the village.

"No idea, it was before her time. She came here four years ago."

"Was it a man or a woman who shot him? Could you work that out from the angles?"

"No, we couldn't, it could have been either. The murderer was right-handed, which didn't help. We asked about cctv, but they'd never had any. They had a burglar alarm instead."

"I don't remember any of this," said van Piet. "I must have been abroad. Was anything taken?"

"Not that we could discover. We checked Mr Johnson's background, and again there was nothing – no professional rivalry, no clients with a grievance, nothing. Not even a jealous lover."

"What happened to the fiancée?"

"She'd been a reporter on the *London Evening Standard*, but when she and Mr Johnson decided to come here, she got a job with BBC Essex. It was on the editorial side, which made it ideal for string-pulling, and without ever being on camera, she made sure everyone knew about Five Willows' sparky new vet. It seems to have paid off, since trade was on the up when he was murdered. He'd made a will - he was organised like that - and the house went to the fiancée, but she'd had enough of Five Willows, so she sold up as soon as she could and went back to her old boss in London. She was never a suspect, if that's what you're thinking. Whoever killed Mr Johnson must have picked up some blood and brain matter, but there wasn't a speck on her, and Forensics looked hard enough. She told us later she'd wanted to wrap him in her arms, but she knew from being a reporter she had to hold back. I'm not so sure about that. I think what she saw was so horrific, she couldn't bear to go near him, but she didn't want to admit it, because it was the man she'd loved – or what was left of him. Either way, it's certain she never touched him."

Van Piet asked if he could remember her name.

"Deborah Watkins it was then. Always Deborah, never Debbie."

Van Piet thought for a moment.

"I know it from somewhere... Yes, I've got it now. She susses out scandals for the *Standard's* business section. She might know something about the Slades, it's her line of country. Have you still got her details on file?"

"Yes we have - as they were then, of course. You can see them when we get back. You don't think the deaths are connected, do you? Ashley Johnson's and Slade's, I mean."

Van Piet was about to say no, but he'd recalled Watkins had hacked into Van Piet Banking's computers once, and the bank had seen her off. He couldn't remember when exactly, but he felt sure it was before Johnson's murder.

"If you get an unsolved death and then you get another one, what do you do?" he asked instead of answering directly.

"We review the first one, just in case. There doesn't have to be a connection, but there could be."

"There's your answer, Eddie. Leave it with me, I'll see what I can come up with."

They walked back to the High Street, where they split up. Gulliver went as far as the field with the horses in it, van Piet walked from the Brace of

Pheasants to the murder house, and Snape did some phoning from his car. When Gulliver and van Piet rejoined him, they were all thinking it was time for lunch. Snape had brought sandwiches and drinks from the canteen in Chelmsford, but he was keen to get away from Five Willows. The place was so small, they must have stood out, and if Hayward was any guide, he might have been recognised. Better to drive to Clacton first, they'd blend in better there. Then it would be on to the Rufuses.

"Ashley Johnson's old house, I see it's still a vet's," van Piet said as Snape drove off.

"Trade's very good round here if you press the right buttons. But it's a partnership now, as you probably noticed, and no one lives on the premises. I asked one of the partners about it once. He said all the partners had families and there was no school in the village. I mentioned call-outs at night, and he said they took them at home. He didn't spell it out, but it's obvious, isn't it – no one wants to live there any more."

Chapter 10

The Rufuses at home

Snape's feelings were mixed as he made his way through Clacton's ageing streets towards the north side of town. The Johnson case irritated him, and the overcast sky made the whole resort seem glum. On the other hand, he'd been going to Clacton from Chelmsford ever since he'd been a boy. The sun had always been shining then, or so it seemed whenever he looked back, and there'd been long hours on the beach, boat trips out to sea, and fish and chips on the prom, before he and his parents had chugged contentedly home in their second-hand Hillman Imp.

He elected to park on the cliff top and enjoy as much of the sea as he could. It was the colour of steel under the cloud cover, the breeze was stronger up there, and the beach looked sadly empty, but he still felt he'd made the right choice. They ate their sandwiches and drank their tea in silence. Before Gulliver and van Piet had finished, Snape fetched out his notebook and tapped a number into his smartphone.

"Willem, I'm talking to Miss Cottrell," he broke off to say, as if van Piet and Gulliver hadn't heard every word. "She'll see us tomorrow afternoon at four in Bishop's Green. Laura Slade will be there as well."

"Five would be better, Eddie. Ask her if that's OK."

It was, and Snape terminated the call.

"I need to keep some time free," van Piet explained. "I want to speak to Deborah Watkins. I'll try for both of us to see her, but it may have to be just me."

Snape asked why.

"You might bring back bad memories. Let me have Miss Cottrell's address in case I have to make my own way there."

Snape wrote the address out and hoped to hear more. But van Piet retreated behind the newspaper he'd bought, and Gulliver picked at a training day she was organising till Snape said it was time to move on.

"We'll go via Clacton police station," he told van Piet. "Sal can change into her uniform there and drive to Walsingham Close while we're with the Rufuses. She'll be asking Pachini's neighbours if they remember him being collected. Maybe Davis's version isn't the only one in town."

The Rufuses lived in a cul-de-sac of blatantly high-income properties. Jaguars, Range Rovers and Mercedes stood in the driveways, and despite the breeze, the heavy quiet that goes with large plots of land was everywhere. The Rufuses' house was of a piece with the rest. Five-bedroomed and timber-frame chic, it headed a drive made of pavers forming pseudo-artistic semi-circular patterns. Despite a three-car integrated garage, two vehicles were standing by the front porch where anyone could see them who approached the house – a Maserati with Rufus For Maseratis neatly signed on the sides, and an Isuzu Trooper proclaiming The Rufus Car Mart in multi-coloured letters that grew larger as they approached the rear wheels. The roof of the front porch rested on wooden pillars made to look as if they'd been formed with an adze, and the door was an upright oblong of solid mahogany. It was held in place by ornate hinges with dents in them to show they'd been made in a smithy.

Snape and van Piet approached the house on foot from a nearby street. As they reached the door, Snape looked at his watch. They were early, he saw, but he hoped it wouldn't matter. He took hold of the rustic bell-pull and gave it a tug. An insistent jangling audible even through the mahogany was followed by a silence, then a key turned in the lock and the door swung open. Snape recognised Anita from her website. She was wearing a dove grey tracksuit and a pair of lightweight slip-on sneakers.

"Mr Snape?" she asked, in a strong, confident voice. "And Mr van Piet? I'm Anita Rufus."

"I'm afraid we're early," Snape answered for both of them and held out his ID. "I hope you don't mind."

"Not at all, we were waiting for you. If you'd like to come in, I'll shut the door."

She led the way through the reception hall into the immense drawing room. It had twin chandeliers, the windows were leaded, and sliding doors gave onto a veranda with a swimming pool beyond it. The marble fireplace was dominated by a state-of-the art log burner, and the two settees with matching chairs that formed a semi-circle in front of it had standard lamps with tasselled shades standing next to them. Rufus closed a copy of *Cycling Weekly* and got casually to his feet. He, too, was wearing a tracksuit – his was maroon – and his choice of footwear was impeccably clean trainers without socks. Anita was taller than he was. Both of them looked as if they'd stepped out of a health club advertisement.

While Rufus was in the kitchen seeing to the coffee, Snape explained to Anita why the enquiries he was making might not seem relevant to a road accident. She said she understood and gave him an encouraging smile. Her teeth were as white as on her website. Snape reckoned she had them done professionally.

"I gather Mr Slade helped out when Mr Rufus wanted to start selling Maseratis," he began, once Rufus had passed round the coffee and made himself comfortable on one of the settees. "Do you and your husband own your two companies jointly?"

"The short answer is no. If Rufus For Maseratis failed, we didn't want the Car Mart dragged down with it, so we put in some firewalls."

"There must be overlaps, surely."

"Not as many as you'd think." Anita was shading Rufus right out, and it wasn't just because Snape's questions were all going in her direction. "However, I do do both sets of accounts. Nothing gets fudged or left out, and I do regular spot checks as well. Derek doesn't like them, but they keep the Revenue off our backs. We've never had a return queried, have we, Derek?"

Rufus shook his head and smiled, then they both waited for Snape, who was writing in his notebook.

"It seems Mr Slade wasn't the best of drivers," he said when he'd finished. He was still talking to Anita. "In fact, Mrs Slade didn't want him to buy a Maserati."

"That's true, but Derek arranged for him to take a course, and that seemed to solve the problem."

"Except we're sitting here now discussing that problem. I'm thinking, you see, that this course he went on wasn't enough. Would that explain his accident, do you think?"

Her tone of voice hardened. Hayward had said she had a temper.

"I hope you're not blaming my husband, Mr Snape. He did what he could to help Mr Slade, and Frinton has it all in black and white."

Snape didn't reply. He could see she was thinking.

"But for all that," she added shrewdly, "if you're saying Mr Slade overestimated his ability, you're also saying his accident was all his own fault. I'd have to agree with that."

Van Piet sensed Snape wasn't going to stop there, and he didn't.

"We've learned Mr Slade had been thinking for some time of buying a Maserati. Maybe he held off because he'd guessed he wasn't up to it. You might conclude he was afraid of such a high-powered car."

"That's perfectly possible. He was a very mature man. I'm sure he had plenty of self-knowledge, despite what I said just now."

"Yet he also badly wanted the car he bought. Your husband told us he snapped it up in fact. Now, if I was caught between being afraid of a car and wanting it badly, I think I'd see if I couldn't try one out first. Then I could make up my mind."

He switched direction.

"Mr Rufus, it says on your website you hire out Maseratis as well as sell them. Did Mr Slade ever hire one of your cars?"

There was a fractional pause. Then, before her husband could speak, Anita answered drily,

"You're a clever man, Mr Snape. Derek, you'd better tell him before someone else does."

So she knew about Rufus and Hayward.

Rufus was still trying to look relaxed.

"Mr Slade hired one of my cars for a week at the beginning of June. It was just as you said, he wanted to buy a Maserati, but he wanted to try one out first and without his family knowing. So I let him hire one, and he garaged it in one of our lock-ups."

"Did you ever go with him when he took it out?"

"Just the once. He asked me to talk him through the controls, so I did."

"Did he have any trouble while he had it?"

Again there was a pause, but this time, Anita didn't say anything. Van Piet thought she'd worked out she'd make her husband look guilty if she had to prompt him all the time.

"He picked up a bad scratch on one side, which I decided to overlook, and then he went off the road altogether. It was near Wivenhoe. I cancelled the hire contract at that point and gave him his money back. The truth is, I lost my temper. I regret that now."

"Did he leave the road on a bend?"

"He did."

"And who paid for all the damage? Your insurance, was it, and then his would pay yours?"

"He didn't want that, his name would get to his own insurer because that's how these things work, and we both knew what that would mean – no insurance for his new Maserati. So I didn't make a claim, I used our body shop instead."

"In other words you made a prospective buyer grateful to you, and not just any prospective buyer but, so to speak, your benefactor, since he'd helped you with your dealership and you were doing well out of Esklivia. That must have made up for taking the hire car back, which some people would see as a vote of no confidence in his driving." He looked hard at Rufus. "You say you lost your temper, but maybe what you really wanted was to stop him turning the car into a write-off."

"Maseratis are worth a lot of money."

"That's one answer, but the big thing about write-offs is, you can't hide them up. The law says you have to report them."

No response.

"There was the lock-up garage as well, wasn't there?" Snape persisted. "Another favour to keep Mr Slade lined up for a sale."

Rufus was looking sweaty.

"Well, yes, if you put it like that. As you say, I owed him a lot. We both did."

"Those repairs you took on, they must have cost time and materials. Could I see the dockets if I asked for them?"

Anita got in first.

"There are no dockets. The damage looked worse than it was, so the jobs went through verbally. We destroyed the hire contract – his copy and ours -

because no money had changed hands in effect, and the costs, well, they were minimal, so we decided to absorb them. I can see that doesn't fit in with what I said about the accounts, but it was a one-off to help Mr Slade."

"And if Mr Rufus sold the car later, it wouldn't have a list of repairs attached to it."

"That's not fair," Rufus broke in. "Everyone knows dealers take out scratches and dents. Customers expect them to."

Snape turned towards him.

"That damage told you Mr Slade couldn't drive a Maserati. You could have refused to sell him one because of that, yet you did the opposite. That got you an accident waiting to happen, and when it did happen, you thought no one would point the finger at you because you'd done everything to cover your tracks. The only question in my mind is why you went through with it all."

"I don't accept any of that. The damage told me he'd need some practice, that's all. That's why I was keen – me, personally - for him to take the New Owner's course."

"A write-off would have killed your cover-up stone dead."

Anita intervened.

"But there wasn't a write-off, Mr Snape, and that's all there is to it. Please try to accept it."

Snape turned back to Rufus.

"Why didn't you tell us all this when we saw you last Wednesday?"

"I should have thought you could work that out for yourself. I didn't want you to think Mr Slade's death was down to me."

Snape sifted through his notes.

"When I spoke to you last Wednesday, you said you and Mrs Rufus were in Clacton Leisure Centre when Mr Slade was killed. I've confirmed that's correct, but it's left me wondering what you do there all that while. Would you like to tell us about it?"

The tension went down a notch. This was something Rufus could handle on his own, and Snape was hoping he might let something slip if he was allowed to talk freely.

"Like I said, Tuesday night is club night for Essex Swimmers. I go there because I do triathlons, and Anita goes because she's one of the best swimmers in Essex. We bike together as well, but swimming's how she wins medals. When we're not training, we coach. And towards the end we play water polo."

"You say you and Mrs Rufus bike together. Is that always around here?"

"Sometimes it is and sometimes we put our bikes in a van we've got and drive off somewhere else. Our son honours us with his presence if he isn't tied up with his friends, and some of the people who work for us come along, if we let them know we're going."

"Like Mr Pachini?"

"Why not? I was always lending him bikes because he never got round to buying one of his own, but he was fun to have around. The sea was what he really liked, though. We keep a Sunseeker motor yacht in The Ship's Log Sailing Club in Brightlingsea - " He paused to let Snape get it all down. "As I was saying, in Brightlingsea, so we'd pick him up from his house and spend the rest of the day on the water.

Holding him back was the problem. He finished with us the last Friday in July, yet he still wanted some friend to bring him to Brightlingsea the following Saturday so he could spend one more day at sea with us. He said if he didn't turn up, it wouldn't be his fault, it'd be his friend not being able to make it. As it happens, he didn't turn up, but he definitely wanted to."

Snape asked him whether he knew the friend's name.

"No, he never said it, and we didn't want to look as if we were prying."

Snape noted the motor yacht's name – The Empress Matilda - and its mooring number, then he asked where the Rufuses kept their van. It was in the integrated garage, and of course Snape could see it on his way out.

Rufus poured more coffee, and they gossiped about the motor trade, cycling and the weather, while in the back of his mind, Snape sorted out his impressions. Rufus was soft, but Anita was hard, clever and determined. That boded ill for Hayward, especially if she thought Rufus would protect her, because there she'd be very wrong. He'd be too busy kowtowing to his wife to do that.

When they were outside, Rufus brought a Vauxhall Movano out of his garage and obligingly opened its doors. It was ink blue, it had The Rufus Car Mart splashed on its sides, and it had six seats, including the driver's. That left plenty of room for bikes, sailing gear, or whatever else needed transporting, and a transit bike rack lay unused on the floor. Snape looked everything over without getting in, then he thanked them for their time and made his way with van Piet down the drive. At the gate he phoned Gulliver to find out where she was, and she said she was parked in a side street near the police station. He gave her a rendezvous point, and asked her not to hang about. They had another call to make yet.

Chapter 11

An angry phone call

"What did you make of all that?" van Piet asked once the Rufuses were out of earshot.

Snape shrugged his shoulders.

"We could have been hearing the truth, the whole truth, and nothing but the truth."

"Or?"

"Or we could have been hearing how Slade was very skilfully got at. Don't ask me why they did it, but I have the feeling Rufus set him up to die, and his wife was in on it."

"The lifeguard as killer, you mean, with Rufus being the lifeguard?"

"Something like that."

Snape gathered his thoughts for a moment.

"Before I forget," he went on, "Barbara Davis is in the clear – up to a point anyway. Colleagues in Bristol have asked around, and there's security footage as well. She was there when she said she was all right."

"So where do you go from here?"

Snape frowned.

"Pachini's a cause for concern, and I haven't got any fingerprints or DNA for him. So, first thing tomorrow morning I'm going to put a team from Forensics into Rufus For Maseratis and another team into The Rufus Car Mart. They'll fingerprint everyone who's there, and they'll take DNA swabs while they're at it - people always go with that, they like to show they've got nothing to hide, even if they have. Then the teams will split up. Rufus will take some of his team home to do his van over, Anita Rufus will take some of hers to this boat of theirs in Brightlingsea, and the rest will converge on Pachini's old house. I'll get a search warrant made out in case there's a problem with Davis. What I'm after is a spread of hairs, prints and whatnot we can't link to a name."

"Why that?"

"Well, Pachini's been in Rufus For Maseratis, the van, the boat, and 32 Walsingham Close, so if those four places produce any three- or four-way matches, we can reasonably say they're his."

"You think the Rufuses will play ball, do you?"

"No question. They're desperate to look clean, you saw it for yourself this afternoon."

They'd turned into a street lined with lime trees, but there was no sign of Gulliver, so they kept walking to avoid attention. It wasn't the sort of area where people stood about on the pavement.

"I'll tell you something else about Pachini," Snape went on. "He had two bank accounts with Lloyds, deposit and current, and he closed them both during his lunch break on July 27th. He cancelled his Lloyds credit card at the same time, and it was the only card he had, Lloyds checked that for me. They also told me he'd transferred most of his savings to an account in his own name with the Credito Emiliano in Parma and withdrawn the balance in cash. So you might say, he wound up the bureaucratic bits and kept enough readies to see him out of England. But that would only figure if he wasn't sticking around for long, so why hasn't he booked his ticket yet?"

Gulliver saw them as she approached from the other direction. She passed them, put in a neat three-point turn, glided alongside and killed the engine. She was back in civvies. As she walked round to the passenger seat, van Piet climbed into the back and Snape took the wheel.

"We're going to The Ship's Log Sailing Club in Brightlingsea," he told them as they pulled away.

Then he asked Gulliver what she'd turned up.

"The living rooms are all round the back, so what goes on in the street doesn't always get heard. That said, three couples in three separate houses recalled hearing car doors slam after dark."

"Did they say what the times were?"

"No, and I didn't put any into their heads, but then there was this man living on his own in a fourth house. He was reading a book in his front room. One of the slams made him look out of the window, and he actually saw Pachini getting into a white saloon. He reckoned it was between half past eight and nine o'clock, and he was definite it was Pachini, because they knew each other."

Snape asked if he'd noticed the car's make or registration.

"No to both, but he said the driver was hooded and could have been male or female. Apparently he heard other slams before and afterwards, but this was the only time he looked out. People think you're nosey if you keep looking out of the window. That's what he said anyway."

"So we've got a positive identification and a likely confirmation of the time," said Snape. "Anything else?"

"A lady at Number 30 told me Miss Davis goes to Germany a lot. Sometimes she goes to see a publisher, and sometimes she goes to family in Bonn. This lady knows that because she keeps an eye on Davis's house when she's away, and Davis usually says where she's going."

Snape told Gulliver about the Rufuses and the Monday blitzes. Van Piet disappeared behind his newspaper.

The Ship's Log Sailing Club was an upmarket development behind a high wire fence on the eastern shore of the Colne estuary. It was familiar territory to Snape and Gulliver. The creek-filled Essex coast is ideal for waterborne crime, so the Armed Support Unit had a patrol boat on permanent standby in Harwich harbour. Once in a while, it put into The Ship's Log, sometimes to check things out and sometimes to feel someone's collar. Wealth and breaking the law had a way of going together.

Snape opened the fortified gate with his Emergency Services pass, and the club's Commodore was soon leading them along the boardwalk to The Empress Matilda. The Commodore was a portly, white-bearded man in an anorak and waterproof leggings, and the ID round his neck said Guy Phillips-Smith. To most club members, he was simply part of the place – efficient, unobtrusive, and easy to get on with - but Snape knew he was a former

Warrant Officer Class 1 in the Royal Navy Police (known in the service as 'the crushers'). That had been useful to know in the past, and it could be useful again. He made a mental note to tell van Piet.

The air smelled of salt, gulls were wheeling and shrieking overhead, and the weather station was signalling a Force 4-5 with gusting. It was good sailing for people who knew what they were doing, and plenty of moorings were empty.

"The Rufuses take her out fairly regularly," Phillips-Smith told them as he scrolled back through the traffic log on his smartphone. "They're good sailors, and once they're out, they like to head for deep water."

They halted by The Empress Matilda, 49 feet of twin-engined elegance and power.

"On July 28th she was moored up all day, but on July 29th she was out," Phillips-Smith read off. "As I remember, they were late casting off, something about someone who didn't turn up, or so they said. Matteo Pachini was the name. He'd finished working in Mr Rufus's workshop, and he was going to have one last sail before he went home to Italy. I can show you what he looked like, if you like. He wanted a photo to send to his parents last Easter, but he'd left his smartphone at home, so I took one on mine and sent it to his. It should be in here somewhere."

He worked his smartphone again, and there were the soft brown eyes and black curly hair Snape and van Piet had seen in Rufus For Maseratis. This time he was sitting astern of The Empress Matilda's cabin. He had a big grin on his face, and he was waving at the camera. Van Piet noticed he wasn't wearing a life jacket.

"No, he never did. He couldn't swim either, but you can't tell some people."

"Are you sure he didn't turn up on July 29th?" Snape asked.

"He didn't while I was standing where I'm standing now. But I had to go to my office to talk to someone whose boat had taken a knock, so I wasn't about when the Rufuses finally cast off."

Snape was becoming impatient. There seemed to be snags everywhere.

"Weren't they on the cctv?" he asked testily.

The answer, please, had to be yes.

Phillips-Smith shook his head.

"Normally they would be, but there was no cctv that day, because the whole system was being replaced. We destroyed the hard drive ourselves. You never know where these things might end up."

"Did the Rufuses know there was no cctv?"

Snape's eyes were narrowed down to slits.

"Mrs Rufus did, she's on the Premises Committee, so I assume Mr Rufus did as well. She saw the replacement through from start to finish, and a very good job she made of it."

While Snape was driving back to Chelmsford, van Piet went into the *Standard's* website to check Deborah Watkins was still writing for them. She was. Hoping he might yet get home more or less on time, he put through a guardedly optimistic call to Celia Tyler. Snape was also hoping for a stress-free end to the day, but once they were back in Police HQ, there were Monday's blitzes to organise and a search warrant for the Pachini house to apply for. There were Deborah Watkins's details to give to van Piet as well. The duty inspector told him they were on his desk in his office.

"We'll fetch them now, Willem, then you can be on your way. You'd better go too, Sal, you're way over shift. Do your report in the morning."

Watkins's details were on three sheets of A4 in a taped-up manila envelope. They comprised her personal data as they were at the time of the murder, plus a summary of the investigation. Van Piet was giving them a first read through when the phone on Snape's desk buzzed. Snape looked at the caller's number - it was Hayward. He mouthed her name towards van Piet and raised the volume.

"Hullo, Steph, Snape here. What can I do for you?"

"Were you in Five Willows this morning, Mr Snape? And were two other people with you, the man you came to see Mr Rufus with and a woman?"

So she had seen them, and she definitely wasn't grateful.

"I have to say yes, Steph, I wanted to see where you live. I'm concerned about you, you see. The other two people were colleagues of mine. I can vouch for both of them."

"I've got very good eyesight, and I thought I saw some people from my upstairs window when I happened to look out, so I got my binoculars out to make sure. Not long after, the woman practically walked up to my front door. You had no right to let her do that. Why are you so concerned about me anyway?"

"You could know more about Mr Slade's death than you realise, and you might say the wrong thing to someone."

"Like to you. Is this a murder hunt then?"

"Mr Slade's death is unexplained, and it means what it says. He might have been driving badly or the car might have been defective in some way. If it was, we have to find out what the problem was and why it was there."

"I'm not likely to say the wrong thing about that, I don't know the first thing about cars. Have you spoken to Mr Rufus yet? You know, about the things I said."

"I saw him this afternoon, and I kept you right out of it. I have to say, he had an answer for everything."

"I bet he did. Was his wife there?"

Snape said she was.

"She'll have worked it out who told you things. Like I said, I think she knows about me and Mr Rufus, so she'll put two and two together, that's how she is. But he wasn't upset when you asked him about what I told you, is that what you're saying?"

"I don't think he could afford to be, not with his wife there."

"Which means he wasn't. Now listen, Mr Snape. I don't want you or anyone else hanging round my cottage. How would you like someone watching who went in and out of your front door? And you don't have to bother about me. I know when to say something and when not to."

Snape could see he wasn't going to win, but he felt he had to keep trying.

"Did you know there was a brutal murder in Five Willows and that the murderer was never caught?" he asked.

"Don't try and frighten me with that. Everyone in Five Willows knows about it, they just don't talk about it, and anyway, it was years ago. It's got nothing to do with me."

"But, even so –"

"Even so nothing, Mr Snape. There must have been twenty or thirty murders in Chelmsford since the one in Five Willows, but I bet you still live there. Why should I be any different?"

Snape was wondering what else he could say.

"Are you sure you aren't keeping something back?" he asked. "You know yourself you'll get done if you are."

"I've told you what I've remembered so far. If I remember any more, I'll talk to you again. What I don't want is you peering at me all the time. Have I made that clear?"

He'd lost, and that was that. He said yes, she'd made it clear, and he'd do his best not to intrude any more. She thanked him ironically and terminated the call.

"She wants to keep the coast clear so Rufus can come creeping round," Snape said to van Piet, leaning back in his chair and lifting his hands in despair. "I'll get an unmarked car to drive past her place now and then, especially after dark. It's not much, but it's the best I can do."

"What about tomorrow? Presumably she'll be on site when your blitzes start. She might take it personally."

"I'll brief someone exactly how to question her. The trouble is, Willem, she's worked out grassing on Rufus hasn't got her anywhere, so she may take him on directly. And that, you'll appreciate, could be very bad for her health."

Chapter 12

Mixed signals from Deborah Watkins

Van Piet reached Gorris Hall not much later than he'd thought he would, and Watkins was seriously on his mind. If he asked to see her on his own, she might recall her run-in with Van Piet Banking and say no. And if he asked to see her with Snape, Snape's name might bring back such bad memories, she'd have a second reason to hang up. So he'd better contact her through someone who might just have a hold over her. He might learn a bit about her as well that way.

Despite the warm weather, the Tylers had prepared roast leg of lamb with trimmings. The scrubbed wooden table in the kitchen, where van Piet preferred to have his meals, was already laid, and the air conditioning was pitched just right. The roast smelled good, but Watkins came first, he told himself, so after an apology he really meant, he went upstairs to his securitised study and called the *Standard's* Business and City Editor. He was Watkins's line manager, and he'd likely still be in his office. That's where he spent most evenings.

"Clive Taylor here," van Piet heard from his smartphone, "and I see Willem van Piet's number in front of me. How can I help, old son?"

"I'm calling about Deborah Watkins, but she doesn't know it yet. I need some background info about her, and then I'll ask you a favour. It's important, Clive. I wouldn't be ringing if it wasn't."

Taylor asked if there was a story in it for him. He'd guessed a long time ago there was more to van Piet than banking, but he'd never found out what it was.

"I can't say yet, but there could be."

"Same old Willem. All right, I'll assume there is, and I'll stand by to be disappointed. I was here when she joined us, and I was here when she came back after she'd left us for a bit, so I know her fairly well. As a journalist she's as sharp as a tack, but as a person, well, let me put it this way: She's friendly enough on the surface, but what she's really good at is fending people off."

"Was she like that before her fiancé was murdered?"

"Ah, so that's where you're at. No, she wasn't nearly so uptight then. She was quite a bit younger, of course, and she had a career to make, so perhaps she was just being nice to the boss. But she didn't strike me that way. The iron curtain definitely clanged down later."

"Has she married since she's been back?"

"If she has, she hasn't told me, and I think she'd have managed that much. Where do you fit in anyway?"

Van Piet phrased himself carefully. Her fiancé's murder was being reviewed in the light of another death, and because there was a money angle, he was lending the police a hand. He asked whether she was still in the building, and Taylor said she was. Should he transfer the call? He'd promise not to listen in.

Van Piet thanked him, but no.

"If I contact her cold, she might hang up on me, so this is the favour I'm asking for. Give her my smartphone number and say I want to meet her urgently. If it comes from you, she might just fall into line. Say the lead officer from Essex Police wants to meet her as well. His name's Eddie Snape – I'm sure she'll remember it. Where we get together is up to her, so long as it happens soon."

Taylor said he'd do his best, then he tried to draw van Piet out some more. When that didn't work, he invited him to have lunch at the *Standard* when he had the time. He hoped he might yet glean something that way.

"I'll make sure Jerome Shaffer's locked up," he joked. "I don't want you having to fight your way in."

Van Piet agreed it might be a good idea.

Shaffer was the *Standard's* Head of Security, and he ruled the building with a rod of iron. What Taylor didn't know was how well van Piet and Shaffer knew each other. Shaffer had been in the Special Intelligence Service, and after three months under cover in Kalilingrad, Russia's weapon-stuffed exclave to the north-east of Poland, he'd been shot across the inter-state border as he'd been slipping back into Polish territory. It had been a joint SIS/SRO operation, and van Piet, who had been waiting for him in the dark on the Polish side, had gathered him up and driven him at speed through thickly falling snow to the Medical University of Warsaw, where Shaffer had fought for his life under round-the-clock protection from the Wojska Specjaine – Poland's élite special force. There had been a delay while the Russians had worked out how to cross the Polish border without provoking an incident, but no one doubted they'd get Shaffer if they could, so with Germany turning a diplomatic blind eye, van Piet had smuggled Shaffer through western Poland and Germany to a British submarine waiting off the coast of Schleswig-Holstein. Shaffer had spent more time in hospital in London, then he'd been invalided out of the SIS with a gratuity and a pension, plus discreet help to get his job with the *Standard*. He and van Piet had stayed in touch.

Van Piet terminated his call to Taylor and scuttled down to the roast, which he acknowledged out loud was more than he deserved. Dessert was rice pudding with nutmeg, and he was poised to make his one contribution to the meal by taking over the serving when his smartphone buzzed. It was Watkins. Once again he excused himself and hurried upstairs. Yes, she remembered Snape's name - he hadn't been in charge, but he'd been involved round the edges and he'd witnessed her statement. She remembered van Piet's name as well. His bank had been one of her failures, she said, and she laughed. It was a good start, but it didn't last.

"Why are you raking up Ashley's murder?" she asked, suddenly harsh. "Can't you leave the dead alone?"

Van Piet found her tone strangely mixed. The surface was all aggression, but underneath, there was hurt and distress. Was she still grieving over Ashley Johnson's death? Was that why the iron curtain had come down?

"Mr Snape is involved in a fresh case – he's in charge this time - and you might have some information he can use. You don't have to come to us. We'll come to London, if that's easier for you."

She didn't respond straight away. When she did, she said,

"I'd better see him then – you as well, if you're helping - but I don't want you to come to the *Standard*, it's none of their business. Come to my flat, it's in Gilbert Mews off Kensington High Street. Can you make 10.30 tomorrow morning? I'm on lates at the moment, I'm pulling in data from the States, so I shan't be missed if you don't keep me too long."

She gave him her full address and the postal code for the satnav. And yes, the number on his screen was her own. After she'd terminated, van Piet called Snape at home. He was in his greenhouse, trying to put the day behind him.

"It's a fishing expedition," van Piet admitted, "but it's worth a try, and we're both invited. I'll tell you more in the car tomorrow."

"Tomorrow's Monday, so we'll have to be on the road by 8.00 at the latest. Then there's the parking at the other end."

"She says she'll park her car at work overnight so we can use her lock-up. She'll open it up when we get there."

"Free parking in London, that has to be a first. I'll tell the Met we're coming, and if they don't like it, I'll get in touch. You never know, they might be after her for something else."

After the rice pudding, which had kept its heat, van Piet made the coffee and loaded the dishwasher. It was tokenism, he knew, but he had to show willing somehow. Afterwards, he went into the conservatory to call Célestine and Jackie. Jackie, who was adopted, had been born profoundly deaf - her parents had rejected her when they found that out, since they didn't think they could cope. He switched on the camera on his smartphone to let her lip-read. Her boarding school had worked miracles, she could understand everything he said, and when she spoke, her intonation was just about perfect. Part of him was glad she and Célestine were in France now things were getting busy. If they'd stayed at home and he'd been out all the while, all three of them would have felt badly about it.

The sun rose at 5.58 the next morning. Van Piet didn't see it – he was shaving, and the bathroom he was in faced north - but by the time he started his car, the sky was bright, and the temperature was on the up. When he arrived in Chelmsford, Snape was in his office waiting to get started. Van Piet gave him Watkins's number, and he phoned through the registration of the car they'd be travelling in. She didn't sound hostile, but she wasn't friendly either.

"Slade's Maserati," Snape said as he locked his office door and they set off down the corridor. "We keep hitting problems we can't solve, so I've asked the NCA to lend a hand. I've kept quiet about Penny Warrener, but it looks as if she was right about the car being meddled with. If the NCA thinks the same, it will cover her tracks."

Traffic was heavy all the way to London, and in town it was worse, so it was 10.29 when Snape finally turned off Kensington High Street into Gilbert Mews - a narrow lane so tranquil, it was like on another planet. A 1930s block of flats took up the whole of one side. It had matt brown garage doors let in along the ground floor, and Watkins was standing in front of one them. As they got nearer, she read the registration, waved to make herself known and opened up with a zapper.

"Mind your doors," she called in as they were squeezing out. "These garages weren't built for modern cars."

Once they were outside on the pavement, she secured the door – it was steel, they both noticed – and led them up the external staircase to the first floor. Again there was the ritual of unlocking and locking, first the outside door, then the door off the corridor, before they were finally in her flat. It was bigger than either Snape or van Piet had expected, and it had, as they perceived through a door standing slightly ajar in the living room, the luxury of a separate dining room. The living room windows looked out on a compact well-tended garth that no one would suspect was there.

"Please, sit down," Watkins said, gesturing towards two of the easy chairs that formed a trio round a low table, "and help yourselves to coffee. It's on the trolley waiting for you."

The room felt snug with its carpet and rugs, its scatter cushions and its vases of flowers, but it was definitely furnished for one, and van Piet thought the easy chairs had been placed where they were so Watkins could keep control. She was in her thirties, shortish, dark-haired and rounding out. She was wearing a lightweight black trouser suit, a white cotton blouse, and dark blue deck shoes that didn't quite match. There were no rings on her stubby fingers.

Snape was uncertain what manner to adopt. Personal contact was there from the past, but so were her memories and his own sense of failure. Once the coffee ritual was over, he got things started the way he'd been briefed in the car, relieved to know van Piet was poised to take over. Van Piet had said he'd worked out a good approach. He'd based it on what he'd heard from Rufus.

"We're grateful to you for seeing us," Snape began. "We're investigating a car crash in which a man called Geoffrey Slade was killed. It happened last Tuesday, and we're treating the death as unexplained. Did you hear about it by any chance?"

"I did. Associated Press flagged it up on my screen, but it didn't happen in London, so I let it go."

"Mr Slade worked for an investment company called Esklivia," van Piet came in. "That's why the police have asked me to help them. When you and Mr Johnson moved to Five Willows, you joined BBC Essex, and you saw to it your fiancé got a lot of publicity, or so I'm told. Now, Mr Slade had lived in Essex for many years. We'd like to know whether he contacted Mr Johnson at all."

She looked at Snape, then back to van Piet, as if trying to gauge how much they knew. Was that why she'd agreed to see them? To find that out?

"Since you ask, Mr van Piet, the answer is he did. It was after a TV item about Ashley we'd put out one tea time. Mr Slade phoned for an invitation, then he came round and offered to help us with our financing. Mrs Slade came with him. He said a veterinary practice was the next best thing to a gold mine, and he offered us a loan below the market rate, because he was certain he'd get his money back. As I recall, he did all the talking. I think he brought his

117

wife so we'd take him seriously. He made sure we knew she was Esklivia's owner."

Van Piet asked whether they'd accepted the offer or signed up for any of Esklivia's investments.

"No to both, Ashley could get all the money we needed from his father, Charles Johnson. Charles was already worth millions, and he's worth even more millions now. He makes industrial fuses and exports them to I don't know how many countries. I told the police about Ashley's father during the investigation. Do I have to go over it all again?"

"If you could, I'd appreciate it."

She pressed her lips together and interlaced her fingers.

"Very well, but I can't say I want to. Charles Johnson's wife left him for someone else, and after that Ashley was everything to him. He paid for Ashley's studies when he was training, and he chipped in with the rent when Ashley got his first job. That was in Bermondsey." She broke off and caught her breath. "I can see Ashley as I talk to you now, Mr van Piet. The partners in Bermondsey were a hundred years old, and Ashley was the fresh-faced junior. He looked so proud. You can't imagine how much I loved him."

Her features had softened, and a wistful look had crept over them.

"Bermondsey was where we first met," she went on. "It was in a pub called The Iron Duke. I was doing a story in the borough, and Ashley was on his lunch break. I can still remember what we talked about - but I forgot, that's not what you're interested in, is it. It's Ashley and his money, as if that's all that mattered."

118

The aggression was back, and the harsh tone of voice with it.

"So let's get it over with. Charles lent us the money for the house we bought in Five Willows. It was a long-term loan at nought percent, and it covered everything Ashley would need as a vet as well."

"I understand housing is cheap in Five Willows," said van Piet.

"You understand correctly, and that was part of the equation. Charles saw the loan as a gift, but Ashley was determined to pay it back. The other part of the equation was the livestock around Five Willows - there was plenty of it. Plus Ashley wouldn't be the junior any more, he'd be the boss."

"So Mr Slade went away empty-handed."

"What else? He was very nice, both of them were, but we simply didn't need him."

"You didn't mention Mr Slade when we were investigating your fiancé's murder," Snape put in.

"No one asked about him. He came, he went, they both did. That was all there was to it."

Snape wondered if she'd had anything to do with him since, but she shook her head and said, "No, nothing at all. I can't think why I should."

She seemed to be starting to stonewall, so van Piet tried another angle.

"You're a trained investigative journalist, Miss Watkins, and six years ago and more, the whole financial sector was being turned over by people like you. Did you ever take a look at Esklivia?"

"When Mr Slade got in touch, I'd changed jobs, remember, but yes, I made one or two enquiries just to be on the safe side. I didn't push it, though, and after Ashley was killed, I wanted to make a clean

119

break, so I destroyed my notes and got rid of the house. I couldn't bear to live in it any more, and Charles forgave the part of the loan I couldn't clear through the sale to help me get rid of it quickly. Esklivia struck me as clean, if that's what you're asking. It dealt in off-shores, which I'm not especially fond of, but that didn't make it illegal."

"Did you offer Mr Taylor anything on Esklivia when you asked him if you could go back to the *Standard*?"

"No."

"You realise we can check that."

"Do as you please, it's still no."

"You told me you were on lates when you phoned me last night. Were you on lates last Tuesday evening?"

"When Geoffrey Slade bought it, do you mean? Yes, I was. I was in my office from something like four in the afternoon till getting on for midnight. It's got big glass windows, and lots of people saw me in there. He was killed in a car crash anyway. He wouldn't need me to help him with that."

"You could be right. Now, you've told us more than we could have hoped, but I'd like to clear up two last points, if I may."

She didn't say anything, but she didn't refuse either, so he pressed on.

"As I understand it, when you went out to look for your fiancé on the night he was murdered, you put the outside light on and saw him clearly enough to realise he was beyond help. Most people's outside lights don't reach very far, and they're usually on the dim side. Can you tell me how you could see so much?"

"Is that all? I thought you were cleverer than that. Ashley believed a country vet should be on call twenty-four hours a day, and he expected people to ring his doorbell at all times as well. In fact, he wanted them to, it was all part of his big, beautiful dream. So he had the drive and the gate widened to make room for farm vehicles and their trailers, and he also had the whole drive lit up so they could see what they were doing if they had to come at night. There's your answer, Mr van Piet – it was bright out there. What's your second point?"

"You didn't have any cctv in Five Willows. Did people know you didn't?"

"Did Geoffrey Slade know, do you mean? The answer is yes, and he wasn't the only one. Ashley was proud of our place, and he liked to show people round. That included the Slades. Geoffrey Slade asked him about cctv, since it seemed an obvious thing to have, and Ashley replied he'd installed an alarm system, and it would have to do. He didn't want cameras everywhere and big notices saying everyone who came to the house was being recorded. He saw it as an affront to his customers, though I expect most of them had cctv themselves. I know he told Geoffrey Slade all that, because I was there when he did it."

"And you didn't agree with your fiancé? About the cctv, I mean."

"Of course I didn't, but I wasn't going to argue." She looked exasperated and tapped her knee. "Looking back, I wish I had. There's not much I can do about it now."

The Rufuses should have been next on van Piet's list of questions. As part of his transformation from town to country vet, Ashley Johnson had traded in his Skoda Fabia for a low-mileage Land Rover Defender. Snape knew he'd done the trade in Chelmsford because it had been traced back, but after Watkins had been asked about the Slades, the next question should have been: Had either of the Rufuses come calling as well? But van Piet didn't ask it, and after a few polite nothings to round things off, he said they had to be going.

"Why did you skip the Rufuses?" Snape asked as he stop-started towards the North Circular Road. "If the Slades could spot a target, so could they."

"We'd heard a lot, and until that point Miss Watkins had been careful not to say anything that could put her in any danger. Bringing in the Rufuses could have changed that."

"Why?"

"She could handle questions about the Slades - they came, they went, and that was that, or so she said. But if we then moved on to the Rufuses, that could sound as if we suspected some kind of organised effort to enrol Ashley Johnson in Esklivia, and if Miss Watkins had said anything to confirm that suspicion, that could have been tricky for her. I thought someone was eavesdropping, you see. When she phoned me yesterday, it struck me as odd someone as private as she's supposed to be would ask us into her home – except that there, either she or someone else could set things up in advance. As you saw, the dining room door was open when we got there, and the coffee was already made, so we couldn't look into the dining room while she was absent in the kitchen. If you ask me, Eddie, she was taking us for a ride. It would be interesting to know why."

Once Watkins was sure Snape and van Piet had gone, she went into the dining room, where Neville Thurston was sitting on a high-backed chair he'd moved away from the table to be out of sight. He was dressed for a summer's day in cotton trousers and a fresh white shirt with rolled-up sleeves. Only his thickened arms and hands connected him with quarrying and building.

"You were sent to keep your ears open," she said, assertive and sure of herself. "How did it go?"

"It sounded fine to me. Better than I could have done."

He looked back at her, equally sure of himself, and in the room's potent silence, the atmosphere morphed from stand-off to sexually charged - at first spontaneously, or so it seemed, but then because both of them wanted it that way. Watkins was good at signalling availability when she chose to, and she was signalling it now. She had all the more effect, because she'd signalled the direct opposite before van Piet and Snape had arrived.

"I've done my job," he added, sensing where things were going. "Do I stay or do I go?"

She'd got him.

"You stay, it's playtime now. Right now, in this flat, and everything else blanked out."

He hesitated.

"You're dangerous for me, you could get me killed. I'm not supposed to have anything to do with you. Personally, I mean."

"I could say the same to you, but who's to know? I'll give you your question back: Are you staying or are you going? It's up to you."

He took longer than she thought he would, then he said,

"I'm staying. I can keep a secret."

As she opened her bedroom door, she felt the steel-cold thrill of victory. She'd give him his pleasure now, so exquisitely he'd come back for more. And if she played her cards right, maybe he'd start telling her things. It was worth a try.

Chapter 13

Pain from the past

When Snape and van Piet reached the M11, the traffic thinned out, and Snape came back to what Watkins had told them.

"She isn't looking too good, Willem, keeping quiet like that. Someone knew Johnson would be on his own by the time he got home. That's got to include her."

"Anyone could have followed him home in the dark. He'd have his torch on, don't forget."

"You live in the country, Willem. Whoever followed him would have needed a torch as well, and you know it."

"Not if they had night goggles."

Snape still couldn't get his mind round what he'd heard. Did van Piet have any bright ideas?

"Well, there's Watkins's notes. You'd think, if she truly got nowhere with Esklivia, she'd junk them straight away, but according to her, she kept them till after her fiancé was murdered. I wouldn't call it a bright idea, but it's one I'd bear in mind."

"Maybe she just hung on to them. People do, you know. We're not all machines like you."

By the time they got back to Police HQ, it was too late for van Piet to drive home before going with Snape to Bishop's Green, so he fetched a sandwich and some tea from the canteen and installed himself in Snape's office to talk to Garry on the secure link. He wanted him to put people who were crossing his horizon into some sort of order. But before he contacted Ashell House, he needed to sort something else out. Watkins had said her office had big glass windows and lots of people saw her in there, but in her line of work, she'd be constantly dealing with people who'd never talk to her if they thought anyone else knew about it. At the same time, she seemed to value her privacy, so did she have somewhere apart from her flat in Gilbert Mews where she could meet people in secret? Taylor would know, but van Piet didn't want to ask him in case he slipped the word to Watkins, so he opted to contact Anke Sweelinck, Head of Van Piet Banking's Intelligence Unit in Amsterdam. When Watkins had tried to hack into the bank's computers, it had been Sweelinck who had warned Watkins off, and that meant Sweelinck had a follow-up file, just in case Watkins was foolish enough to try again. The trouble was, Sweelinck wouldn't be in her office just yet, since she preferred to work at night. So he settled for a text, though he wasn't happy about it. He liked talking to Sweelinck about Amsterdam. It was nearly as good as being there.

Finally, after he'd told Garry what he wanted, he asked Celia Tyler not to cook for him any more. He was getting so unreliable, it was painful.

Letting van Piet have his office didn't bother Snape much, since he had his own calls to make and any other room would do, as long as he could shut the door. The coroner was first on his list. He didn't want an inquest till he'd firmed his enquiries up a lot more, but he had no idea when that would be. He rang Tait's office in County Hall, but she wasn't there, and her secretary was in evasive mode, so he guessed she was on the family farm near Tiptree. He tried her mobile and found he'd guessed right.

"Let me see what I can do," she said amiably – her Red Polls always put her in a good mood. "I can't register the death until after the inquest, but now the post mortem's out of the way, I can issue an interim death certificate to let probate be applied for. That usually makes the relatives friendlier, but if that's not enough, why don't I open an inquest and adjourn it, if it looks like the best thing to do? Bear with me a moment." She downloaded her schedule onto her smartphone. "Wednesday 23rd at 10.00 is available. Will that suit you?"

Snape thought it would, he'd let her know if anything got in the way. And thanks.

Thurston came next, but Snape had to call Leicestershire's Chief Constable first, since Thurston lived in his bailiwick. He might get some background as well.

"Neville Thurston? He's a fine man," he heard down the line. "The Rotary Club, the Food Bank, the Air Ambulance fund – you name it, he's always in there somewhere. He's done well for himself over the years, and he likes to spread it around."

"What about his private life? Anything I should know?"

"He's never married. The word is, he likes the ladies, but there's never been any scandal. Legally he's got a clean sheet. I know that because a couple of months ago he applied to have his firearm certificate renewed, so I had a search made. He goes to a shooting club in Leicester, and his weapon's a Sig Sauer P320. I'm told he's pretty good with it."

Snape didn't mention the Sig Sauer when he called Thurston on his mobile. Thurston sounded as if a visit would make his day.

"Why not come tomorrow? Come to the quarry, that's where I am now, you can have a look round while you're here. And bring whoever you like. What was the name again?"

Snape said van Piet, spelled it out and arranged a time. Van Piet was all for it when he heard. He had his own questions to put to Thurston.

"That Sig Sauer, it's quite a weapon," he said as they left Police HQ for the car park. "You might get the word to Sal. Tell her what we've learned about Watkins as well. She needs to know these things."

Bishop's Green was just a short drive away, and they soon found the detached Georgian house they were looking for. Cottrell answered the door, and they followed her through the entrance hall into a roomy high-ceilinged drawing room with typically symmetrical windows. Laura Slade, smart-casually dressed like Cottrell, was sitting in a leather-covered easy chair, part of a suite that centred on the Adam-style fireplace. The hearth was fronted with a mock-tapestry screen they'd bought in Athens. It depicted Artemis destroying Acteon with his own hounds. A low rosewood table on a fluffy rug dominated the space between the hearth and the three-piece. Van Piet took the second easy chair, Snape seated himself on the settee with his notebook next to him, and Cottrell slid a leather-covered pouf next to Laura's chair with her foot.

"Tea or coffee, gentlemen?" Cottrell asked, still standing, and when they said tea, she brushed Laura's hair with her fingertips as she disappeared into the kitchen. Laura looked bone weary. When Cottrell brought the tea things in on a large heirloom-looking serving tray, she looked up with an affectionate smile. But the effort it took was obvious.

"Help yourselves to milk and sugar," Cottrell said as she set the tray down, and Snape wondered what kind of impression she was trying to create, with or without Laura's connivance. Loving and domestic for sure, relaxed and confident as well. If either of them was nervous, it wasn't showing. Snape asked Laura how she was coping.

"I haven't enjoyed today, but I simply had to go in to work. My mother was there, and that helped me a lot. I was just telling Millie, I've booked a seat in the Festival Hall for tomorrow evening. I feel if I sit at home, I shall be losing a battle I have to win. My mother's taking the same line, and I think she's right."

Snape asked what she was going to hear.

"Brahms's *Requiem*. It will remind me of my father, he liked it a lot. He always went to it on his own, it affected him so much, and he'd drive a long way to take in a performance." She gave a sort of laugh. "I'll try not to burst into tears in the middle of it."

"Will you be on your own yourself?"

"I'm having tea after work with an old friend in Islington, but yes, after that I'll be on my own. That's how I want it. I may stay in town on my own as well. I'll take a small bag with me, just in case."

Cottrell, now seated on the pouf, took her hand and kissed the back of it. She was taller than Laura and, close up, visibly older – Snape thought around forty – but her girlish face and her easy way of dressing made her seem a lot younger.

It was time to move on.

"Miss Cottrell, I understand Esklivia's gain was J.P. Morgan's loss," he began. "Would you like to tell us about it?"

Her mouth tightened and her gaze became hard.

"I'd really rather not, but since you're here to do a job, I'll do as you ask. I went to J.P. Morgan from university because I liked what they offered, but there was a Tarzan culture there like you'd never believe. They soon worked out I preferred my own sex to theirs, but instead of leaving me be, they started a kind of war of attrition. I suppose they felt threatened if I didn't see them as every woman's dream. E-mails went round headed 'Dildos for the workers', or 'Who needs Holland when there's a dyke in the office?' - that sort of thing. Some genius scrawled 'Excepting Millie Cottrell' on the door of the ladies' loo, and another Einstein daubed 'Plus Millie the Man' on the door of the gents'. It was stupid and pathetic, but it kept on and on, and whenever I complained to my line manager, all I got was, 'It's just the boys having fun', as if I was the one who was peeling bananas."

130

She was visibly stressed now. Laura put her hand on her shoulder.

"But they were the apes, not me, Mr Snape. I'd been laughed at and bullied at school, my parents didn't even try to hide their shame, and now the life I'd dreamed about – just being me and working for J.P. Morgan - was disappearing down the pan. I was actually shedding tears in a bistro one lunchtime when Mrs Slade sat down opposite me. I didn't know her then, but so far as I recall, she said there were no other single seats free, so did I mind? She can't have seen I was crying at first, but then she did. We became close after that, and after she'd made the enquiries you'd expect, she told me Head of IT at Esklivia was being advertised, but if I wanted the job, it was mine, and she'd pull the advertisement, because she'd heard good things about me.

"Naturally I wanted it, and it's been bliss ever since. Laura was at university then, but she was in Esklivia House a lot while she was qualifying, and we felt, well, attracted to each other. Mr and Mrs Slade were unbelievable about that, they positively fostered our feelings for each other, and once Laura had eased herself into Esklivia, Mrs Slade made her Head of Compliance so we'd have equal status."

Van Piet said it was a moving story. Cottrell must have felt very loyal to Mr and Mrs Slade.

"Totally. And now Mr Slade is gone, I'm totally loyal to Mrs Slade. Why should I hide it?"

"I've no idea. I understand you're salaried. Are you content with what you earn?"

"Esklivia pays me top dollar, it always has. Much more than J.P. Morgan, for all the money they're sitting on. So yes, I'm entirely content with it."

"If I might put a delicate question to you, Miss Slade," van Piet went on, moving his attention from the one to the other. "Miss Cottrell has been open about her sexuality. Were you aware of yours before you met your partner?"

Laura blushed, then she giggled.

"You think I might be offended, don't you, but the answer is yes, and I'm proud to say it. My parents knew as well, and unlike Millie's, they took it in their stride. Can you tell me why you ask?"

"Not at the moment, but I'm grateful for your answer. It's helped me a lot."

He sat back in his chair as a signal for Snape to take over again. Snape turned to a fresh page in his notebook and, calling it his routine question, asked where they'd been the previous Tuesday after 5.00 in the afternoon. It was Cottrell who answered.

"Laura and I came home from Esklivia after lunch. We came on the underground as far as Theydon Bois, and Mrs Slade came with us. Then we went our separate ways. Laura and I came back here in my car, and Mrs Slade drove to Lower Mindle in hers. We had a lot of work on we simply had to get through, but Mrs Slade wanted to be in The Lodge to get things ready for Mr Slade. It's why we left London early and split up in Theydon Bois.

"Laura and I got started pretty much straight away, and we stayed here till Mrs Slade called Laura to say the police had been round. Laura was in her study on this floor, and I was in my computer room under the roof, but we've had a three way Skype link between Laura, me and The Lodge for some time, and we used it repeatedly through the afternoon and evening because the work we'd brought home required a lot of discussion. You're welcome to check the metadata, and I'll open up our in-house data, if you think that's not enough. Ours is a smart home, so you'll see Laura opening the fridge, me putting the TV on and so forth, all fully logged. All three of us were using our smartphones as well, it was that kind of evening. I can assure you, Mr Snape, no one left the house till Laura went to The Lodge, and we can prove it."

"Did anyone ring the airport when Mr Slade looked like being late?"

"No, it happened all the time. He'd come back with people he'd been on conference with, and they'd stay talking together, especially if there was a deal in it."

Snape confirmed he'd check their Skype and smartphone data. He might as well see their in-house data while he was there. As much out of curiosity as anything, van Piet asked if he could see it as well. It meant going up to Cottrell's computer room, and what struck them both was how much it resembled a juvenile's den. There were brightly coloured bean bags instead of easy chairs, pens and pencils in a Goofy mug, and a soft-toy Cheshire cat smiling benignly from the top of an old-fashioned radio. The radio reminded van Piet of the one his mother's parents had had in their cottage in Wales, and he allowed himself to say so.

"It stood on a silk runner on the sideboard. They used to call it the wireless."

"They're one of my hobbies," Cottrell smiled back. "I buy them in sales, do them up and give them to people I'm close to. I gave a very nice Grundig to Mr and Mrs Slade some Christmases ago. Laura's been resistant till now, but I've got a Mullard in my workshop she rather likes, so I think she's coming round. What sort did your grandparents have?"

"A Philips."

"They were quality, and they had such lovely designs. I build VHF into mine, there's plenty of room in their casings, and I make it so the tuning knob can find the new channels as well as the old ones. But - true confessions - my heart's with valve technology. It crackles a lot, I know, but I love it."

Van Piet allowed himself to agree. It was a shared moment of pleasure.

"More gold-plated alibis."

Snape was grumbling again as they motored back to Chelmsford.

"The Skype and the smartphone calls put Mrs Slade in the clear as well. I'll have them checked, but I might as well not bother. These alibis are made to hold up, you can see it from here. Proving it's the problem."

Whenever anyone asked Snape how he ran his cases, there was always one thing he came back to:

"My biggest problem is, the people who help me are never there when I want them. They might be out asking questions, they might be in court giving evidence, or they might simply be off shift. Whatever the reason, they're always somewhere else. To beat that, whenever they've got something to tell me, they write it down and leave it for me to find. It doesn't take much doing, and it's a sight better than hanging around waiting for me or sitting through endless update meetings."

That was why, as Monday afternoon became Monday evening, Snape and van Piet were in Snape's office reading through notes from Forensics. There'd been no resistance to Snape's blitz, they learned, not even from the engineer – they'd learned the word early – who'd let Forensics into his locker because it had been Pachini's. Pachini himself was a fading memory, and Hayward presented herself as a shy and retiring workhorse who kept her paperwork straight, knew where everything was, and went home knowing she'd done a good job. Davis had been at home and had willingly opened up Number 32, so the search warrant hadn't been needed. She'd been all smiles and had kept making tea for everyone. And there might be a lead of sorts already. Some facial hairs, probably from an electric razor, had been removed from the S bend under the sink in what had been Pachini's bathroom. They were being compared with three cranial hairs from The Empress Matilda and a single one from under some seat padding in the Vauxhall Movano. There could be some fingerprint matches as well.

What the notes didn't say was that after Rufus got back to Rufus For Maseratis, Hayward made sure the intercom was off, went into Rufus's office and shut the door behind her. Had he enjoyed having the fuzz snooping round, she asked.

"I wish I had, Steph. If this gets out, it'll send trade through the floor."

"That's not the only reason, is it? What if you, personally, have got something you want to keep from them? Something very important, you might say."

"Such as?"

He shifted uneasily. He was afraid.

"I know about Geoffrey Slade's Maserati before he got his hands on it. You wouldn't want that to come out, would you?"

He believed her one hundred percent, it would be just like her to know things she shouldn't. He pressed his fingers hard onto his desk.

"What are you trying to tell me?" he asked and swallowed hard.

"I want you to start seeing me again, Derek. Just like you used to."

She'd moved in close to him. He could smell her perfume and her skin.

"It's what I want as well, Steph, but I can't and you know it. Anita watches me like a hawk these days."

"Don't give me that. You can give her the slip when it suits you, that's something else I know about you. Think again, Derek, and think very carefully."

He took his time, then he said,

"You're right as always. I can't make tomorrow, I'm due at the Leisure Centre with Anita. I'll try for Wednesday, though, and if that doesn't work, I'll make it Thursday, honour bright. I'll let you know during Wednesday."

"What time will you come?"

"It'd better be after dark. Let's say 9.00."

"You've lied to me in the past, Derek, but you'd better not lie to me this time. I might as well tell you, I've got a direct line to the police these days. What's more, I know exactly what to say if I have to use it."

She closed her hand on the door handle.

"Don't say a word to Anita, she's a witch. And don't try to harass me either. I want you to be nice to me again, then I can be nice to you. Try hard to make it Wednesday. Waiting till Thursday might make me impatient."

He looked up at her open-faced.

"Leave it to me, Steph, I'll make it Wednesday for sure."

"Honour bright?"

"Honour bright. You've got me where you want me, and I'm pleased about it."

Chapter 14

Thurston's Quarry

"An hour earlier and you'd have heard the big bang," Thurston said, as he ushered Snape and van Piet into the quarry control room. "We blast once a day, and we always do it at 10.00 so people in the villages know what they're hearing."

He looked much as he did on his website – greying hair, lines round the eyes, big smile – but he was wearing off-white overalls, not dungarees, and like his steel-capped boots and his lime-green safety jacket, they were ingrained with dust. The sunny weather was holding up, and he'd been waiting for them by the entrance gate. When he pulled off his hard hat, his forehead was sweaty.

His quarry was a great big hole in the ground. The sides had become terraced as the granite had been split away, but it was still in essence a great big hole. A roadway linked the outside world to the site, as Thurston liked to put it. It ran through the gate, passed the admin compound on the lip of the quarry and spiralled ledge-like down to the excavators and dumper trucks on the quarry floor.

"I own 368 acres in all," Thurston told them without being asked as he set out three mugs and waited for the kettle to boil, "and the quarry takes up 122 of them. If you see it from the air, it looks like an asteroid has smashed into a gigantic piece of scrubland. That's how big it is."

He had a self-made-man's streak of vanity. Van Piet asked how much granite he got out in a year.

"2·9 million tonnes last year, and I'll beat that this time round. The crusher's getting most of what we blasted this morning, but setts and building blocks always sell well, so we'll pick out the bigger bits for them. I'll show you how we cut them when we're down there."

"I suppose the guided tours you advertise take that in, do they?"

"That and the older parts of the quarry. We've got a fair few caves and tunnels, and we've set some up like in the old days. Some of the children find them spooky, but most visitors like them."

There were several other people in the control room, so once Snape and van Piet had finished their tea, Thurston led them into a side room that served as an office, saying they wouldn't be overheard in there. The in- and out-trays were full of invoices, correspondence and hand-written notes, and the windows had even more dust on their outsides than the ones in the control room. A whiteboard with targets for the week written up in felt-tip dominated one of the side walls, and on either side of the door they entered by were enlarged, framed photos of birds, some perching and some on the move. They were all birds of prey, and each photo had a punctiliously handwritten card between it and the glazing stating what kind of bird it was, where the photo was taken and when. There were red kites, buzzards, kestrels and hawks, but it was the owls that caught van Piet's eye. In one, a snowy owl was rising with a squirrel in its talons, in another a tawny owl was descending onto a field mouse, and in a third a long-eared owl was seizing a vole.

Snape sat down and opened his notebook.

"You know why we're here," he began. "Some years ago you did a lot of work for Mr and Mrs Slade, and you've been back to their house since then. How did you come to know the Slades?"

Thurston leaned back in his chair and stretched his legs out in front of him.

"I didn't, they came to know me. They'd bought this grand house, and they wanted a wall built round it, plus a new drive and an outhouse. They were keen on granite setts for the drive, so they went through the websites and asked around for quotes, and I for one duly provided one. It got me a whole-job contract, plus Essex Police on my back. I expect you've still got files on that somewhere."

"We're good at storing paper. Now, as I said on the phone, we're treating Mr Slade's death as unexplained, so we want to find out all we can about him. Most of the work you've done for him makes sense, but there's a question mark over the outhouse you mentioned. You'd think he and Mrs Slade had enough rooms already."

Thurston tapped the side of his nose knowingly.

"The Slades were on the way up, Mr Snape. They were making big money, and they bought a big house to go with it, but it wasn't enough, they had to make it bigger. So they asked me to build another outhouse for them, and they called it the boulting house, with a 'u' if you please, as if anyone would know what a boulting house was. It's like these footballers and pop stars you read about. They buy a ten-bedroom mansion, then add on a whole new wing. They don't need it, but it makes them feel good when they show their mates round."

Not the sort of thing Thurston would do, van Piet suggested, and Thurston prickled.

"My property's inherited, and that makes a difference. I live on quarry land, as I expect you've found out. My great-great-grandfather had my house built near his quarry, and what suited him has suited the rest of us down the years. When I moved back in after my parents died, I modernised it inside and let the trees all round it grow taller, but essentially it's the house I inherited."

Van Piet apologised and asked whether Thurston knew what was in the boulting house.

"I've got no idea what's upstairs, I've never been up there since the job was signed off. But downstairs there's a desk, some chairs and a couple of computers. I know that because I was in there last Thursday about a job. I saw you arrive, in fact. I don't think you saw me, but you might have seen my Range Rover parked by the garages. I've been putting in a chemical damp course for Mrs Slade. The foundations must have moved a bit somewhere, but I couldn't dig down to find out where with Mr Slade just passed away, so I've gone for the chemical option."

Van Piet was intrigued he'd stayed in touch with the Slades. Why was that?

"I've got a maintenance contract with them, and if anything extra crops up, they give me a call because they know I do a good job. It'll be Mrs Slade doing the calling now, I'm sorry to say - I had a lot of time for Mr Slade. As I understand it, he was going to use the boulting house to write a history of his investment company in, but he won't be able to do that now. Mrs Slade's investment company, I should say, since she's the owner and always has been. I don't want to tell you wrong."

"Have the Slades ever loaned you money? To finance the building side of your business, for instance?"

"Never. My father helped me get started, but I was soon financing myself. Where the Slades have helped me and still do was with investments - all declared and taxed, of course, and I keep copies of everything to prove it."

He was altogether a hoarder, he explained, as if that made him more interesting. Some of the clothes bills he kept were years out of date, but he still hung onto them. And he could give them plenty of other examples.

"If you throw something away, you can be sure it's the one thing you'll need, and then where are you? Up the creek without a paddle, that's where."

Snape had been peering through the dust on the windows. How did Thurston keep a big site like that secure?

"I've got my own team, and they cover the site twenty-four seven. You passed some of them as you came through the gate. I keep explosives as well as plant here, so I have to be doubly careful. You can see the inspection certificates if you like. They're all in order."

142

"If I need them, I'll call them in. Do you stop quarrying at night?"

"I have to. Nine o'clock and that's it. It's in the by-laws."

Snape added it to his notes.

"Now, a question you must have seen coming: Where were you last Tuesday evening between 5.00 and 9.00?"

Thurston took out his smartphone and flipped back through his calendar.

"I was with an architect on a building site near Quorn till 4.15 or thereabouts – I've always sub-contracted a lot, but I keep a close eye on things. Then I went home and got ready for a 7.30 meeting of the Leicester Rotary Club. I can't remember what time we broke up, but it'll be in the minutes. It wasn't before ten, that's for sure, because it never is, and my name will be logged, because the Secretary always records who turns up. In years to come, his minutes will be in a museum, and my name will be in there with them."

He took a piece of paper from his desk and wrote two names on it.

"The first name is the architect's," he said, handing it to Snape, "and the second one's the Rotary Club Chairman's. I've put their phone numbers as well. I don't mind you contacting them, but I'll ask you to make clear I'm not under suspicion for anything. Mud sticks in this life, and I don't want any on me."

Snape said he'd take every care, and then it was time to be shown round. Thurston found them some orange overalls, orange hard hats, and lime-green safety jackets with 'Visitor' on the back, and bounced them down to the quarry floor in a Jeep Grand

Cherokee with 'NT1' painted big on the bonnet and sides. Wearing ear protectors because of the noise, they watched the crusher and the cutters, and they silently confirmed what they'd already begun to notice - the overalls and hats were colour-coded. Management wore off-white, manual workers wore black, and visitors wore orange. When Snape asked how the overalls were cleaned, Thurston said he had his own laundry further along from the admin compound. He also took them into some of the tunnels left over from the old days. In one he turned the lights off to show how dark it would be if the oil lamps ran out. It was totally dark, more a sensation of pressure than an absence of light, and it made Snape and van Piet feel suffocated.

"I don't like it myself," Thurston admitted as he switched the lights back on, "but that's how it was back then if there was a rock fall. Not a nice thought, is it?"

"You could destroy a lot of things in that quarry and no one would know," Snape opined later, when he and van Piet were back on the road.

Van Piet asked him what he had in mind.

"A laptop for a start. Thurston's got permanent access, and they stop working at night. He could slip it in the crusher, and no one would ever know. There'd only be his security, and he could tell them anything."

"What about his alibi? Can you break it, do you think?"

"Not a hope, it's solid like the others. I'll have to think of another way to get at them."

He pulled off the motorway at a service centre near Northampton. Thawed out fish and chips looked the best of a dismal menu, and as they were making a start, van Piet's smartphone buzzed. He signalled to Snape and drew out an earpiece on a thin cable. It was Sister Agnese, and again she switched to English once she knew Snape was in on the call. As she'd sort of expected, she'd had to wait for permission to leave the convent, but she'd found out *Signore e Signora Pachini* had last heard from Matteo on July 28th. That was a Friday. He'd called a little after 10 pm Italian time, just as they were starting to clear up in the restaurant, and he'd said he didn't have a reason for calling, he just wanted to know how they were and say he wasn't coming home just yet. He'd assured them he was fine, but they couldn't call him back, because he'd lost his mobile. He was using a friend's to talk to them, and he'd call again when he'd got himself a new one. His parents had said it was just like Matteo, losing things and being hard to find, he'd been like that since he was a little boy. No, they weren't worried at all, and they'd ring the convent the minute he came through the door so Sister Agnese would know everything was all right.

"A little after 9 pm our time," Snape said, going back to his fish and chips. "That's not long after the white saloon showed up. Did he really want to talk to Momma and Poppa Pachini right then, or did someone put him up to it, complete with an untraceable phone?"

Back on the motorway, the traffic was moving freely, and Snape was able to reel off the miles without too much trouble.

"Laura Slade," he said as they passed Milton Keynes. "She's going to that concert this evening, and I'm thinking we should be keeping an eye on her. I know what she said, but someone's playing games, and it could be her. You can meet a lot of people in a concert hall."

Van Piet looked up from his smartphone. He'd been texting Célestine and Jackie.

"Relax, Eddie. Miss Slade's seat is in the front stalls – she bought her ticket in her own name, so it was easy to find that out – and someone from the SRO will be watching her from the side stalls. He'll have an archive photo from the *Financial Times*, and he's been told what she looks like as well, so there's no chance he'll watch the wrong person. I fancied the job myself, but I might have been recognised."

"You got him a seat he could see Laura Slade from just like that? Who do you people know the rest of us don't?"

He'd tried for a *Messiah* once as a Christmas treat for his wife, and he'd had to take separate seats right at the back.

"There'll be an extra usher on duty, and he'll be sitting in a staff seat. We're putting a team of three on, one in the side stalls and two analysing the cctv, since you never know who else might show up. Tom's setting up a gallery of everyone we've met or heard about so far, and we'll use it to trawl with tonight. You never know, we might be lucky."

"How come the SRO is getting so involved? I thought you were on secondment."

"Money talks, Eddie, and Esklivia's is talking loudly. We want to know what's really going on. It goes with the job."

146

Chapter 15

The heyday of the blood

When Laura took a taxi from her friend's flat in Islington, she already knew the Festival Hall was out, even though, automaton-like, she told the driver to take her there. The music would be too upsetting, and getting to Lombard Street in time could be tricky. So, as her taxi neared the Thames, she leaned forward and told the driver to drop her near the National Gallery. It was a place she went to a lot, and it was open till midnight all through August. As the taxi was slowing to a halt, she switched off her smartphone. Nobody who thought she was in a concert would expect her to have her smartphone on, but not everyone knew where she was supposed to be going, and she didn't want to get caught out by answering. Leaving her bag at the desk, she made her way up to Room 41- the one she always went to, whatever else she went in to see. There she sat down to contemplate Seurat's tranquillity-inducing paintings. Other visitors blocked her view from time to time, but she was content to sit quietly till they moved on.

Then it was time to reclaim her bag and go. It was dark outside, but the air had stayed warm, and there were still plenty of people about. Like her, they were mostly without coats. A lot of them had to be tourists making the most of the friendly weather. Pacing herself, she walked to Charing Cross station and took a taxi to Potter's Yard, a cul-de-sac off Lombard Street. It was an easy walk from there to Esklivia House.

The Square Mile was virtually empty, and when she stepped into Lombard Street, she was the only pedestrian. She made the most of the shadows between the street lights, but she was still afraid Verity would recognise her if she should pass her in a taxi or a private car. And there was always the chance Verity would be waiting by the door of Esklivia House for whoever was coming to see her. Laura had an excuse of sorts ready for if that happened, but she didn't find it credible herself, so she hoped she wouldn't have to use it.

By 10.16 by her watch, however, scarcely any traffic had gone past, and Verity was nowhere in sight. There was no light leaking past the blinds in her office either. From inside a pool of darkness Laura watched the last porter of the day turn his Chubb in the lock and activate the burglar alarm via the keypad. Then he left for the underground.

The burglar alarm was like a stockade. It guarded the outside doors, the windows and the roofspace, but anyone could move around inside, provided they didn't open an outside door or window, or go up into the roof. If they did, a silent alarm would flash to HastaPrees, the Square Mile's premier security firm. It was headquartered in nearby Birchin Lane, and it would be on site in seconds. Its tactics had been honed in armed conflict, and its interpretation of minimum force was notorious. Just having its logo about the place made most villains go somewhere else.

Laura's plan was simple. Her zapper included a mini-transmitter, and with the porter out of the way, she'd use it to shut down the burglar alarm remotely after she'd put in a date-related code to tell HastaPrees the zap really was from her and wasn't made under duress. HastaPrees wouldn't react till the end of the quarter, when it would service the system and discuss the activity log with Verity. By that time Laura would either have devised a good story or reached a position where she wouldn't have to.

The cctv would come next. She'd zap it out before it caught her on camera, and once she was in the basement room where the controls were, she'd re-activate it along with the burglar alarm. After her mother had come and gone, likewise using her zapper each time, Laura would shut down the cctv and the burglar alarm one last time, leave the building herself, and re-activate them from outside. Then she'd book into a hotel for what was left of the night. The first porter on duty in the morning wouldn't matter. He'd log the fact the cctv had been off, but that was all he would do, since Verity, unlike her husband, thought cctv was something Esklivia House didn't really need – like the vitamin pills she took every morning but didn't believe in. Cctv was fine for a country house like The Lodge, but in Esklivia House, what counted for Verity was the burglar alarm.

Laura left her hiding place and opened Esklivia's outside door. The silence inside got to her, and she had to stop in her tracks to get her nerve back. The low-glow emergency lights were on, but they were the only sources of light apart from pinpricks of red and green behind the porters' desk to her left. Thick curtains covered the ground floor windows, and where the emergency lights didn't reach, the darkness was total.

Ahead of her was the staircase with the lift to its right, but this time, instead of going up to her office, she'd be going down into what looked like the mouth of a pit. And she had to do it now or she never would. So scarcely daring to breathe, she stepped towards the top stair through the gloom and went down one stair at a time till she reached the basement corridor. Some of the stairs creaked like gun shots, but she forced herself to go on, telling herself that if anyone else was in the building, they'd know by now where to lie in wait for her.

To her left in the basement was the copier room. During the day, its door would be open, all the ceiling lights would be on, and the sounds of photo-copiers, printers and people talking would all be spilling out. But now there was just a locked door glistening dully in the low-glows and a pervasive uncanny stillness. Beyond the copier room was the cleaners' storeroom – it was also locked - and at the end of the corridor, secured with a keypad as well as a lock, was the cctv room. As with the zappers, access to it was limited to the Slades. Even Cottrell had to get permission to go in, despite the fact that the cctv was nominally part of her empire. Laura tapped in the code, inserted her key and opened up. Thanks to her mother's attitude, not all of the in-house cameras worked. The ones in the offices did, her mother had her reasons for that, but several in the corridors and, more particularly, the one in the cctv room had been out for some time and looked set to stay that way. Laura knew that from Cottrell, who griped about it regularly when they were alone in Bishop's Green. Laura had built it into her plan.

The cctv room was windowless, small, and ventilated through inlets in the skirting and a silent extractor in the ceiling. The controls were in a single labelled console, with an array of monitors neatly stacked behind it. Right now, the monitors were all dead, excepting those showing the fire exits. Using the console, Laura could see into whichever offices she liked without anything being recorded. She could do that even when the cctv was officially off. And if she did do that, she'd leave no trace of what she'd done in the firmware.

"The cameras in the offices of our staff can read most printed material with ease," Verity had told her when she'd been explaining the zappers to Laura, "but they don't have lights on them that come on when they're active. That means we – that's you, me or your father, my sweet – can watch the rest of the staff, and they don't know we're doing it. They know the cameras are there because we point them out when they join us, but they have no way of knowing whether they're on or off - just knowing they're there is enough to stop them slacking off. If they decide to cheat us, they'll persuade themselves they can outsmart them, because that's the way the minds of cheats work. But they can't, of course, and that lets us flush them out."

That had left Laura with some questions.

"What about the cameras in our own offices?" she'd asked. "Yours, mine and Daddy's, I mean. Will you watch me, for instance?"

Verity's response had been serene.

151

"Not in the sense you mean, poppet - you're a Slade like your father, so you're trusted. But some of our clients can be people we're better off not being alone with, so you may need to be watched when you're in your office with them. Don't worry, you'll be told when it happens. You'll thank me for it as well."

There were no emergency lights in the cctv room, only the yellowish console lighting plus the glow from the monitors that were in use, so Laura left the door open while she placed her bag where she wouldn't fall over it, put the burglar alarm and the cctv back on and moved a swivel chair in front of the controls. She glanced back down the corridor, then round the room, and everything looked good, but she needed to try the door in case it squeaked when she pulled it to. She stood up, tapped in a code to stop the lock being activated, and the door made no sound at all as she closed it. But she opened it again quickly, because it was claustrophobic with it shut. She had nothing to do now but wait. Occasionally she more felt than heard a vehicle go past outside. Everything else was at a standstill.

As each second passed, she felt more and more foolish for being there. Why had she got so worked up about an attaché case? Her mother had probably bought a replacement and not got round to saying, that was all. She might not even turn up. She'd looked stressed during the day, and she'd left early, telling everyone who mattered not to contact her, she had things to do in Chelmsford, including seeing the undertaker. Laura looked at her watch - it was showing 10.38. Well, there was still time for something to happen. She'd hang on a bit longer, then she'd let herself out and find a hotel.

But at 10.41, the cctv monitors excepting only the ones showing the fire exits went blank, and she faintly heard a key turn in the outside door. Her mouth went dry and she felt like screaming as she darted towards her own door and pulled it almost shut. The next thing she heard was the sound of shoes being wiped on the doormat. It was two people. There was a pause to re-set the burglar alarm, and as Laura expected, the cctv stayed off. Laura thought they were about to come downstairs, but then she heard the lift open, close, and clank up to the second floor. Before long, it would automatically come down again, and when it did, she had the nightmare feeling someone who knew she was there was in it. Not until it was clear it was staying on the ground floor did she shut herself in completely and sit down in front of the console. Willing her hands to relax, she double-checked that nothing would be recorded, then she switched on Camera 1- the one in her mother's office - and one of the blank screens sprang into life.

The view was from the back wall, and the camera had enough tilt to take in most of the office. It was a week to the day that Slade had been killed, and Verity, who was making drinks at the drinks cabinet, was dressed in a dark grey suede jacket, a high-neck black knitted top, a black, grey and white plaid skirt and black shoes with medium heels. Around her neck was a diamond and gold pendant necklace Slade had brought back for her from a business trip to Davos. There were no overhead lights on in the office, just the soft, warm glow from three standard lamps, and someone had drawn the curtains over the blinds. Her mother looked as drawn as she'd done during the day, yet her eyes were lively, and she seemed to be laughing as she spoke.

Watching her from an upright chair near one of the windows was a man in his late fifties. Laura had never seen him before. He looked like an ageing academic who'd drunk too much beer with too many generations of students. His thinning fair hair was cropped short as if he was clinging to earlier years, his blue eyes were bleary, and three-day stubble covered the lower part of his face, which was flushed. He was wearing a lightweight navy blue woollen suit, a maroon tie over a white windowpane shirt and brown slip-on shoes. His left hand held a pair of designer spectacles with rounded lenses set in a deep brown carbon fibre frame, while his right hand was steadying what looked like Verity's attaché case on his knees. It was open, and Laura could see it contained bundles of twenty pound notes. The attaché case's twin lay on Verity's desk next to her appointments diary, her memo pad and the usual row of files. It, too, was open, and inside it were sheets of paper neatly packaged together in coloured translucent folders. So it *was* an exchange – the papers for the money. But who was getting what? Why be so secretive about it? And why cash? Laura operated the zoom, but the top sheet was blank, and none of the others stuck out enough for her to see what was on them.

Verity left the drinks cabinet, a glass in each hand, and headed towards the coffee table. Laura could see they were drinking gin – the East India Company's opaque bottle told her that. Verity's guest, companion, or whatever closed his attaché case with a nod and a smile, and placed it on the carpet.

So he was getting the money and her mother was getting the papers. Standing his spectacles on Verity's desk, he moved across the office to an easy chair she'd waved one of the glasses towards. On the coffee table near his hand was a stack of patterned coasters in a gun metal holder. He leaned forward, and as if he'd often done it before, he placed two of them so Verity could put the glasses down on them before she sat down close to him. As they clinked glasses, Laura lip-read, "Cheers!" and she was struck once more by the contrast between her mother's drawn face and her sparkling eyes.

For a while, there was nothing much to see. They talked and laughed easily, and the gin in the glasses went steadily down. When both glasses were empty, they looked expectantly at each other. Verity closed her hand briefly on her companion's, and heaving himself to his feet, he picked the glasses up. Laura thought he was going to re-fill them, but instead he carried them towards the ensuite as if he was intending to rinse them out, while Verity crossed over to where the settee was, stacked the cushions on the floor and began methodically to turn it into a bed. When it was flat, she laid an undersheet over the thin mattress that was already in place and turned off two of the standard lamps. Her companion, meanwhile, had put the glasses back in the drinks cabinet, closed its doors and slipped off his jacket. Verity put her arms round his neck and, standing a little on tip-toe, kissed him hard on the mouth, pressing her body against his. When they separated, she laid her necklace carefully on her desk and began to take her clothes off, pacing herself with her companion, who was doing the same. She let him take off her black bra and panties, then she lowered his underpants over

155

his erect penis, which she fondled with her tongue and, moving easily, went with him towards the makeshift bed, where she lay with her legs apart and let him heave himself on top of her. She was visibly hungry for it, and it showed even more as they moved into a rhythm, he thrusting hard with his lumpy buttocks and she drawing her knees up, then pushing back.

Laura snapped her head away from the monitor and screwed her eyes up tight. This was her mother, still mourning her father, and doing *that* – she had a prim mind and a prim way of speaking to match. When she looked again, her mother was reaching ecstasy, and she was probably groaning or gasping, since her head was back and she was opening and shutting her mouth. Laura was somewhere between hurt and massively angry. She'd never had sex with a man herself, she'd never had the desire to. All she'd ever wanted were affection and re-assurance, and Millie wrapped those round her like a warm blanket when they had their intimate times. What did her mother see in this man? He was pudgy and balding, and his frantic face had gone from red to crimson. And what did he see in her mother, come to that? Her body, for all its residual trimness, was showing clear signs of being over fifty. Laura had only ever seen her with clothes on, and even in their most relaxed domestic moments there'd always been an aura of properness about her. Could she really be naked and orgasmic when no one was looking, excepting the man who was turning her on? It must have happened with her father, though Laura couldn't really imagine it, but with a stranger? And at her mother's age? Surely she had to be past it. Not knowing what else to do, Laura went back to watching with white-hot fury as they climaxed, peeled apart after a pause, and relaxed side by side. She couldn't help herself, they reminded her of animals rutting in nature films, and that filled her with disgust. Much worse than that, though, her mother had visibly enjoyed betraying her father. That hurt existentially.

They were in no hurry to go. Still complacently naked, Verity fetched a new-looking porno magazine out of her desk and lay with her head on her companion's chest while he browsed through it. From time to time, he showed her one of the pictures, and they both laughed. When his penis began to rise again, she put the magazine on the floor, led his hand over her nipples and stroked his foreskin up and down till he parted her legs and clambered on her again. They paced themselves more this time, and when they finished, they looked entirely content.

Verity went into the ensuite first, and while her companion was in there, she put the magazine back in her desk and reconverted the bed into a settee, stowing the rumpled sheet in a drawer in the base. Then, neatly and efficiently, she got dressed. When her companion re-emerged, she slipped back in to do her hair, and then they were ready to go, he with his glasses back on and both of them with the attaché case they'd come for. Laura gave them ten minutes after the cctv came back on and then, distressed and bitter as she had never been before, she picked up her bag and made her own way out. Lombard Street was deserted. At the top of Potter's Yard she phoned a hotel in The Strand she sometimes used after a show, and then she called a taxi. She had no idea what she'd be like at work the next morning, all she wanted to do was climb into bed and never wake up again. But that changed as she waited for her taxi. The more she thought about it, the more she was certain what she'd seen was connected to her father's death. Somehow she had to find out how it was connected, and why.

Her taxi arrived quickly - she'd said she was on her own in an empty street - and when she was gone, a shortish female figure moved out of an unlit passage opposite Esklivia House into the penumbra of a street light. It was Watkins. Out of reach of Esklivia's cctv, she was putting the night camera she'd recorded the evening's comings and goings on into a leather shoulder bag. Then she, too, called a taxi, to take her back to Kensington. For her it had been an excellent night's work. A bonanza, in fact.

Chapter 16

Rufus makes an arrangement

Laura was in Esklivia House by 9.30 the next morning. She was impeccably dressed and made up, but inside she was blown apart. Cottrell must have asked the porter to let her know when she arrived, since she'd scarcely stood her bag down in her office when Cottrell was opening the door and asking how the concert was. Laura had no idea how to answer. She desperately wanted to tell her partner everything that had happened, but her mother had blown her trust so much, she didn't know who to confide in.

"It was beautiful," she started to lie, but she was sure she'd get found out. "No, Millie, that's not true."

She faltered, then she buried her face in her hands. Cottrell locked her office door, drew her close to her, and held her firmly till her weeping stopped.

"I'm sorry," Laura said as she wiped her eyes with a tissue from a box on her desk. She was searching desperately for something to say that was true, but which kept all the big things under wraps. "I didn't go in the end, I couldn't face it. I sat in the National Gallery, and then I went to a hotel. I've hardly closed my eyes all night, but I had to come in this morning. I couldn't think what else to do."

Cottrell said she'd make her some tea, it would make her feel a whole lot better, and while Laura hurried along the landing to repair her face in the ladies', Cottrell took the lift up to the staff kitchen, switched one of the kettles on, and joined in the gossip while the water boiled. She might be senior management, but everyone liked her, and if she was a girls' girl, that was her business and no one else's. When she re-appeared in Laura's office, she had a tray in her hands with two cups and saucers on it, a dumpy teapot, and a small jug of milk. She set it down carefully on the desk and left the door unlocked.

"Good things are worth waiting for," she said brightly as she poured, and she gave Laura a smile Laura read as love in capital letters.

Just a few moments later, there was a knock at the door and Verity came in, saying the desk had told her Laura had already arrived. Unlike Laura, Verity had slept like a log, and she was carrying what looked like the attaché case she'd taken with her during the night. She, too, asked Laura how the concert had been, and Laura, looking up from where she was sitting, repeated what she'd said to Cottrell.

Verity went over to her and put a motherly arm round her.

"You poor dear," she said gently, her scarcely-lined face touching her daughter's forehead. "I know just how you feel. But we have to be strong for each other now Daddy's gone. We're all we've got left, remember?"

160

She kissed Laura's temple, and as she moved towards the door, she seamlessly transformed herself from concerned mother into the owner of Esklivia Investments.

"Since you're both here," she said, the handle in her hand, "I'll remind you of the middle and senior management meeting at 8.00 this evening in the committee room. I'm expecting resistance from some of our younger colleagues, so I shall expect you both to attend. I don't have Geoffrey to support me now."

She gave Laura a parting smile and let herself out. Cottrell kissed Laura's cheek, patted her fleetingly on the head, and followed Verity through the door.

In Chelmsford, Snape had arrived at Police HQ at 6.00 that morning, and his first port of call had been Forensics. He'd wanted to catch the night shift before it disappeared, so he'd gone straight from his car to the Second World War left-over Forensics was housed in. The night shift team leader and overall man in charge was Dr Michael Craske, a civilian who'd been with Essex Police almost as long as Snape. He'd been on duty for twelve hours, and he was looking forward to going home.

"How far have you got, Mike?" Snape asked, pulling up a grey-painted tubular chair in Craske's airless office.

Craske removed his glasses and rubbed his eyes. Why, after all these years, did Snape still believe in miracles?

"The DNA samples are being processed," he replied in the unhurried way he'd honed over time. He could like his job a lot, if it would let him. "As soon as the results come through, someone will let you know, but not before. We've identified as many fingerprints as we can, but there are still a lot we can't account for. They could be from customers, postmen, aliens even. We've simply no idea."

Snape asked him whether he'd found any blood in the van or the boat.

"Sorry, not a drop, but don't take it to heart. Run your eye over these."

He rotated a monitor on his desk so Snape could see it as well, typed in his password and opened a folder titled Crossfinds.

"We found this one inside the Vauxhall Movano," he said, displaying part of a fingerprint captioned Poss Pachini/Right Index. "The top fifth's missing, and what's left is smeary, but the ridge pattern's unusual, so we had something to go on. This next one is less smeary, and there's still a bit missing from the tip, but not so much. It was on the underside of a tool drawer in Rufus For Maseratis' workshop. Then there's this one, which is pretty much complete and nice and sharp as well. It's from the Rufuses' boat. And finally this one, which is also pretty much complete. It comes from the garage in Walsingham Close. If I make these images a bit bigger, you'll see the ridges on all four form arches, and as I've told you many times before, that's extremely rare. About 70% of the population have loops, 25% have whorls, but only 5% have arches, so we're not likely to find two people with arches in the same sample. That supports our micro-analysis of the ridges, which tells us these prints all come from the same index finger. And since they come from four places connected with your Mr Pachini, including where he lived, I'd say they're what you're pestering me for."

Snape perked up. This was worth getting up before dawn for.

"Have you got any more prints with these arches on? People don't go through life using one finger."

"Fingers, thumbs, left and right hands, you name it. I'll ask my relief to put them on the intranet for you, when she eventually shows up. You can access them whenever you like then."

Snape left Forensics feeling something had gone right at last, even if he didn't know what to do with it, and he had the same feeling when he found two hand-written notes on his desk. One was from Gulliver: Davis's neighbour at 30, Walsingham Close had rung in to say Davis had flown to Bonn via Cologne/Bonn airport first thing Tuesday. It was one of her family visits, and she expected to be back late Thursday. The other note, which was more of a scribble, was from the leader of the NCA team working on Slade's Maserati. It read, 'The firmware's been tampered with to accept external instructions. Poss intended to destruct on impact, but didn't!!! Thought you'd like breaking news. Report to follow - Danny Chilvers.' So Warrener had got it right. Better yet, she needn't testify, Chilvers could do that for her. That would cheer Willem up.

Snape had skipped breakfast to get in early, and now it was catching up with him, so he walked down the corridor to the incident room, where he knew he could make himself some toast. He wasn't the only one to think like that, he could smell toast in the air as he walked in, and it smelled even better as he spread butter on his slices. He was thinking of treating himself to double rations, when his mobile buzzed. It was van Piet.

"I'm calling from home," he said. "I'm leaving for Ashell House in about ten minutes, and I think you should come with me. I'll collect you in half an hour or so, and we'll go in my car. It'll be easier at the other end."

While van Piet and Snape were setting out for Chelsea, Rufus was checking his dealership was ready for the day. The workshop came first, and that meant twenty minutes or so with the Chief Engineer going through the bookings and sorting out supplies. He liked it in the workshop, it had its own atmosphere, and it told him how right he'd been to start selling Maseratis. Even when they were up on lifts, they looked the best around. The Sales Manager came next, a portly, middle-aged man with a knack for getting people to spend far more than they intended to when they came through the door. Finally there were the day's appointments and the inevitable pile of letters. They both meant Stephanie Hayward, so he pressed the right button in his designer console, and when she came in, she brought with her a notebook and pen, a desk diary, and the letters duly opened and flattened. He asked her to sit down, he talked to her across his desk, and he kept the door firmly shut. The letters came first, then the desk diary. Both of them stuck to business till, glancing at the door and lowering his voice, he said,

"I'm going to Harwich this afternoon to look at some new shipping arrangements, and I've tacked on some other contacts that more or less matter as well. I've already told Anita," he added as he slid a sheet of

A4 across his desk, "and the details for the diary are on this piece of paper in case she phones in to check. Write them in word for word and give me the A4 back when you've done it so I can shred it. Anita thinks I'll be there all evening, but I won't be, so put something on with not too many buttons on it, I'll be at your place by 9.00. If you still want me to come, that is."

She gave him a quick glitter of triumph and smoothed her Rufus For Maseratis one-piece over her hips and legs.

"You've taken a wise decision, Derek," she said coolly. "Have you still got your key?"

"No." He looked furtive. "I had to destroy it, Anita was going through my things. I'll knock four times, then you'll know it's me."

Her face hardened.

"Be warned, Derek, if you're teasing me, you'll regret it. And no torch, remember. Half the village would see it, and they'd probably call the police. Have you still got your night goggles? I don't want you breaking your neck."

"Don't worry, everything's taken care of, and I'll come by taxi as usual. I'm glad you got on to me Monday, Steph, and I'm not just saying it. Now be on your way, before I start to sample the goods. I'm in the mood already."

She blew him a kiss and let herself out. She'd taken him on, she'd won hands down, and all her spite had evaporated. She'd put Snape in his place as well, though he didn't know it yet. Next time she saw him, she'd sort of hint at it, just to watch his face. It would be like Christmas come early.

Chapter 17

A photo gallery and some shell companies

Ashell House was located between the Chelsea Royal Hospital and the Pimlico Road. The name next to the glass swing doors at the front said Scrite and Associates: Architects, and Scrite and Associates was a genuine firm. But Avery Scrite, who had had to accept abnormally tight security clearance to get the lease, needed only a fraction of the building. The rest was the SRO's, and its entrance was round the back. It was a roll-up door that looked like the entrance to a garbage bay. Directly behind the door and out of sight was a crash-proof portcullis that went up and down with it.

Van Piet halted his blend-into-the-background Ford Mondeo in front of the roll-up door and waited for the registration to be scanned. While more cameras looked to see nothing was lurking behind it, van Piet's face and Snape's were biometrically read, and when the door clanked up, van Piet drove at walking pace into bleached, shadowless lighting, where a concrete barricade halted him till the door clanked down. Another wait, and steel doors in the barricade parted to let him through. Garry was waiting on the far side. Once he was in the back, van Piet turned into a continuously lit slope that wound down to the underground car park. From there a lift took them up to the floor van Piet's office was on. The Director General's room, as his office was always called, was one floor higher, and the floor above that was the top one. It housed Signals, plus sleep-in accommodation for whenever a crisis was on, which was often.

Van Piet's office reflected the SRO's tight budget. It contained two featureless writing desks, one for himself and one for Garry; a Formica-topped table with half a dozen upright chairs round it; a similar table supporting a computer and three screens; and by the walls, four armless easy chairs. In-house rules prohibited family photographs (too risky), flowers (could provoke an allergic reaction), reading lamps from outside (could contain spyware), and any kind of heating device that wasn't SRO-issue (fire hazard). An SRO electric kettle stood on a grey metal filing cabinet, and Garry switched it on to make a jug of filter coffee. Snape didn't want to sit down after being so long in the car, so he walked over to one of the windows. The glass was bullet- and wireless-proof, and the venetian blinds couldn't be raised. But if he pushed the tilted slats far enough apart, he could see the trees in the Ranelagh Gardens and, beyond them, the Thames. The weather was holding up, and everything outside looked postcard-placid.

Van Piet called him over to where he was standing.

"I figured Watkins might have a second address in London," he said, "so I asked a colleague in Van Piet Banking about it. Here, the text's in Dutch, but you can still read the address bit."

He held his mobile up, and Snape copied Flat 16, 25 Primrose Place, Paddington into his notebook. There was a landline number as well.

"It belongs to the *Standard*," van Piet added, "and if it's too small to hide an eavesdropper in, it could explain why she asked us to come to Kensington."

As soon as the coffee was made, he stood three upright chairs in front of the computer and said he was ready to start. Garry was his usual self-effacing self. Ashell House folklore had it, if he was in a room with just one other person, that other person wouldn't notice he was there. Two or three inches taller than van Piet and vaguely in his fifties, he matched everyone's idea of a Whitehall civil servant, which he allowed his neighbours in Barnet to believe he was. Snape prided himself on his awareness of faces, but he routinely had difficulty recalling what Garry's was like when he wasn't right in front of him. He sometimes wondered whether van Piet had the same problem. If he did, it would be ironic, since Garry was one of the very few people van Piet halfway trusted.

The coffee tasted good after the journey in the car, then van Piet got down to business.

"We'll look at some pictures from Tom's gallery first, that will give you an idea of what's in it so far," he told Snape as Garry got the computer up and running. "You can access it with your mobile, Tom will give you the code before you go. As you'd expect, he's still adding to it."

Davis came up first. The pic was from *Translation Journal's* archive, and she was looking straight at the camera. Then came Ashley Johnson as Five Willows' new vet, followed by his father, a small skinny man wearing flip-flops, Bermuda shorts and sunglasses. He was waving from a luxury yacht anchored off Antibes. It was a pic van Piet hadn't seen before. He asked Garry where it came from.

"*Entrepreneurial Engineer*, it was taken two years ago. Mr Johnson had signed a major contract with Boeing and acquired a new yacht on the strength of it. It's cruising off Monaco at the moment. He seems to like that part of the world."

"What's its name? It's not clear on the photo."

"Electric Calamine. It's a mineral, Sir. You may know it as hemimorphite."

Van Piet didn't reply, and Garry paused again when he came to a picture of Pachini. It was a head and upper-body shot, and it came from the *Essex Chronicle's* archive. Pachini was looking jubilant. He was well wrapped up against the weather, and he was wearing two different football rosettes, one on each side of his overcoat. The caption read, 'Football-mad Matteo supports Colchester United *and* Arsenal in Saturday's Cup-tie thriller'.

"It was taken outside Colchester Community Stadium," Garry commented. "He'd just collected his ticket for the match."

He skimmed through several stills of Pachini from Border Force cameras – he'd been to Europe a lot over the years - and there was also a copy of his passport photo. Thurston came next, and then Cottrell. She was chairing a panel event organised by *ComputerWeekly*.

"I didn't think these computer types liked being seen," Snape commented.

"It depends," replied van Piet. "A pic in *ComputerWeekly* will have done her no harm, but this next one might."

Garry moved on to a less than sharp black-and-white still that showed Cottrell standing in what looked like a drinks area of some kind. She was smartly dressed, and there were a lot of people around her, but they didn't look as if they had anything to do with her.

"This one," van Piet explained, "comes from the cctv in the Festival Hall. It was taken during the interval last night, and Tom fed it to me at Gorris. Laura Slade wasn't at the concert, her seat stayed empty all evening, but Cottrell was there, and her seat was in the rear stalls. It was well behind Laura's, and Laura probably wouldn't have seen her unless she knew where to look. Cottrell went home on her own by taxi – we took the cab's number and asked - but where Laura was is anyone's guess, including, by the look of it, Cottrell's. Cottrell could have been meaning to spy on Laura, though the pics don't say that for certain. She could certainly have sat a lot nearer to her if she'd wanted to. A ticket was available."

Snape made a note in his notebook, and van Piet asked Garry to change programmes. As he did so, van Piet explained he'd been struck by how Verity Slade, the Rufuses, Davis and Thurston had all insisted their bookkeeping was beyond reproach. So he'd applied for a Crown warrant and he and Garry had started taking a look. GCHQ was doing the finding, and Van Piet Banking was helping with the analyses. It was like wading through treacle, but already networks of shell companies were beginning to emerge.

"You'll have to tell me what shell companies are," Snape put in. He knew the phrase, but that was all.

"They're bogus companies set up in tax havens to help with bogus deals, and one of their biggest attractions is, the lawyers who create them can register them under proxy names, so the real owners' names stay hidden. We started with Thurston, though it could have been any of them."

He turned to Garry.

"Can you show Ambilly One, Tom?"

Garry brought up a colour-coded network of company names linked by arrows.

"Don't let the daft name fool you, Eddie, this is serious money. Ambilly One is a trading company registered on Nevis in the Caribbean, and as far as we can find out, it's legal. Thurston has invested a lot of money in it over the years, and his annual profit has averaged 13·6% gross, which he's religiously declared to the Revenue. He's got four other investments like it, and they're all brokered by Esklivia. They also yield big returns, and they're also fully taxed. The problem is, our analysis of Ambilly One's trades doesn't show how these returns are generated. The same applies to Thurston's other investments, which are just as complex –" Garry brought up Ambilly Two, Three, Four and Five – "and it also applies to investments Esklivia's brokered for the Rufuses and Davis, which we're just beginning to untangle. So, either we're missing something or money is being pumped in at one end from an outside source, being laundered through a mixture of real and fake trades, and being paid out at

171

the other end disguised as a profit. We think it's the second one, but we don't know yet what the outside source is because the proxy registration is in the way. Geoffrey Slade had similar investments, by the way, and Verity Slade still has."

Snape wondered where the profits were finishing up, and van Piet asked Garry to show Davis's relevant bank accounts, since they were easiest to read.

"The pattern's the same for Thurston, the Rufuses and the Slades" van Piet said. "The profits go into a current account that already has money in it from sources no one could fault. That account's got a pre-set ceiling on it which looks suspiciously low to me, so some of the mix gets pinged into other accounts – that happens automatically as soon as the ceiling is hit. The rest stays where it is till it's spent or whatever, but whether it goes or whether it stays, the money's so completely mixed by now, it's hard to tell the good from the bad, if bad is what it is."

Snape ran his eye down the figures.

"If they're all like Davis, they like their ready cash," he said, pointing his finger at the withdrawals. "What about Cottrell?"

"No investments we can find, but that may be a feint – she's on a very high salary and she makes her share of cash withdrawals. No investments for Laura either, and virtually no cash withdrawals. She prefers cards."

"So what are you saying, Willem? That Davis and the rest are being bought?"

"I think it's more complicated than that, but the jigsaw's still a piece short. When I find it, I'll give you a proper answer."

On their way back to Chelmsford, Forensics texted Snape to say the DNA analyses were provisionally complete, and the facial hairs, the cranial hairs and the single hair from the Movano all had to be Pachini's. Snape felt that was another step forward, but he was uneasy about the Crown warrant van Piet had mentioned. It was a powerful authorisation - it dated back to Henry VIII - and it gave van Piet direct authority over him and any other police officer. He didn't mind that, van Piet had used it before, and Snape was the last person to let vanity stand in the way of solving a case. But he had to know how it would work in practice, so, raising his voice above the Mondeo's road noise, he asked van Piet how he saw things.

"Geoffrey Slade and Ashley Johnson are still your cases, Eddie," he replied as he eased past a girder carrier. "It's up to you how you run them, and I'll do what I can to help. But when I take over, you'll do as I say, Sal as well. And you'll do it on the button."

Chapter 18

Another death

Hayward didn't feel like going home straight after she'd finished work, so when she left Rufus For Maseratis, she drove into Clacton to have tea with her mother and father. She knew she'd be welcome, they were always glad to see her, and she'd cook them some tea while they got things ready for the morning. The holiday trade meant they hadn't done their shopping, so tea was odds and ends from the freezer, and they ate it in the flat above the shop with the windows open. It was low tide, and they could smell the seaweed and the salt on the breeze that wafted in, making the curtains rustle. The sounds of footsteps and voices came in with it, plus, in bursts and from further away, more raucous noises from the amusements on the pier. Like the scratch meal from the freezer, they were all part of being home again. She wouldn't have her parents forever. It was up to her to make the most of them.

Gradually, however, it became time for her to go, and she felt her mood change as she looked forward to having Rufus to herself again. She took her time over the kisses and hugs, and then she was off down the stairs, with her father following not quite so fast, the key to the side door ready in his hand. She gave him another kiss, said, "See you soon, Dad," and as she walked to her car, she looked up and waved to her mother, who was leaning out of the window. They'd be off to the bingo before long. During the summer, that was their Wednesday treat. They didn't win much, but it got them away from the shop.

Daylight was almost gone when Hayward reached Five Willows. The Brace of Pheasants was lit up inside and its car park was full, but the rest of the village was like a cemetery. She could see why some people might find Five Willows boring, but she liked it, it gave her privacy and independence. It also meant Rufus could keep a low profile. He always came in a taxi, since his Maserati would stand out a mile even without his name on the sides. That didn't mean people in the village didn't know about him, but it allowed them to pretend they didn't. For Rufus as for them, that was good enough.

She made the turn-off to the right with the ease that came from doing it just about every day. Her Mini Cooper's headlights lit the road up, but they made everything else seem twice as dark. To get to her cottage, she had to turn off left into a narrow lane that meandered past her front gate and on through the Essex countryside to an equally bendy road leading to Colchester. Virtually no one used the lane apart from her. Here and there it was wide enough for a car to turn round in, but mostly it stayed narrow, and a little way beyond her cottage was a ford with a bad reputation. It was always full of water even when the summer was dry, and it dropped off so sharply, it

175

threatened the underside of any car that went through it. There was no lane behind her cottage, just a hedge marking her land off from the meadow it butted into. A deckchair out the back on a hassle-free summer's day - that was her idea of bliss. Being all on her own at night didn't bother her.

She reversed through the gate and stayed in reverse as she swung through ninety degrees, passed her front door and came to a halt. Making ruts wasn't a problem since the ground was all paved, and anyway, her mind was on Rufus. She'd cleaned the whole cottage the evening before – not thoroughly, she hadn't had time for that, but no one was going to look in the corners - and when she switched the hall light on, she was pleased with what she saw. Even the air smelled good, although it had been shut in all day. She de-activated the burglar alarm, locked the front door, put more lights on, and drew the curtains. Then she cleaned her teeth, took a quick shower and slipped on a pink cotton frock over some filmy underwear that made her giggle as she posed and tried to pout in front of her full-length mirror. Rufus had said not too many buttons, and the pink frock didn't have any, just a zip up the back. She was sure he'd be happy with that.

Drinks came next. Rufus wasn't much of a drinker, he said alcohol damaged his fitness, but he liked enough to get him started, so she opened a fresh bottle of vodka, put some ice cubes in a jug, and filled it with orange juice. She added two tall glasses and carried the tray through to the living room. He wouldn't want anything to eat, it was sex he came for, and he wouldn't waste time once they'd got their drinks out of the way. She was happy with that, she was all for sex herself, and she hoped he might love her one day if she went along with the rest. The big thing right now, though, was that he was coming to see her again. That would be one in the eye for Anita, if she ever found out about it. He'd be a lot better off if he dumped her altogether. He often said just seeing his Steph turned him on, and she knew he was telling the truth.

Outside in the dark, Police Constable Neil Massie parked his unmarked Prius hybrid in a farm gateway between the sign warning about the ford and the ford itself. If he'd kept to the schedule he'd put together in Clacton, he'd have coincided with Hayward outside her cottage, and that could have been awkward, since he was in uniform and it had been drummed into him she mustn't know he was there. But just as he was leaving Clacton, he'd booked a cyclist for riding on the footpath, so Hayward was already in the shower when he silently cruised past on battery, looking for he wasn't sure what. When he parked, he wrote the time down and then that her car was there, parallel to her cottage and looking ready for the morning. The downstairs lights were on as well, and the curtains were drawn – she had to be inside. He wouldn't want to live there himself, all isolated like that, but she ought to be all right if she locked her doors and windows. Keeping his eyes peeled, he walked carefully back along the cottage's frontage, using his torch to see where he was treading, but being careful not to flash the beam around. When he got back to the Prius, instead of getting in, he continued over the ford, crossing it on a metal span with a handrail attached that was bolted in place for pedestrians. He walked another fifty yards or so, then decided he'd done all he could. He had no idea he was being watched. He turned the Prius round on battery. It took some doing in the narrow space and with only the sidelights on, but he'd been told explicitly not to drive through the ford and not to alert Hayward, even indirectly.

It was gone nine o'clock and Rufus still hadn't shown up, but at 9.12, when Hayward was browsing in a magazine with one eye on the clock, she heard four knocks on the front door. She sort of noticed they sounded muffled, but she didn't give it any thought, she simply laid the magazine down on the small table next to her chair and hurried into the hall with a big happy smile on her face. The key was still in the lock, but when she turned it and pulled the door open, all she saw was night goggles over a black ski mask, black zipped up clothing despite the warm evening, and a silenced pistol pointing straight at her. It was held in gloved hands, and before she could leap back and slam the door shut, one bullet struck her in the chest, knocking her backwards, and a second one passed through her brain, killing her instantly. A gloved hand reached into the hall to switch off the light, then it pulled the door shut. All around was silence, and it seemed safe for the killer to relax for a moment. Off came the goggles and the ski mask, and a black-clad forearm wiped the sweat away. Then came a thumbs up into the darkness, where a second person was waiting. After ten to fifteen seconds, the mask and the goggles went back on, a quick ground check was made to remove all traces, and the two of them set off towards the ford, leaving Hayward's gate bolted behind them. They'd

178

parked about eighty yards beyond where Massie had called it a night and on the farther side of a bend. The lane was wider there, and their car was already turned round. Its engine sounded loud as it sprang into life, but there was no one about to hear it or see it as, like Massie's Prius, it was driven away on sidelights. It made for the Colchester road.

Chapter 19

The body is found

At 9.25 the next morning Rufus walked into the office of Tony Pendery, his junior sales manager. He had a sheaf of correspondence in his hand, and he looked worried. Steph Hayward hadn't showed up, he said, and she wasn't answering her landline or her smartphone. Would he mind running over to Five Willows in his car to see if she was all right? Petrol and mileage would be on the house. He had Hayward's address and postal code already written out, since Pendery's answer had to be yes. Penderey had a job to hang on to.

"Put this in your satnav," Rufus told him. "And while I think of it, just past this cottage of hers there's a ford across the lane. I've heard it's a bad one, so don't go through it."

Although he was quite a bit younger than Hayward, Penderey had fancied her from the time he'd joined Rufus For Maseratis four and a half months previously. One or two colleagues had warned him off, but it wouldn't have mattered if they hadn't, since she made a point of looking straight

180

through him. But Penderey couldn't switch off so easily, so he was more than willing to go to Five Willows, a place he'd visited obsessively on his laptop but had never been to for real. With luck Hayward would ask him in, and then who knew what would happen?

The day had dawned with clouds about, but they were just about gone as he threaded his Peugeot hatchback through Five Willows till he reached the left-hand turn to Hayward's cottage. The gate was shut, so he drove past it and turned where PC Massie had turned the evening before. If he parked outside Hayward's gate, he'd block the lane, so mentally composing an apology in case she came to the door, he unbolted it, reversed in, and left it hooked open to show he hadn't come to stay unless, of course, she asked him to. When he shut his car door, he cringed at the noise it made. It might fetch her out in a rage before he could get his explanation in.

Under the porch, the day's *Daily Mirror* was still poking out of the front door, there were some letters jammed in on top of it, and all the downstairs curtains were drawn. He could just make out the downstairs lights were on as well, so maybe she really was ill. Or maybe she'd fallen off some steps and knocked herself out. In that case, he'd have to call an ambulance, and he'd like doing that. She might start noticing him more if she knew he'd come to her rescue – maybe saved her life even. He located the bell push, and when he pressed it, he heard a ring from inside and then nothing. He pressed it a second time, but nothing again. His first thought was to contact Rufus and ask him what to do, but he didn't want to sound like a ninny so, scared and bold at the same time, he tried the door handle. The door was unlocked. He opened it a fraction, afraid the alarm might go off – there was a sign for one under the gutter – but it didn't. Then he opened it some more. The hall light was out, but he didn't need it to see Hayward's dead body in a smart pink frock with blood on it. It was lying supine beside a low cupboard that had a vase of flowers on it. The lower part of her face seemed intact under the dried blood that covered it, but her forehead was visibly holed. And although he couldn't see it, a much larger section of her skull had been blown out at the back.

The shock was total. His stomach contracted automatically, and the adrenalin surge was so strong, he thought he was going to black out. Instinctively he pulled the door towards him and clung onto the handle to get his breath back. When he was certain he wasn't going to faint, he felt he had to look once more to see whether what he'd seen was really there. It was, and it transfixed him with fascinated horror. Then he became terrified someone would call by and think he was the one who'd done it. That made him slam the door to, lower himself onto the step and, as if in a trance, drag his smartphone out of his inside pocket to tap in three nines. He'd never rung the emergency number before, so he expected to get Clacton police, but the voice he heard could have been anywhere, and the questions went on and on – which service did he want, what was his name, where was he, what had happened, was he on his own? He became more and more overwrought. Here he was telling them someone had been shot, and all they could do was ask questions. He started to shout, then he thought someone might overhear him, so he dropped his voice again. That was when he started to cry.

"Please come," he wept into his smartphone. "Yes, I'll stay here till someone arrives, and no, I won't switch my phone off. But please be quick, you've got no idea what it's like in there."

The police arrived first, and they made sure they saw him before he saw them. He was still on the doorstep, staring in front of him and holding his smartphone loosely in his hand, when he heard a female voice call, "Mr Penderey?"

It was Gulliver. Startled, he looked up.

"This is Essex Police and we're armed. Raise your hands high in the air and walk slowly past the car in the drive towards the gateway."

His Peugeot didn't entirely block his view, and he soon made out someone was crouching behind one of the gate posts and the part of the hedge that grew up against it. He also made out the Glock 17 that was pointing at him. He'd reported a shooting, and Gulliver wasn't taking any chances. Two more armed police were out of sight in the lane, three more were in the meadow behind the back hedge, the approaches to the cottage had been sealed off and – Penderey took in the noise for the first time – a helicopter was holding position overhead. Further down the lane, Fire and Rescue was putting metal spans across the ford for itself and for an ambulance on its way from Colchester. In the other direction and spilling out into the lane that led past the field with the horses in it were four marked patrol cars, plus an unmarked car with Snape in it, and two teams from Forensics in their vans. Snape had already contacted van Piet, who was in Ashell House expecting a call from the SRO's Monte Carlo resident. He said he'd rather not come to the site, he didn't want the media to see him, but he'd like the details and pics when they were ready.

Penderey did exactly as Gulliver told him. When he reached the gateway, she ordered him to stay where he was and keep his hands in the air while one of her back-up very carefully frisked him. She wasn't showing it, but she was as tense as he was. He could be a killer trying to bluff his way out, or there could be a killer in the cottage, maybe more than one, waiting to force a get-away. She'd called the cottage a death trap the last time she'd seen it. It looked as if she'd been right.

"We've been told there's been a shooting," she said as she allowed Penderey to put his hands down. "Is there anyone else in the cottage or the grounds?"

"I don't know, I haven't been inside," he managed to say before he broke down again.

"A woman's been murdered," he wept. "She's behind the front door. Please don't ask me to go in there. I can't take it again."

Penderey seemed harmless, but he might not be, so Gulliver had her back-up take him to their car before she organised getting into the cottage. As he was being escorted away, the opening bars of Colonel Boogie sounded loudly from inside his jacket, and one of his escort took his smartphone out for him. Penderey looked at the number.

"It's my boss, Mr Rufus. He owns Rufus For Maseratis. Shall I answer? He's the one who sent me here."

It was still playing Colonel Boogie.

"Sorry, Sir, but you talk to us first. If it's that urgent, he can leave a message. We'll tell him why you didn't answer when we speak to him ourselves."

Hayward's body was photographed, a forensic pathologist put the time of death at between 9.00 and 11.00 the previous evening and saw the cadaver away. Both bullets had passed through Hayward's body. They were dug out, their locations were marked, and analysis of the wounds showed they'd been fired from close range. Snape put an up-and-coming CID officer, Detective Inspector Leonard Parnaby, in charge of evidence-gathering, but he kept overall control. He also set up the questioning of the Rufuses, Verity and Laura Slade, Cottrell and, with the agreement of Leicestershire Police, Thurston. He didn't want them to get any idea what the police knew about them already, so the line was, there was an outside chance Hayward's murder and Geoffrey Slade's death were connected, and where had these people spent the previous evening? Beneath the endless arranging, he felt depressed. He'd tried hard to protect Hayward, but it hadn't been enough. Nothing could persuade him her murder wasn't down to him.

"You want me to postpone this inquest till you've got further with the Slade business, do you?" Tait asked him when he phoned her, and he said, if she could, he'd appreciate it.

"And the deceased's name is Hayward, you say? Stephanie Hayward?"

"I'll give you a qualified yes. It's not official yet, but I've met her in the past, and there was enough of her left for me to think it was her. Why do you ask?"

"If it is her, I know her parents. They've got a toy shop near Clacton pier, and I've bought things for my granddaughter in there. Go easy on them unless you've good reason not to. They thought the world of Stephanie. She was the only one they had."

He knew that already, he'd had background enquiries started the day Hayward had talked to him in Starbucks. As soon as he'd heard about Penderey's call, he'd contacted the two officers he'd sent to Verity Slade. They were to get to the Haywards before the media broke the story, and they were to treat them gently unless they got word not to. But if they really had nothing to do with the killing, what then? Grief for the rest of their lives – and her belongings, the photographs, the anniversaries all making it harder to bear. The body would have to be identified too, and one or both of them would have to see their daughter with her shot-in chest and skull. He'd snatched a word with the fp while the latter was spraying his hands with disinfectant. He was a locum from Yorkshire he'd not met before, and he was doing holiday cover in Essex to supplement his pension. Hayward was just another corpse to him, but he was eager to have his contract extended, so he'd said Snape could leave it to him, it was just a question of wrapping her up right. And he could start the post mortem as soon as the ID was over. How did that sound, Mr Snape? Snape had said it sounded just fine and wished he didn't feel so badly about it.

It was past 7.00 in the evening when he finally got back to Chelmsford, leaving Parnaby on site to organise a police guard for the night. Penderey had been taken into Clacton to make a formal statement and then been allowed to go, but he'd had to leave his car in Five Willows, so the police had driven him home for the rest of the day with Rufus's blessing. The Rufuses, Verity and Laura Slade, Cottrell,

186

Thurston and the Haywards had all likewise been questioned, and copies of their statements were in front of Snape on his desk along with Penderey's as, red-eyed and weary, he allowed himself a cup of fresh tea and a moment of absolute stillness. Border Force had told him Davis was in flight from Cologne/Bonn, arriving in Stansted at 20.05 British time. Snape had two officers waiting for her. She'd be interviewed when she got off the plane.

Stifling a yawn, he activated the secure link to Ashell House. He talked to Garry first, who told him the national news had gone big on the story, then he had van Piet in front of him. He summed up how things were, transmitted the pics – two wounds and only two shots fired - and moved stolidly on to the alibis. The Rufuses had been in a Harwich restaurant all evening with two logistics supervisors from Container Traffic and a manager from Maserati UK. The logistics supervisors, the manager and the restaurant staff had all been questioned, and the Rufuses had definitely been there. This tallied with an entry in Rufus's desk diary. It was in Hayward's handwriting, as confirmed by a police graphologist. The two Slades and Cottrell had been in Esklivia House attending a management meeting – that was also confirmed. Thurston had been playing darts in a pub in Leicester – confirmed again. Davis was at that very moment approaching Stansted from Cologne/Bonn, and Mr and Mrs Hayward had been playing bingo on Clacton pier. That was witnessed too. They'd been devastated by their daughter's murder, but they'd promised to do the identification in the morning. Both of them. They'd said they had to, they felt it was their duty.

"What about the person who found the body?"

"Tony Pendery? He's a drummer in a rock band when he's not working for Rufus. He was playing in a club in Felixstowe all evening."

"It was Rufus who sent him to Nightingale Cottage, wasn't it?"

"That's the story."

"And Hayward was expecting someone, you say?"

"So it seems. The burglar alarm was off, she'd trimmed herself up, and there were two glasses set out for drinks that hadn't been used. She wasn't assaulted before or after she was shot, and nothing seems to have been disturbed or removed. If you ask me, it was an execution."

Van Piet glanced at his watch.

"I'll be out of town tomorrow, Tom as well, I've had a message I want to follow up. If anything breaks, you can reach me by mobile. I'll talk to you as soon as I get back."

He terminated and contacted the SRO's high-security heliport. It was downstream from central London on the Isle of Dogs. Notices all round its perimeter fence said 'Ministry of Defence land – keep out', and they were true enough to conceal who owned everything else. He talked through a flight plan with a scheduler and OK-ed it when she'd finished. Take-off would be at 6.30 sharp the next morning. Time of return: Uncertain.

Chapter 20

More about Barbara Davis

The air off the Thames was still dawn-fresh when an SRO driver brought van Piet and Garry to the heliport. Armed guards checked them through the gate, then the driver dropped them off outside the nondescript concrete terminal. Inside, staff were doing their best to look awake, but the six o'clock shift was definitely the one to avoid. Van Piet and Garry put their watches forward an hour to align them with German time. It gave them something to do while they waited for their pilot and co-pilot, Kenny Efflin and Tamsin Springer, to come and collect them.

The Agusta Westland 109 took off exactly on time. It stuck to its cruising speed of 170 mph, and before long they had a bird's eye view of Cologne/Bonn Airport. Berlin has been Germany's capital for many years now, but plenty of government still goes on in Bonn, and the secluded area they landed in reflected the fact. A Federal Police BMW ferried them to a screened-off transit area where, after detailed security checks, they were handed over to

Dominic Beecher, the SRO's resident for Germany West and North. The Agusta would stay where it was.

"Good to see you, Mr van Piet, Mr Garry," Beecher said as they climbed into his Mercedes. "I'll take you to my place first, then we can go visiting, if that's what you still want."

The SRO didn't use apartments if it could avoid them, it regarded them as a security hazard, so Beecher, who was in his early thirties, had the use of a detached house in the fashionable district of Poppelsdorf. The neighbours thought it belonged to the UK Consulate-General in Düsseldorf. Eileen Beecher, Dominic Beecher's wife, had just got back from the supermarket when they arrived, so they all went through the front door together. She was two years younger than her husband, and they had a six year old daughter, Jade, who was out for the day with friends. A pair of fluffy pink slippers in the middle of the hall marked her departure. Beecher stooped down without thinking and put them in the shoe rack. He also unloaded the groceries while Eileen made the coffee. Then it was work time in Beecher's securitised workroom at the back of the house. The sun was high in a cloudless sky outside, but the blinds were drawn and the spy-proof windows were locked.

"I've had to call in a whole load of favours since Mr Garry first got in touch," Beecher began, "but you were definitely on the right track. Barbara Davis's nationality is a real can of worms, so it's a good thing you've come over. It's true her parents were working for the V and A when she was born, and it's also true they had a place in Hampstead. But now look at this."

He brought up a German birth certificate on a VHD screen. Barbara Sarah Winckler was the name, the parents were given as Andreas and Francisca Winckler, and the place of birth was Schaabstrasse 21A in Bonn. So Barbara Winckler was born in Germany, and her nationality was stated as German. Van Piet, like Garry, could read German fluently. He asked what Schaabstrasse 21A was like.

"It's the upper part of a house that's been converted into a duplex. When Barbara Winckler was born, it all belonged to Andreas's elder brother, Friedrich, and it's still Friedrich's today. He and Andreas grew up there when it was all one big house, and Friedrich inherited the lot from their father, who was a widower when he died. Andreas wasn't left out. He got a nice sum of money, and he seems to have stayed there as a sort of non-paying guest till he decided to move on. Friedrich, on the other hand, has never lived anywhere else.

"He's never married either, so it's likely he didn't need all that space on his own, but that doesn't have to be the reason he split the place into a duplex, since he did it when Francisca was pregnant with Barbara. 21A was called 'self-contained family accommodation' on the planning application, and that's what the paperwork still calls it, because it's never been changed. Now here's why it matters.

"You presumably know as well as I do, when you move out of an address in Germany, you have to inform the authorities. But no one ever did that for Barbara, and she's never done it for herself to this day. Her surname has never been changed over here either. As far as this country's concerned, she's still Barbara Sarah Winckler of Schaabstrasse 21A."

He brought up some more images.

191

"These documents make that clear. They're duplicate copies of her German ID, her German driving licence, and her German health insurance, which she pays regularly. This is one of her German tax forms – she has some of her translation work paid for and taxed over here - and this is her most recent application to renew her passport. Her German passport, that is. During her school years, her parents gave her address as Schaabstrasse 21A, but they also declared she was living with them in their second home in Hampstead and going to school in London. That kept Child Protection off their backs. Later on, she played the same sort of trick herself. Whenever she had to, she told the Germans her primary residence was Schaabstrasse 21A, but she had a second home in England. The result is, she's got a complete identity as Barbara Winckler, a German national who's currently living in Clacton."

Garry had taken his smartphone out and was quietly making some searches. Van Piet said,

"She told me the Wincklers had all become British when she was ten. And they changed their name to Davis at about the same time."

"She's probably good at telling the truth when it suits her, but what I'm sure she didn't tell you was that Mr and Mrs Winckler didn't inform the British authorities they wished to retain their German and Spanish citizenships even though they were now British, although they were entitled to do that under the European law of the day. And they treated their daughter's German citizenship in the same way. That meant that in the UK, all three Wincklers were British and nothing else.

"As for the new surname, that was of course an entirely separate action, though if you ask me, the

192

timing wasn't a coincidence. If you're British, which the Wincklers now were, you can change your name whenever you like, and that's precisely what they did. They changed their name by deed poll, the Royal Courts of Justice duly enrolled the change, and all the newly minted Davises had to do after that was inform their banks, their employer and so forth who they now were, not forgetting Barbara's school in London. The upshot was, Barbara Sarah now had two parallel surnames as well as two parallel identities, one in Germany and one in the UK. And as an adult she's hung on to both of them."

He selected some more images.

"This is her British driving licence, this is one of her British tax declarations – you'll see it's mostly buy-to-let income plus some investments – and this is her British passport. You'll notice they're all in the name of Davis. And whenever an address is called for in Britain, she gives her British one as if it's the only one she's got."

It was getting stuffy in Beecher's workroom, but van Piet was too busy thinking through what he was hearing to be bothered by it.

"It's beginning to look," he said finally, "as if when Mr and Mrs Winckler became British, it wasn't out of any love for Britain, it was part of setting their daughter up for some kind of trickery later on in her life, and her Uncle Friedrich was in on it from the start. But surely, once their British citizenship became official, the British authorities informed their German and Spanish counterparts as a matter of course, even if Andreas and Francisca Winckler were personally happy to let their original citizenships lapse. And that ought to have killed any scheme they had right there."

Beecher rubbed his hands.

"I'm glad you mentioned Uncle Friedrich, Mr van Piet. Britain informed Spain about Francisca just as you say, but as I see it, Spain didn't count, it was the German side that mattered. Britain tried to inform the German authorities as well – it sent the information to the Federal Office of Administration, because that's the outfit that deals with these things over here. But the FOA is in Cologne, which is an easy commute from Bonn, and Friedrich Winckler happened to be the official who would have received that information, since he ran the relevant section till he retired. The word is, incidentally, he could have been promoted out of it - more than once, in fact - but he turned all the offers down. Strange to say, there's no trace of that information from Britain in Cologne, it's as if it never arrived. And what the FOA isn't told about, it doesn't know about, because that's how bureaucracies are."

Van Piet asked him if he was sure of his facts.

"Absolutely. The Davises are retired now, by the way, they live on the south coast in Brighton. Apparently Mr Davis, as he's known over there, needs some kind of nursing care. His brother Friedrich, on the other hand, seems to be still going strong."

Beecher gave the Brighton address to Garry. He'd already printed it off.

It was time to take a look at Barbara Winckler's home in Bonn. Schaabstrasse was a busy street near the Kennedy Bridge, and the duplex, which pre-dated the Second World War, had a central European look about it. It stood on a corner, and its smooth front wall and one smooth side wall bordered directly onto the pavement, as if it was turning its back on the

194

outside world. The front wall had a door in it that was shut. It had 21 next to it. In the side wall was another door that was also shut. It had 21A next to it, and according to Beecher, who'd been through it pretending to deliver fliers for a laundromat, it opened onto a staircase. Neither of the doors had letter flaps in them. German-style, the letter boxes were in a vestibule behind each door. They were made of metal, they were bolted to the wall, and they were lockable. At the far end of the side wall was a post-war extension with two garage doors in it. They were also numbered 21 and 21A, with Schaabstrasse added each time, since the side street had a different name.

Van Piet had borrowed a grubby denim suit Beecher used for jobs in his garden, plus an equally grubby sun hat with a wide brim. Over his shoulder he was carrying a cloth satchel with fliers for a pizza service in it. They looked exactly like the ones they were copied from and, like the laundromat ones, they came from a stock Beecher kept for when he wanted to move around Bonn without being noticed. The denim suit was too big for van Piet, but that simply helped his image, as did the well-worn trainers he'd borrowed that were also too big. He'd had to lace them up extra tight, and he was glad he wouldn't be walking very far in them. Beecher had opted for everyday jeans and a grey T-shirt that was into its final summer. Garry kept to his two-piece suit. Anything else would have drawn attention to him.

He and van Piet got their first sight of the duplex as Beecher's Mercedes crawled past it at the same low speed as all the other vehicles. Schaabstrasse was a sort of local high street, and strategically placed traffic lights and crosswalks kept the through speed down to a minimum.

"Andreas and Friedrich's father bought this place after the Second World War," Beecher explained as he turned off well beyond the duplex and hunted for a space to park in.

"His name was Karl Winckler, and he was a doctor. He'd qualified after war broke out, and he was called up straight away as a medical officer. His record says he was in Greece, and he was nearly shot as a traitor there because he'd treated two wounded men who'd turned out to be National Liberation Front. He claimed he had to treat anyone who was hurt, regardless of who they were, which would normally have got him nowhere. But reading between the lines, his unit was getting slaughtered and he was the only medic they had, so he survived. The record goes quiet after that. So far as I know, he was never in the Nazi party."

Van Piet got out of the Mercedes first and began to work his way back with the fliers. Garry gave him a few moments, then he got out, crossed Schaabstrasse and kept van Piet in sight from the other side. Finally Beecher locked the car and followed van Piet, hanging well back. He pretended to talk into his smartphone, which he held ready to use as a camera.

At Schaabstrasse 21A, van Piet pushed open the door and went in, thinking it was a miracle the place hadn't been bombed like most of the rest of Cologne. The air smelled hot and dusty, as if the door hadn't been opened that day. He took in the staircase at a glance and pushed a flier into the letter box. He didn't dare do anything else in case he was on cctv, but he felt he hadn't been wasting his time, since in the corner of the vestibule he'd noticed a small safe. So, a lockable letter box wasn't enough for Fräulein Winckler. He went from 21A to 21, where everything seemed as it should be, and from there he carried on further up the street. He didn't see a figure emerge from the flow of pedestrians and enter 21, but Beecher did and photographed him as he opened the door. Garry saw him as well.

When van Piet judged he'd delivered enough fliers to look convincing, he crossed over to work his way back. Beecher reached the Mercedes first. He'd bought some jam doughnuts he didn't want in order to change direction, and he put them in the boot, meaning to bin them later. Garry arrived next carrying a news magazine, and Beecher opened the passenger door for him. When van Piet got back, he opened the rear door for himself. If anyone was watching, the chances were they looked like a driver, an employer, and someone down on his luck trying out for a mini-job.

Once they were clear of Schaabstrasse, Beecher said he'd photographed someone going in to 21, but he didn't know who it was. At the next set of lights, he handed his smartphone to Garry, who checked the image and reached the phone to van Piet without comment. It showed a pudgy, academic-looking man, apparently in his late fifties. His hair, which was fair and going thin, was cut short, the lower part of his face was stubbly, and his glasses had a deep brown frame. He was wearing beige chinos, a light blue shirt open at the neck, and brown suede shoes. His lightweight jacket was also beige, but a darker shade.

"I don't know him either," van Piet said, passing the phone back to Garry. "What about you, Tom?"

"I'd have to think about it, Sir," he replied, and he slipped the phone into the all-purpose holder by the hand brake.

When they were back in the Beechers' house, van Piet changed his clothes and, with some relief, his footwear. While Beecher transferred the Schaabstrasse image to van Piet's mobile and deleted it from his smartphone, Garry contacted Efflin.

"Ask for take-off in two and a half hours' time, please. If there's a problem, call me back."

But Efflin didn't call back, and after a quick meal with Eileen Beecher and Jade, who had just been dropped off, Beecher was taking them to the airport. On the way, van Piet made it clear to Beecher that on no account was he to go back to Schaabstrasse unless he was told to, and Beecher took it on board. His career mattered to him.

"What were your searches all about, Tom?" van Piet asked as they waited for Efflin and Springer by the Agusta. The airport was busy, and it was noisy and smelly in the restricted area, but they could speak there without being overheard.

"Well, Sir, Miss Davis left Stansted airport for this one early last Tuesday morning. She could have left Schaabstrasse for Düsseldorf airport the next day – I make it between one and two hours' drive away – and she could have caught the 10.55 from there to Heathrow as Fräulein Winckler, landing at 11.30 British time. From Heathrow to Five Willows is three to four hours by road, and Stephanie Hayward was murdered at something like 9.00 in the evening, so Davis alias Winckler would have had plenty of time to hire a car and pick up any clothing she needed

198

from a hiding place, plus the murder weapon. Or she might have had an accomplice to help her out, but either way, time wouldn't have been a problem. She could have spent the night anywhere, but if - still as Fräulein Winckler - she took off from Heathrow on Thursday morning at 9.30, she could have been back in Düsseldorf by 11.55 German time. From there she could easily have got back to Schaabstrasse, re-organised herself and caught the 19.55 from this airport as Miss Davis, landing yesterday evening in Stansted at 20.05 British time."

"Thanks, Tom, that's brilliant. Ask Border Force whether she really made those trips as soon as you get the chance. And who was in the photo Mr Beecher took? I'm sure you recog- "

He broke off, his mobile was buzzing. The caller was Snape, and he had a lot to tell.

"First, Willem, Forensics has found Pachini's fingerprints in Deborah Hayward's cottage. There may be some DNA traces as well, that's being looked into.

"Second, the officer who was outside her cottage just before she was shot went back there this afternoon and located a place her murderer may have waited in till the coast was clear. We still don't know whether more than one person was involved, but the officer found some minute traces of black fabric, and they're being analysed as I speak. We've got some faint footprints as well that could be connected with the murder. They're men's hiker's boots, size 11. Stephanie Hayward's parents have identified her body, and the post mortem says it was the shot through the head that killed her. The bullet came from a Beretta 92 that was fitted with a silencer.

199

"Third, Davis dissolved in anguish when we stopped her on the airport and told her about Hayward's murder. She said she'd met her just once, it was at Rufus For Maseratis, and she'd taken an immediate liking to her. But she didn't see how she could help us, because she'd been in Germany when poor Miss Hayward lost her life."

"Did she say precisely that?"

"Yes, and it's in the signed statement we asked her to make. Word for word."

"That could blow her wide open, if she's been flitting back and forth," van Piet thought to himself.

"Leave Davis alone for the moment," he said, and before Snape could protest, he added, "Something else has cropped up, and I need to deal with it first. Be in Ashell House tomorrow around midday, we've got a lot to talk about. Hang on a moment."

He paused to get his thinking straight, then,

"You've got a search warrant for the house Pachini lived in. It's valid for three months, isn't it?"

"It is."

"Get search warrants for Davis, Verity Slade, Laura Slade and Cottrell, the Rufuses, Thurston and Watkins. Paddington as well as Kensington for Watkins. There's a new name to add to the list, but I can't tell you what it is yet. Perhaps tomorrow. It's the new name that's causing me problems."

Van Piet terminated and nodded to Garry.

"Your turn, Tom."

"His name's Jesse Kett. He's GCHQ, and at the moment he's with the National Cyber Security Centre. He's an expert on Infrastructure Protection, and I happen to know it, because I attended a seminar he addressed just after you went on leave. I thought it best not to say anything in front of Mr Beecher."

Van Piet went on full alert – he remembered what Snape had said about ready cash. This could be the missing piece of the jigsaw. At that moment, a Federal Police BMW drew up, and Efflin and Springer got out. As soon as it had swished off, van Piet told them to get into the Agusta, prepare a new flight plan – destination: Gloucestershire airport - and get an emergency take-off slot from the control tower, citing European Flash Code Red. Garry was to contact Benjamin, asking him to stand by for an emergency message, and once Efflin and Springer were in the Agusta, van Piet used his mobile to call a Cheltenham number.

"Kossler here. What's up, Willem?"

A plane was coming in to land, but van Piet instinctively kept his voice down.

"Ian, I'm giving you a formal instruction under a Crown warrant. Speak to your Director and get Jesse Kett of the National Cyber Security Centre quarantined as of now. Yes, Jesse Kett in Infrastructure Protection. Don't let him know anything about it. I'm out of the country at the moment, but I'll be landing at Gloucestershire airport in something under four hours' time. Where will you be?"

"I was going to be at home. Do you want me to stay in GCHQ?"

"No, I'd better not be seen there, I'll come to your place. Tom Garry will be with me."

Garry had meanwhile made contact with Benjamin. Van Piet took his mobile from him and gave Benjamin a full briefing.

"We have to assume the worst, Sir," he said, and Benjamin had to agree. He'd start making arrangements.

Van Piet finished by requesting SRO transport from Gloucestershire airport to Cheltenham, plus reliefs for Efflin and Springer for the flight back to London. Putting his mobile into his pocket, he moved to where Springer could see him and indicated he and Garry were coming on board. The Agusta had a ferry range of 570 miles. A westerly was springing up, Springer said, as she secured the cabin door, but they should be all right for fuel. It was bringing rain with it, she tacked on as she bustled into the cockpit. It was always the same with westerlies. They brought moisture in from the Atlantic, and dumped it on England as rain.

As the Agusta was crossing the Channel, Thurston, feeling smug, was driving home from Watkins's Kensington flat in his Range Rover. She'd asked him to come – a quick call from a central London pay phone had been enough - and they'd had a good time together, he thought. The sex alone had been worth it, he reckoned, as he weighed it against working time lost and his travel costs. They'd talked a lot as well, and one way and another, he was sure something was happening between them. In the end, she'd had to go in to the *Standard*, but before they'd split up, she'd said she'd like to see him in his own place to really get to know him, so how about the following day? She couldn't spend the night with him, she had to spend Sunday and Monday on an article she was finishing. But they could still spend a lot of the day together.

The following day was Saturday, and that created a problem for Thurston, though he wasn't going to say so out loud. Every so often, Anita Rufus liked to drive over to his house and, as she told him in her unvarnished way, be fucked by a real man for a change. It made her feel how she felt entitled to feel. Rufus knew it was happening, but he never said anything, and she'd arranged to spend Saturday with Thurston some days previously. But Watkins was Thurston's priority now, so he mentally deleted Anita and suggested Watkins come over late morning, say 11.00 or so. He told her how to get there, saying he'd look in at his quarry early to make sure things were running right, then he'd take the rest of the day off. He often did that on a Saturday, so no one would give it a thought. She should look for Thurston Mansion when the satnav said she'd arrived. The house's name was inscribed on each side of the gateway.

As soon as he got the chance, he stopped his Range Rover and texted Anita, using end-to-end encryption, as he always did with her. He said a rush order for granite would keep him busy all Saturday, and there was nothing he could do about it. She couldn't be as fed up as he was, but there'd be other times soon for sure. He tacked on some kisses and a dejected-looking emoticon, restarted his car and drove on. That, he chuckled, solved that one.

Chapter 21

A question of money

The evening sky was an angry red as the Agusta powered its way towards Gloucestershire. While it was touching down on the airport, a Nissan Qashai from the SRO moved into position. The driver had brought Efflin and Springer's reliefs, plus make-shift meals and flasks of tea for anyone who wanted them.

Cheltenham was just four miles away, and the Kosslers' ivy-covered Edwardian villa was on the eastern edge. Van Piet phoned the Nissan's registration ahead, and the front gate swung open as they approached it. Kossler was waiting in the doorway, and he locked the door as soon as van Piet, Garry and their driver were inside. Judith Kossler, an A and E consultant in Cheltenham General Hospital, was off shift for the night. She'd be keeping an eye on the driver in a separate room. There was no one else in the house.

Kossler led the way into a small room on the ground floor. The curtains were drawn, and hot coffee in an insulated jug stood on a small table near the hearth. Van Piet took Kossler through everything that had happened since Slade bought his Maserati. He didn't want there to be any gaps.

"Some connections look to be certain," he said as he drew to a close. "Davis knows or knew the Rufuses, Verity and Geoffrey Slade, Heinrich Winckler, Hayward and Pachini. The Rufuses can be linked to Verity and Geoffrey Slade as well as to Hayward and Pachini. Thurston knows or knew all three Slades, and the same goes for Cottrell. Watkins met Verity and Geoffrey Slade while her fiancé was still alive. Pachini's fingerprints have been found in Hayward's cottage, and Kett and Heinrich Winckler appear to know each other as well. I'm sure there are more connections, but I'd need hard evidence to say what they were."

There was a spattering noise on the windows. The rain had arrived, and the wind was growling in the chimney. Scarcely hearing it, van Piet turned to the bank accounts GCHQ had been opening up for him. The people they belonged to were regularly drawing out cash, he explained, including Millie Cottrell, who didn't have any traceable investments but whose salary was high even by London standards. The exception was Laura Slade. Her salary was high as well, but she used cards for just about everything. All these people were affluent enough to carry well-stuffed wallets and purses, so their cash withdrawals needn't be sinister. But cash was difficult to trace, and if Verity Slade, Cottrell, Davis, the Rufuses, Thurston and, until recently, Geoffrey Slade, were drawing out an average of £500 a month each, someone else could be £42,000 a year better off, and no one would be any the wiser. Was that where Jesse Kett came in? Was he the missing piece of the jigsaw?   Speculation wasn't proof, and £42,000 wasn't an especially large sum of money, but a lot of people had sold secrets for less. Kossler agreed - it had happened at GCHQ. But if van Piet was right, why was Esklivia financing a cut-price traitor?

"I don't know the answer to that, Ian, but if you can go into all of Esklivia's accounts – yes, all of them - and sort them by name, nationality, profession and possible criminal records, I think I can come up with one. Can you do that without Kett knowing?"

"We should be able to. I'll make it a separate file. What name shall I give it?"

"Call it Capricorn, it's easy to remember. Send everything to Tom as soon as you can, and I'll take it from there. Now, what can you tell me about Kett?"

Kossler found it strange to treat someone he'd worked with on top secret projects as an enemy, but he could see it had to be. In security, suspicion is enough.

"He built an academic career in IT at Oxford, then we asked him to come to us. When the Russians cyber-attacked Estonia, we asked him to work out how it was done, and fending off Russian hacking was his thing from then on."

"Just Russian?"

"Just Russian – we compartmentalise everything these days. Anyway, he helped with Firewall Britain while he was here in Cheltenham, and when we set up the National Cyber Security Centre in London, we transferred him there to work on protecting British infrastructure – again, just from the Russians. He's often in Germany, because we talk a lot to their intelligence services, and Bonn is easy to get to from most places over there.   I'll be honest,

Willem, I'm concerned, and so is the Director. With a background like his, he's got a lot to leak."

Van Piet asked about military secrets and NATO. And what about his personal life?

"Nothing military, he's always been on the civilian side - that's where the action is these days, of course. Why use bombs and missiles when computers will do? As for his personal life, he's divorced, he's got no children, and he lives on his own in a detached house in Oxford. He'd already bought it when he came to us."

"With a mortgage?"

"Yes, he could just about afford it then, and he can certainly afford it now. Maybe he's just got greedy, it can happen, you know, and maybe they're pampering him a bit as well. But I'll tell you one more thing while I'm at it, Willem. When we vetted him, we asked some of his students about him, and one of them was Millicent Cottrell. The name didn't stand out then, but it does now."

Van Piet asked what she'd said about him.

"What the others said: He liked his pleasures, he never mentioned politics, and behind the friendly façade, he was completely caught up in his work. That figured. His wife told us it was his computers that drove her out, and when she left him, she let him know by e-mail so he'd get the point."

There was an uncomfortable pause, and the rain became more noticeable.

"We couldn't find a security breach, however hard we looked, but we have to assume there's one now," he said finally. "We're sorting Kett's quarantine out, but it isn't easy, because he'll notice if we start holding things back. What about you?"

"The murder hunts go on because they have to," van Piet replied. "So does the hunt for Pachini. Kett is now part of these hunts, so Mr Snape will have to be told about him. So will the Head of his Armed Support Unit. I'll see to that tomorrow, unless you think I shouldn't."

Kossler rubbed his eyes wearily.

"What can I say, Willem? The most I can ask is that, when you speak to these people, you quote what the Official Secrets Act says about information entrusted by a Crown servant on terms requiring it to be held in confidence. You'll do us all a big favour if you make it clear that if people break that confidence, they end up in the slammer."

Van Piet said he would. Did Kossler know where Kett would be over the next little while? Kossler consulted his smartphone.

"He's due back from Germany tomorrow. Sunday he's got off, so he'll probably be in Oxford, and Monday – well, well – Monday he'll be talking to Lloyds Bank and Barclays in Chelmsford. It's part of his job to help national assets with their hacking defences, and he's splitting the day between them. Thereafter, he'll be in London, unless he decides to work at home. That's always possible."

Van Piet wondered about tailing Kett, but Kossler was strongly against it.

"He'd know straight away. Bonn was a one-off, so we'll hope you got away with it, but try it again and he'll see you, because that's how we train people these days. Be thankful we live on an island, Willem. People can do all sorts of things while they're here, it's getting away that's the problem."

Van Piet took the point and asked for some photos of Kett to be sent to Garry. Then he said,

"Thurston built a brand new outhouse onto the Slades' house in Essex, allegedly to make it grander than it already was. According to Thurston, it's got an upstairs he's not been into since he finished building it and a couple of computers downstairs. If he's telling the truth, I want you to find out what's on those computers. Can you do that?"

"If they're online I can. It may take time, that's the only thing."

"What if there are more computers upstairs?"

"Same answer. If they're online I can."

"Why shouldn't they be online?"

"Plenty of reasons. A personnel manager can list his staff, organise shifts and cover absences without going online. For him, being offline's a firewall. Or someone preparing a hack may keep his servers offline till the very last minute so no one knows they're there. For that person, being offline's like preparing an ambush."

Van Piet knew he should have seen that for himself, but he'd just about had it, and there was still the flight back to London to get through. The coffee in the jug had gone cold, and no one except him wanted any more, so he emptied it into his cup and drank it down. While they were all getting to their feet, he asked Garry to book two emergency rooms in Ashell House, arrange transport across London from the Isle of Dogs, and find out whether Efflin and Springer needed help to get home. Not to worry about the Nissan driver. Someone else would see to him.

It was raining hard outside, so they got into the Nissan fast. The airport terminal was a ghostly place now – only security and the cleaners were in there. As the Nissan approached it, van Piet's mobile buzzed. It was Snape, he was still in Police HQ. Could he speak freely?

"Hang on."

Van Piet asked the driver to wait in the terminal, then he told Snape to go ahead. He turned the volume up so Garry could hear.

"I know it's late, but this is hot off the line, Willem," they heard through the rain beating on the Nissan's roof. "You'll remember Laura Slade said her father liked to go to these Brahms things, on his own and distance no object. Well, I put a team onto that, and we've found performances in Croydon, Ipswich and Cambridge he bought single tickets on-line for within the last eighteen months. We've checked them out and turned up zilch, but now listen to this. At 8.38 am on 13th February of this year he bought a ticket on-line for the Theatre Royal in Bury St Edmunds, and the performance was the same evening."

"Just like that? How did he manage it?"

"The 13th was a Monday, February is February, and Bury isn't London, so it was a thin house. Perhaps Slade had a sudden gap in his diary or something, but the point is, Bury's about sixty miles from Lower Mindle, and when we asked who sat next to him or near him, the manager came up with an unidentified customer who bought a ticket in person at 4.52 pm the same day. This customer paid in cash and sat five seats away from Slade in the next row back. Theatres are archiving their surveillance pics these days in case anti-terrorism wants them, so we linked up with the Theatre Royal, used Tom's gallery pics to base a search on, and Customer X turned out to be Deborah Watkins. We think she knew Slade was going to be there, so she checked the theatre's website for empty seats, travelled all the way from London, and bought her ticket without having to say who she was."

"What happened after that?" van Piet asked. All the fatigue was gone.

"You'd be surprised. During the interval, she attached herself to Slade in the bar. He didn't look too pleased at first, but he seemed a lot more cheerful when they went back to their seats, and they left the theatre as if the night wasn't over. What do you reckon, Willem? It can't be coincidence, not in Bury St Edmunds on a February Monday."

"You've got three choices, Eddie. He could have told her where he was going, someone else could have told her the same thing, or she hacked into his computer and found out for herself. Listen, when you come to Ashell House, bring Sal with you. Tell her to wear civvies and not to come armed. I'll get Escorted Clearance for her, and Tom will see you in."

Snape was happy with that, but he sounded less than happy when he asked,

"Is Watkins in danger, do you think? I mean, her fiancé was murdered, we think Geoffrey Slade went the same way, and Stephanie Hayward certainly did. I shouldn't want Watkins to make a fourth."

Van Piet had zero trouble with that.

"Watkins is a lot smarter than Hayward ever was, and my guess is, she's come up with an equally smart plan to keep herself alive. That doesn't mean it will work, it simply means, if anything happens to her, she won't have seen it coming. She can always ask for protection if that's what she feels she needs, but if I've got her thinking right, she won't. So step away and stay there, Eddie. We owe her precisely nothing."

Chapter 22

Watkins goes to Thurston's house

It had rained all through the night and it was still tippling down as Deborah Watkins eased her Mazda coupé out of her garage and set off for Thurston Mansion. The house's name made her laugh out loud, but Thurston had the taint of death about him, and that wasn't funny at all. She'd left a message on her office ansaphone saying where she was going and when she expected to be back. She did that when she was meeting someone dangerous. The problem was, Thurston could be useful. But there was no chance she'd be staying the night.

Once she left the motorway, she had to rely on her satnav. The roads dwindled into lanes full of tilted and rusting signposts – just like the lanes around Five Willows, she recalled with a sinister chill - and then she was in low gear driving parallel to a barrier of high, black railings topped with sharp spikes painted gold. When her satnav said she'd arrived, she was opposite a gateway on her right. She put her winker on, but instead of making the turn, she thought she ought to make sure she'd got the right place, so she lowered her side window and peered through the teeming rain.

The gateway was set back from the road, and both gateposts had dressed granite slabs fixed to them with 'Thurston Mansion' spelled out in mock-imperial chiselled letters. Below each name, a pair of heraldic beasts held up an engraved coat of arms, and below the beasts, 'Faber Suae Quisque Fortunae' unfolded on a wave-like scroll. She had no idea what it meant, and she didn't think anyone else would know either. "Self-regarding prat," she thought to herself, and she was about to raise her side window to keep the rain out when a Hyundai saloon coming from the other direction slowed down when it saw her and flashed her to get her to cross over. Feeling harassed, she crossed over too fast, and then she had to brake hard, which unsettled her more than she was already. An intercom was let into the gatepost on the driver's side. It was a bit high for her in her coupé, and when the mini-screen lit up, she saw Thurston beaming down at her. She flashed a bright smile on in return, spoke into the grill under the screen, and finally shut her side window as the gates swung back. As soon as she was through, they closed behind her.

The lowering sky and the rain made the tall trees seem grim and hostile, and it was only because Thurston Mansion was made of red Victorian stock bricks that there was anything light about it. It was clearly built to impress, but Watkins found it overbearing. Cluttered as well. Its obsessively escalloped blue-black tiles had dormers, chimney stacks and a belvedere shooting out of them, an oversize conservatory dominated one corner, and massive steps disappeared into a basement between the pompous front porch and a thrusting bay window.

The front door was open, and Thurston, in bottle green corduroys and a purplish merino pullover, was standing under the stained-glass fanlight with a rolled golfing umbrella in his hand. He moved forward as Watkins drew to a halt and pushed the umbrella open. She dropped her side window again and flashed on a second smile.

"Leave the car where it is and come straight in," he told her, tilting the umbrella so she could get out underneath it. "It won't be in anyone's way."

She raised the window once more, grabbed a hold-all from the passenger seat, and scrambled out.

"I've brought some indoor clothes," she said as they wiped their feet on the doormat. She was wearing Goretex rainwear and hiking boots. "And I've brought a pair of slippers as well. Your carpets came first, but my comfort came a close second. I want to enjoy myself."

She was finding it hard going already.

He showed her upstairs to a guest room where she could change. He'd told Snape and van Piet he hadn't altered the house much since his great-great-grandfather's days, and that was how it struck Watkins now. The entrance hall was floored with brownish encaustic tiles, the staircase and the corridor it led up to were narrow and gloomy, and the guest room contained a bed with a polished brass bedstead that stood, Victorian-style, on a fringed carpet that didn't reach to the walls. She looked out through the rain-bespattered window, but all she could see was tall wet trees, so she left the lace curtains open while she changed. There was no chance anyone could see in.

When she came downstairs, Thurston's living room, which was larger than she'd expected, had the same dead-hand feeling about it, despite a large-screen television and wrap-round sound gear. The overstuffed three-piece suite had button backs, the cast iron fireplace had a halo of glazed patterned tiles round it, and twin gasoliers – converted to electricity, but still looking authentic – hung from the ceiling like throwbacks. A Davenport desk with cabriole legs stood by one wall. It looked like something stolen from a schoolroom, then ornamented to conceal the theft. In the kitchen, which in contrast was fully modernised, peeled potatoes and cut broccoli stood ready to go in their saucepans, a pot roast was simmering in a slow cooker, and a bottle of Cabernet Sauvignon was waiting on one of the counters. They agreed 12.30 or so would be soon enough to eat, so they made some coffee together, and then they sat in the living room looking uncertainly at each other, their heads backed by hand-stitched antimacassars. Watkins badly needed to gain control, so before long she was saying,

"We've both got big things to hide, Neville, there's no point pretending we haven't, and we'll have to tell each other about them at some point. But if we go into them now, we might kill this nice thing between us before it's had a chance to grow. So let's make today work and see where it takes us."

Thurston was hard to read, but he seemed to like what he'd heard. The rain was sheeting down now, and the low cloud was making the room dark. As he put some table lamps on with his smartphone, she turned towards the bay window, hoping she didn't seem too stagey.

"When I left London," she said, "I thought we might take a look round your quarry, that's why I brought my waterproofs with me. But I want to stay indoors now and see how close we can get to each other."

Thurston was still hard to read, but he seemed to like that too.

The meal went well. Watkins made sure Thurston had most of the wine, plus most of the cognac after the dessert. He seemed more settled after that.

Some 110 miles away in Chelsea, at about the time Thurston and Watkins were sitting down to lunch, Garry was seeing Snape and Gulliver into Ashell House. The rain had made them late, but Garry said not to worry, they weren't ready for them yet anyway. When they got out of the lift, they saw why he'd said it. They'd gone up to the topmost floor, been ushered past Signals with its heavy armoured doors, and been shown into a corner room that was being hastily converted into an operations room. While some desks were in place, others were standing where they'd been put down, there were screens and computers still in boxes, and a team of technicians was cabling up where it could. In the middle of the room, Selina Mitchie – stocky, middle-aged, in jeans and a Breton T-shirt - was talking animatedly to van Piet.

Mitchie was in charge of the operations room. She and van Piet had had hardly any sleep - they'd been bundled into a crisis meeting as soon as van Piet had got back from Cheltenham, and it had seemed to go on and on as GCHQ, the NCA and Border Force had been linked in one by one. They broke off when they saw Garry, Snape and Gulliver come towards them. Garry had had just as little sleep, but it didn't seem to show.

Mitchie was senior management, and when she went off shift, someone equally senior would take over, though who that would be was still being sorted out. Snape had met Mitchie before, but Gulliver hadn't, so to give her some standing, van Piet explained she'd helped him catch Alex Trilling, the former Director General who'd betrayed the SRO[1], and Russell Burney, the murderous oil millionaire[2]. Mitchie smiled wanly, said, "Well done" in a tired voice, and shifted her attention back to the operations room, where in the parts that were functioning too many agencies were sending in too much data at once.

"We'll use the conference room across the corridor," van Piet decided. "It'll be less stressed in there. Get some water from the dispenser, if you want something to drink right now. We haven't got as far as tea and coffee yet."

They seated themselves on moulded plastic chairs round an old wooden table that was too large for four people. Van Piet wanted Snape and Gulliver to be as fully briefed as Kossler, so after he'd cited the Official Secrets Act with Kossler's warning attached, he went over old ground to help Gulliver, then he moved onto Davis's two identities, the strong possibility she'd murdered Hayward, and the sighting of Jesse Kett. Davis had definitely entered and left the UK as Barbara Winckler, Garry had got that from Border Force, but van Piet was against pulling her in till he could nail Kett. He thought Watkins was a key player, especially after what had happened in Bury St

---

[1] *Death by Drowning*
[2] *Dangerous Knowledge*

Edmunds. He also had hopes of Capricorn once it got going. There was nothing against Kett except suspicion, he admitted, but he was too big a risk to ignore.

When he'd finished, Garry took Gulliver through all the people whose names she'd heard, with Snape and van Piet looking and listening. That way, they all had the same mental database. As Garry closed his laptop, Gulliver asked van Piet where her Armed Support Unit came in.

"Thurston can shoot, and it looks as if Davis can, so we have to assume the others can as well. How many people have you got?"

"Three shifts of eight, plus me. I've also got one specialist driver and a helicopter crew for each shift, plus shift crews for our off-shore patrol boat. If I need more personnel, I go begging to other units. If you think your budget's tight, try mine."

Van Piet turned to Snape.

"Re-group them and put them on twelve hour shifts, Eddie. Sal, you're on twenty-four hour call as of now, and you'll be based in Chelmsford. Tom and Selina will sort out communications with you as soon as they get a minute, and one of our drivers will run you back. Eddie, you're staying here. Have what you need sent up from Essex, you might be here for some time. Anyone want to say anything else right now?"

"You might like to know this," Snape said. "There are DNA traces in Hayward's cottage that definitely come from Pachini, and that's on top of his fingerprints. I thought Rufus was her fancy man. Maybe I should think again."

Van Piet didn't respond, so Gulliver asked him why he'd flagged Watkins up. He hesitated before he answered. He could be on the wrong track.

"As I've said, not too long before Ashley Johnson was murdered, Watkins hacked into some of Van Piet Banking's computers. We know that because she got found out. When the Slades came into her life, she took a look to see what they were about, or so she told us last Monday. She said she didn't find anything, but she didn't destroy her notes till after her fiancé was murdered. She's kept herself to herself since she rejoined the *Standard*, or so her boss says, but she hasn't forgotten the Slades. Her zeroing in on Geoffrey Slade proves that, so she may have been tracking them all the while. If she has, she almost certainly knows more than we do, and she may also be preparing to make some kind of move. It could well be a hostile one."

In Clacton, Anita Rufus was having real trouble keeping her temper under control. She hadn't begun to believe Thurston's text about the rush order for granite, it was the sort of excuse he'd made more than once, and there'd always been a woman behind it. So, good and early, she'd driven to The Rufus Car Mart in her Isuzu Trooper, helped herself to a used Hyundai saloon to conceal who she was, and accelerated off to Thurston's quarry, leaving a message for her manager to look after things for the day. The weather hadn't brightened her mood, and when she got to the quarry, she found out Thurston had come and gone, but no one knew about a rush order.

"OK, Neville Thurston, we'll sort this one out right now," she'd said to herself, and despite the rain, she'd set off at speed for Thurston Mansion. She'd felt humiliated at the quarry, since everyone had guessed why she was there, and for all she knew, they were still laughing about her. They'd been smirking enough when they'd thought she wasn't looking.

As she approached Thurston's gateway, she saw a Mazda coupé stopped in the oncoming lane. It had its winker on, and she was near certain it was the scrubber Thurston had dumped her for. She had half a mind to tell whoever it was to clear off there and then, and her foot briefly dipped the brake pedal. But she wouldn't hurt Thurston that way, she'd just make him grouchy, and she might be wrong anyway. So, eager to do real damage but not sure how to do it, she switched on the dash-cam, flashed the Mazda and balefully captured its registration as it turned in front of her. She couldn't really see the driver through the rain, but there was no doubt about it, it was a woman all right.

Her anger stayed with her all the way back to Colchester, where she cleared the Hyundai's dash-cam and told the manager he might as well shut up shop, since the rain was turning the day into a write-off. Then she motored to Clacton in the Isuzu, brooding malevolently on what to do.

Rufus had left a note with a time at the top saying he'd gone out for a training run, so the house was empty when she got home. That was what she wanted. She phoned Driver and Vehicle Licensing, explained who she was, and dictated the Mazda's registration down the line. Could she have the name and address of the owner, please? Someone had called her manager about a sale, and she needed to check the caller was genuine.

"There'll be a fee," she heard back. "If you want to know something, you have to pay for it these days. It's like with the car park operators. We can tell them who's parked without paying, but they don't get it for nothing."

"I know, I know, I make these calls all the while. Just give me an answer and put the bill in the post. I don't need a sermon."

The DVLA man took his time – Anita thought he was making a point – and she was beginning to worry Rufus might come back early when "Deborah Anne Watkins" came down the line, plus Watkins's Kensington address.

She was afraid she'd been too snappy with the DVLA man – she didn't want trouble the next time she called - so she thanked him fulsomely for his trouble, and no, there'd be no follow-up, she could handle things from her end now. She was sorry to be such a pain, but she always checked these things. Not everyone was honest in the car trade.

"Deborah Watkins," she said out loud into the empty room.

She'd never met her, she'd had no reason to, but she knew the name all right, and not only because it had been in the news lately. She took out her smartphone and went into the blacklist Verity supplied to her inner circle. Under Watkins's name were a range of recent photos, her Kensington address, her place of work, and Verity's comment in bold and underlined: 'Completely untrustworthy, manipulative, and highly dangerous to Esklivia. All contact forbidden. Inform me immediately if any is attempted.' Then came a list of places Watkins was

222

known to frequent, followed by the address of a flat in Paddington. It was marked, 'Used for confidential interviews. Never accept an invitation to this place.' Finally came Watkins's smartphone number and the landline numbers of her Kensington and Paddington flats. 'If you get a call from any of these numbers,' she read, 'do not respond in any way. Call me immediately instead.'

So, Anita mused, this Watkins woman was really bad news, and now she was hanging round Thurston. She stared in front of her, and her temper became more focused. If she asked Thurston about Watkins, she knew he'd lie to her face, so despite what the blacklist said, she'd take Watkins on directly and tell Verity afterwards. That would drop Thurston in it, and a good thing too, but it was Watkins she was after. She wasn't just angry, she was jealous. She had to make Watkins pay, and she didn't care how she did it.

Chapter 23

A shock discovery

After lunch, Thurston made himself comfortable in his living room. Watkins made a show of doing the same, and soon he was telling her about the fortunes his great-great-grandfather had made. The first one had been in textiles. Then, instead of retiring to count his money, he'd seen the new-fangled railways would need something to lay their tracks on, so he'd bought a run-down quarry plus as much land around it as he could and made a second fortune selling crushed granite. As Thurston talked, he kept sipping from a large glass of liqueur he'd placed near his elbow, while Watkins stayed with coffee. Years of being a journalist had taught her how to look interested even when she wasn't, so he asked her to wait while he fetched a book he'd put together from upstairs. It was about the quarry, the house and the Thurstons, he explained, and he kept it in a safe because in years to come it would be valuable.

"We've got our own coat of arms," he said proudly when he came back. "You must have seen it on the gateposts when you arrived, and it looks even better in colour. Great-grandfather Thurston fetched it personally from the College of Arms, and the motto means, 'Every man makes his own fortune' – but I expect you knew that already."

"I'm afraid I didn't," she admitted, happy to make him feel superior, "but now you've told me, it sounds just right."

He glistened with satisfaction.

The book was a glorified scrap book. In it were drawings and photos - mostly sepia or black-and-white - of the Thurstons, their wives, their children and their business associates, along with hand-written letters and invoices. There were water colours and pen-and-inks of the house as well. A carefully mounted photo of Princess Margaret talking to Thurston's grandfather served as a frontispiece, and the coat of arms was on the cover. Its colours were losing their brightness, and the cover showed signs of wear. The book had obviously been handled a lot.

After Thurston had talked Watkins through it, he asked her if she'd like to see round the house. She thought he meant his bedroom, but he was eager to give her a complete tour first, so she was shown into the dormers, the bedroom he'd had as a boy, the upstairs room his safe was in, and the room he described as his business headquarters. As they went from room to room, he pointed out darkening oil paintings depicting his forebears and told her who had added what to the house.

"We've all done our bit," he said as they paused in the upstairs corridor, "and this thick carpeting is down to me. When I took the house over, I upgraded the central heating, and that made the floorboards you're standing on creak when anyone walked on them. People who needed the bathroom during the night were embarrassed by that, so I put this carpeting down. It doesn't go with the house, but my guests all like it."

Did he often have company, she probed and, smiling grandly, he said he knew a lot of top people through his charity work. If he had them over for dinner, they often stayed the night. It was like the country weekends people had years ago. He'd read about them in a book about Churchill.

As they were passing through the entrance hall on their way to the basement from indoors, he paused by the door under the stairs and said she must tell him if was talking too much about his family. The thing was, it was preying on his mind. He was the wrong side of fifty and he'd never married, so when he died, the Thurston line would die with him. It had been bothering him for some time, but then Watkins had come into his life and, well, as she'd said, there was this nice thing between them, and it seemed to be blossoming.

"Have I said more than I should have, Debbie?" he asked shyly. He'd been calling her Debbie since she'd arrived, and it made her want to screech each time. But she also saw a chance to get him to open up.

"Not at all," she replied, sounding as warm as she could. "I'm glad the barriers are falling. I still think we mustn't hurry things, but I did say, 'Let's make today work', and it looks as if that's what's happening."

The indoor steps down to the basement were made of granite. After she'd admired his wine collection and allowed herself a small glass of port to go with his larger glass of the same, he showed her into a leisure room with a full-size snooker table, easy chairs and a corner bar. One wall was wainscoted, and the other three were decorated with light floral wallpaper. He offered her another drink, and she asked for orange juice, so he emptied two tins from the refrigerator into jazzy-patterned tumblers from the 1950s. He put a large splash of vodka into his own glass first, but she said no thanks, it'd only make her sleepy. His confidence was in full flow again, and when they'd finished their drinks, he said,

"I've got something special to show you. Watch this."

He reached under the bar counter, pressed a button, and part of the wainscoting swung forward to disclose a narrow wooden staircase with carpet pads on each stair. The staircase lit up automatically. The air became cooler as they went down, and then they were standing in front of a heavy metal door. He released the locks and switched on the lights beyond it with his smartphone. Inside was a shooting range hollowed out of the granite the house was standing on.

"In this gun box here," he said once they were in, "is a Sig Sauer, if that means anything to you. It's my favourite gun, and I put it down here before you came, thinking we might come this way at some point. The police know about it, and I normally keep it in a box upstairs in case they ask to see it. But they don't know about my shooting range, and they don't know about the other guns I keep down here, because I don't tell them. I know quite a few shooters who can keep their mouths shut, and we have competitions down here. No one can hear from outside. The ventilation's hidden, and we're completely surrounded by rock."

227

She said she couldn't shoot, but she'd like to learn. He talked her through the basics, took a 9mm Smith and Wesson out of a cache in one of the walls and let her try to hit a target with concentric circles marked on it. She missed it altogether at first, but after a magazine and a half and plenty of advice, she placed two consecutive shots near the bull's-eye.

"Let me see the expert do it," she flattered him with as she eased her ear protectors off, so he showed her how the target console worked and asked her to set up some moving targets. Firing his Sig Sauer, he killed them all without wasting a shot, re-loaded, and did the same thing again, this time with head shots instead of shots into the chest.

"It comes with practice," he said, "and I practise a lot."

She had another go and achieved a respectable spread on the target. He made a ring with his thumb and index finger, then he cleared up and locked the guns away.

He'd been touching her a lot while she'd been using the Smith and Wesson, so when she suggested they go back to his bedroom, he was hot for it. She took a perverse pleasure in hiding her loathing of him, and after she'd scrubbed herself in his ensuite, she said she ought to be thinking about getting back to London. His mood switched to peevish, and he insisted she stay for something to eat first, it was a long way to go on an empty stomach.

She didn't dare cross him, so she said yes please, if it wouldn't put him out. He made some open sandwiches and a fruit salad with cream, and they ate them in the breakfast room - it was more snug than the dining room, he explained, implying it was for people who were already a couple. He asked her if she'd like whisky in her tea, it was something his father and his grandfather had sworn by. She shook her head, saying she couldn't even try to keep up with him, so he put some Johnny Walker in his own, and they clinked their cups together. She still hadn't got much out of him and time was running out, so doing her best to sound innocent, she asked,

"After you listened to what I said to the police in my flat, who did you tell it back to?"

For a second he tightened up, but he'd drunk a lot since she'd arrived, and she looked so matter-of-fact, he saw no harm in answering.

"Mrs Slade – Verity, as I call her, when it's just her and me. She was the one who sent me, I thought you knew that. She told me you'd phoned her to let her know what was happening."

"So I did. You know Mrs Slade well, do you?"

"I certainly do. You might not think so, me being a working man, but we're like that."

He crossed the middle finger of his right hand over his index finger and clamped it tight.

It meant a lot to him to be in with Verity, he confided – Geoffrey, too, when he'd been alive. He told her how they'd found him on the internet, how much building he'd done for them, the chemical damp course he'd been putting in, and how he'd made lots of money through their investment company. He didn't like talking about his money, he said, since it sounded like boasting, but the truth was, he was a lot richer than most people thought. If things worked out right, she'd never have to worry about money, he could say that right now.

"Do you think they will, Neville?" she asked, and then she opted to take a very big risk. "The reason I'm asking is this. Mrs Slade and I don't get on at all, and she can be ruthless when it suits her. I shouldn't want you to go the way of her husband."

There was a long silence broken only by the sound of rain on the window panes.

"I didn't think you knew as much as that," he said slowly. "But – " and he brightened up again – "it doesn't really change anything. You know things we don't want you to know, but you can't have told the police yet, and that's the main thing. You see, Debbie, what I'm hoping is, you'll come onto our side. Then you won't be enemies with Verity any more, you'll be one of us."

It was Watkins's turn to be surprised.

"I hadn't thought of that," she said, as though she wished she had. "You'll have to let me sleep on it, but it's good to have a secret to share. It bonds us even closer together."

He was relieved by the fact she sounded keen on the idea. His wariness fell away, she played him along, and eventually, as he poured more tea for both of them with more Johnny Walker for himself, he said he'd be driving over to The Lodge Tuesday evening. The chemical damp course he'd told her about, well, Mrs Slade was pressuring him to finish it, so he'd agreed 9.00 Wednesday morning, and he'd stay till no one would know he'd been. His speech was becoming draggy, but his vanity was riding high, and he badly wanted to impress her by telling her something special, so he hinted there was more to the job than putting paid to some damp, if she cared to ask him about it. She did care.

"I'm only telling you because we're getting on so well," he replied, pumped up with insider knowledge, "but it's not a chemical damp course I've put in, it's dynamite from my quarry, and the detonator's already connected. It's in a dummy humidifier, and I've put incendiaries in the floor and the ceiling. If the detonator's triggered, the whole place will go up like a Roman candle."

She felt her stomach contract with excitement. This was three cherries in a row.

"Dynamite and incendiaries!" she exclaimed, and she beamed admiration at him like a searchlight. "That's awesome, Neville! But what are they for?"

It was jackpot time for him too. He couldn't wait to tell her.

"It was Verity's idea. She told me she'd got some top-secret stuff in there she needed to destroy quickly if she had to, and she knew I used dynamite in my quarry. Well, I never say no to Verity, so she sent Geoffrey over to sort out the detonator, and he brought her smartphone with him. He surprised me how good he was, given it wasn't his line of work, but Verity knew, and Geoffrey said she was in a hurry. He started by linking the detonator to her smartphone while the detonator was still unhooked, since if that bit worked, we knew everything else would. It didn't take him long, and the rest was down to me. It's a shame he won't see the finished product. It'll be like a memorial to him, you might say."

"So Mrs Slade can blow everything up. Can anyone else?"

He asked her whether she knew a Miss Davis.

"Of course."

"Well, Miss Davis can, but only her. She's the one who's really in charge of us, but I've always been closer to Verity. I don't know what Verity meant by top-secret stuff, and I wouldn't expect to, it's all very carefully locked away. But she trusted me with the rest."

What else could she wring out of him without making him turn nasty? Her mouth was as dry as the Sahara.

"What about Mr Slade's own smartphone?" she asked, trying desperately to read his face. "Did he link the detonator to it while he was at it?"

"Not a chance," he laughed, "Verity had put her foot down about that. She didn't think he was serious enough, and he agreed. That's how he was."

"I hear what you're saying, Neville, and I can't tell you how impressed I am, but could Mrs Slade really blow a whole building up and hope no one would notice? And where would she live afterwards? Wouldn't the whole house be wrecked?"

He folded his hands over his stomach. This was bliss.

"You're educated, Debbie, and I'm just a quarryman and builder, but you're the one who's getting it wrong. All of us working with Verity, on the dark side that is, know something could always go wrong, and then we'd have to get out of the country. We've got more than one plan for doing that, but we'd have to destroy everything first, because the country we'll go to doesn't want anyone knowing what we've been up to. So there's your answer, Debbie: She could do what she liked, because she'd be on her way to somewhere else."

Watkins had got as much as she needed, so she let things taper off, and finally she said she really must hit the road. There was an awkward moment when Thurston asked about Monday, but the answer she gave him sounded genuine because it mostly was.

"Sorry, Neville, but, like I said, I'm completely tied up from now on. I've promised my boss I'll have my article finished late Tuesday so he can see what

I'll be asking him to print. That means locking my door and keeping it locked till I've tapped in the last full stop. That could be midnight Monday or even Tuesday first thing, but I'll come here again just as soon as I can, and we can talk some more about me joining your side. I like the idea a lot."

That brightened him up.

"You might hear me moving about while you're changing upstairs," he said, wanting to show he wasn't going to argue. "I'll be putting my book back where it came from."

It didn't take her long to put on her outdoor clothes, but the zip on her trousers snagged as she was pulling it up. Tugging at it only made it worse, so she thought she'd let Thurston free it for her. He'd enjoy doing it, and it would keep him benign till she was out of his way. So, not bothering to put her slippers back on, she stepped out onto the thick carpeting and walked silently down the corridor. He'd left the door to the room he was in ajar, and through the gap she could see him kneeling with his back to her in front of his safe, which was open. He'd taken some boxes and files out, presumably to make room for his book, and it looked as if an elderly document had caught his eye, since he was holding it up to read it. But what caused her almost to faint with horror was next to his knee. Clearly visible in a labelled transparent bag was a semi-automatic pistol with a silencer lying next to it. She saw straight away it was a Walther PPK ·380 – she'd studied them closely since her fiancé's murder – and it looked as if Thurston had put it and the silencer in the bag to keep them together. With her heart pounding, she backed slowly away, and as silently as she'd come, she returned to the room she'd left and shut the door. No one kept a gun in a labelled bag in a safe without a reason. It had to be the gun that had killed Ashley Johnson.

Sucking in air, she sat on the bed and thrust her head down as low as she could – she'd caught a glimpse of her face in the mirror above the washstand, and it had been chalk white. She had to force some colour back into it before Thurston saw her. When she stood up, the faintness came back, but she managed to free her zip at the cost of some of the fabric, and finally she was ready to return downstairs. She hadn't heard Thurston pass her door, but he was already waiting in the hall. He had one hand against the wall to stop himself swaying.

"Sorry to take so long," she smiled. "The zip on my trousers got stuck."

"You should have called me. I'm good at undoing zips."

So he hadn't noticed anything.

"Next time, naughty boy," she compelled herself to laugh, and she lightly patted his cheek.

He caught her hand, kissed it hard, and his mood darkened. His sour breath made her feel sick.

"Whatever you do, Debbie, don't tell anyone about us," he urged, keeping his voice down as if someone might be listening. "It'd be the death of both of us, and I mean it."

"I give you my word," she responded solemnly, and she gave him a long kiss on the cheek, though she really wanted to scream at being called Debbie yet again.

He pressed her against him and their faces touched, but she'd assured him she'd be back, so he didn't hang on to her. The rain was easing off, and after she'd turned her car round, she stuck her hand through her open window and waved goodbye to him. He waved back, a menacing figure framed by an empty house. Then she was gone.

Chapter 24

A Sunday morning in Colchester

Watkins was up bright and early the next morning as she had a two hour drive in front of her to the Camulo Wellness and Social Club in Colchester. She had zero interest in keeping fit, but she'd found out Cottrell and Laura used the club a lot, so she'd become a member to spy on them without being seen herself. It was something she was good at. Cottrell was away on a cyber conference in Coventry, and Watkins knew she'd be there till Wednesday tea-time because she'd posted it on Facebook. That meant Laura would be in Colchester on her own. Camulo's website said she had a squash ladder match at 10.00, and Watkins had studied Laura enough to know she wouldn't spend time with her opponent afterwards. If Cottrell wasn't there, she'd keep herself to herself.

Watkins stopped on the way just once - to post an envelope with some papers in it and to make a call from a nearby payphone. She reached the club at 10.28, and, taking her time, she headed upstairs to the John Constable cafeteria. In her hand was a patterned cloth carrier bag. Laura's squash match would be just about over by now, and after she'd showered, she'd come up to the cafeteria. That was her routine. Watkins bought a cup of coffee and picked a table where she could blend into the background.

Laura's hair was still damp when she joined the queue for refreshments and bought a large fruit cocktail. The cafeteria was barely half full, and she soon found a free table in the area she normally sat in. Outside, the sun was shining as if rain was something you read about in books, and the well-manicured lawn that sloped down to the River Colne was dotted with wrought iron tables and chairs, all painted glossy white. The grass was less than dry, but plenty of people were out there, and Watkins felt things were definitely going her way, since if everyone had been inside, Laura wouldn't have been able to sit on her own. Patiently Watkins watched her settle herself, then she picked up her half-empty coffee cup and made her way towards her.

"It's Miss Slade, isn't it? Do you mind if I join you?"

Laura, who'd started to read a magazine she'd taken out of her squash bag, looked up in annoyance, but Watkins was already sitting down, and Laura was too well-mannered to ask her to go away. Watkins slid her business card towards her.

"I'm Deborah Watkins," she said. "I work for the *London Evening Standard*."

Laura read the card. She knew Watkins's name and face from her mother's blacklist, and Watkins's name was in any case fresh in her memory, because Essex media had linked Hayward's death to Ashley Johnson's as soon as the Hayward story broke. 'Five Willows: Another Murder Mystery!!!' had been one

237

headline, 'Will The Police Find Out Whodunnit This Time?' had been another, and BBC Essex had emphasised Watkins had been working for it when the earlier murder had happened. Watkins had followed the coverage minutely, and she'd been relieved to see hardly any pictures of herself had been used, except for an archive shot on BBC Essex. She'd also put on weight since her time in Five Willows, she'd changed her hair style from long to short, and she'd switched from big-framed glasses to contact lenses. All of that generally stopped people from recognising her now. But Verity paid a detective agency good money to keep her blacklist images current, and Laura checked through the updates once a week at least, because it was part of her job. Yet she'd never noticed Watkins in Camulo before, and she wondered whether she should have.

"I'm afraid I'm not allowed to talk to the media," she replied, politely but firmly. "It's a house rule of the company I work for. If you insist on sitting there, I shall have to go somewhere else."

She was rolling up the magazine as she spoke, but before she could get to her feet, Watkins took twelve sheets of A4 from her carrier bag and placed them face up next to Laura's fruit drink. They were prints from Watkins's night camera, they were clearly dated and timed, and they were held together with a ⅝" bulldog clip. The top one showed Laura arriving at Esklivia House on August 15th.

"I'd be sorry if you did," Watkins said, ignoring what Laura was doing. "I thought you might like to see these photos."

Laura let the magazine unroll. Her face was pale and her eyes were wide.

"Take as long as you like over them," Watkins added, invitingly removing the bulldog clip. "I don't have to be anywhere else just yet."

While Watkins finished her coffee, Laura took in pics of Verity and Kett arriving and leaving, followed by Laura herself. The other pics were of Verity and Kett arriving and leaving in April, May, June and July. Laura didn't say anything. The pics brought back memories of her mother peeling off her mourning clothes and fucking with a stranger. Laura had forced herself to come to Camulo to help her control the trauma that had caused her. But now there was this.

"Do you know who the man is?" Watkins enquired as Laura struggled to maintain her composure. Laughter was coming from the middle of the room, and everyone else seemed to be having a good time. Laura shook her head and asked whether Watkins had shown the photos to anyone else, meaning Verity.

"No, no one at all. Amazing what you discover when you watch people," Watkins went on, unaware how painful her words were for Laura. "I won't tell you the man's name, but he's big news in national cyber-security, and when he comes to Esklivia House, he brings an attaché case that looks just like your mother's. You can probably guess why I'm here, Miss Slade. I want to know what's going on."

Watkins was pleased to see she'd unsettled Laura. It gave her something to work on.

"I'm sorry, but I don't see how I can help you," Laura came back, and her tone of voice was Arctic. "I know almost as little as you do. Adultery isn't illegal, if that's what you're insinuating. And my

239

mother's a widow now, so she can meet whomever she likes."

It was a lawyer's defence, and Laura knew it – it conveniently left out the attaché cases. But her eyes gave her away, and Watkins was sure she'd guessed right: Kett was selling secrets, and sweet little Laura had found out about it. Could she get Laura to fill in the details, she wondered. But Laura was staying defensive.

"If you think there's more to it than that," she was saying, "you must take your suspicions to the police."

She regretted saying it as soon as the words were out. The media thought the police were failures, and so did she. If they investigated her mother's activities, she might never get her father's death cleared up. She had to keep them out of it.

"Come, come, Miss Slade," Watkins responded amiably. "If I went to the police, I'd lose my story. That's why I'm talking to you instead."

But Laura was thinking ahead. Watkins's night photos showed how dangerous she was to Esklivia, but she'd as good as said her mother hadn't seen them, so what had she done already to get on her mother's blacklist with 'untrustworthy', 'manipulative' and 'highly dangerous' fastened round her neck? Laura hadn't forgotten the crossed out photo of her father she'd found in her mother's drawer. Maybe Watkins knew dark things she needed to know herself. She nerved herself and started at a tangent, hoping Watkins wouldn't see how desperate she was for information. She didn't want Watkins to take advantage of her.

"Is losing your story all you're worried about?" she asked. "Or are you afraid, if you went to the police, your name would come out and you'd be open to physical attack? You must know as well as I do how often it happens."

Watkins smiled complacently.

"It won't happen to me. I document everything and use it to keep me safe. As you can see, it works."

The atmosphere between them had become suddenly strange. Watkins was more puzzled by Laura's question than Laura had meant her to be, so she let a silence develop. If she kept Laura waiting, Laura might yet come out with something Watkins could get a handle on. It took a moment, then she did.

"I was remembering my father, Geoffrey Slade, when you joined me. He was well-known in the City, as I'm sure you're aware, and there's an article about him in this magazine I brought with me. I expect you've heard he died recently when his car left the road not far from here, but the police aren't satisfied it was an accident." She hesitated. "I know from my mother you keep a close watch on Esklivia. It would mean a lot to me if you could tell me anything about his death."

More laughter was coming from the middle of the room, and a bright-eyed twenty-something with a squash racquet in her hand was making her way between the tables to speak to Laura. Watkins slid the photos into her bag before she got there. The interruption gave her time to work out her response.

"Did you win?" the twenty-something asked Laura, and Laura said she had, adding, "Fenella, this is Deborah. Deborah lives in London."

"Gosh, you must like this place," Fenella replied airily. "Pleased to meet you."

241

She'd never noticed Watkins before, and she didn't recognise her now. She returned her attention to Laura.

"You'll never believe this, Laura, but I lost – yes, really! - and that drops me to next above you on the ladder. Do you want to challenge me for next Sunday right now? It'll save you ringing me during the week."

Laura made a show of being keen and suggested 10.00. Fenella said she'd book a court on her way out, waved a breathless goodbye, and hustled towards the exit. The strange atmosphere re-formed, and Watkins delivered her reply.

"I know quite a lot about his death, as it happens. It wasn't an accident, it was contrived, as you seem to suspect, and I could name you names as well. But first you must tell me exactly what you witnessed in Esklivia House when you were spying on your mother. That's the deal."

Laura fiddled with the magazine.

"So my father was murdered, was he?" she asked.

"Yes, he was."

"And you know who did it?"

"I do."

"Do you know how it was done? The police don't, they'd have said by now if they did."

"That's up to the police, but yes, I know exactly how it was done."

Laura flashed back to what she'd seen in Esklivia House that evening. The insult to her father's memory had outraged her, and her mother's naked delight had destabilised her so much, she still couldn't put it into words. She could never tell anyone about either of those things, certainly not a journalist, but, of course, she wouldn't have to. Watkins didn't know they'd happened because she'd been outside when they did, and her mother and the man she'd been with would never let on, it wouldn't be in their interest to. They might say something if they were arrested and put in the dock, but Laura believed she could cope with that, it would be sort of distanced if it came from a court of law. All of which meant she could tell Watkins about the trade of secrets for money as if that had been all that had happened. It would effectively amount to betraying her mother to the law, but her mother had betrayed her father, so she thought she could bring herself to do it. But could she trust Watkins to keep her side of the bargain? She thought everything through again - all the things Watkins had told her, her mother's blacklist, and her desperate need to clear up her father's death. Then she made her mind up.

"I can't do what you ask," she said, "and I'm not prepared to say why."

Watkins couldn't believe it.

"Then it's no deal, Miss Slade, and I must say, you surprise me. Would you like a moment to think things over?"

Laura said no, there was no chance she'd revise her opinion, so Watkins settled for saying,

"Keep my card at least, you can always phone me if you change your mind."

It was the best she could come up with.

"And if you decide to involve the police after all," she went on, "may I ask you to contact me first? I feel you owe me that."

Laura said the police weren't part of her thinking, she'd go about things in her own way. Then she asked whether Watkins would say anything to her mother or the man she'd been with to let them know they'd been seen. Watkins looked astounded.

"I wouldn't dream of it, Miss Slade. They can find out what I know when I publish, not before."

Laura had to find out when that would be.

"What you write will be less than complete, thanks to me," she said, "but it will still get the police involved. I'll be honest with you, Miss Watkins, I'm afraid they'll sweep me aside without solving anything themselves. You'll forgive me for mentioning it, but they still haven't established who killed your fiancé. When are you thinking of publishing your story?"

"When I'm ready, and not before. It'll be a Friday, so it can pick up speed on Saturday and Sunday. Then it will run and run."

Laura picked the card up, slipped it into her magazine and finished her drink. She thanked Watkins for taking her into her confidence, but she wanted to get off home, and Watkins, unaware she'd just experienced why Laura was an exceptional Head of Compliance, said she'd be staying till she'd had some lunch. They shook hands like courteous enemies, and Laura made her way out. As she left the club building for the car park, she put Watkins's card in the bin by the front door.

Watkins had a second cup of coffee while she waited for Laura to get well away, then she went down to a payphone in a fully enclosed kiosk that was standing in the lobby. Sure no one could hear her, she called Verity at home. It was like glass cracking whenever they talked to each other. The hatred on both sides was total.

244

"Is anyone with you?" Watkins asked. "Including this afternoon?"

"I'm on my own at the moment, and the way things are looking, I shall stay that way for the rest of the day. Does that answer your questions?"

"Looks can deceive, Verity, as you know better than most people. I'll be arriving at 2.30, and I want Barbara there as well. Switch the cctv off ahead of time and keep it off till I've gone. If anyone else fancies coming to see you, tell them not to. You and Barbara won't want anyone else to hear what I've got to say."

After lunch in the cafeteria, Watkins went back to her car and set off for Lower Mindle. Her way out of Colchester took her past The Rufus Car Mart, but although she'd watched Anita a lot over time, she saw no need to make a detour, since she didn't think she'd be recognised in her car. As The Rufus Car Mart's banners and bunting came into view, she noticed someone jabbing impatiently at the button of the crosswalk just ahead of the forecourt. It was Anita, and she was in a hurry. A dealership in Harwich had gone out of business, and the liquidator was coming to see her about buying the stock. It could be a mega-deal for her, and she was sure Verity would help with the money. She just had time to fetch a bag lunch from across the road and eat it before he arrived.

The crosswalk lights changed, and as Watkins slowed to a halt, Anita recognised the Mazda first and then the driver. The road was empty, and her anger and jealousy overrode her anxiety not to be late, so she strode round to the driver's side window and knocked on it hard. More bewildered than frightened, Watkins let the window down. Anita bent down to

245

see in, gripping the door with her swimmer's big right hand.

"Don't pretend you don't know me, Deborah Watkins, because you do," she said straight into Watkins's face. "I was planning to get in touch with you, and here you are. There's something very important I want to discuss with you."

The crosswalk lights went back to green, but Watkins made no attempt to lose Anita's grip and move off. Going to Lower Mindle was too important to put back, but she had to find out what was upsetting Anita. And how come Anita had known it was her just from seeing her car? Watkins knew all about Verity's blacklist, so maybe that was the answer, though she didn't entirely believe it. She glanced at her dashboard clock. Time was on her side.

"I'll pull onto your forecourt, Mrs Rufus," she said evenly, making no attempt to fight back. "We can talk things over right there."

"You'll do nothing of the kind, I've got someone coming to see me. He'll be here any time now, and we've got a lot to get through."

So the afternoon was blocked off for Anita as well - that made things a lot easier. Watkins rootled around in her glovebox till she found one of her business cards. If nothing could happen till evening, she could make sure she'd be on home territory. Not in her sanctuary in Kensington - letting Thurston, Snape and van Piet in had been bad enough - but in her working flat in Paddington. It was the only address and landline number her cards carried, that was for self-protection. The only problem was the Mazda. She had street parking rights in Primrose Place, but a snazzy coupé like the Mazda was a powerful magnet for thieves, so she virtually never used them. She'd take it back to Gilbert Mews and lock it up there, then she'd go to Paddington by taxi.

"This is where I'll be after 7.00," she said, holding her card out. "I promise you I'll be there, and I'll give you all the time you want."

Anita took the card almost in slow motion – she wasn't going to demean herself by snatching it – and she clamped it between her big-nailed finger and thumb while she read it.

"I'll be there too," she said, thrusting it into the pocket of her summer-weight gilet to show she meant what she said, "but you'll wish I wasn't. You'd better move on now. You've got a Renault right behind you, and I've got to be getting back."

Watkins glanced into her mirror just as the Renault flashed its lights. She raised her hand to apologise, and as she drove off, she gave Anita a friendly wave, which she ignored. Watkins put her out of her mind after that. 7.00 would come round soon enough, and she had some highly important things to do first.

Chapter 25

The quittance

The Lodge's gates were already open when Watkins pulled up in front of them. She took a scanner out of her glovebox and checked the cctv was off. It was.

The front door opened as soon as the bell rang, so Verity must have been waiting in the hall. She took Watkins through to where Snape and van Piet had asked their questions, and she seated herself in the armchair she'd sat in then. Davis was sitting on the other side of the hearth and Watkins made herself comfortable on the settee in the middle. There was no tea or coffee on offer, and neither Verity nor Davis even tried to smile. Watkins looked from one to the other.

"Same arrangement as always," she said briskly. "Everything I'll show you is copied and stored where you can't reach it, along with everything else I've got on you. It's known I'm here, and I'm expected to call back when I leave. I've also written out a summary of what I'm going to say, because it's such a big deal. That's in a safe place as well. Are we agreed?"

Davis nodded.

"Your antics have kept you alive so far," she said, not in the least chatty now. "They can keep you alive a bit longer. What's on your mind?"

Watkins took the A4 sheets out of her bag, unclipped them and reached them over to her. Davis went through them frozen-faced and handed them to Verity without comment. Verity couldn't stop a sharp intake of breath when she saw Laura about to enter Esklivia House and checked the date and time. So that's where she'd been when she'd skipped the concert! After Verity had seen them, Watkins clipped them together and put them back in her bag. Verity shot an anxious glance at Davis, but Davis stared straight ahead.

"I've identified the man with you," Watkins said, speaking mostly to Verity, but taking in Davis as well. "His name is Jesse Kett, he lives in Oxford, and he's big in the National Cyber Security Centre."

Thanks to Laura's refusal, she had to bluff the next bit.

"The attaché cases you bring with you, they always match each other, so I asked Laura about them this morning when I went to see her in Colchester. I'd already told her who Kett was, and the long and the short of it is, Verity, you're buying state secrets from Kett, Laura's seen it happen, and I know about it too." She turned to look Davis full in the face. "You can see what that means, Barbara. You and your clique are blown."

There was high tension in the room now – high tension and wariness.

"So Laura's seen these photos, has she?" Davis asked.

Watkins said she had, and Davis asked her whether she – Watkins - knew who Verity was passing the secrets on to. Watkins said no, Laura hadn't told her that, but the police could easily find that out. All they'd have to do was do it.

"Believe it or not," Watkins went on, turning back to Verity, "I've never spoken to Laura before, I've always believed she's got nothing to do with your criminal outfit. But she must have had some reason for poking her nose in, so I'm wondering what it was. She said her father's death was still looking suspect, so perhaps that was it. She certainly asked me a lot about it."

"What did you tell her?" Verity asked sharply.

She'd remembered Thurston had seen Laura in her and Geoffrey's bedroom.

"That it wasn't an accident and that I knew who did it. But I didn't want to tell her everything at once, so that's where I stopped. I'm sure we'd all like to know what she'll do next and when she'll do it. She must be very wound up if she's spying on her own mother."

Verity wiped her palms on the one-button blazer she was wearing. Laura must have seen her having sex with Kett - gagging for it, in fact, because that was how it had been. And Laura was so fragile, she'd have been completely taken apart by it.

"I think we should put our cards on the table," Davis said into the hostile atmosphere. "Tell us what you want, Deborah, and we'll see what we can do. You can leave Laura to us. We'll manage her separately."

Watkins gave her a fake-friendly smile.

"One thing at a time, Barbara, it's my meeting, not yours. When Snape and van Piet wanted to see me, I asked Verity to send someone to listen in, so you'd know I hadn't betrayed you if you found out about it. That was for my protection more than your peace of mind, and in her breathtaking wisdom, Verity sent Neville Thurston. Were you in on that decision?"

"I was. I approved it."

"So neither of you foresaw things might happen between two consenting adults in a private flat, but they did happen, Barbara, because I made sure they did. Thurston fell for it like the fool he is. He couldn't get his dick in fast enough."

She switched her attention to Verity.

"I'm surprised you didn't see that coming, Verity. He's been here often enough when Geoffrey's been away, and it hasn't been to mend the drive."

Verity made as if to snap back, then she thought better of it. She'd never lost control of things before, but she had now. It was upsetting her badly.

"I spent a lot of yesterday in Thurston's house making them happen again," Watkins continued, "and in his swollen-headed and half-drunk way he told me, if everything went pear-shaped, the outhouse he built for you would get blown up, and you'd all escape abroad. I know all about the explosives and the incendiaries he's installed, but I don't know about the escape, so you're going to tell me about it right now. After that I'll put a deal to you that will save your lousy skins, but be warned. It comes at a price."

Verity looked towards Davis and got the same treatment as before.

"You mentioned the police just now," Davis said to Watkins. "When you saw Laura this morning, did she say she'd go to the police?"

"No, whatever's on her mind is personal, and she wants to keep it that way. If you ask me, she's a much bigger danger to you because of that. You'd do well to feel threatened by her."

"Save your breath, Deborah, we know her better than you do. You're not going to the police, of course. You wouldn't be so foolish."

"Even when you don't say much, you still gibber, Barbara. Just tell me what your escape plan is, and we'll take it from there."

"That's your sticking point, is it?"

Watkins confirmed it was.

"Very well. Since you know so much, you might as well know the rest. We'll see if it does you any good."

Davis settled back in her armchair as if she was guest speaker at a coffee morning. Watkins had expected her to break up, but she hadn't. Watkins wondered why.

"Jesse Kett's secrets are going to the Russians. Sometimes Cyber Security comes up with something to protect this dreadful country, and Jesse sells it to Verity. Or sometimes they know what they want, and they ask for it. I hope that much is clear."

Watkins said it was, but what about the escape?

"I'm coming to that, if you'll let me. We've got a whole fund of ready-made plans agreed with our Russian friends, and which one we use depends on circumstances. One is the obvious one - we make a beeline for the Russian embassy in London - but they don't want us to do that unless we're actually on the run, since the political fall-out could be awkward, and they'd still have to get us out of the place. So the plan I'm selecting is this one. I'll send an emergency message to what you call our clique to get to the sailing club in Brightlingsea where the Rufuses keep their yacht. We'll get there by a set time and day, and Derek and Anita will take us out to one of the Russian commercial vessels that sail between the Baltic and the Atlantic much more frequently than the stupid British realise. Once we're under a Russian flag, we'll have nothing to worry about, since we'll be on Russian territory. Excuse me for a moment while I see how things stand."

She took a key from her handbag, crossed the room to a sideboard by the rear wall and helped herself to a smartphone from inside it. Watkins noticed there were several more smartphones lying near it. Davis explained she needed a phone that couldn't be traced back to her.

"All ships at sea use the Automatic Identification System," she went on as she activated the smartphone. "It's GPS-linked, and anyone can see which ships are where through the internet. I use Lloyds of London's website when I make my routine checks, but there are plenty of other providers, and right now I'm looking at a container ship coming north from Spain and Portugal. She's on her way to St Petersburg, and – give me a second – yes, her projected route will see her off the Essex coast mid-afternoon on Tuesday. She's called the Elena Andropova, and she's the closest Russian vessel to us time-wise that's going in the right direction." She closed the smartphone down. "I'll tell the Embassy what's happened, and they'll ask Moscow to alert the captain we're on our way. So you see, Deborah, no panic and no scrabbling about. It's as simple as that."

Watkins looked at her in disbelief. Could she really call the shots without asking Moscow first?

Davis bubbled over with loyalty.

"You watch too many American films," she flashed back. "We Russian agents aren't stooges. We're trained to take decisions in emergencies, since we're the ones who are closest to the action, so of course I don't have to ask Moscow first." She tapped the smartphone with her fingernail. "You've got everything you've asked for, Deborah. Now what's this deal you're so proud of?"

Watkins could scarcely contain her excitement. She'd waited a very long time for this.

"Your plan's a good one, Barbara, and I'm sure it will work. I'll let you use it on one condition."

"Only one? You disappoint me. What is it?"

"That one of you kill Laura first."

"Please, Deborah, no! Not that!"

It was Verity, she was wide-eyed with horror. Watkins looked at her with total contempt and continued as if nothing had happened.

"With Laura dead, I'll be satisfied, and I'll have no reason to spoil your escape. On the contrary, I shall be glad to be rid of both of you. And you, Verity, before you lose your wits altogether, fasten your mind on this: One of you would have to kill Laura, even if I hadn't asked for it. She's seen my photos, she knows about you and Kett, she knows her father was murdered, and she's made up her mind to do something about it. So what else can you do except get her out of the way?" She leaned forward, her face flushed and her eyes gleaming. "As I look at you now, Verity, and see you squirming just at the thought of it, I don't want Barbara to kill her while you watch, even though that would give me so much

254

pleasure I'm not sure I could take it. I want you to do it, you personally. I need your direct and immediate pain to make everything perfect."

Verity was whining soundlessly and plucking at her blazer. Watkins watched her for a moment, then she took two smartphones out of her carrier bag, turned back to Davis and said she, too, preferred phones that couldn't be traced back.

"I found this one in a taxi and this one, which is for me, in the National Theatre. They've got brand new SIM cards, they're prepaid, and they encrypt, so if they're intercepted, it won't matter."

She handed one to Davis, along with a number she'd already printed off.

"When Verity kills Laura, Barbara, you'll photograph her doing it, and you'll send the picture to this other smartphone with the date and time on it. Make Laura very obviously dead, Verity, I have to be certain you've taken her life, otherwise you won't escape. In fact, I positively want to enjoy her death, so make sure I get all the details."

Gently but firmly, Davis told Verity she'd have to go through with it. Verity didn't reply for a long time, then she wiped her eyes and face.

"You're right, Barbara," she said, breathing in hard. "I can see it for myself, there's no other way. I'll use the gun Neville gave me."

Davis got out of her armchair and kissed her on the temple.

"Then we need to sort out when it will happen," she said as she sat down again. "How about this evening, then Deborah will know we're as good as our word? Laura's on her own at the moment with Millie away in Coventry. It'll be the easiest thing in the world to drive over and do as Deborah wants."

Verity shook her head emphatically.

"This evening's too soon, Barbara. We can't have Laura dead tonight and us not getting away till Tuesday. It's too big a risk."

"So what's the alternative?" Watkins asked.

Verity's mind had left her emotions behind. She was taking decisions again.

"I'll get Laura to come here tomorrow after work. We'll have tea together, and you'll be here as well, Barbara, I'll say a legal problem with your buy-to-lets has cropped up. After tea, I'll kill her, and we'll hide her body in the lake. No one will know it's there if we weigh it down, we can use the chains the gardeners use when they're dragging out trees. I'll e-mail them tonight not to come for a week so we have a clear run."

"What about Millie? Will you leave her in Coventry?" Watkins asked.

Davis said they couldn't. If they left her behind, she'd tell tales, and that would upset the Russians. They'd make sure Kett escaped as well. He was their admission ticket to Russia.

"What about Thurston?"

Watkins couldn't keep the loathing out of her voice, and Davis picked it up.

"We couldn't leave Neville behind, even if you asked us to," she replied, not bothering to hide her *Schadenfreude.* "He'd talk as well."

She interlaced her fingers.

"Now, let's see where we've got to. First, Laura gets killed tomorrow night, but we can't leave England till Tuesday afternoon. That's your insurance policy, Deborah. If we don't kill Laura on time, you can betray us before we can get away, and there'll be nothing we can do about it. Second, once we're under a Russian flag, we'll be safe. Third, we'll blow up the boulting house once we're on our way. How does that sound, Deborah?"

Watkins liked it, but in the back of her mind she was thinking Anita mustn't learn about the escape before she turned up in Paddington. She'd been angry enough in Colchester with her big swimmer's hands and her gleaming white teeth, and if she knew she was going to be yanked out of the good life thanks to Deborah Watkins, there'd be no telling what she'd do. Watkins didn't know who'd murdered Hayward, but she was sure Anita had had a hand in it somewhere. Like Thurston, she was as dangerous as a snake.

"When will you contact your little gang?" she asked Davis.

"As soon as you leave. Why do you ask?"

"I'll not tell you that, but if you contact anyone at all before 10.00 tonight, I'll find out and your getaway will fail. That's not a threat, it's a statement of fact, and I wouldn't advise you to test it. Do I make myself clear, Barbara? Verity?"

Davis said yes for both of them, and Watkins checked her bag and stood up. There was no point staying any longer. Verity made no attempt to move, so it was Davis who saw her to the door.

Watkins couldn't help herself, she had to ask.

"Tell me," she said in the hall, as if it were neutral territory, "why do you do all this? Verity's lost her husband, her daughter's next on the list, and you're losing a lifestyle a lot of people could envy."

Davis's face filled with self-righteousness. It was like throwing a switch.

"We've got things we believe in, that's why - unlike most people in this day and age. We see

257

America's war-mongering and the uselessness of Western democracies, and we say, there are better ways to do things. That's why we support Russia and President Putin. He stands for peace, honour and national pride, and he doesn't need me to say that, his record speaks for itself. Verity and I will have to make sacrifices, and so will the others in our fellowship. But if we make the world a better place, they're worth it."

"So you fancy a poky Moscow flat and a weekly vodka allowance, do you? That's all people who spy for Russia get, if they make it that far."

"Nonsense, Deborah, we'll be stars! We'll give interviews, we'll be linked into global forums, and President Putin himself may have a word with us. Watch us on RT – you probably know it as Russia Today - you'll soon see how well we're treated. Verity's been hit hard and she'll be hit hard again, but she'll bounce back, because she knows she's on the winning side. For me it will be a dream come true. That's why I've been so calm all afternoon. I could thank you, if I didn't detest you so much."

After Watkins had driven out through The Lodge's gateway, she stopped and re-checked the cctv. It was still off. The sun was bright and warm, so she stowed everything that might blow away in the boot and put the coupé's roof down. It had been a long day, and it wasn't over yet. But she was still alive, and her victory was beyond sweetness.

On a whim, she decided to detour to a café she knew from her BBC Essex days. It was on the road to Chelmsford, and apart from being nostalgic, it had a payphone. When she pulled onto the car park, she put the coupé's roof up, fetched her carrier bag out of the boot and found herself a table on a veranda that overlooked open fields. Overhead was an awning that made for a kind of open-air cosiness, so, completely content, she started on the coffee she'd bought, took a reporter's notepad out of her carrier bag and was just about to write on it when a voice said,

"Hullo, Deborah. Not on an assignment, are you?"

She looked up, but she knew the voice anyway.

"Oh, hullo, Fergus," she replied. It was a television reporter she'd worked with. She still saw him from time to time, it was purely platonic, and that was how they liked it. "Just signing one off, if you'll give me a minute."

"Your coffee smells good, I'll get some for myself. Make sure you've finished writing by the time I get back. It's been weeks since we last talked to each other."

When he returned, the pad had gone, and they settled down to catching up. Fergus had been covering a 5k family run in Chelmsford, but that was over, so he'd come out to the café to unwind. Watkins mostly lied to him, though she threw in some truths about her America project to make the rest sound authentic. Five Willows was wholly taboo.

She could have sat there indefinitely, she felt so pleased with herself, but there was no avoiding getting back to London, so she said she'd give Fergus a call once she'd got her week straight, and got up to go. On her way out, she called her office ansaphone from the payphone. Everything was coming good.

Since Davis couldn't contact anyone till after 10.00, she told Verity she'd leave it to her to alert the others. She'd interrupted a translation in order to come to The Lodge, and – ever the committed professional - she wanted to get back to finish it because she'd agreed a deadline. However, she'd contact the Embassy after 10.00, that went with her role as leader.

But Verity didn't want her to go.

"Please stay a bit longer," she begged, and as she stood up and caught the light from a window, Davis was startled to see how much she'd aged during the afternoon. "You've no idea how lonely I am now Geoffrey's not here, and I won't have Laura for much longer either." Her tears had come back - they were making her blazer smell – and she was becoming maudlin. "I ache daily for Geoffrey, Barbara. Every day was happy when he was around, and Laura will always be my little one. I've shielded her from what we've been doing as if it was radiation, and now I've got to take the life I gave her. I accept it has to be, but please try to understand what it's doing to me."

Davis held her tightly.

"I do understand," she told her, since it was what Verity wanted to hear. "And of course I'll stay longer, if that's what you want. What are friends for, if not to see things through together?"

Verity broke down entirely at that, and convulsions of grief racked her under her expensive clothes. She wouldn't back out, she was too dedicated for that, but in a small corner of her consciousness, she knew that with Laura dead, no one would know how she'd behaved with Kett except

Kett himself. If she couldn't erase having been seen with him, she could at least outlive the person who'd seen her. It wasn't the main reason Laura had to die, but it helped in its way.

During the evening, she and Davis talked a lot, sometimes about the good times that were fading into the past, sometimes about the escape, and sometimes - because Verity felt she had to - about Laura's murder. It was while they were discussing the murder that Verity suggested a change of plan.

"The chains we'll use to weigh her down, I think they'll be too heavy for us," she said tentatively, "so I'll ask Neville to help out. He can take the photo as well, Deborah won't know it isn't you, and you can go straight to Brightlingsea rather than come here. You'll be needed more there anyway."

Davis bridled. She didn't think Thurston could be relied on, not after what Watkins had told them about him.

"Neville's got an escape plan just like the rest of us," she said sharply. "It doesn't include coming here."

"That doesn't solve the problem, Barbara. Neville won't cause any trouble, he'll want to get away as much as the rest of us."

Davis thought about it further and had to agree. Verity could put it in the message she'd be sending to Thurston, and Davis would leave Watkins's smartphone for him to take the photo with.

After Davis had gone, Verity went up to a small room next to her bedroom she used to store personal things in, and in a collection of albums dated by year she found a photo of Laura when she was about to go to primary school. There was the brand new uniform, the enormous grin, and a satchel almost as big as she was. The photo wasn't glued in, its corners were let into slits in the backing card, and for a long while Verity sat looking at it, reliving the moment it was taken in. Then she eased it out, slowly crossed it out with a black marker pen and took it into her bedroom, where she put it in the same drawer Slade's photo was in.

During the rest of the evening she couldn't settle to anything. The silence preyed on her nerves, and the darkness in the rest of the house disturbed her so much, she put all the lights on from a central control. She got her messages out after 10.00, but she couldn't face talking to Anita, since she just knew she'd be beside herself, so she used one of the computers in the boulting house to contact the Rufuses. After that, she tried hard to calm herself down. But when she finally put the cctv back on and plodded upstairs to bed, a sleepless night in a large empty house was all she had in front of her.

Behind The Lodge in an unlit lay-by, screens flickered on in the light-proofed rear of what looked like a high-roofed British Telecom van as the cctv returned to life. Robert LeVine, an SRO inland operations agent, stirred in the doze he'd fallen into waiting for the screens to re-activate. His first sensation was pain. He'd stretched out on some rain-proof sheeting on the floor of the van, and now his back hurt. But the outside pictures were clear despite the darkness, and once he was mobile, he checked through The Lodge's entire array. He'd been told to expect wireless cameras, that's what they were, and they were definitely all working. He contacted Ashell

House and was linked through to Garry. The cctv had just come back on, he said, and he was switching some pictures through. How did they look from his end? And could he finish now? He'd installed a receiver/transmitter high up on a telegraph pole near The Lodge's grounds. No one would see it up there, and Ashell House could run the cctv as easily as he could.

"No fault found, Rob. Come in when you like."

Garry terminated, told van Piet and Snape how things were and moved on to sending images to Chelmsford. After a trial run through, Gulliver got back to him. No problems on the wall screen in front of her, and her smartphone was taking the relay as well. She sampled a run of cameras using her override. No problems anywhere, she reported. It was like being right there.

Chapter 26

Taken by surprise

The clocks in Ashell House were nearing midnight, and a canteen assistant was trundling tea, coffee and snacks between the desks of the operations room. She was the only one who looked well rested. Van Piet, Snape and Garry had retreated to some upright chairs in one corner, and on a table in front of them were neat piles of print-outs, images and faxes. So much data was streaming in, they'd gone over to sorting out hard copy just to get away from the screens. Mitchie was back on duty, and the screens were getting to her too. She helped herself to some coffee and made her way over to them.

"Anyone else?" she asked, holding her cup up, but they shook their heads, so she pulled up a spare chair to see how things were going.

"It's mostly loose ends," van Piet replied, rubbing his face with his hands. "Davis visits her parents in Brighton towards the end of every month, but is that all there is to it? Cottrell's definitely in Coventry, but is it a front for something else? So it goes, Selina - we know a lot, but we don't know nearly enough."

"What about Kett?"

"He was in Oxford when he phoned some friends this morning, but we're not sure he's still there."

His mobile buzzed, it was Kossler calling from GCHQ. Van Piet turned the volume up so the others could hear above the chatter in the room.

"Those computers in the boulting house, Willem - at least one of them is in a virtual private network. We caught a message from The Lodge to the Rufuses just after 10.00 tonight. We're working on the encryption and tracing who else is in the network."

Van Piet was about to reply, but Kossler wasn't finished.

"There's been some broadcasting late this evening on short wave, and we can't account for it. It came from Radio Moscow and it was *en clair* in English, so don't get too excited. It could be aimed at anyone in the world who understands English."

Van Piet asked what was being broadcast.

"It was someone reading out long lists of page, line and word numbers, and the programme went by the name of Statistics Revision Exercises for Advanced Students. I'd say you can disregard that, since the numbers are almost certainly linked to a book code, and if you don't know what the book is, you can't crack the code. It's a trick the Russians used during the Cold War, and they could be at it again. As I say, what we heard might have nothing to do with you, but we've established similar broadcasts were made before Ashley Johnson, Geoffrey Slade and Stephanie Hayward were killed, so it might. I'll get back to you when we find out more.

"Oh, one last thing. The Bristol couple, Linda and Gregory Hales, they're as clean as a whistle. No dodgy investments, no large cash withdrawals, nothing. Does that fit in with what you know at your end?"

Van Piet glanced at Snape, who nodded OK.

"The police say yes. We think Davis likes to look good by hanging around with good people. It's the sort of thing she would do."

He terminated, and Snape asked Garry what a virtual private network was. His grandchildren would know, but he wasn't as young as they were.

"It's a closed array of servers, Sir. They use the public networks, but they're set up so they only talk to each other and no one can eavesdrop on them – that's the theory anyway. They're called virtual because they're not really private, but they function as if they are."

Mitchie had to get back to the screens, and as she finished her coffee, a co-ordinator handed Snape a fax. It was from Chelmsford, and if Essex Police hadn't been so short-staffed, it would have been sent a lot earlier. Even so, Snape was pleased with what he read. He'd had one of Garry's pictures followed up, the one showing Pachini wearing his football rosettes. It turned out Pachini had had a Colchester United season ticket for the previous four seasons, and Watkins had had the seat next to him for the last three of them.

"Watkins, Pachini, Hayward," van Piet mused after Snape had passed the fax over. "I wonder if there's a link there."

Snape thought he might be able to follow that up, so he sent a text to Craske at Forensics.

"If you ask me, Watkins is the kiss of death," he said to van Piet when he'd done. "Ashley Johnson's gone, Slade's gone, Pachini could be, and now we're looking at Hayward."

"You could be onto something, Eddie. Things hang together strangely sometimes."

Snape wondered if they could have another go at Watkins without rocking the boat. He expected van Piet to stall again, but he didn't. Instead he said,

"Clive Taylor," and he took his smartphone out. "You'll remember the name, Eddie. He's Watkins's boss at the *Standard*."

Snape said he did. Once he'd been told a name, it stayed with him.

"What about him?"

"He's married to a lady named Elsie. He's estranged from her now, but he wasn't when Watkins went back to London. I'll ask Elsie if we can see her tomorrow. I want to know how Watkins got her job back so easily."

"Why so?"

"Because normally, once you leave a job, someone else gets it, and that's you gone. But Watkins seems to have waltzed back into hers without any trouble at all. I don't see her or Clive telling us the truth about it, but Elsie might, if she knows what it is, and that could let us have another go at Watkins."

He tapped out a text and sent it. There was no immediate reply, which didn't surprise him.

"Elsie might still be busy," he explained. "She does lighting and sound designs in theatres, so she often starts when the punters have all gone home. I should have asked her about Watkins before, it's been on my mind long enough, but maybe it's still not too late."

Monday dawned sunny and clear, and a hot day was forecast. In Oxford, Kett was up good and early – he was due to collect a brand new Alfa Romeo before he caught the train to London. He felt he could risk splashing out on it, as long as he paid on instalments. No point selling state secrets and driving a Volkswagen Passat. In London, van Piet noticed the sunshine through the curtains of his Ashell House bed-sit, and he was sorely tempted to go outside just to feel it on his skin. But the operations room came first, and that was the end of that.

Snape was in there already, talking on his smartphone. When he saw van Piet, he said, "Hold on a sec" and waved him over.

"It's Mr Chatsley senior, Willem. You'll remember, he's looking after Slade's mortal remains. He's called me about a wreath that's just been delivered. He says the card is in Russian, and he wants to know whether to display it or no. He's afraid it might be political."

"We can soon answer that. Ask him to send a picture."

Snape passed the message on, and by return he had the card on his screen as Garry was walking past to a desk on the far side of the room. Van Piet asked him what he thought.

"It's in Russian all right," Garry said. "It says 'From friends to a friend', but I don't think any Russians sent it. Close on thirty percent of Ukrainians speak Russian, and the yellow and blue shield under the text is the Ukrainian coat of arms. My advice is, replace the card with one carrying the message in English. It's harmless enough out of context."

"What about the shield?"

"Transfer it onto the new card, but make it smaller. If anyone recognises it, they'll already know what they think about the Ukraine. If they don't, they'll think it's a trademark or something."

Snape passed Garry's reply on to Chatsley and told him to keep the original safe till the police could collect it. Chatsley asked for plain clothes and an unmarked car, and Snape said he'd arrange it.

"Have you had many wreaths for Mr Slade?" he asked.

He always liked talking to Chatsley.

"An enormous number, Eddie. He must have known no end of people, and they all seem to have liked him."

Snape tapered the call off and asked van Piet what he made of the card.

"Difficult to say. We've got no clear proof Slade was helping the Russians, but if he was, you'd think Ukrainian nationalists would be the last people he'd be in with. So maybe he'd infiltrated them and was shopping them on the quiet, or maybe he was simply getting a commission out of them. He might even have had a soft spot for them, who knows? It'd be useful to find out whether he had any strong beliefs at all. I'm inclined to think he didn't, but I could be wrong."

Elsie Taylor had texted back in the early hours. Van Piet could come and see her, and he could bring Snape along as well. So, after he'd had some breakfast and brought himself up to speed, he booked a car and driver, and soon he and Snape were threading their way to Hampstead in a venerable beige Saab. The spacious condominium Elsie had once shared with Taylor was in the loft of a four-floor new build. The brickwork was pale red, the windows had smooth white surrounds, and the roof had white-clad dormers reaching out of it. Two of the dormers were close together and formed part of Elsie's living-cum-dining area. They were firmly shut since the air conditioning was on. When Elsie opened the door, the smell of fresh coffee wafted out. The driver, Lily Quinnell, had been told to park where she could, van Piet wasn't expecting to stay long. He was starting to get nervous about time. On the one hand, he felt things were gathering momentum; on the other, he wanted to give every new detail all the time it needed.

"So, Willem, you're helping the police solve Ashley Johnson's murder, are you?" Elsie said as she invited them in.

Snape had expected to see some kind of exotic in the doorway, but Elsie could easily have been a successful establishment lawyer or the CEO of a large company. Her short white hair was immaculately coiffured, her blue-black two-piece could have been bought the day before, and her cream cotton blouse was ironed to perfection. She wasn't wearing a wedding ring, but a depression on her ring finger showed where one had been.

"Something like that, Elsie. There's a money angle cropped up, and money's something I know about."

"Well, Clive didn't kill him, if that's what you're thinking, and neither did I come to that. Clive was in St Thomas's having a pacemaker fitted, and I was stuck in New York because my flight home had been delayed. The way we live now, I'm sure these things can be checked."

"So am I, but that's not why Mr Snape and I are here. Can we speak in confidence?"

"Come off it, Willem, you know me better than that. What do you want to know?"

"How Deborah Watkins got her job back so easily."

"I see. And you don't want to ask her or Clive."

"No."

She didn't respond straight away. Snape paged through his notebook, van Piet drank most of his coffee, and a large-faced clock on the wall ticked stolidly. Finally she said,

"I think Clive fell for Deborah the day she showed up for interview. If it wasn't then, it was very soon after she joined his staff. He tried to hide it, of course - he was a lot older than she was - but she didn't miss much, and she didn't miss that. Ashley Johnson made the big difference. Once he'd entered her life, all she could think about was him, so Clive donned the role of amiable uncle, and he was actually relieved when she left, because the role was stressing him out. He told me it was like getting off heroin, though he's never taken more than Warfarin in his life. We were still close then, and he rather enjoyed confessing to me. Absolution was one of the games we played.

"Unfortunately, addictions have a way of returning. According to Clive, Deborah's replacement was actually better than she was, but when Deborah asked to come back, he got her replacement promoted to the *Telegraph* and rolled out the red carpet for her.

"But it wasn't the Deborah we'd known before. Clive had always liked to invite her round here, and as long as Ashley was in tow, I hadn't minded too much, since she could be lots of fun when she wanted to be. But when Ashley was killed, something in her died with him, and she became an out and out schemer. Getting her job back was clearly part of a much larger plan, but Clive couldn't or wouldn't see it.

"Now, the *Standard* owns a flat in Paddington for when reporters want to meet people on the quiet. Clive got her exclusive rights to it by misusing his senior status, and they started to meet there in secret. I found out about it, of course, and I made Clive choose between us. He was eating out of her hand by then, so he chose her and moved into a rented place in the Barbican, which is where he lives now, as you may or may not know. That's the story, gentlemen. I hope it helps you, since it's cost me a lot to tell it."

Snape asked whether Taylor would break the law for Watkins if she asked him to.

"Clive's a good man for all his faults," Elsie replied, spreading her fingers and studying the backs of them, "but, as you see, he can also be very silly, so yes, I think he would. I doubt he'd rob anyone at gunpoint, but anything less and Deborah would get her way. He probably wouldn't even see it as criminal."

Snape brought her back to the age difference she'd mentioned. How old was Taylor exactly?

"He'll be sixty-five next March." She gave him a wry smile. "It's pathetic, isn't it? He's done well at the *Standard*, everyone there thinks he's the bee's knees, yet in his private life he's an idiot. I think if

272

he wrote about himself instead of other people, he'd come to the same conclusion."

Van Piet felt they'd found out all they needed to know, so they gossiped a bit about theatreland, and then it was time to call Quinnell, who'd found a space for the Saab on a cricket ground car park. The heat was aggressive outside, and there was no shade in the street, so they opted to wait in the lobby for her. Van Piet thought they should try calling on Watkins on their way back to Ashell House - Primrose Place first, then Gilbert Mews, and the *Standard* if they had to. But no advance notice this time.

"We'll ask her about the Slades to start things off," he said. "She's got away with blanking them out so far, and she'll know it. We'll see where that takes us now we know a bit more."

They were getting into the Saab when Snape's smartphone buzzed. It was Craske calling from Chelmsford. Snape turned the volume up.

"You asked me to go back to the fingernail scrapings Deborah Watkins provided at the time of the Ashley Johnson murder. Their DNA matches the DNA of two hairs Forensics found in Nightingale Cottage that didn't belong to Hayward."

"Ask him which room they found them in," van Piet said.

"The cottage has two bedrooms," Craske came back, "and the hairs were in between the carpet and the skirting in the spare one. The room was clean, but they'd be easy to miss, and there's no telling how long they'd been there. There's something else, Eddie, if you've got a minute, which I'm sure you have, since I'm working all hours to suit you."

Snape grunted and told him to go ahead.

"Those fibres Neil Massie found near Nightingale Cottage. The dye and the weave are unique to an Edinburgh factory called Forraloy Industrial Fabrics, and one of Forraloy's lines is heavy-duty overalls. It could be something to go on."

Snape thought it was and terminated. The overalls he and van Piet had worn in Thurston's quarry had been made by Forraloy. He'd made a point of reading the labels.

A burst water main in Maida Vale slowed the traffic up badly between Hampstead and Primrose Place, and van Piet spent a lot of the time talking to Garry. When they reached Number 25, he told Quinnell to stop a few numbers further along and park near Paddington railway station. Quinnell's ID should get her into a police bay, but she wasn't to say why she was there.

Number 25 was part of an elegant terrace that formed one side of an equally elegant square with railed-off bushes in the middle of it. The freshly-painted façade was an attractive off-white, the drainpipes had little shields on them with '1905' curled across them, and the porches over the front doors were pillared in neo-classical style. Snape, who'd done his homework, said the ground floor counted as zero, so Flat 16 was on the first floor, and as they walked back, he told van Piet where it was without pointing. It didn't look as if it was air conditioned, not with the windows open. It could be hot in there.

There was a brass-slatted list of residents' names by the front door, and each name had a bell push next to it. Van Piet was reluctant to use the one next to Watkins's name in case she refused to let them in, but as they got nearer the porch, a take-out

274

courier cycled past them, leaned his bike against the railings and pushed the button for 22. Snape and van Piet fell in behind him, and while he waited for the lift, they made their way up the imitation marble staircase. The air was cooler there, but Snape and van Piet were both sweating by the time they found Watkins's flat.

Snape pressed the bell push, and they both dimly heard the chime through the solid wooden door, but there was no response. They waited a few moments, then Snape tried once more, but again nothing happened. If it hadn't been for the open windows, they would have moved on to Gilbert Mews, but Watkins might just be in the bath or something, so they gave her enough time to put on a bath robe and Snape tried a third time. Still nothing.

There was no sound in the corridor, and Snape reckoned most people were at work. He lifted the flap of the letter box and tried to see in, but the letter box was a real one, namely a box attached to the door, so all he saw was darkness. The box was probably deliberate, he thought. Who would want anyone looking into their flat?

"What do you think?" he asked. He knew already what the answer would be.

"I don't like it, not with the windows open. Has your search warrant come through?"

It had, so van Piet took what looked like a thin, translucent piece of plastic out of a holder in his inside jacket pocket. It was less wide than a credit card, but it was longer and more flexible.

"It's graphene," he said. "I'll see if it'll get this Yale lock open. The burglar alarm won't be on, not with the windows open."

He began to ease the graphene in.

"If there's a smart lock built into the door, I'll have to think again," he said.

But the graphene pushing the Yale back was enough.

There was a heavy stillness inside, and as van Piet shut the door behind them, Snape noticed the smart lock hadn't been set. The safety bolt hadn't been slotted in either.

"Miss Watkins," he called into the silence. "It's the police. Mr Snape and Mr van Piet."

No answer. He made his mind up.

"We keep going," he said. "We'll open each door as we reach it. We don't want anyone hiding between us and the door we've just come through."

They were in a softly carpeted hallway, the overhead light had come on automatically, and all the doors they could see were shut. To their right was a walk-in clothes cupboard, and they opened it first. It was almost empty – just a shower-proof coat, a pair of outdoor shoes, and some left-over winter wear.

"This is the bedroom," Snape said, pointing to his left, "and behind the door in front of us is the bathroom. The rest of the flat is round to the right."

The bed was made, and a nightdress and dressing gown were neatly laid out on it. The curtains, which were lined to keep out the light, were drawn back. They flapped and swished occasionally, but mostly they hung motionless. The furniture was conventional for a bedroom, but against the wall under the open window was a writing desk with a reading lamp, a computer and a printer on it, and next to the desk was a locked security box. So the bedroom doubled as an office, and someone hidden in there wouldn't have heard what was said in the living-cum-dining area. That could have been why Kensington had got the nod.

"Not much of a love nest, is it?" Snape commented, and van Piet agreed. However tenderly Watkins might feel about Taylor, it didn't show in the bedroom, and it didn't show in the bathroom, where everything seemed to belong to Watkins. There wasn't even a spare toothbrush in there.

"Maybe the Barbican's the new bower of bliss," van Piet offered, but he didn't sound convinced. Watkins had to be stringing Taylor along.

There was no door to the living-cum-dining area, which was also carpeted, so they took it all in at once as they closed the bathroom door. The living part consisted of a fawn three-piece suite covered in leather, a coffee table and some standard lamps, while a circular cloth-covered table and four matching chairs supplied the dining part. To their right was the galley kitchen. The lighting came on automatically as they opened the door - there were no windows, only a hood over the hob and an extractor grill in one corner - and on the white-and-grey tiles which covered the floor, Watkins lay flat on her back, her blood-flecked eyes staring sightlessly at the ceiling. Her forehead was bruised, and so was her throat, which was engorged above and below the bruising that discoloured it. Her plaid summer shirt had been unbuttoned, her bra had been pushed up - more on her left side than on her right - and a 150mm flat-headed screwdriver had been forced between her ribs and through her heart. Blood had dried into her clothing and there was more on the floor. But there wasn't a lot of it.

Van Piet and Snape had both seen death before, but for a brief moment they were dumbstruck. Then clinical efficiency took over. Snape knelt down by the body and carefully tried one of the arms for movement. It was conspicuously stiff.

"She's been dead for some while," he said, glad to be workmanlike, "but not long enough for rigor mortis to disperse. This is a crime scene, Willem. We'll not touch anything else."

He looked closely at the screwdriver's handle, changing his position to see it from different angles.

"It's not a new screwdriver," he concluded. "And it's not the sort of thing most people keep in their kitchen. It looks as if whoever did it came prepared."

He stood up and looked round. There was water in the electric kettle, two cups had been set out, and an opened jar of Nescafé stood next to an unopened pint jug of semi-skimmed.

"There's a chance she knew her killer," he said, "since everything says she let him or her in. I think she came in here to make some coffee, her killer stunned her by banging her head against the wall, then strangled her. To make sure she was dead, he or she undid her clothing and pushed the screwdriver into her heart. I'd be surprised if she fell as she is now, I think she was moved to make the stabbing easier. She's still got her jeans and slippers on, and I don't see any smears or stains, so it's likely the attack wasn't sexual. I'm going to call the Met, Willem. They have to know, and the sooner the better."

Snape already had his smartphone in his hand when van Piet stopped him.

"When she was alive, she wouldn't help us," he said. "Now she's dead, she might do just that."

It sounded like an order. Snape looked at him sharply. He'd remembered something van Piet had said.

"Were you counting on her death when you told me to step away and stay there that time?"

"Counting on it, no, but I could see it might happen, and I thought we might gain by it, so I put the two together. She asked for it and now she's got it, Eddie. It's up to us to use it."

He called Garry on his mobile and told him rapidly what had happened.

"Ask Mr Benjamin to call me right now, I need to speak to him urgently."

Garry speed-dialled the Director General's mobile, and within seconds van Piet was telling him what he'd told Garry.

"Sir, I want you to call the Metropolitan Police Commissioner on his personal mobile without delay," he went on. "We can't stop Watkins's murder being investigated, but I don't want any news about it to leak out for at least an hour and for longer than that if he can manage it. He won't like it, but if you tell him there's a Crown warrant out, he won't have any choice. Make sure he understands that, please. He's got no choice."

He terminated and called Jerome Shaffer on his smartphone.

"Jerome, when I reach the *Standard*, get me out of sight quickly. I'll tell you what I want when I get there."

Next came Quinnell – she was to pick him up from Number 25 straight away, and he'd be waiting in the porch on his own. Destination was the *London Evening Standard* in Derry Street.

Snape came after that.

"I want you to guard this murder site till the Met shows up, and when they do, make sure they understand that no leaks means what it says. I'll call you from the *Standard* when I'm ready, and I'll send Lily to fetch you."

Finally, he called Garry again.

"Start Blue Zebra now," he said, "and let me know as soon as it's finished. We've run with the hares long enough, Tom. From now on we hunt with the hounds."

Chapter 27

Decline and fall

As soon as van Piet saw Shaffer walking in his direction, he was out of the Saab before it had come to a halt. Shaffer didn't show he'd recognised him, he simply turned into the *Standard*, and van Piet followed him in. The lobby was busy as always. The *Standard* was one of London's village voices, so people felt free to come in, say their piece, feel part of the place or whatever.

"Don't stop," van Piet said through the chatter as he closed the gap on Shaffer. "It's the blood bank I'm after."

All major newspapers store dirt on famous people. A lot of it is hard copy to prevent hacking, and it's guarded more closely than the gold in Fort Knox. The *Standard's* hoard was in a dedicated sub-basement nick-named the blood bank. A cramped security lift mostly hidden by a rubber tree was the only way in, and Shaffer's face and left thumbprint had to be scanned before he could open the lift door.

The blood bank was permanently lit, and its humidity and temperature were kept constant. Round the walls were numbered safes of different ages and sizes. Some, especially the older ones, were large and free-standing, while smaller ones were in blocks like lockers in a changing room. The larger ones were effectively armoured archives. The secrets inside them could go back years, and only the most senior editors had access to them. The smaller ones were for foot-soldiers like Watkins when they were working on something best kept under wraps, and the house rule was, they could access them on their own up to the point of publication, but if one of their seniors wanted to consult their work-in-progress and they weren't there, that senior had to get a second senior to come down with him or her. That protected everyone's interests. There were reading desks by the walls. Each desk had two chairs under it and a reading lamp on top with a vase-shaped upright. Next to each desk was a shredder. Any paper put into it ended up as powder. There was a clearly marked fire door, but it was strictly exit only.

Like the rest of the building, the blood bank was cleaned daily. Shaffer had declared it a security hazard almost as soon as he'd arrived, and he'd had a windowless storeroom built into one corner to stop the cleaners carrying things in an out. It contained everything they needed, including a sink and running water. The door was thumbprint-recognition plus a code lock, and every cleaner in the blood bank and the storeroom was supervised by Shaffer or one of his staff. The cleaners themselves brought nothing in with them, and they took nothing out except garbage. That, too, was supervised.

Van Piet liked what he saw, namely, that the blood bank was empty. He quoted the Official Secrets Act at Shaffer, though Shaffer knew it as well as he did, then he briefed him. That included explaining who Snape was. When he'd done that, he asked whether Taylor was in. Shaffer consulted the tablet he was never without.

"Looks like it. He's logged in at the desk, and the green light over his office is on."

"What about his secretary?"

"She's on maternity leave, so he's using the pool."

Van Piet took out his smartphone, and Shaffer told him to move to somewhere else if the signal broke up - there was a lot of steel and masonry overhead. Van Piet called Snape, found a good place for the signal, and gave him Taylor's direct number.

"Call him right now," he said. "Say Watkins has been murdered in her flat in Primrose Place and he's entitled to know before the news gets spread around. Say you're sorry she's dead if you have to, but don't take too long over it."

He walked back to Shaffer, who was leaning against one of the reading desks.

"We'll hide in the cleaners' storeroom," he told him. "If I've got this right, Mr Taylor will be joining us shortly. I want to see what he does when he gets here."

Like the blood bank, the storeroom was permanently lit, the air in it smelled of detergent, and there were some cleaning cloths on a drying rack. Shaffer accessed his tablet again. It showed the room they'd just left from a range of angles and then the corridor outside Taylor's office. The images were good.

"I'll make a small alteration while I'm at it," he said, and he superimposed a control panel. Van Piet watched to see what he'd do, then they waited, but not for long. Taylor came out of his office, and Shaffer tracked him to the security lift. Then he was in the blood bank.

Shaffer's tablet was high definition, and its treatment of Taylor was harsh. His face came across as blotchy, and his wispy, brown-white hair looked as if it had been scorched. The lenses of his glasses were thick, and while he'd had a stoop for years, the tablet made it seem worse. His pacemaker went with the general impression, and van Piet could easily guess how Watkins had hooked him and kept him. She'd made him believe he was young again.

Taylor looked round furtively to see whether anyone else was about, then he opened a safe in one of the blocks. He'd obviously done it before, but to van Piet's disappointed surprise, only a few sheets of paper came out. They were held together with a ⅝" bulldog clip, the top A4 sheet was face down, and a piece of paper on top of it, which was also face down and smaller, looked as if it had been torn out of a reporter's notepad. Van Piet had expected a lot more to be in there, but that seemed to be it. Taylor slipped the bulldog clip into his jacket pocket and smiled at the smaller piece of paper once he'd turned it over. As he went through the A4 sheets, he seemed to be torn between hurrying through them and looking at each one carefully. Finally he took the first four sheets and tried to feed them into the shredder, but it didn't respond. Flustered, he struggled down onto his knees and clicked the mains switch off and on, but again no response. He was still on his knees when Shaffer opened the storeroom door and came out with van Piet.

"I'll have to take those papers from you, Mr Taylor," Shaffer said. "You know you can't access the juniors' safes on your own."

Shaffer held out his hand. Off balance with guilt, Taylor handed them over, then the bulldog clip, and van Piet signalled to him to stand up.

"We figured you might come down here, Sir," Shaffer said, "so I turned the shredder off from my tablet just in case. I didn't turn the cameras off though. They've caught everything."

Van Piet took the papers from Shaffer and went through them one at a time. They were Watkins's night photos of Laura Slade, Verity Slade and Kett outside Esklivia House, and on the smaller sheet there was a hand-written note saying, 'Dropped these off after job was done. Nearly over now – Deborah.' The words were followed by some kisses and a quickly sketched heart with an arrow through it. Van Piet noted the photos' dates and times, plus the matching attaché cases, then he called Snape on his mobile. Could he come over straight away? Snape said he could, give or take a minute, so van Piet called Quinnell, who had gone back to Paddington railway station, and asked her to pick him up. Then he asked Shaffer to go up to the lobby and wait for him, but not to bring him down till he'd called down to van Piet for clearance. Aware Taylor could hear every word, van Piet described Snape in detail, emphasising his rank and the police force he headed. Snape must have told Taylor who he was when he called him, but van Piet wanted Taylor to feel the police were closing in. Snape would arrive in a beige Saab, he added, turning the screw some more. Not many Saabs about these days, so if it was a Saab, it had to be Mr Snape. As the lift disappeared, van Piet gestured to Taylor to sit down by the desk the switched-off shredder belonged to. He took the other chair, and they faced each other.

"What are you doing here, Willem?" Taylor asked. "And how come you know Jerome so well?"

He was completely bewildered. Bewildered and very frightened.

"I talked to Elsie this morning, and Mr Snape was with me. After we found Deborah Watkins's body, we had to get to you next, and I came on ahead."

"What about Jerome?"

"Tell me who doesn't know him, Clive. He's a legend."

That was all he was getting.

Van Piet wanted to make Taylor believe he was on his side.

"We can talk things through before the police get here," he suggested, sounding like a good comrade. "If you go through your answers with me, it might help you when they take over."

Taylor nodded eagerly.

"Good idea, Willem. I need a friend right now."

Van Piet got things moving.

"You pretended to me you scarcely knew Deborah Watkins, but I've learned from Elsie it wasn't true. Deborah needed her job back, and you eased her replacement out so she could have it. What line did she take to win the glittering prize? Did she say you could have her if you did what she wanted, but you'd never see her again if you didn't?"

Taylor shrugged abjectly. He wasn't crooked enough to lie.

"She meant everything to me, Willem. I don't know what I'll do now she's dead. Perhaps Elsie will have me back."

Van Piet let that pass. He wanted to firm up some ideas he had.

"Why was Deborah's safe nearly empty?" he asked. "I was expecting a great bundle of stuff to be in there. I thought she'd set things up so she could tell the Slades, if anything happened to her, their whole dirty story would come out. It seemed such an obvious thing to do."

"You're almost right, it's just she preferred a strongbox in a solicitor's safe. Don't ask me who the solicitor is, because she never told me. What Deborah kept here was temporary. If she wanted to go back to old stuff, she'd fetch it personally from her solicitor and take it back personally when she'd done with it. New stuff she'd take as soon as she'd finished with it. I doubt her solicitor ever saw more than the packing it was in. She was good at keeping secrets.

"I ought to tell you, she got herself a solicitor because she didn't trust me," he felt obliged to add. "She thought, if she was killed, I wouldn't pass what she'd found out on to the police, I'd destroy it on the quiet, so I wouldn't get dragged in. She was right, of course, that's why I'm sitting here now. I knew she'd left something in here for me to see, she left a message on her office ansaphone saying she had."

Van Piet asked him when that was.

"Towards the end of yesterday afternoon. If she left something for me, I'd normally bring a colleague with me, so everything she put in her safe

287

had the top sheet face down, like now. Then the colleague couldn't see what it was."

"Didn't they ask to see?"

"Why should they? I've been here a long time, so they found it easier not to. As it happened, I was taking time off last night, so I didn't come into the building to look when I got her message, and when I came in today, the usual Monday hoo-hah got in the way. But nothing had ever gone wrong before, so I guessed I could hang on till things quietened down. Then Mr Snape phoned me, and I realised I couldn't and, well, you know the rest. I came down on my own, because I was going to use the shredder. I didn't want a witness for that."

"What about the cameras? They'd have picked you up."

"I'd have thought of something, if I'd had to. Like I said, I've been here a long while."

Van Piet asked whether Watkins ever discussed her investigations in detail. Taylor said they went through some things together but not everything, and it was the same with what she showed him. Van Piet was inclined to believe him.

"Did Deborah know who killed Ashley Johnson?" he asked suddenly, hoping to jolt the truth out of him.

Taylor bit his lip.

"Yes, she knew who did it, but she never told me who it was. I repeat, Willem, she didn't tell me everything, just enough to keep me, well, protecting her, I suppose."

"What about Geoffrey Slade's death? Come on, Clive, you know these names. Did she talk about that?"

288

"She said it was murder and she knew who did it, but that was all."

"What about Stephanie Hayward, who's been shot, and Matteo Pachini, who's disappeared? Was she silent about everyone?"

"Don't crowd me, Willem, I'm not up to it. She knew Hayward was in danger, but she didn't know who killed her. And she used to moan nonstop about Pachini. She went to football matches with him, but she hated the game, and she'd get frozen stiff as well. Then she stopped talking about him altogether. I didn't push it, it wasn't my way. It was up to her what she said."

Van Piet asked him straight out if he was telling the truth. He insisted he was, and van Piet went back to sounding friendly.

"You must have been worried about Deborah at times. What was she tracking these people for anyway?"

"She was a bit vague about that. I got the impression there was something wrong with Verity Slade's business, and she was after a scoop. I keep saying it, Willem - I didn't ask questions. I was afraid to, she might get tired of me."

He broke off for a moment.

"She always took good care of herself. If things looked tricky, she'd leave a message on her office ansaphone saying where she was going and how long she'd be there. Apart from her, no one can access her ansaphone except me, not even her secretary, and it automatically sends the messages she leaves on to my smartphone. If everything went well, she'd ring in and delete the message afterwards, and my smartphone would pick that up as well. I liked that, it put my mind at rest."

"The police think they know where she spent Saturday and who she spent it with. What about yesterday? Do you know where she was?"

"I can piece it together for you. Will that do?"

Van Piet said it would. Everything would be checked anyway.

"Well, in the morning she went to a sports place in Colchester called the Camulo Wellness and Social Club. She met Verity Slade's daughter, Laura, there, and she showed her the pictures you've just seen, but she didn't tell me why she was doing it. In the afternoon she saw Verity Slade and a friend of Mrs Slade's called Barbara Davis – that was in the Slades' house in Essex. She showed them the same pictures, but again she didn't say why. All I know is she was very excited about it. Laura Slade isn't dangerous, Deborah was certain of that, but she thought Verity Slade and Barbara Davis could be, so she played extra safe with them. She wrote out a summary of what she was going to say to them, as well as leaving a message on her ansaphone."

Van Piet asked where the summary was. Watkins had written, 'Nearly over now' on her note. That had to mean something.

"She posted it to me Sunday morning. She liked the post, she used to say it was as good as an armed guard, but there's no collection on Sundays, so it'll arrive here tomorrow. It'll be addressed to me personally and marked Confidential. No one else will open it."

Van Piet asked where Watkins went after she'd left Verity's house. He said she dropped off the photos they'd been looking at in the blood bank, then she went to Primrose Place.

"She was going to spend the night there and stay on today to finish some work for me."

"Was she meeting anyone in Primrose Place, do you know?"

"Yes, a Mrs Anita Rufus at 7.00 pm. She said Mrs Rufus was in a bad mood about something, but she didn't see her as a threat, so I needn't expect a message to say she was all right. I sound as if I'm pointing a finger, don't I, but it's what I heard. I took Deborah at her word and deleted the call myself. She said I could."

"And you were where exactly when you did it? You said you'd taken time off."

"I was in the Barbican. That's where I live these days, I expect Elsie told you. I was chairing a Tenants' Association meeting in the evening, and I had to get it ready beforehand. I wasn't obliged to chair it, but I feel a bit lost when Deborah isn't around, so I got on with it. To be honest, I sort of welcomed it."

Van Piet asked whether he knew the people in the photos.

"Verity and Laura Slade, that goes without saying. I don't know who the man is though. I've never seen these pics before, nor any like them."

"But she wanted you to see these, didn't she, because that gave her a hold over you, like all the other things she's let you know about, complete with little notes. Maybe she was planning something you'd dislike so much, you might turn against her, unless she had you over a barrel."

Before Taylor could answer, van Piet's smartphone buzzed. It was Shaffer. He was in the lobby with Snape, and the Saab had gone back to

Paddington station. Van Piet asked him to bring Snape down.

Snape and Taylor had never met before, and with old-fashioned courtesy, Taylor stood up as he came in.

"You'd better sit down again, Clive," van Piet said, and the good-friend tone in his voice was gone. "You're not going to like this next bit."

He gave the photos plus Watkins's note to Snape, then he went through everything Taylor had said before he felt behind the reading lamp and detached the miniaturised recorder Shaffer had placed there.

"It's all on here, Eddie," he said, handing it over. "Mr Shaffer's got cctv pictures as well. Mr Taylor's all yours now."

Snape told Taylor he was under arrest and recited the caution. He'd be taken to Paddington Green police station, and the charge would be seeking to pervert the course of justice. Other charges could follow. He'd be detained after he'd been charged, then transferred to custody in Essex. He could contact his solicitor from Paddington Green. Essex Police would oppose bail.

Van Piet looked at his watch. Time was pressing.

"Your security lift's on the small side," he said to Shaffer. "Take me upstairs first, then come back for Mr Snape and Mr Taylor. Secure Mr Taylor's office and Miss Watkins's as soon as you can. No one to go in except the police. That will kill my attempt to keep things quiet," he added wryly. "No newspaper's going to ignore one of its editors being arrested in its own basement."

When they were in the lobby Shaffer made sure no one could overhear.

"That was a textbook sting you organised down there, Willem. You'd think Mr Taylor would see through it, he being a newspaper man."

"You would, wouldn't you, but he didn't. Mrs Taylor told me he enjoyed confessing, so I thought I'd see how true it was. Thanks for the bug, by the way. I reckoned old habits might die hard, and it was easy to guess where you'd put it. The only chance you had was when you told me to move with my smartphone."

Getting Taylor to Paddington Green and into the cells took more time, and so did the follow-up paperwork. While he was waiting, van Piet asked Benjamin to put Watkins's murder entirely under Crown warrant control. Then he brought Kossler and Garry up to speed.

Taylor couldn't co-operate enough. He'd been brought up to help the police, and he couldn't stop doing it now. Elsie would help them as well, he said, he was totally sure of that, and he'd gladly identify Watkins's body, if her parents couldn't go through with it. Snape said he'd bear it in mind, but it was the last thing he wanted. He'd had Watkins's parents checked out. Her father was a plasterer, her mother was a cleaner in a care home, and they lived in a terrace house in Swindon. It must have lit their lives up to see their daughter doing just fine at the *Standard*, and now she was murdered. Taylor, he felt, would contaminate everything.

"We've got no choice, we've got to pull them all in right now, Anita Rufus and Kett included," van Piet told Snape as Quinnell was driving them back to Chelsea. He sounded tense. "The chances are they're packing already. Get Brighton and Hove Police to shut down Andreas and Francisca Davis. They mustn't talk to anyone from now on, and if Andreas can't be moved, I want a round-the-clock guard put on him. That leaves Friedrich Winckler. We have to take him as well."

Snape said he'd get an Interpol Red Notice issued. The Extradition Act would take care of the rest.

"What about Laura Slade?" he asked. "She seems to be out of it, but she keeps cropping up."

"We find her and we hang on to her till we know we don't have to. And get someone onto the Post Office. If Watkins has sent something to Taylor, we need to know what it is."

He was reaching for his mobile when he recalled something he had to get out of the way.

"Ashley Johnson," he said. "You told me there was nothing in his background to explain his murder. You still stick to that, do you?"

"We looked hard enough. Did we miss something?"

"I'd have to say you did."

He leaned forward to talk to Quinnell.

"Lily, when we get back to Ashell House, get something to eat and drink for us three plus two more, and bring it to the car. I'm fetching two technical assistants from the top floor, then we'll be taking off fast."

He turned back to Snape.

"We need to sort out where our villains are, I'll get Tom onto it pronto. Tell Sal to get her people readied up. I know she's short on numbers, but we should be able to cope. We just have to be smart about it."

If the sun was hot in London, it was even hotter in Monaco. Dynamic positioning was holding Electric Calamine, Charles Johnson's yacht, in place off the entrance to Port Hercule harbour. She was waiting for a cruise ship to leave Quai Rainier III and head for the open sea. Then she could move in and tie up in her usual place.

Johnson was relaxing on a recliner overlooking the stern. He was expecting guests on board later, but for the moment he was on his own, and that suited him fine, since in the years after his son's death, he'd got used to his own company. He was reaching for a magazine on a nearby table when his personal steward brought him a message from the bridge: The *Police Maritime* wanted to talk to him in confidence. He sighed tetchily and said he'd take the call in his cabin. As he was speaking, two motor launches left Quai Antoine 1er, where the *Police Maritime* had its headquarters. Quai Antoine 1er was deep within Port Hercule, so no one on Electric Calamine saw them. There were too many yachts in the way.

The accented English Johnson heard in his cabin was fluent and polite, but it was still the opposite of welcome.

"M. Johnson, two of our launches are approaching your vessel. One of them is bringing two officers of your National Crime Agency with it.

They wish to board Electric Calamine under the armed protection of our *Police Maritime.*"

Johnson said they didn't need protection, they could come aboard anyway. What was the other launch for?

"It is carrying a special unit to ensure that everything goes smoothly, since we've been informed your crew carries firearms. That is a clear breach of Monégasque law, as you know, and we shall take it further at an appropriate time. But for now, we want you to understand that if you or your crew offer resistance at any point, you and your yacht will be taken by force."

"So what do these officers want then?"

It had to be crossed wires.

"They want to arrest you, Mr Johnson, and take you back to England. They've been here for some days, and if I may say so, you would be well advised to co-operate. They have our full support, and Monaco is the most intensely policed country in the world, including at sea."

Listening in through a headset and watching through binoculars was the SRO resident in Monte Carlo. His balcony was deep in shade under an awning. When he finally eased his headset off, he took his mobile out and contacted Garry, who in turn contacted van Piet. Operation Blue Zebra was over.

Chapter 28

Preparing to get away

While Quinnell had been driving van Piet and Snape to Elsie Taylor's, Cottrell had been talking to the organiser of the conference she was on in the privacy of his hotel room. Looking as upset as she could, she explained a text message had reached her late the previous evening saying her mother was dying in a Belfast hospital. If she hurried, she might still be able to see her for one last time, and so – regrettably - she would have to leave the conference straight away. The organiser, a generous man and known to be so, was entirely sympathetic. Of course she should go, he understood perfectly how distressed she must be. When he asked her whether he could help in any way, she said thank you but no, she'd packed her suitcase before breakfast, and she'd booked her flight from Manchester as well. But she was grateful for the offer, his kind words meant a lot to her.

Cottrell knew Coventry well - she was a popular speaker, and this was the fourth conference she'd taken part in there, since she kept being invited back. She enjoyed exploring the city during her free time, and she knew there was a vehicle hire company seven or eight blocks over from the conference hotel. She drove to it now through side streets she was confident wouldn't have surveillance cameras in them. She needed a van to move some furniture for a friend, she told the Customer Reception Assistant, and she hired a Toyota Hiace for three days. Could she leave her car on the car park, she asked, and there was no problem there. She transferred her suitcase to the van before she drove off, but her laptop and the smartphone she normally used remained switched off and stowed beneath the carpeted board in the boot of her car that covered the spare wheel recess. If anyone tried to locate her through them, they'd be disappointed. They were both wrapped in metal foil she'd managed to buy in a hurry.

From Coventry she motored to Cambridge, secure in the knowledge her car's registration wasn't being caught on camera. Once she was there, she booked into a small commercial hotel that wasn't part of a chain and parked behind it on its private car park. All she had to do now was blend in with the tourists till it was time to head for Brightlingsea on Tuesday. She still had the emergency smartphone Verity had called her on to tell her about the escape. Everyone in the conspiracy had one, they had to carry it with them at all times, and like the ones in Verity's sideboard, they were untraceable. A Beretta 92 Compact and a clip of ammunition were packed in her suitcase. Leaving England would be a wrench, but she could see why it had to be. And as Verity had assured her more than once, Russia welcomed its friends with open arms.

Monday morning found Thurston equally busy. First, he drove to his quarry to say he'd be going into a clinic for a minor operation. He expected to be in there for three days, and he'd be keeping his phone switched off. Back in Thurston Mansion, he made his routine Monday calls, then he put a recorded message on his landline phone that repeated what he'd said at the quarry. His laptop and his everyday smartphone came next. He wrapped them in lead sheeting from his home workshop and locked them away in an underfloor strongbox. Finally, he packed a suitcase, changed into a suit and tie, and drove into Leicester in his Range Rover, where he hired a Renault Mégane, likewise for three days. He said some good building land had come onto the market, but he didn't want to be spotted driving around to look at it in case he put the price up. He, too, left his car on the company car park.

He had plenty of time to get to Lower Mindle, since he'd been told not to arrive too early. He wasn't to phone ahead either. He felt wretched about leaving his quarry and his house behind. He'd often thought about turning Queen's evidence and making a fresh start away from Davis and the Slades, but he'd never followed it up. It was too late now, the die was cast, but it didn't stop him wishing bitterly he had. He'd made a point of leaving his book about the Thurstons in his safe. He didn't care about anything else in there - he'd be out of the country when it was turned out - but he positively wanted the book to be found so it could be admired by generations to come. He'd left a note to that effect addressed to Leicester's New Walk Museum. He'd left a generous cheque as well, just to make sure.

Around the time van Piet and Snape were arriving in Primrose Place, Davis was signing out a Skoda Octavia from The Rufus Car Mart on a three-day trial. On Tuesday she would drive to Brightlingsea in it, leaving her everyday smartphone wrapped up in her safe in Walsingham Close. If she noticed how angry Anita was behind her spray-on smile, she didn't show it. She was well into living her dream, but Anita wanted to leave England as little as Thurston did. The deal she'd been looking at Sunday would make her very rich, and it didn't help that Rufus seemed to be taking it all in his stride. It showed how useless he was, she thought. If she could get rid of him in Russia, she would. Perhaps she could denounce him or something, and he'd be shot. Things like that happened over there. She'd be driving home in a Ford Focus from stock - it had had a new clutch plate fitted, and she wanted to make sure it worked properly, or so she'd told her manager. Both the Rufuses would leave their everyday smartphones in the safe in their house, wrapped in foil like Davis's and Cottrell's. The Empress Matilda was fully fuelled – that happened every weekend anyway.

Kett drove to Chelmsford in his new Alfa. Like Davis, he was looking forward to going to Russia. He was bored in England, the work was too easy, and it was making his nerves twang living constantly in fear of arrest. The Russians had promised him an élite career in cyber-warfare if he ever left the UK, plus the pay and the perks that went with working for Putin's friends. Tuesday he had to be in London to begin with, but he had a lock-up garage in Bethnal Green, so he'd drive in first thing in his Alfa, see what was doing, tell everyone he was taking some work home and hit the road for Brightlingsea. He knew how long Highways England took to feed new registrations into its systems – too long for his Alfa to be picked up. Leaving it behind didn't bother him - he'd have a Daimler in Russia, it would be one of his perks. His briefcase was lined with a Faraday's cage. He'd lock his laptop and smartphone in it when he left London for good, and they could stay in there when he abandoned them and his Alfa.

Verity was badly on edge through the whole of Monday morning. She did her best to hide it, but it wouldn't go away. Her clients left her office feeling, as always, they'd found the money tree, but each time her door closed, she lowered her head to her desktop to ease the splitting headache she had. Lunch didn't help. Diary permitting, she liked to eat early, and on Mondays she lunched with two or three staffers on a rotating basis so she could keep in touch with them all. But today her appetite was nil, and she felt infinitely depressed discussing a future she knew wouldn't happen, since without her Esklivia would fold. When they got back from a restaurant in London Wall, she knew she couldn't hold out much longer. She saw the two clients who were still in her diary, e-mailed her senior managers with instructions for the following forty-eight hours, and that was it. She told her secretary she'd be spending the rest of the day at home with Miss Slade and all day Tuesday as well. Under no circumstances were they to be disturbed, they had a lot of fourth-quarter planning to get through. No, there was no need to ask Miss Slade to come up, she'd call into her office on her way out.

"Please don't mention what's in store for Miss Slade if you should happen to see her before I do," she added, placing her index finger on her lips. "What's in store for her is tedious beyond belief. I don't want her dismayed before she has to be."

Laura's office, like Verity's, gave onto Lombard Street, and when Verity knocked and opened the door without waiting, she saw the blinds were up and Laura was looking out without wanting to be seen from outside. She tried to hide what she'd been doing as Verity came in, but she wasn't fast enough. She looked terrified as she turned full-face towards her mother. For one alarming moment, Verity thought she must know she was going to be killed.

"Are you all right, Laura?" she asked, making her nervousness look like concern. "I seem to have made you jump."

Laura sort of laughed, but it sounded phoney.

"That's exactly what you did do. I've looked out of this window three or four times today because someone unpleasant seemed to be hanging around. But they're gone now."

Verity said she'd call HastaPrees, they'd soon sort that one out. What did this person look like?

"No, really, I don't think you should," Laura came back. "I could easily have been mistaken, and then we'd both look foolish. You know how restless I get when Millie isn't there. I didn't sleep at all last night, all on my own in the house, and now my tiredness is making me see things."

Verity didn't believe her, she thought Laura hadn't got over the previous Tuesday, but Laura's spying was something Verity wasn't even going to hint at. She gave Laura a hug and sneaked a look out of the window, but everything seemed normal. As she broke contact, she planted a mother's kiss on her forehead and told her she was to come back to The Lodge with her – yes, right now, why else was she standing in her office? She said Mr Chatsley had been phoning about the cremation, and there was still a lot of preparation to get through. Whatever Laura was doing, it could wait, her father's departure with dignity came first. As Verity spoke, she fingered a black choker she was wearing to make it clear she, for one, was still in mourning.

While Laura was putting her desk straight, Verity asked her how she'd come in to work. She replied she'd caught the underground in Theydon Bois, and she was expecting to go back the same way. But Verity had a better idea. She said it would be cooler and quicker to take a taxi, that's how she'd come in herself. Laura's car would be perfectly alright on Theydon Bois car park, her twelve-month permit would see to that. Laura wasn't persuaded, but she deferred to her mother because that's what she always did, and after one last look round, she said she was ready to go. Her eyes still showed fear, and her make-up only partly concealed the deep rings under her eyes. Esklivia's air conditioning kept her and Verity cool till the taxi was at the door. Then they were gone.

Chapter 29

At The Lodge

"I'm expecting Mr Thurston to come here before the day is out," Verity said as she used her everyday smartphone to unlock The Lodge's gates. She had no reason to stop using it yet. "That's why I'm leaving the gates open. And don't look like that when I mention his name. His contract comes up for renewal shortly, and I need to discuss it with him. There are some things in the gardeners' barn I want him to move as well. He can do that while he's here."

Verity had shut the cctv off as well. She'd made sure Laura hadn't seen her do it.

"I thought he was coming Wednesday," Laura said, making no attempt to hide her annoyance.

"So he is, but he happens to be in the area today, so it makes sense for him to call by this afternoon. I don't know what gets into you sometimes, Laura. We'll make a cup of tea for now and have something to eat when he's gone. Perhaps that will cheer you up."

Laura said she was sorry for being grumpy and left it at that. She seemed depressed and all fired up, both at the same time.

Slade's cremation papers were laid out on a coffee table in a small ground floor room called the patio room. It was in the angle where the main part of the house ended and the outhouse terrace jutted out from it. The patio door that went with the room's name opened onto the knot garden via a small paved area.

Laura couldn't really see the outhouses from where she elected to sit - just most of the knot garden plus the wall, the oak door, and the wing of the house at the other end of the garden that ran parallel to the outhouses. The air conditioning was on, but the room still smelled musty, despite a bowl of potpourri on a gate-leg table that was covered with a white linen cloth. A canvas bag containing wool and some knitting needles stood next to the chair Verity tended to use when she was in the room, and it made Laura smile wanly when she saw it. Her mother had knitted a lot while she'd been growing up, she'd said it reminded her of when they didn't have much money. Laura had no idea her mother still knitted, but it looked as if she must do. Perhaps she gave the things she made to charity, since – she glanced at her mother's perfectly cut peach dress and matching top - she never wore anything that looked hand-knitted now.

Outside, the afternoon was slipping into decline. The temperature was still high, but they were out of London now, and a breeze was springing up. Cloud was forming as well. When it parted, the sun made everything bright. When it re-formed, everything dimmed down.

Verity had brought two cups of tea with her on a tray, and she'd just opened a folder marked Invitations when the doorbell extension rang in the corridor.

"That will be Mr Thurston," she said, and she put the folder down. "Stay here, I'll go and open the door for him. He can have my cup of tea, I haven't touched it, then he can busy himself in the barn till I'm ready to speak to him. I'll fetch the key for him while I'm at it, and he can let himself in and out of the house through the side door. I'll unlock it with my smartphone for him."

She was talking too much, but Laura didn't seem to notice.

Thurston had exchanged his suit for a freshly laundered version of the off-white overalls he wore in his quarry. He'd shed his necktie as well. His Sig Sauer was in one of the pockets in his overalls, but they were baggy, so its shape didn't show.

"Laura's here," Verity said in a low voice as he came through the door. "Don't forget, I'll shoot her once to keep her still, then the second time, I'll have to shoot her through the head. It's the only way Watkins will believe she's dead."

"What about the cctv? We can't take any chances now."

"I switched it off before you arrived. All of it. And before I went to work this morning, I used nail varnish to blank out the cameras between where we're standing now and the room Laura's in. See for yourself."

The cameras were tiny, but he knew where they all were. He looked up at the one let into the ornate

306

door frame, and sure enough, the normally glassy pinpoint lens was just a dull blob.

Verity handed over the smartphone Watkins had given her, together with the piece of paper with the number on it. She'd kept them hidden in an ottoman by the shoe rack that was next to the front door. Her face was gaunt and her eyes were glittery. The only thing holding her together was the conviction she was doing the right thing.

"We'll do it straight away and get it over with," she said as she led the way into the house. "I'm glad you're staying the night. I'll go mad if I'm on my own knowing Laura's dead in the lake. I've made up a bed up for you in a room near mine, but don't get any ideas. You're here to do a job, and that's all."

Once they were in the patio room, Thurston tried to make small talk with Laura as he stood and drank his tea, but Laura stayed hunkered within herself, so he switched to chatting to Verity, who was also standing. Laura idly watched the garden brighten once more as the sunlight came through, but as Thurston put his empty cup down, she suddenly looked up, terrified, and made a dash for the corridor. Instinctively Thurston grabbed at her shoulder, but his hand slipped on the silk frock she was wearing, and she wriggled free, knocking the coffee table over in her panic. Reacting almost as quickly, Verity scrabbled an unsafed Smith and Wesson out of her knitting bag, followed Laura at speed into the corridor and shot her twice in the back. The noise made her ears ring, and Laura was thrown forward onto her face. Verity caught up with her and rolled her over. She was still conscious and in searing pain.

"Why did you run away, you silly girl?" Verity asked in a puzzled tone of voice, transferring her gun to her left hand and cradling her as best she could. It was something she had to know.

"Police," Laura managed to say. She was bleeding heavily, and bloodstained froth was dribbling from her mouth. Her blood was warm on Verity's arm and hand, but Verity let it be. "I ... police," Laura managed again, and then she passed out.

Thurston had joined them. He heard what she said.

"She must have got wind of something, she was going for the police," he surmised. "I'll drag her back into the room, the light's better there. I'll take the pictures while you finish her off."

He bent down to take hold of Laura's ankles, but Verity stopped him.

"How dare you, Neville!" she exclaimed. "Can't you see she's suffering? Take her by the shoulders and move her gently. I don't want her dress riding up either. It would disgust me."

He walked obediently past Laura's unconscious form, turned her round and pulled her back into the patio room, leaving a trail of blood on the carpet. He was careful not to get any on himself.

"Do you want her in a chair?" he asked as Verity followed them in.

"No, leave her on the floor, it'll be easier for her as well. Take one picture of her as she is now and another one afterwards, and make sure you get me in both of them. One of me as I fire would be best of all, but that's probably asking too much."

Thurston wiped the sweat from his hands on his overalls and took the first picture. Then he backed away from Laura in case any blood or bone splashed up, while Verity cleaned the palm of her gun hand on a tissue.

"Goodbye, my love," she said solemnly. "You'll always be in my heart."

The shot pierced Laura's head, and again the noise was immense in the confined space. Thurston took a final picture, he and Verity stood looking at each other, and the smell of spent ammunition took over from the potpourri. Verity forced back the anguish that was threatening to overwhelm her, and Thurston checked the pictures. He'd taken three in all, they'd come out well, and the second one had caught Verity pulling the trigger. He showed them to her without saying anything. She took the smartphone and Watkins's number from him, wrote, 'Deborah – as you can see, I've done as you asked – Verity,' and sent the message with the pictures attached.

"We'll put Laura in the lake now," she said, tearing up the piece of paper. She absolutely had to keep moving. "I must see her go before I do anything else, then I'll change out of these clothes and take a shower. Don't bother to clear up. We won't come into this part of the house again."

She was putting her gun and Watkins's smartphone into her knitting bag when they both heard a buzzing noise. It was Verity's emergency smartphone - it was in her handbag, which, like Laura's, was standing next to the potpourri. Verity's everyday smartphone was on the table as well, but it had a different buzz.

"Verity, it's Barbara," she heard. "Are you at home? And has Neville arrived yet?"

Verity said yes to both questions and raised the volume.

"I've just heard on the news," Davis continued. "Deborah Watkins is dead, she's been found murdered in London. Yes, murdered, and the police are saying she'd been dead for some time when they found her. I want Neville to bring you to Brightlingsea right now, we're all getting out as soon as we can. Are you listening, Verity? I must ask you both to hurry. And don't try to contact anyone else. Things will only get muddled if you do."

Davis terminated, and Thurston reacted fast.

"Rinse that blood off and get changed, Verity. I'll wait by the front door for you."

But Verity didn't move. She was staring at Laura's shot-up body, and her face was contorted with grief.

"We didn't need to kill her, Deborah was already dead," she wailed. She dropped her emergency smartphone and covered the sides of her head with her hands. "She could still be alive, Neville, it wouldn't have made any difference."

She fell to her knees, lifted Laura's hand against her cheek and howled as if all the anguish in the universe was inside her. Thurston shouted, "Come on, come on!" and tried to prise her fingers loose, but he only made her cling to Laura more obstinately.

"We could have worked out the other things between us, I know we could, my love," she wailed into Laura's senseless ear. In the shock of the moment, she believed it was true. She looked up at Thurston.

"It's your fault, all of it," she forced out between sobs. "If you hadn't opened your big mouth on Saturday, none of this would have happened."

So she knew about him and Watkins, and that had to mean Barbara knew as well. But Barbara hadn't cut him out of the escape – she wanted him to take Verity to Brightlingsea. He drew his arm back and slapped Verity hard across the head, knocking her off balance.

"Get up and get changed, you stupid cow!" he shouted at her, emphasising each word separately. "We've got to leave right now!"

She re-grasped Laura's hand and looked up at him like a volcano about to erupt, but before she could do anything, her everyday smartphone buzzed. Thurston shook his head: She wasn't to answer it. It buzzed a while longer, then it stopped.

"Say goodbye to Laura, then get moving," he ordered, not shouting any more, but still loud and forceful.

He wanted to kill her right there and take off, but he was firmly convinced, if he went to Brightlingsea without her, Davis would stop him boarding the Rufuses' yacht. He was part of Davis's organisation, but, he often felt, not as much as the others. He supposed it was because he worked with his hands.

Verity kissed Laura's fingers and whispered, "Goodbye, sweetheart. Your mother always loved you."

As she got to her feet, her everyday smartphone buzzed again.

"That's the second time, it must be important," she said, and she moved quickly to pick it up before

311

Thurston could stop her. She hoped it was Cottrell, she needed her support.

"Hullo?" she said, her voice rising. "Is that you, Millie?"

"Mrs Slade?" she heard. "This is Essex police. My name is Gulliver, and we've surrounded your house. Your cctv is under our control, and if you open it up on your smartphone, you can see for yourself that we're here. The pictures will come from us. We'll start them now."

Without breaking voice contact, Verity saw a marked car straddling the gateway, another one parked behind the garage block, and a third behind the gardeners' barn. She didn't see any personnel because she wasn't meant to – Gulliver needed to keep her guessing about numbers.

"I believe you," she said. "What do you want?"

"We want to ask you some questions. We know from your cctv that you, your daughter and Neville Thurston are in there, and that's all. We think you're in the small room between the main part of the house and the outhouses, the one with the patio door."

Verity asked why they thought that. It was a reflex response.

"When your cctv is switched on, there's a line from your front door to that room that doesn't show anything. We think you've blacked the cameras out, and where the line ends is where you are now. Can you confirm that, please? I should warn you, we're armed, and we're prepared to shoot if we have to."

Verity was calculating fast. Once again, she'd decoupled her mind from her emotions.

"Call me back in two minutes," she said. "I'll answer you then."

She terminated.

Thurston was learning the hard way what fear is like when its size is XXL. It was a new experience for him, and he was handling it badly.

"Some of them must be hiding behind the garden wall," he burst out, and a thought struck him. "I bet Laura saw them arrive. She said something about the police before she ran off."

But he couldn't explain why she'd done it.

Verity ran her gaze along the wall and saw the oak door move fractionally. They wouldn't have a clear view into the room from there, she reasoned, and they wouldn't have heard the shouting, maybe not even the gunshots. Not that it mattered – she was still trapped.

She reached her decision what to do. It would take all her cunning, but she knew Thurston well enough to believe she could manage it.

"We'll fight our way out," she said without a hint of doubt in her voice. "If we kill one, the rest will back off. We may even be able to take a hostage."

Thurston's reaction was instant.

"You're mad," he protested. "There must be hundreds of them. The first shot we fire, they'll be after us like hornets."

So he was thinking negatively. Good. She doubled down.

"So what do we do instead? Invite them in for tea? We can't make a run for it, we're completely surrounded, so either we fight our way out or we lose." She touched his arm. "If you can think of a third way, you're smarter than I am."

313

She paused to let it sink in.

"Perhaps I am," went through his mind. "You've done my thinking for me for too long."

He pulled his Sig Sauer out of his pocket and unsafed it. Pointing it at her and reaching into her knitting bag, he helped himself to her Smith and Wesson and Watkins's smartphone. They went into his pockets. Then he jerked the white cloth off the gate-leg table, making the potpourri and the two handbags fall heavily onto the carpet.

"I'm going to talk to them," he said, and he sounded bizarrely triumphant. "On my own, that is. I'm going to turn Queen's evidence. I've often thought about it, and now I'm going to do it. I know a lot of things they'll be interested in."

"I really believe you will," she snapped back in best bad loser mode. "A broken-backed rat like you, what else can you do? But at least you won't shoot me, that would ruin everything for you. Not that I imagine you would, you haven't got the nerve. You like women, but you're afraid of us. That's why you've never married."

That hurt a lot. He had to get away from her, or he'd kill her and ruin everything, just as she'd said. He snatched her everyday smartphone to open the patio door with, but instead of backing off, she remained stubbornly where she was.

"Give it back," she said, holding out her hand. "They'll come pouring in if they hear a different voice, and then where will you be?"

She was right, he believed, and it was like salt on an open wound, but he shoved it into her hand. As he did so, it buzzed, and Verity took the call. It was Gulliver again. Did Mrs Slade have an answer yet?

314

"Your deduction was correct, we're in the room with the patio door, and we know where some of you are as well," she said, entirely matter-of-fact. "Mr Thurston is coming out to talk to you. I'm unlocking the door for him now, and Miss Slade and I will stay here till you're finished with him. Mr Thurston will walk along the outhouse terrace and then along the wall to where you are. That way you can see him coming without having to open the door in the wall too far."

She terminated and looked at Thurston as if their spat had never been.

"I'm sorry, Neville, I was completely in the wrong," she said, oozing fondness and concern. "Of course you must talk to them, it's your only chance, and go the way I said, it's what they're expecting. Don't worry about me, I'm finished anyway. Tell them if they want me, they'll have to come and fetch me. Tell them Laura is dead as well, and I did it. That way, you'll look better by contrast."

The patio door clicked as she unlocked it, and Thurston stepped outside. The sun had gone in again, but he still blinked in the extra light. Looking towards the oak door, he held his Sig Sauer up high and dropped it conspicuously onto the knot garden. The Smith and Wesson went the same way. Then he raised both hands and waved the white cloth like a flag of truce, while behind him Verity gently closed the patio door. Gulliver watched him through the slightly open oak door, talking softly all the while into her radio microphone. As he drew level with the boulting house, she suddenly heard through her earpiece,

"Sal! Get yourself and everyone else behind the wing of the house! Run, run, run!"

315

Gulliver had five of her team spread out behind the wall, waiting for the word to climb over. Thankful she had grass underfoot, she raced silently to the first one, whispered into his ear what he had to do and pushed him hard on his way. The rest saw what she'd done, she beckoned them frantically to follow, and she went last. Within seconds the back of the wall was clear.

As she moved away, light appeared in the slightly open doorway where she'd been. She knew it would happen, but she hadn't wanted Thurston to see the door close in case he thought it was being shut in his face. Nevertheless, the sudden light made him stop to think what to do next. Perhaps he could make out what was going on if he stood a little higher. Taking care not to lower his hands, he made his way backwards up the three steps in front of the boulting house door. The door was let into an archway, and seeing him support himself against it while he stood on tiptoe, Verity, who had merely been waiting for him to get close to the boulting house, gratefully noted the extra he'd supplied. She operated the electric door opener with her smartphone, the door swung inwards, and as he teetered backwards, she activated the detonator, causing the incendiaries and the dynamite he'd installed to go off in a pre-programmed sequence. The incendiaries in the downstairs ceiling cindered everything upstairs in an upsurge of flame reaching 4000F; the incendiaries under the downstairs floorboards engulfed the two computers plus the debris falling from upstairs; and the dynamited walls crashed down to smash anything that was left. A descending clump of bricks pinned Thurston down while, fully conscious, he burned alive. The adjacent outhouse was ripped open, and sparks roiling up from the boulting house ignited its tinder-dry roof timbers. The breeze ensured the fire took hold and spread quickly.

Behind the patio door, which had taken a volley of brick fragments without cracking, Verity felt she'd got it all right. She'd destroyed everything in the boulting house – that had been her duty. She'd punished Thurston for causing Laura's death - that was her personal revenge. And by letting Thurston keep Watkins's smartphone, she'd made life just a little harder for the police. Now she had to warn Davis and the others what had happened. She picked up her emergency smartphone and tried it, but it was blocked, so she let it fall again. She tried her everyday smartphone, but it was blocked as well. So was the landline extension that stood on a shelf in one corner, and so was Laura's smartphone when she tried it. She was completely cut off. It was time to take the last step available to her. She'd give herself up and face the law with pride. It could take away her freedom and it would. But it couldn't deny she'd always been in the right.

Chapter 30

The Renault Mégane

Too far away to be noticed, van Piet and Snape had been watching Thurston's bid for a deal from a converted Sikorsky Executive S92 helicopter. The SRO had bought it fifth hand three years before and had had it re-fitted as an operations support aircraft. On the ground, ambulances and fire engines were converging on The Lodge, road blocks were going up along the county's land boundary, a forensic pathologist on his first full day back from the Caribbean was on his way in from Chelmsford, and three hearses were on the move from Co-op Funeralcare in Harlow. DI Parnaby would take charge of the site when Snape gave the word. Snape was convinced Davis had murdered Hayward, so he had no qualms about taking Parnaby off the Five Willows hunt. Putting a detective inspector in charge of a large operation was no problem for him. He routinely trained people above their rank and promoted them when the money was there.

"What made you pull the alarm on Sal?" van Piet asked him, as one of the TAs he'd brought from

Ashell House put a person-to-person print-out into his hands.

"Thurston's overalls. They reminded me he'd said he kept explosives on site. You don't take chances with people like that."

"Sharp call, Eddie, I'd have missed it."

He speed-read the print-out - it was from Kossler – and passed it over. Radio Moscow had interrupted a scheduled programme to put out more page and line numbers, but Kossler still couldn't say what they meant. Also: An encrypted signal had been sent from a smartphone in The Lodge to a smartphone in Primrose Place, Paddington. Both smartphones – possibly stolen - were old technology, and decryption looked problem free. Someone hadn't been so clever after all.

"Those broadcasts," Snape said, handing the print-out back. "It'd be nice if they actually told us something."

Van Piet didn't reply straight away – he was studying the fire billowing up from the outhouses.

"I'm inclined to be grateful for them," he said finally. "We might not know what they say, but where they come from and when they're put out confirm it's the Russians we're up against. They also tie in with Cottrell's old radios."

"How so?"

"Old radios had short wave as standard, so they're ideal for Radio Moscow." He went back to studying the burning outhouses, then he said, "I wonder if Laura and Verity Slade have left that corner room yet."

"We can lift the blockade and phone in."

"I'd rather someone took a look. Sal reported some shots, don't forget. Wait a minute, someone's coming out."

A screen showed the patio room as seen from the Sikorsky's underside camera pod, and Verity was emerging with her hands up. She made no attempt to move towards the Smith and Wesson or the Sig Sauer, though she knew where both of them were, and she left the patio door open, as if closing it didn't matter any more. The fire was making a roaring noise, but as soon as she became aware of the Sikorsky, she guessed it was the police and raised her hands further. Van Piet zoomed in on her. The blood on her dress and top had gone dull, but it was obvious what it was. It was on her skin as well. Van Piet gave a quick nod, and Snape told Gulliver to bring her in, since that seemed to be what she wanted.

"Call to her from across the knot garden first – it might be a trap," he warned. "And route her away from the blaze. One thing first, though, and I'll make it quick."

He brought up a plan of The Lodge on his smartphone and told Gulliver to do the same.

"That side door near what's marked as a barn," he said. "Get some people into the house through there. Laura Slade's still missing, and that's all we know. She may be armed, so be careful, and don't take longer than you have to. That fire's hungry."

While Snape was talking, van Piet was telling the pilot to land near the wall, but to leave enough room for Fire and Rescue. As soon as they touched down, he sent everyone out, including the flight crew - he had some calls to make that mustn't be overheard. When he finally emerged from the

Sikorsky, he had a small metal box in his hand. He waved Snape over.

"Did an unmarked car come in with Armed Support? That's what usually happens, isn't it?"

Snape said there was one, and van Piet asked him to get the driver to him. He had a job for him.

"And ask Leicestershire Police to seal off Thurston's house. Tell them not to go in, just make sure no one else does. Same with his quarry. If they argue, say it's Crown warrant. We'll get back to them when we know what we want to do there."

Gulliver put Verity under armed guard, formally detained her for questioning and had her escorted out of the garden. Armed Support found Laura's body, and because of the fire, Snape had it photographed where it was, then brought out on a rug and placed behind the garden wall not far from where Verity was standing. Verity deliberately turned her back. Snape felt he ought to cover the body, but he had to accept Forensics would want it as it was. The Smith and Wesson and the Sig Sauer went into evidence bags, along with everything Armed Support had scooped up in the patio room. The officers who'd moved Laura's body were sent to the Sikorsky. There was some bottled water in there they could clean their hands with. No one was to go into the house from now on.

Van Piet was standing a little way off. He caught Snape's attention, and when they'd finished talking, they walked over to Verity.

"I'm going to ask a colleague to take over from me now," Snape told her, "but as you can see, there's a lot going on, and I'm staying on site till I'm sure he's got everything under control. I also need to free up a car for you, and that could take time, so I suggest we wait in that hut of yours by the lakeside. It'll be less public for you than standing out here. Cooler as well, I should think."

Verity said that was just fine – the hut was never locked in summer, because there was nothing worth stealing in it, and there were some chairs inside they could sit down on. She made no objection to van Piet coming with them. She was past believing van Piet was just a banker, but whatever he was, she felt strong enough to take them both on. Snape asked Verity's escort to take her to the hut while he did some phoning about the hand-over. He and van Piet would join them as soon as they could. He stepped away and contacted Parnaby.

While van Piet was waiting for him, Gulliver rested her carbine on the ground and told him the car Thurston had arrived in was hired. Chelmsford had checked the registration, and she'd got the call-back instead of Snape, because he seemed to be permanently on the phone. Van Piet was only half-listening. More out of politeness than anything, he said he'd have been surprised if it hadn't been hired, but as he spoke, the penny dropped. PC Massie had found some fibres near Hayward's cottage that could be linked to the overalls Thurston used in his quarry, but no one had explained how the fibres had got there.

"What's the registration and the hire company?" he asked.

Gulliver contacted Chelmsford, wrote the answers down on a pad, and van Piet routed them on to Garry.

"Ask Mr Kossler to go into the company's computer," he told him. "I want to know when else Thurston has hired a car from there. Get back to me as soon as you can."

He switched back to Gulliver, who was feeling the heat in her body armour.

"Stand down for now, Sal, and get a drink from the helicopter. You'll be on the move again shortly, so get as much rest as you can."

Snape and van Piet were on the point of entering the lakeside hut when the same TA as before came running from the Sikorsky and handed van Piet some print-outs in an envelope. He took a good look at them, showed them to Snape, then put them away again.

"Not much doubt there," Snape grunted. "If I can, I'll fit them in."

As he'd guessed, the air inside was cool. To the left of the doorway were trestles for standing the rowing boat on, and above them were brackets for the oars. Further along were more brackets for a pair of kayaks and their paddles, and at the back were clothes cupboards, shelves with folded towels on them and some deck chairs, all neatly folded and standing upright. The corner to the right housed a toilet and a shower, then came a mini-kitchen with a fridge, followed by four canvas director chairs round a low table. The flooring was wooden boards, and the matting on it, which was freshly laid, smelled of fibre. Verity had already sat down, but the two Armed Support officers with her were on their feet, their fingers on the triggers of their carbines. Snape asked them to wait outside till their relief came and shut the door. Four lilac monogrammed bathrobes were hanging in a row on the back of it. He found one with Verity's initials on it and asked if she'd like to cover up her dress with it – she couldn't go back to the house to change because of the fire. At first she said no, then she appeared to change her mind and slipped it on. That made it her decision.

"There's some spring water in the fridge," she said. "Glasses are in the cupboard above the sink. Mr van Piet can have some too."

Over the glasses of water, Snape became his amiable best. She wasn't charged with anything yet, he told Verity, but did she realise it was only a matter of time before she was? She said she did, and she'd answer her accusers in court. She'd done nothing to be ashamed of.

"What puzzles me," Snape persisted, "is that your own family's involved so much. Your husband for a start."

Her grip tightened on her glass.

"He died in a motor accident. He was driving a car he couldn't handle."

"I'm sure you're right, but there are accidents and accidents, and we're still treating this one as unexplained."

"That's your decision, Mr Snape, but I was at home at the time, remember, so you know more about it than I do. I'm not afraid of your questions, but if you don't mind, I'd rather not talk about my husband. His death caused me immense distress, and it still does."

Snape took the envelope from van Piet.

"Then I'll talk about your daughter, if I may. She was shot and killed this afternoon, and we believe you fired the gun. Are we wrong there as well?"

She said she wouldn't answer without legal advice, and Snape said that was fair enough, he'd probably say the same. Nevertheless, he opened the envelope and laid out the print-outs.

"Can I ask you to look at these, though?" he asked blandly. "They reached me literally moments ago. This first one shows Miss Slade before she was shot through the head, this one shows her afterwards, and this one shows you firing the gun. You're in all three pictures, Mrs Slade, and the message sent with them ends with your name."

Verity forced herself to look at them. Pain distorted her features, then she brought them under control again.

"You have the advantage of me," she said, doing her best to remain composed, "so I'll say this by way of reply. Because of the cause I believe in, I've broken the law in certain ways. My daughter knew nothing about it, because I didn't want her to. She was an open-hearted, innocent child, and it was not in her nature to do anything wrong at all. You may find this strange, but her innocence made me love her even more than I would have loved her anyway, if that was possible. No mother loved her daughter more."

"If I may ask you, Mrs Slade," van Piet put in, "why does your message say, 'I've done as you asked'? Were you compelled to shoot your daughter?"

She shut her eyes and shook her head.

"Please, Mr van Piet," she replied. "I've said no mother loved her daughter more, and I meant it. I beg of you, let that be enough."

Snape put the print-outs away and began a new tack.

"Those pictures, they were sent from here to a smartphone that's been found in a flat in Paddington. That makes the Deborah in your message Deborah Watkins. You obviously know her, you're on first name terms with her."

Verity conceded their paths had crossed.

"Did you know she's been murdered?"

Verity hesitated. If she said yes, she'd have to invent how she knew and why, and she didn't think she could do it without entrapping herself.

"No, you take me by surprise. Do you know who did it?"

Snape's expression didn't change.

"The Met is handling the investigation," he began, "but as you can imagine, the Met and Essex Police talk to each other. Miss Watkins was a journalist who specialised in undercover work, and her entire Paddington flat was wired for sound and vision. She received someone by arrangement at 7.00 yesterday evening, and it seems she was expecting trouble, since she pre-set both systems to run for a full three hours, presumably as a precaution. She also shut her windows. In the event, there was a lot of shouting, including in the entrance hall, but no physical harm was done, and she would probably have switched her systems off when her visitor departed, if she'd been left to her own devices. But just as she was opening her windows again, the doorbell sounded, and she let in someone else who'd possibly heard the shouting through the door and knew when not to press the bell push. That person was Miss Watkins's murderer, and they knew each other. Do you want me to go on, Mrs Slade?"

Verity looked surprised.

"Yes, of course. Why shouldn't I?"

"Very well. Earlier in the evening this person had rung another number Miss Watkins had – a Kensington landline number. The call was made from a payphone on a London railway station, and when there was no answer, that same person went to a payphone on a different station, tried the Paddington number, which was also a landline one, and hung up when Miss Watkins said, 'Hullo'. So this person had both numbers and now knew which address to go to. That was clever, but what was not so clever was to overlook the fact that payphones on London railway stations have video surveillance these days. Or perhaps this person didn't think it mattered. With help from various people, we've worked backwards from Miss Watkins's two phones, so we know who made the calls. It was Laura, your daughter. And it was Laura who murdered Miss Watkins. It's recorded in detail, and she brought her weapon with her."

Verity was shaken rigid.

"Did Laura know she was being recorded?" she asked, struggling to absorb what Snape had said.

"In the excerpts played to me, she doesn't behave as if she did. My impression was, it wasn't part of her thinking she might be. Perhaps she was hyper-focused, that can happen sometimes. She also left her weapon behind, which is definitely unusual. She just stood up, looked hard at Miss Watkins's body, and let herself out of the flat. She didn't even close the windows."

"That was her innocence, Mr Snape, if what you say is correct. When did you get these excerpts, as you call them?"

"After one of my colleagues reported hearing shots from your house. A lot was happening at once, so excerpts were all I had time for."

"And the murder took place last night."

"It did."

So that was why Laura had been jumpy, going back to when she'd been in Esklivia House. Tired too. She'd killed Watkins, but she hadn't been able to control her fear of being caught. She must have seen some of Snape's police from the patio room and thought they'd come for her. If only she could see her mother now. That would teach her how to take the police on.

Van Piet signalled he'd like to ask something else.

"Can you explain why your daughter should want to kill Deborah Watkins, Mrs Slade? I ought to add, when we came to your house on August 10th, she said something intriguing as she showed us out, and Mr Snape noted it down. Mr Snape?"

Snape took his notebook out of his jacket pocket and leafed through it till he found the page.

"She said, 'I loved my father more deeply than you can imagine. If anyone has harmed him, I want that person destroyed.' I wrote it down from memory, but I'd answer for it in court, and Mr van Piet heard it too. She definitely said, 'destroyed'."

Verity didn't reply. She was recalling Thurston seeing Laura in her bedroom, Laura lying about going to a concert in order to spy on her, and Laura being talked to by Watkins in Colchester. So that was how it was! Watkins had told Laura she knew who had murdered her father, and Laura had worked out or found out that if Watkins were killed, the truth would come out, because Watkins had set things up that

328

way. One by one, Verity worked in silence through the implications of all she'd heard in the hut, sensing van Piet had already done the same. When she'd finished, she drained her glass and said, quietly but firmly,

"I won't answer your question, Mr van Piet. In fact I don't want to answer any more questions at all. Whatever happens to me now, it can't be as bad as this."

Snape put his notebook in his pocket, took out his smartphone and asked Parnaby to come to the hut by the lake. When he arrived, Snape formally arrested Verity for the murder of Laura Slade, cautioned her, and told her her rights, adding that other charges were in preparation. The Armed Support officers outside had been replaced, and it was two unarmed colleagues – one male, one female – who, followed by Parnaby, led Verity away in handcuffs to a police car waiting on the drive. She still had her daughter's blood on her skin and clothes – Snape, with Forensics in mind, had seen to that – and although she was wearing a bathrobe, she carried herself with something close to dignity.

Snape and van Piet watched her go from the doorway.

"Well, it went pretty much according to the script," Snape remarked. "Perhaps now you can tell me why we did it."

"Verity Slade is smart enough to grow rich without any help from the Russians, so if she's working for them, it's because she wants to. That indicates she's some kind of ideologue."

329

"She said as much in the hut just now when she was blithering about the cause she believed in."

"Exactly, and the trouble with ideologues is, they wrap themselves in their beliefs so tightly, you can't get anything out of them. On the other hand, Verity showed some normal human feelings when we interviewed her in The Lodge, and I figured if we could play on those, her beliefs might begin to waver. There's still some way to go, but if we can press her some more and get her to talk freely, most of our problems will be solved. And I've got an idea how to do it."

Snape felt he ought to take a last look round the site. The background noise had been rising while they'd been in the hut, and now they could see why. A police helicopter was on station over The Lodge, and the drive and the outer part of the forecourt were filled with police cars, a police bus, a fire chief's mobile control vehicle, and an incident caravan with its own power generator. Fire appliances were in position behind the garden wall, and the oak door was blocked open to let firefighters and their hoses through. Laura's body still lay where Armed Support had set it down. Someone had put screens round it, an unarmed police officer was guarding it, and the firefighters, who knew what was there, were taking care to keep clear of it.

Snape and van Piet picked their way through the doorway into the garden, and that was as far as they got. It had become a mud bath, with grit and fragments of bricks trampled into it, and there was no paved path across it. Snape, who was a keen gardener when he had the time, instinctively thought it should have been divided into four and suspected the Slades had had it laid out in one piece to make it

330

look grander - in their own eyes if in no one else's. The gardeners must have used duckboards to tend it, there was no other way. Now it was just a mess, and beyond it, the outhouses were an inferno. Firefighters were jetting water in through doorways and window hollows, and from behind the terrace, a firefighter on a turntable ladder was directing water into the open roof. But it was a losing battle. Flames were encroaching on the patio room, and more firefighters were setting up hose lines to tackle them. A lot of smoke was being generated, and it was causing problems of its own. The breeze was swirling it away, then swinging round to drive it over the garden. Dry heat came with it, and each time it happened, it became difficult to breathe.

Nearer the boulting house, the grit and brick fragments were thicker on the ground. What was left of it was buried in foam, bits of which were blowing away. Standing separate from the other firefighters and talking into her radio was someone Snape recognised. It was Wendy Pollard. When she saw him, she gave him a wave and trudged over to him, keeping her eye on what was happening all the while.

"We were told it was a scene of crime" she said, raising her voice above the noise and nodding towards where the boulting house had stood, "so we used foam instead of water to protect it better. The casualty's still underneath it. We could never have saved him, he was burned up when we got here. A load of bricks fell on him and the fire did the rest."

She broke off to answer her radio.

"Sorry," she said, her attention back on the fire. "I'm doing blaze assessments for the Chief. I can talk to you later if you like, but not now, unless I really have to."

Snape said later would do, and she went back to where she'd been.

"These Slades, they had it all, and now look," he said. He and van Piet were back on the other side of the wall. "All they had to do was keep their noses clean."

He shook his head wonderingly as he spoke. Van Piet shrugged his shoulders.

"No sacrifice too great, Eddie, that was Verity Slade. Her house, her family, you name it. The cause topped them all."

They were between the fire appliances and the Sikorsky when van Piet's mobile buzzed. Attached to a text from Garry was a spreadsheet of all the times Thurston had hired a car from the company the Renault Mégane came from. It turned out he'd done a lot of hiring. The mileage totals varied, but so many of them equalled round trips to Lower Mindle, van Piet thought they couldn't all be coincidence. He concluded Thurston hadn't always wanted to be noticed when he came to The Lodge, and Garry had concluded the same, since along one edge of the spreadsheet, he'd collated Slade's trips abroad as registered by Border Force, and more often than not, Thurston had hired a car when Slade had been out of the country.

Three hirings stood out as van Piet scrolled through the data. They were each for two or three days, and they covered the dates of the deaths of Ashley Johnson, Geoffrey Slade and Stephanie Hayward. The mileages fitted as well. He showed them to Snape, then contacted Garry. He knew now what he wanted done in Leicestershire.

"I want Thurston's house searched, and it has to be us who do it," he said. "The house may be booby-trapped, so Safety and Sabotage will have to go in first. Ask Mr Benjamin to give them the word. When the searchers go in, you'll go in with them, but I don't want anyone searching before – let me think - 10.00 tonight. That's important. I'll be controlling the search remotely, because I know what I'm looking for, but I'm likely to be tied up till then. Is Mr Benjamin still in the building?"

"He's said he's staying till you finish, Sir. What about transport?"

"You'll need a helicopter to get there. Ask him to help you book it in case someone else wants one at the same time. And one more thing. Thurston said he'd let the trees round his house grow tall, so everyone and everything will probably have to be winched in and out. Be ready for that. Leicestershire Police are guarding the house, but they're under orders not to go in. I'll ask Mr Snape to let them know you're coming."

He terminated, looked at his watch and turned back to Snape, who'd been listening in and who nodded assent to the last bit.

"I'll brief Sal next, and then it's our turn to move on," van Piet said.

Snape asked him where they were going.

"Back to London," he replied as if it was obvious. "We've got a lot to get through before ten o'clock. The sooner we start, the better."

Chapter 31

Breaches of trust

Anita collected Rufus in the Ford Focus. They threw as much as they could into two rucksacks, then they locked up their house for good and drove to The Ship's Log. Phillips-Smith was near the gate when Rufus opened it with his card. They were surprised to see him, since Monday was his day off. He hadn't been there long, he said, but he had a job to do, so he thought he'd come in and get it out of the way.

"How about you?" he asked. "Going out anywhere?"

Rufus said they were taking some guests out for an after-dark run. They'd be getting back around midnight.

"Should be fun. You'll have a Force Two to Three from the east veering to south, so watch out for mist and fog. And can you let your guests in yourself, please? Staff's thin on the ground today."

Anita parked on the visitors' car park – she didn't want any of the members to see her with a Ford Focus - and they made their way to The

Empress Matilda. They had no idea where they were sailing to. Davis would tell them when she arrived.

That was later than they expected. They were killing time on the afterdeck, when Rufus's emergency smartphone buzzed, and he took the call in the cockpit so as not to be overheard. It was Davis, she was waiting for the gate to be opened. Anita said she'd do it, she couldn't sit still any longer, and with her Skoda parked well away from the Ford, Davis was soon on the yacht. She'd brought her things in a rucksack too, and when they went down to the master cabin, it struck Anita Davis seemed to know her way around. Davis apologised at length for being late, but she'd been sorting out their new rendezvous.

"The Elena Andropova can't get anywhere near us in time," she explained, taking a folded sheet of A4 out of her rucksack, "but a Russian freighter that was on its way south is turning round to pick us up here – " she showed Rufus the co-ordinates – "at 20.45 on the dot. That suits us fine. Sunset's at 20.19, so no one will see what we're up to."

She made it sound like a dormitory jape.

Rufus pulled out a chart from one of the overhead lockers. Paper was safer than electronics, he said, and anyway, he'd learned on charts. He soon found the rendezvous. It was east by south from Brightlingsea and just into international waters. His tides timetable told him the tide would be on the ebb.

He ran his eye down the A4.

"AIS to be on," he read out. "The freighter will signal contact with her lights, and we're to use the pilot's ladder on the port side – it's the only ladder on that side, so we can't go wrong there. She's called Irinushka 052, and – well done, Barbara - you've printed the name in Russian letters so we can read it when we see her. You say she was taking sawn timber to Morocco before the change of plan. What was she bringing back - camel dung?"

He looked round with a big grin on his face, expecting the others to join in the joke.

"Do you have to clown around all the time, Derek? You really get on my nerves sometimes."

It was Anita - seeing Rufus and Davis looking full of themselves was getting to her. Rufus said he was sorry and patted her arm. She wiped her hand across where he'd touched her.

"What's her excuse for turning round?" she asked, still as prickly as cactus. "Freighters don't just turn round in mid-ocean."

"An owners' recall," Davis replied brightly. "The captain's reported an engine bearing is running hot."

"There you are, Anita," Rufus chipped in. "Just another Russian rust bucket falling apart." Then his tone changed. "What about our yacht, Barbara? What's the plan for her?"

He had to ask before Anita did. He could guess what the answer would be.

"They'll sink her with their grabs, Derek. What else can they do? They can't leave her floating around, can they?"

Anita covered her mouth in horror and bottled up her anger some more. In the fraught silence that followed, Davis wondered if they had any spare waterproofs for her for when they were at sea. Rufus asked Anita to find her some – and some thermals as well - while he set the cockpit up, and as Anita and Davis moved about the boat, Anita again got the feeling Davis knew her way around.

When Kett arrived, Davis went with Rufus to let him in, since Rufus didn't know him by sight. Team meetings in The Lodge referred to him as 'our agent', and he never turned up in person.

"I've come without any luggage, would you believe?" he prattled affably as they were walking along the boardwalk. "It's all been a bit of a rush."

But once they were on The Empress Matilda, his mood darkened. There was something they had to talk through.

"I heard it on the car radio," he began. They were in the master cabin with the door shut. "There's been an explosion at The Lodge, and the whole place has gone up in flames. The police are saying two people are dead, but they haven't named them yet, and they've taken Verity to Chelmsford in handcuffs."

No one spoke at first. They'd all missed it, and when Davis said it must be Neville and Laura who were dead, no one asked how she knew. Kett thought Verity might give them all away, but Davis said he was wrong there. Verity was stronger than any of them. The yacht was bobbing gently, and through the portholes they could see people moving about. It was like looking into another world.

"What about Millie?" Rufus asked Davis. "Have you contacted her?"

"I have, and she's got her own plan," she replied. "When we see her in Russia, she can tell us how it went."

She had to stop them brooding, so she asked whether they could get some food and maybe start out after they'd eaten it. Anita said she'd get some from the clubhouse, but she wanted to look at the TV first, there might be something about the fire on it.

Rufus zapped it on, riffed through the channels and put the sound on low when BBC Essex came up. It was still broadcasting live from near The Lodge. Much of the house was gutted, neighbouring homes had been evacuated, and the cause of the explosion was under investigation. They sucked it all in till they were sure they'd absorbed every detail, then Kett said what they wanted someone to say: The police weren't looking beyond Lower Mindle.

That lowered their anxiety, and a kind of euphoria took its place. Even Anita felt more positive as she passed a printed menu round to find out who wanted what. After they'd eaten, however, she quietly transferred a loaded Beretta 92 from her rucksack to a pocket in her waterproofs. Better safe than sorry.

They slipped on their buoyancy aids, cast off, and manoeuvred away from their mooring. Some of the other yachts had their cabin lights on, people were eating and laughing on deck, and a cheerful hubbub was coming from the clubhouse, which had its windows wide open. Once they rounded Colne Point and entered the North Sea, however, the air freshened and portents of night-time marked the sky. The wind across the tide was causing a swell, and there were clear traces of sea mist about.

Rufus was in the cockpit. He could feel as much as hear the twin Volvo diesels, and the yacht's wake was signalling they were seriously on the move. There was the usual clutter of traffic on the radar, and a wide-reaching southerly arc looked the best way to get through it. He copied the Russian-alphabet version of Irinushka 052 onto an electronic notepad in the bulkhead so anyone could see it when the time came. They were all wearing thermals and waterproofs, and in the lee of the open-backed cabin Kett was sitting between Davis and Anita on a padded bench that was bolted to the deck. Kett was doing most of the talking. He felt he had nothing to hide now, and he liked being the centre of attention, so in his detached and donnish way he chattered through his time at Oxford, how Cottrell had worked her charms, and how he'd been helping the Russians ever since.

"All for money, of course," he laughed. "I leave the politics to Barbara here, she's much better at them than I am. Verity, too, poor dear. They put me to shame, both of them."

Thickening mist was making the afterdeck chilly and wet, and Kett, Davis and Anita had moved into the cabin. Rufus locked the rudder, swung round in his captain's chair and called for someone to get him a coffee from the galley. Davis said she'd do it. She asked if anyone else wanted one, and went below deck to make four. She re-emerged with them in a plastic mini-crate, and after she'd handed Anita and Kett theirs, she moved on to give Rufus his. Anita was stirring cream in when something made her look towards the cockpit, and she was certain she saw Davis brush-kiss Rufus as she reached his coffee into a holder fixed to the bulkhead. So that was why she seemed to know her way around! She'd been on board when Anita hadn't been there! Anita's anger flared up, jealousy, too, but she couldn't see what she'd gain by shouting, so, with even more effort, she bottled her temper up yet again.

She was nearly through her coffee when she felt the yacht slowing right down, and she heard Rufus call out,

"Anita! Come here, can you?"

There was tension in his voice. The remains of her coffee went over the side, and she moved swiftly alongside him.

The mist was becoming fog, and it was blanketing itself round the windscreen. The wipers weren't achieving much, nor were the yacht's forward lights. But none of that was what was bothering Rufus.

"We're on schedule, and we're pretty much on course," he said, nodding towards the automatic course setter. "But take a look at the radar."

All Anita saw at first was the usual splurge of dots as the two-second pulses of the high output antenna were reflected back and converted into points on the screen. But then she, too, saw the problem. One of the dots had an afterglow – it meant one of the boats out there was going fast. She called up the pop-up to take a better look.

"She's doing 16 knots in this weather," she read off. "Anything to do with us, do you think?"

"Could be. She's in a hurry, that's for sure."

"So what are you going to do?"

"Assume it's the police, I can't do anything else. And if they're on our radar, you can bet we're on theirs."

Anita didn't like that at all.

"How are you going to get us out of this?" she fired at him. "Come on, genius, don't keep it to yourself."

Irritably he told her to get off his back and pointed towards the screen.

340

"Look at where the dots are instead of grizzling all the while. We've got something big and slow-moving to starboard – my guess is it's a container ship coming up from the Thames. I'll tuck into her radar shadow, that'll wipe us off the fast boat's screen. Then I'll move from radar shadow to radar shadow till we can make a dash for the rendezvous. The fast boat won't have seen us get that far, so she'll have no idea it's us when we go. Here, work it out for yourself, Dumbo. It's all right in front of you."

Anita shook her head.

"It won't work, Derek. If it's the police, they'll be asking everyone if we're near them. We'll be lined up before we get there, and they'll take us when they like."

"They can ask as much as they like, there are umpteen languages out there, and there's a whole load of traffic swirling about in the fog. They'll never pick us out. Tell Barbara and Jesse to hold tight. I'm going to go dark."

While Anita called back into the cabin, Rufus switched off all his lights, including his navs. His AIS, his anti-theft tracker and his VHF radio went off as well, and he put his course setter into receive-only mode. As he moved through the fog towards the big ship, it sounded its foghorn in great warning blasts, but he ignored it. His radar told him he had enough room, and when the fog thinned for a moment, he could see he'd guessed right. It was a Chinese container ship, and its massive size meant the fast boat couldn't pick up the yacht's radar signals or ping the yacht with its own. After a glance at his chronometer, he adapted his speed and direction to the container ship's. Problem solved, he told himself, and mentally gave himself a gold star.

341

Patience, patience - he needed a lot of it. The fog was thick again, and in The Empress Matilda's cabin no one was saying anything. The container ship had kept its foghorn going, and other vessels were deploying theirs. Some were close, others were further away, and they filled the sodden air with lingering wails of despair. Finally Rufus judged he'd done enough waiting. He arc-ed away in reverse, crossed the container ship's wake once its propellers had thrummed clear, and moved into the next radar shadow. It was a nerve-racking game. He didn't have infra-red cameras on board, and away from his radar, visibility was virtually nil. If he went too fast, he might hit something. But if he slowed down too much, he'd miss the rendezvous.

Sea mists and fogs form when the wind passes over warmer water way out to sea and then over cooler water inshore. Rufus had sailed for too long not to know that, which meant he also knew the further he got from land, the sooner he'd reach clear air.

When he did, it was a complete break, and suddenly he could see navigation lights sprinkled everywhere. A grain carrier sheltered him briefly, then a liquefied natural gas transporter and a coaster with a full load of scrap metal. When he was clear of the coaster, he opted to re-assess.

"Find the fast boat on the radar," he told Anita as he dropped his speed right down. "She must be out there somewhere. Go on, she won't know it's us, not by now."

But Anita couldn't find her. The afterglow wasn't there any more, the screen was just all dots.

"Radar shadows cut both ways," she bitched. "She's lost us, or so you hope, but we've lost her as well."

But she watched the radar closely as Rufus raised the tempo, and before long she noticed a dot ahead and to port that was exactly matching The Empress Matilda's speed and direction. Rufus stiffened when she pointed it out. He raised the tempo some more, and they watched it a while longer.

"It's the fast boat all right," he said, speaking only as loudly as he had to. "She's never lost us, she was waiting for us."

Anita looked at him furiously.

"I thought you could stop that happening."

"I was sure I could. I switched everything off as well, but – " He broke off, and he had to stop himself from hitting the bulkhead with his fist. "Phillips-Smith! He was hanging around when we got there, and it was supposed to be his day off. Wasn't he in the navy police?"

Anita nodded sourly, and he said it for her:

"He's put a tracker on us. They've known where we are all the while."

Her eyes dilated with fear.

"So the fast boat really is the police," she said. "They want to see where we're going, and they'll take us before we get there." She made to touch his arm to steady her nerves, but she remembered the brush-kiss from Davis and held back. "I think we should go back," she said firmly. "We've got a start on them. If we beat them to Brightlingsea, we can get to our cars and hide up inland."

"Like where?"

She had no idea. Then she did.

"The Embassy. We can go there if we're being chased, Barbara's said so more than once."

"Not a hope. I know that boat, she's faster than us, and her infra-reds can see through fog as if it isn't there. They'll radio ahead as well. We're keeping going, Anita. If they get in our way, I'll ram them. They won't stop us now."

He raised the tempo some more to show he meant what he said.

He didn't know how much the others had overheard, so he told Anita to spell out how things were and to ask whether they had their guns with them. He had his, and he didn't have to ask about Anita's, he said, since he'd noticed it in her pocket. That was another blow to her self-esteem. Davis had a Smith and Wesson, Anita reported as she clambered back into the cockpit, but Kett had never fired a gun in his life.

Rufus checked his chronometer again, set an adjusted course for the rendezvous, and the fast boat, keeping ahead and to port, stayed with them. Anita alternated between watching the radar and scanning the darkness for lights, but in the back of her mind she was sorting out what she had to do to get herself out of this mess. She hated leaving England, but she hated the thought of gaol even more, so she had no option, she had to go to Russia. But did she have to go there with her useless husband and Davis? She'd dearly like to prevent that, what she'd really like would be for them to get caught and spend the next hundred years behind bars. She gave it some more thought and reckoned Kett was the answer. He was the one the Russians really wanted, and there was only one port-side ladder onto the Irinushka 052. If she could get herself and Kett onto it, they'd be on

Russian territory, and all she'd have to do then was make sure Davis and Rufus didn't follow them up it. She reached for a pen and scratchpad that were next to the radar, glanced over her shoulder to make sure no one could see, and in the dim light coming from the instruments, she wrote: 'Forget about ramming the police boat. We'll use Kett as a hostage to get past them. He hasn't got a gun. If I keep mine in his back, they'll have to let us through - XXX'.

She slid the pad towards Rufus. He read the note, took the pen and wrote, 'Brief Barbara on the quiet. You're in charge – XXX'. It couldn't be better. She pocketed the note and asked Davis to come and hold a torch for her downstairs – she had to check some gauges. When they re-emerged, she said they were all just fine, and then she had to clamber back into the cockpit fast, because Rufus was calling her. A dot was on the radar that hadn't been there before, and it was heading for the rendezvous. She checked the chronometer - it had to be the Irinushka 052. It was angling in over the horizon, and the area approaching the rendezvous was handily clear of traffic.

But the radar also showed the fast boat was shedding speed and beginning a looping curve that would place it between The Empress Matilda and the rendezvous. Rufus shed speed as well, but the distances were collapsing, and soon Anita and then Rufus could easily see both vessels through the night vision binoculars she'd pulled out of a lockerette. The fast boat was facing The Empress Matilda by this time. It was unlit apart from its navs, but Anita could still read POLICE in large capital letters on the white wedge-shaped foredeck that sloped up to the bridge.

It was a word she didn't want to see. It made her stomach cramp up.

"It really is them, Derek," she said nervously. "They know who we are, and they're waiting for us."

Before Rufus could reply, the Irinushka 052's bridge and deck lights all came on at once. Anita checked the electronic notepad and peered through the night glasses again. It was her all right. The pilot's ladder was lit up like an invitation, and the gate at the top was open. She turned round to speak to Davis and Kett.

"We're nearly there," she told them. "Just do as I say, and we'll be all right."

She didn't want them doing anything on their own.

"The police are staying dark," Rufus murmured, as he slowed down almost to a standstill.

He was glad Anita had taken over, it was what he was used to. He'd tried to lead, but it hadn't worked. He had to accept she was better.

"They don't want to get shot at, that's why," she retorted, just loud enough for him to hear. Then she raised her voice to include the others. "Listen all of you, because I'm not going to say it twice. Jesse, you and I are going onto the right hand foredeck. We're going to pretend we've taken you hostage, so you'll have my gun in your back. Barbara, you'll stay in here out of the way. Derek, put our navs and deck lights on as soon as Jesse and I are outside, and call the police on our VHF. Don't let them try to negotiate, just agree a speed and say we'll pass them on their starboard side. We've got nearly twenty minutes to rendezvous time. We should just about make it."

She drew her Beretta, put the cabin lighting on low and told Kett it was time to get moving. He looked eager as he stood up and steadied himself against the cabin's side – what she'd said made complete sense to him. Once they were on the foredeck, she told him to hold onto the front railing with one hand but to hold the other one in the air. When the navs and the deck lights came on, he felt the Beretta press hard against his spine.

"We get onto the freighter's ladder first, then Barbara and Derek," she whispered in his ear, and he nodded.

What she didn't say was, she'd be the only one with a gun already in her hand and that she'd use it when the time came.

There was a wait, then one of the cockpit's side windows opened.

"Anita, I've been talking to the police," Rufus called out. "We've met the officer in charge in Brightlingsea. Her name's Gulliver, and I think we can trust her. She'll let us through if we don't do more than 4½ knots, but that will take us past 20.45. What do you think? It would help if they weren't in our way, but they're saying that's our problem, not theirs."

Anita assessed the relative positions and speeds.

"The freighter won't stop because she can't, but she'll slow down as much as she can. Take a chance with six knots and steer more to port. That should do it."

Rufus was at six knots almost instantly, and straight away the VHF was telling him to slow down or be stopped altogether. He slowed down to four, just to make sure. As they got closer to the police boat, which continued to stay dark, Anita used her gun to make Kett reach up higher. The yacht's tempo seemed painfully slow through the inky swell. They'd be late, but only fractionally. That had to be all right.

Once they were between the police boat and the freighter, Rufus speeded up and shaded still more to port. At the same time, the police boat put in a fast turn and tucked in at a distance astern. Rufus raised his speed again, and the police boat did likewise, but she made no attempt to catch up. Anita's ruse had to be working. 20.45 showed on the chronometer, and they were almost there. But just as Rufus's tension was giving way to relief, all the lights on the freighter went out except for the navs, and turbulence at the stern told him it was moving on. At the same time, a searchlight on the police boat drenched the yacht in a harsh white light, and through a loudspeaker mounted above the bridge they heard Gulliver call out:

"Your transport's gone, Mr Rufus! Stop your engines and stand on deck with your hands up! We know there are four of you, and we want you all in plain sight! If anything happens to Mr Kett, we shall open fire!"

Davis reacted like greased lightning. She drew her Smith and Wesson, scrambled forwards onto Anita's vacant seat in the cockpit, and ordered Rufus to make for Brightlingsea as fast as he could. Yes, Brightlingsea!! Just do it!! As long as they had Kett, they'd be all right, he'd get them to the Embassy. She'd call Gulliver herself and tell her to keep out of it. Rufus couldn't believe it. Use Kett as a hostage to get to the Embassy? Why hadn't he thought of that when Anita had wanted to go back?

Anita heard Davis's voice but she didn't catch her words as Rufus reversed round at speed, shielding his eyes with one hand and sorting out a line to take him past the police boat. Also shielding her eyes, Anita saw Davis pressing against Rufus as she tried to reach for the VHF microphone, and a fresh stab of jealousy would have made her try to shoot her through the windscreen, except she thought she had a better idea.

Kett had grabbed the railing with both hands as The Empress Matilda had surged round. Anita had seen he had had no choice, but she still shouted at him to stay where he was, if he moved from the railing she'd kill him. Then she raced along the deck to the back of the cabin, looking for Davis. Davis thought she was coming to kill her, and as she twisted round to get her shot in first, Anita, unfazed by the yacht's heaving and pitching, put three bullets through her shoulder with the clinical skill she'd acquired on Thurston's shooting range. Davis's buoyancy aid was nil protection. She shrieked with pain and kept on shrieking as her Smith and Wesson fell onto the cabin floor. Anita moved forward and scraped it up one-handed.

"Kill the motors, Derek!" she screamed. "Kill them now!"

He obeyed straight away, it was a Pavlovian reflex. She didn't bother about his gun, she knew he was too scared to use it.

Except for Davis's yowling, everything seemed eerily quiet. As the yacht drifted and the swell tipped it up and down, the police boat put in an unhurried turn of its own, all the while keeping its searchlight trained on the yacht, and cautiously closed in from astern and to starboard. Anita pocketed her Beretta, lunged forward and grabbed hold of Davis's waterproofs. Deliberately targeting her shoulder, she wrenched her out of the cockpit, through the cabin and onto the afterdeck, where she stood over her while she whipped her Beretta out.

"Get up to the front with Kett!" she shouted at her, gasping for breath and kicking her hard to get her to move. "Get up there now, or I'll kill you!"

Losing blood and in pain beyond belief, Davis dragged herself forward, not realising Anita couldn't afford to kill anyone right in front of the police. Anita allowed herself a split second to gloat over Davis's agony, then she shouted to Rufus to put his gun on the bulkhead and go to the bow as well. Once he was there, she moved up to the open side window of the cockpit, reached in, and yanked the VHF microphone out full length. By this time, the police boat was drawing level with The Empress Matilda, and the searchlight's brightness had been dimmed down. Clicking to 'Speak', Anita asked for Officer Gulliver. Gulliver's voice came to her through the bulkhead loudspeaker.

"Officer Gulliver, I was brought onto this boat against my will," Anita panted, knowing Rufus would hear her and hoping Davis would as well. "Thanks to you, I've been able to free myself and capture the others for you. I'll hand all the guns over to you when you come aboard to arrest them, mine included, which I've only ever used to protect myself. The other three have pressured me into everything I've done. I ask you to take note of that. You can come alongside when you like, I've got everything under control."

She ostentatiously dropped her Beretta as soon as she saw the carbines of two Armed Support officers trained on Kett and Rufus. Gulliver transferred Kett and both the Rufuses to the police boat, making sure Anita was kept well away from the other two. Davis was bandaged up and kept on The Empress Matilda under guard, and a set of infra-red cameras was rapidly installed to get the yacht back through the mist. One of the police boat crew would take it back to Brightlingsea with the police boat following behind. Armed Support's helicopter, which had been virtually invisible against the night sky and downwind so as not to be heard, tracked them till Kett and the Rufuses were on their way to Chelmsford in three separate police vehicles. Rufus had one fleeting opportunity to vent his fury at Anita before he was driven off, and he took it.

"You stupid, stupid fool, Anita!" he screamed. His rage gave him courage, and he was past caring who heard him. "Kett would have got us all the way to the Embassy! All we had to do was keep a gun at his head and we were there, but, no, you had to come crashing in and ruin everything! I hope you're pleased with yourself, it's what you usually are! We'll see how pleased you are when you go down for twenty years!"

Use Kett to get to the Embassy? She thought about it quickly, and her heart sank. She was sure it would have worked.

"I'm sorry, Derek, really I am," she said humbly. But he was already being escorted away.

An ambulance took Davis to Chelmsford and Essex Hospital. It was a light night in Casualty for once, and she didn't have to wait long to be operated on. Her surgeon thought her shoulder would never be right again, regardless of what anyone did to it. It was something she'd have to live with. When he asked what she'd been up to, no one was allowed to say.

In a quiet moment on the police boat, while it was following The Empress Matilda on the way back to Brightlingsea, Gulliver sent an informal text to van Piet (copy to Snape) to tell him how things had gone. '1) Your tracker worked a treat,' she wrote. '2) The coastguards kept the approach to the rendezvous clear. 3) I obstructed the EM, as you asked me to. 4) The freighter took off at 20.45 and 13 seconds – unlucky for some!!!' To Snape (copy to van Piet) she texted, '1) Targets detained for questioning – Davis shot three times in shoulder but should survive. 2) AR claiming she did everything under pressure. 3) Full report when I get back.' Snape couldn't resist a reply. 'Thanks for the warning about AR. A/V in Watkins's flat has AR saying she's helped with two murders and been glad to do it, but she'll kill Watkins single-handed if she doesn't stay away from Thurston. That's pressure, is it??'

Van Piet saw what he'd written and supplied a couple of spelling corrections.

"What line will you take when you question her?" he asked after Snape had sent the text.

"We'll let her tell her tale to see how much she gives away, then we'll warn her about lying in court. That's to protect ourselves. My guess is she'll keep lying if she thinks it will help her out, and if she does, we'll get perjury tacked on to the other charges. That should keep her off the streets for a good long while. I'm not hoping she'll lie, of course, but I shan't be upset if she does."

Chapter 32

Proofs positive

Cottrell was in King's Parade when Davis contacted her. Davis didn't speak for long, and as soon as she terminated, Cottrell bought a souvenir T-shirt in a tourist shop opposite the chapel, since she wanted the plastic bag. Back in her hotel, she showered, tidied her hair, and changed into the smart-casual clothes she'd put into her luggage for Coventry. The T-shirt came out of the bag, and in went some toilet things, the lightweight trainers she'd been wearing and a cardigan, which she wrapped round her Beretta and the clip of ammunition. It wasn't much, but it would have to do. When she came downstairs, the lobby was empty except for the receptionist, who was idling away the time with a TV magazine. House rules said guests had to hand in their keys if they went out, so Cottrell slid hers across the counter and said she was dreadfully sorry, but she'd had a surprise invitation to dine with some friends in Trumpington. The receptionist told her not to worry and languidly crossed her off the diners' list. Then she went back to her magazine.

Traffic was light on the motorway, and Cottrell kept well within the speed limits. The sun was hot through the Hiace's windows, so she put the air conditioning on, but the empty van was noisy, so she let the radio be. She wasn't allowed to make any phone calls, Davis had emphasised that, so she felt cocooned from everything, and she liked it. It made her feel snug.

She was heading for Kett's lock-up in Bethnal Green. She had a spare key, and she knew from Davis Kett had taken his car to Chelmsford. She and Kett were close. He liked her because she was bright, and she worshipped the ground he walked on because, like Verity, he made her feel wanted. He'd do well in Russia, she was certain of that, and maybe some of his stardust would fall on her. It was a shame they couldn't go there together, but there it was. She'd just have to make sure she got there safely. She didn't want to let him or Verity down.

Kett's lock-up was one of a block of eight someone smart had thrown together fast. The paintwork was peeling and the concrete apron was cracked, but the underground station was just around the corner, so the rents were galactic and the waiting list had a life of its own. Cottrell was well within schedule. She couldn't be sure when her next meal would be, so she strolled to E. Pellicci's, the greasy spoon in Bethnal Green Road that was hallowed with a Grade II listing. She and Kett had eaten there a lot. The weather was too hot for its trademark steak pie and chips, so she ordered spinach and ricotta cannelloni and let a stream of good memories take over.

She was still well within schedule as she made her way down the steps to the underground. She'd wanted to say goodbye to Peter Pan's statue in Kensington Gardens, but she didn't fancy the park in less than broad daylight, so she stayed in the underground till Queensway. When she emerged, she kept to the Bayswater Road till she was ready to cross over to Kensington Palace Gardens, the Crown Estate street with the almost identical name. The Russian Embassy was Number 13, and she had to be outside it at 20.45. She checked her watch and calculated she'd make it to the minute. She was surprised how smoothly everything had gone. She'd always thought, if she had to escape to the Embassy, she'd be running for her life, but it had been nothing like that at all. She paused to take a lingering look at Millionaires' Row, the popular name for Kensington Palace Gardens till the billionaires moved in. She'd never be in London again, and she wanted to make the most of every moment. She also had to decide what to do about the armed police on guard at the end of the street.

The armed police were always there, they went with the money, and there was a traffic control as well, though that was manned by Crown Estate employees. Since the Embassy was expecting her, she'd likely only have to say her name and the police would let her through, but one thing was certain – she'd have to get rid of her gun. She looked all round and saw a litter bin. It was three quarters full, so the Beretta went in without a noise. The ammunition clip clinked a bit as it hit the pistol, but the sound was masked by the traffic. With that done she steeled herself and made her way towards one of the police. He used his radio to check her name, and he searched her plastic bag using a torch. Her shoulder bag came next. A policewoman asked her to come to a control booth with her. There was a security alert on, she explained as she patted her down behind a screen, but she didn't say what kind it was. Cottrell was tense now, but she let it happen. Then she was through.

The street lamps were discreet rather than bright, and the air smelled fresh from the plane trees that lined either side. The houses were immense. Their wrought iron railings looked black in the artificial light, and their lit-up windows made them seem alien and remote. There were just three cars parked in the street, and they were at the far end.

As she approached Number 13, a shadowy figure detached itself from a gateway just ahead of it and came towards her. She made out a tallish male who, she guessed, was still in his twenties. He was wearing a dark poplin jacket over an equally dark open-necked shirt, and suede shoes that made no sound. She tingled to think he might be Russian, but when he asked if she knew where the Tanzanian Embassy was, she was sure he was English.

"I think it's Number 6," she replied. "No, sorry, it's Number 17. I always make that mistake."

They'd both come to a halt.

"Well done, Miss Cottrell," he smiled. "You got that word perfect."

He pulled the top of his jacket out and said, "Contact confirmed" into the microphone inside it.

"You'll want to check my ID," he went on, taking a plastic-encased card from an inside pocket. "Here, you'll see better with this."

He pulled a flat LED torch out of another pocket, and instead of switching it on, he held it out towards her free hand. She stood her plastic bag down, switched the torch on and gasped in shock.

The ID said PC Neil Massie, and the logo said Essex Police.

Having something in her free hand made her hesitate – that had been the intention – so when she threw the torch at his face and tried to bulldoze her way past him, he was pretty much ready for her. Number 13 was one of the biggest houses in the street, and despite the subdued light, it was within such easy reach, she could make out its Gothic façade in detail. Massie evaded the torch and grabbed the strap of her shoulder bag. It didn't stop her, but it slowed her down till the strap slipped and she could wriggle her arm out of it. By this time the three cars from the far end of the street were moving towards them, and two armed officers who had been concealed behind plane trees had moved into position between her and the Embassy gate. They'd been told she didn't have a gun, but they still kept their hands near their service pistols. Desperately she made to outflank them, and when one of them caught her arm, she went for his face with her nails in the hope he would loosen his grip. Instead, he seized both her wrists, while the other one clamped hold of her shoulders to stop her forcing her way forward. She squirmed and kicked frantically, and it was not until she'd been wrestled to the ground and pinned there that she stopped struggling. Her wrists, which were slippery with sweat, were handcuffed behind her back, then, still gasping for breath, she was allowed to stand up. She hadn't screamed or shouted, and the police hadn't raised their voices either. It was as if the night-time quiet of the wealthy must on no account be disturbed. In the stillness that followed, she distinctly heard a door shut. She didn't see it happen, but there was no mistaking the sound, and it

357

definitely came from the Embassy. A movement behind her made her look round, although it hurt her to turn her neck. Massie was standing a little way back with her shoulder bag and her plastic bag in his hand. Some way behind him, a policewoman in plain clothes was holding up the Beretta and the ammunition clip, both in evidence bags. She must have been tailing her. If Cottrell had gone into Kensington Gardens, she might have seen her follow her in. But she hadn't.

Cottrell recognised Snape as soon as she saw him get out from the first of the cars. Instinctively she looked for van Piet, but he was out of sight in the second car. Snape told her she was under arrest, since – he lapsed easily into the formula - he had reasonable grounds for suspecting her to be guilty of three offences. The first was being an accessory to a breach of national security. The second was being in unlawful possession of a firearm.

"And the third?" she asked, trying to project defiance. "Hurry up, Mr Snape, don't keep me in suspense. What's the third one?"

"The third one, Miss Cottrell, is the murder of Geoffrey Slade."

Her denial was total.

"Geoffrey Slade?! You must be hard up for an arrest. I was nowhere near him when his car went off the road. I was at home and you know it."

She spat in his face. Calmly he wiped the saliva off with a handkerchief, and equally calmly he went through the caution and her rights. She'd be taken to Chelmsford for questioning.

As the three cars restarted their engines, Snape gave a wave to the Met officers guarding the end of the street. They stepped to one side and signalled to a

Crown Estate employee, who was watching them through the glass of his control hut. He pressed a button, retractable bollards sank into the ground, and the three cars moved through. The first and the third continued on to Chelmsford with Cottrell in the back of the first one. The second one, an SRO Kia Sorento, drove the short distance into Chelsea, and van Piet and Snape got out in Ashell House.

They were in the operations room when they received the texts Gulliver sent from the police boat, and shortly after Snape texted back, van Piet went to talk things through with Benjamin. When he came back, he told Snape COBRA had been meeting in Downing Street and had decided on some actions he – Snape - should know about. COBRA is short for Cabinet Office Briefing Room A, which sounds harmless enough, except COBRA only meets in times of national emergency. This particular meeting comprised the Prime Minister and the Home Secretary, plus senior figures from the NCA, MI5, GCHQ and the Met. The Met has legal authority throughout England and Wales. It can invoke it at any time, if the situation is serious enough. Benjamin had taken part via a secure link, and one result was, the Met was sealing off the houses of the Rufuses, Davis, Cottrell, and Kett pending searches for booby traps. Once the houses were declared safe, specialists from GCHQ, the National Cyber Security Centre and MI5 would take them over to hunt for breaches of national security. Only when they were finished would Essex Police be allowed in.

"They'll box what they find and take it away, so you shouldn't be kept out too long," van Piet said to Snape. "Esklivia House is the exception. It will be sealed off indefinitely, there's too much in there to do anything else."

Snape saw straight away COBRA must have been meeting before Kett, Cottrell and their friends had been arrested.

"What are you saying, Willem?" he asked uneasily. "Are the murder enquiries being downgraded?"

Van Piet looked astonished.

"Certainly not, not when they're almost complete. We're still in charge of Thurston's house, Mr Benjamin made sure of that for me. And once we get Verity to talk, we're pretty much home and dry."

By midnight, Safety and Sabotage had cleared Thurston Mansion for entry, van Piet had spelled out to Garry what to look for, and the waiting in Chelsea had begun. Mitchie was still on duty – like Benjamin, she'd opted to stay till van Piet called time – and Snape was behind a corner desk talking to night staff at the Crown Prosecution Service and the NCA. Francisca and Andreas Davis had been added to the list of arrests. Francisca was in Brighton gaol, and Andreas was in a secure ward in the Royal Sussex Hospital, which was also in Brighton. Friedrich Winckler had been arrested as well. He was in a police cell in Bonn pending an extradition hearing. Watkins's solicitor was still missing. The NCA was taking that forward.

When Snape was done, he helped himself to a hot cup of tea from the trolley and made his way through the bustle to van Piet. Van Piet's mobile was on a nearby desk, and next to it was a monitor. He was waiting for Garry to get back to him.

"It was a trade-off, wasn't it," Snape said as he sat down.

It was a statement, not a question. Van Piet opened his hands, raised them and lowered them again.

"It had to be, Eddie, we had to get them. That was the bottom line."

"So how was it done?"

Van Piet glanced at his watch. Garry would need more time yet.

"Verity Slade, Esklivia Investments, the boulting house, Kett and the Russians," he began, ticking them off on his fingers. "They were scattered items at first, but over time they formed up like beads on a string, and that helped me when the boulting house got blown up. I had mostly no idea what was in it, but the Russians weren't to know that, and everything said, whatever it was, it mattered a lot to them, so I decided to take a chance. I chased everyone out of the Sikorsky and bluffing hard, I put a deal to a contact we have in their embassy with the backing of Mr Benjamin, the Prime Minister and the Home Secretary. I said, with the boulting house and everything in it destroyed, the Russians could deny they'd been meddling in British affairs if they helped us catch Kett and the rest. They, of course, had to be heading for the exit, Watkins's photos alone would have seen to that. The Russians are keen on meddling, but they're not so keen on getting found out, so they warmed to the idea fairly fast, and that confirmed for me I was on the right lines. The snag for them was, they don't like letting their agents down any more than we do, so we agreed Kett & Co could go ahead with their escape plans, and if they worked, the Russians could crow and we'd put up with it. However, if blundering British flatfoots just happened to get in the way, the Russians would accept it, provided it looked as if they'd done everything they could do to get their people out. So, at 20.45, the Russians were waiting with open arms on the North Sea and in Kensington, but, sadly, blundering British flatfoots did get in the way, and the rest you know. Now all we've got to do is play everything down. That suits us because the Russians got past our guard, and it spares their blushes as well."

"Did you know where Kett and the rest were escaping to?"

"No, but realistically they only had two options: They could either skedaddle to the Embassy, or the Rufuses could get them out to a Russian boat. I ran both of them past our Embassy contact, and since her masters wanted the deal as much as mine did, she kindly filled in the details."

Snape thought that one through.

"So Kett wasn't important after all."

"I wouldn't go that far, but they could manage without him if they had to. Presumably they've got plenty more Ketts tucked away where we don't want them to be. It's just we haven't found them yet."

He stood up to fetch some coffee, the indoor air was getting to him. When he sat down again he said,

"I learned some interesting things about Davis while I was talking to our contact. We already know Grandfather Winckler stood out against the Nazis. Well, Francisca's pedigree was pro-Communist in the Spanish Civil War and anti-Franco thereafter, so on both sides of the family, Davis was destined for the

362

Left from the day she was conceived. In practice, that meant helping the Russians as soon as she was old enough, and they started her with courier work between this country and the Continent. To finance her, they put some London buy-to-lets her way, the same as they did later on in Clacton. She and the Slades didn't know each other then, but the Russians liked her so much, they eventually moved her from London to Clacton so she could take over."

"What did they do that for?"

"Putin was on the up by then, and they wanted the Slades to rally behind him. The Slades began as Communist idealists, but Putin was ditching all that, and there was a chance they might not like it."

"Your contact told you all that just like that, did she?"

"Pretty much, except she was careful what she said about Putin. The Russians like to pass things on you can find out for yourself. They think you'll feel obliged to them."

Normally Snape was good at waiting, but not now – he was as anxious as van Piet to hear from Garry. As the time ticked away, van Piet opened an e-mail attachment from Amsterdam detailing how Russian money was finding its way to Nevis and then on to Esklivia in London. A postscript flagged up a Russian connection with Samoa that was still being worked on. It seemed stale news now, but it was all part of the evidence chain, so he took Snape through it and had a copy printed off for him. Info was arriving in no particular order, but at least it was still arriving. As he was fetching more coffee, Mitchie told him GCHQ had traced a second virtual private network. One kept Davis, the Slades, Kett and the rest in contact with each other, and the other connected Davis, the Slades and the Russian Embassy in London. 'A couple of computers downstairs' – the phrase came back to him as he listened. Now he knew what both of them were for.

"Why are you so focused on Thurston?" Snape asked.

Garry still hadn't called back.

"His car hire patterns for starters, then those fibres PC Massie found. He was a hoarder as well – he told us that himself."

Snape leafed through his notebook.

"He kept out-of-date clothes bills," he read off. "That's hoarding all right. You think he might have kept more than that, do you?"

Van Piet said he might have. Most people just put their hands up when they give themselves up, but Thurston was waving a white cloth about like someone in a film, so perhaps he had something to bargain with. Like who killed Ashley Johnson.

Snape looked startled.

"What makes you say that?"

"Johnson was killed for a reason, and I believe I know what it was. I also believe Watkins recognised the killer when she lit the drive up. I doubt it was Thurston, because it's unlikely she'd met him then, but I'm hoping he was involved. You'll remember, in his office -"

His mobile buzzed, and the monitor next to it lit up. It was Garry. The first sweep through was complete, he said, and amongst other things they'd found a largish safe in one of the upstairs rooms. It had some interesting things inside it. Some had been bagged and some hadn't. He'd relay the photos he'd taken now.

"There was this laptop," Garry said, as the first photo filled the monitor's screen. "Not what one would expect to find in a safe, but it was in there all right. As you can see, it's a grey-white Apple. Then there was this pistol -" the monitor showed a Walther PPK and a silencer "- and this one." It was a Beretta 92 and a silencer. There was also a rubberised torch.

"Towards the back was this pair of black overalls, size small. You told me Thurston had a laundry at his quarry, but I don't think this pair has been cleaned. It doesn't smell, so it's probably not been in the safe for too long, and any body traces should still be intact. Possibly that was Thurston's intention. There was also this pair of size 11 men's hiker's boots. They're padded inside, as if someone with smaller feet has been wearing them, and they don't smell either. Next to the boots and in a bag were a pair of night goggles, a black ski mask and a pair of black gloves. The mask and the gloves don't look laundered. You also asked me to look out for a night camera and any photos Thurston might have taken with it."

Snape realised what van Piet had been about to say when his mobile had buzzed. The owl photos in Thurston's office had been taken at night.

"He'd turned one of his rooms into a photo-lab, and we found a night camera in there," Garry continued, "but these photos were in a folder in the safe."

They were black and white and diamond sharp - Thurston must have used an infra-red flash. One showed Verity. She was wearing dark clothing and gloves, but she was bare-headed. She was standing by the side of a figure on the ground - also bare-headed - and she was pointing a silenced pistol at its head. The head was lit up by a torch on the ground, which was covered with something to limit its brightness. A pair of night goggles was round Verity's neck.

On the photo's reverse side, which Garry showed next, it said in the same clerkly handwriting Thurston had used to label his bird-of-prey photos, 'Verity Slade of Esklivia Investments about to shoot Ashley Johnson, vet, on the vet's drive in Five Willows, Essex. Verity has shot Johnson in the back, and the torch is Johnson's. Verity has used her ski mask to stop it spreading too much light around. She used the torch because her goggles were misting up'. A second photo showed much the same thing, except the skull was badly damaged. It was captioned, 'Verity Slade has shot Ashley Johnson in the head for the second time'. Both photos were dated and timed. A third one showed someone in a dark pair of overalls and a head covering with some kind of strap round it approaching a front door. It was taken from behind, and it was captioned, 'Barbara Davis, landlady and translator, going to shoot Stephanie Hayward, secretary, in Nightingale Cottage (Five Willows, Essex)'. A fourth one showed Davis with her head bare. She was about to wipe her forehead with her sleeve, and her face could be seen clearly. These photos were also dated and timed, and the last one was captioned, 'Barbara Davis has just shot Stephanie Hayward.'

"Thurston took a risk with this last one," Snape said. "Davis must have been looking straight through the darkness towards him."

Van Piet covered his mobile with his hand.

366

"His owl shots were good as well."

He took his hand away.

"Anything else, Tom?"

There was a handwritten diary of Thurston's various journeys in hired vehicles, the book about Thurston's family, the note he'd written to the museum, and the cheque. Then came a sequence of shots showing Thurston's underground shooting range, his stash of illegal small arms, and his underfloor strongbox, first closed, then opened. Garry asked whether he should bring anything back.

"No, everything stays there until we can take the place apart. I'll get someone sent up to look at the laptops and the smartphone sharpish, and Leicestershire Police can keep guard for the time being. Mr Snape will make sure they don't go away."

He terminated, and Garry shut the monitor off remotely.

"It looks," Snape said, "as if Thurston was chauffeur, armourer and bin man all in one. Verity and Davis must have given him their things to destroy in his quarry. Cottrell as well, by the look of it."

"But he hung onto them instead, complete with body traces. Presumably he hoped for a deal, if ever the time for one came."

"By betraying his friends, you mean?"

"How else could he do it? Unfortunately for him, Verity seems to have got in first."

Chapter 33

A means to an end

Hettie Tait liked things done properly. She read the documents she needed for the Slade inquest in detail, and she made sure the witnesses would be in court when they should be. They included Rufus and Verity. She also spent a long Tuesday evening in Tiptree talking things through with van Piet and Snape. They sat indoors, and she kept the windows and the door tightly shut. With August drawing to a close, the evenings were starting to cool, she said.

"I can still postpone the inquest if you want," she offered to Snape, but he was happy for it to go ahead as scheduled.

She looked at van Piet, who said nothing.

"So be it. And if you can show it was homicide, I'll adjourn at that point."

She gathered her notes together and looked pointedly at her mantelpiece clock.

"We'll leave it at that then, shall we? Make sure you're punctual tomorrow."

They said they would be.

The following day everyone stood when she entered her court at 10 am sharp, and no one sat down till she said they could. She explained she was there to establish four things: Who died? Where did they die? When did they die? And why did they die? Testimony would be given under oath or affirmation, lying under either was a criminal offence, and everything would be recorded. Determining guilt or innocence wasn't part of her job, so no one should expect it of her.

"One witness will be late," she finished with. "That person has been held up in traffic on the way from London, but I shall proceed anyway."

Identification of the body, the medical cause of death, and where and when Slade died were all taken from documents and read into the record in short form. Then Tait called Verity, who looked frail and worn, but also defiant. Two police officers in uniform were escorting her, and one of them supported her as she stepped onto the witness stand, where her handcuffs were removed before she took the oath. She was wearing dark clothes and shoes, she was devoid of jewellery apart from her wedding ring, and she had no make-up on. Tait allowed her to sit down, and an usher poured some water into a glass for her. Van Piet was watching from one of the seats at the back that were set aside for the public and the media. He wouldn't be called as a witness - Snape's evidence would be enough on its own. Snape was sitting ahead of him on one of the seats reserved for witnesses, and two rows in front of him were Rufus, his uniformed police escort – also two officers - and his legal adviser. Rufus was still in handcuffs. When

Verity wasn't on the witness stand, she sat in the front row. Her police escort had seats either side of her, and if she wanted to talk to her legal adviser, she had to lean across one of them. In a coroner's court, witnesses are allowed to hear everything, including each other's evidence. They can question each other as well.

Tait knew exactly what to ask Verity. She questioned her about Slade's line of work, his character, his purchase of the Maserati and his driving ability, and in a subdued but unwavering voice, Verity told her what Laura had told Snape and van Piet two days after his death: That he was not the best of drivers, and that she – Verity - had done everything she could to stop him buying the Maserati.

"It was the wrong car for him, he was bound to have an accident," she said, and then she gave way to the stress that had already been peaking when she'd entered the building. "It's tearing me apart to go through all this again," she managed to say. "I loved him when he was alive, and I love him now. I miss him indescribably, and everything I say reminds me I'll never have him back."

Tait was used to grief. She gave Verity time to recover, said she could pause at any time, and then she continued her questioning. By the time she finished, Verity looked on the point of collapse, and when Tait asked her whether there was anything else she would like to tell the court, she said, whey-faced and haggard, "All the while I was speaking, I felt my late husband was in your court with me, but I couldn't reach out to touch him. I wanted to do that more than anything else, but I couldn't do it."

Tait told her she was free to leave now she'd answered all her questions, but she might wish to hear the remaining testimony, since new facts about her husband's death could yet come to light. Verity, who had been wanting to go, looked apprehensive at that and said she'd stay. She held out her hands, her handcuffs were clicked back on, and she returned to the front row.

Rufus was called next. His handcuffs came off, and he declared by affirmation he'd tell the truth. He, too, was wearing his own clothes, they'd been fetched for him from his house. He looked white and frightened, the opposite of the confident triathlonner Snape and van Piet had interviewed in his office. Tait asked him about the sale of the Maserati to Slade, and he told her the damage Slade had done to the hired Maserati showed he needed some practice, so he'd recommended a New Owner's course to him, and he'd made good progress as a result.

"Were you surprised when you heard he'd had an accident?"

"Not entirely, if I'm honest," Rufus replied, looking as honest as he could. "If he'd had the car longer, he'd have probably got used to it, but being a new owner, well, it's like when you've just passed your test. The law says you can drive, but you don't have the experience, and that can catch up with you. It was his own decision to buy, though. I just went along with it."

While Snape was being sworn in, the usher quietly set up a beamer and screen so Tait and the public could see the images. Snape worked the beamer from a laptop he placed on the broad rim of the witness stand, and after he'd explained why he was on the Roman road, he showed Tait the same images he'd shown Warrener in Brunel, plus the images Warrener had made, all without mentioning her name or university. Towards the end of his presentation, a second usher slipped into the courtroom and placed a note on Tait's desk.

"Mr Slade was in a powerful car he wasn't used to," she said after she'd glanced at it. "Isn't it possible he simply lost control?"

"It's possible, Ma'am, but we believe the vehicle was illegally manipulated."

Tait had her reply ready.

"Then I must ask you how it was done, Mr Snape. Can you tell me that?"

"The witness who has yet to arrive can. May I ask for an adjournment?"

Tait picked up the note from her desk.

"There's no need. He's here now, and you can stand down for the time being."

She asked for the beamer and screen to be removed, and beckoned towards the second usher. He opened the courtroom door, and, looking tentative, Matteo Pachini came in, followed by a Met officer in plain clothes. The Met officer quietly sat down behind Rufus and, leaning forward, shook hands with Rufus's escort. Pachini's black curly hair had been freshly cut, and he was wearing a new-looking suit and tie. Tait asked the second usher to conduct him to the witness box, where she allowed him to sit while she explained what her court was about. She also told him he was to address her as 'Ma'am'. For the record, she told the court he was under police protection, not under arrest, then she asked him to stand. He preferred an oath to an affirmation, and after he'd explained who he was, Tait asked him what it meant to be the Maserati's named engineer.

In fluent and only lightly accented English, he explained he had to set the car up and install any extras before it was released to the customer. For example, there was Mr Slade's anti-theft package.

"And what did the package contain?"

"Mostly a state-of-the-art tracking device. Standard trackers are accurate up to 15 feet or so, but this one was accurate to within three inches. We called it military grade."

She asked him whether there were any problems with it.

"Not with the tracker, Ma'am, but yes, there was a problem."

Normally, he explained, he and Rufus calibrated the trackers together, and they often used the Roman road, because he could stand on a footpath with his laptop and see Rufus driving on the road. There was never much traffic about, and if Rufus wiggled the car around or if he went through the bend where he'd heard Slade had been killed, Pachini could check the moving map on his laptop to see it had got it right. But this time Rufus said he was getting someone else to work with him.

"I didn't like that, Ma'am, I felt made small, you know, so I wanted to know who this someone else was who was supposed to be better than me. I found out when Mr Rufus was going to do the calibrating – I heard him arrange it on his mobile when he didn't know I was there. It wasn't going to be in working time, it was going to be in the evening, and that made me even more curious. So after work, I drove to my house in Clacton, I put my own laptop and a bike Mr Rufus used to lend me in the back of my car, and I drove out to near the Roman road. I knew how to get up to the footpath on a bike. I also knew how to switch the tracker on and download the moving map, but Mr Rufus had already switched it on, so it was easy for me to see when he was getting near in the Maserati. He stopped where he always did, and the person with him got out to climb up to the footpath. I was some way off and hidden by some bushes, but I saw it happen."

He hesitated and looked towards the Met officer who'd come in with him. He couldn't avoid seeing Rufus as well, but he was back in handcuffs and hemmed in by police. The Met officer gave a faint nod of re-assurance, and he began again.

"When Mr Rufus drove off, he did the sorts of thing he always did, but he also did crazy things like accelerating very fast. And he kept repeating the same run down the long straight where the footpath is and through the bend I talked about just now. After a fair amount of time, when he had driven right out of sight, there was still plenty of light about, so I put my laptop into my rucksack and pedalled along the footpath as if I was out for a ride. The person who was helping him was a lady. When she'd got out of the Maserati, I'd I thought, 'Aha! That's why it's not me,' and I thought it again now. Then I made a long detour back to my own car."

Tait asked whether he knew the lady. Pachini replied he'd never seen her before, and he didn't think it mattered she'd seen him – not at the time, anyway - because he could have been anyone.

"But I had a close friend," he went on. "Her name was Deborah Watkins, and I am very sad about her, because I have heard she's been killed. I asked Deborah about this lady, because Deborah knew everything about Mr Rufus and his dealership. She worked for a newspaper, and she investigated businesses for a living. She asked me what this lady looked like, and then she showed me a photo on her smartphone. I said, 'That's her!' and she said, 'Her name is Millie Cottrell.'

"Then Deborah became very serious. She said some of the people Mr and Mrs Rufus knew were very dangerous. There had even been a murder in the past, and she knew that because it had been the man she'd been engaged to who had been murdered. I was very worried, because Deborah was sure this Millie Cottrell had described me to Mr Rufus, but I was also going home to Italy after not too long, and Deborah knew that, because I'd talked about it a lot. 'Tell me about it again,' she said. 'I need to get it right.' So I said a friend would pick me up after my last day at work, I'd stay in England a little bit to say goodbye to people I knew, and then I'd go back to Italy, where I hoped she'd come and see me. 'Is there anything else?' she asked me, and I said I was going sailing one last time with Mr and Mrs Rufus the day after I finished work. I'd done a lot of sailing with them, and it was all arranged. I hadn't told Deborah that before.

"'You've seen too much to be safe,' she said, 'and it would be easy to fake an accident when you're out to sea, so this is what we'll do. You'll tell your friend not to pick you up, but you won't tell anyone else. I'll hire the same sort of car your friend has, and I'll pick you up in it. I'll also wear a hoodie so no one knows it's me. Then I'll take you to Stephanie Hayward's cottage – ' Miss Hayward was Mr Rufus's secretary, Ma'am. I hardly knew her, but Deborah did. Someone told me she's also been killed, and I'm sorry about that too, but it shows Deborah was right to worry about me.

"Deborah said I had to disappear completely – maybe for some time - and Miss Hayward's cottage would be a good place to hand me over to someone who would help me to do it. She'd have to tell Miss Hayward what was happening to get her to agree, but her cottage would be better than a hotel, because hotels have cctv, and her cottage doesn't."

Tait intervened.

"Was it really safe to trust Miss Hayward, do you think? Might she not tell someone what she heard?"

"Deborah said, if Miss Hayward told anyone, she'd be in the same danger I was. She'd make sure Miss Hayward understood that."

Tait thanked him and asked him to go on. He said Watkins would hand him over to the father of the man she'd been engaged to, and she'd change into her normal clothes there and drive back to London in the car she'd hired to fetch him.

"This father's name was Mr Charles Johnson, and he's very rich. He had a yacht moored off the Isle of Wight, and his crew brought it to a place off the coast of Essex where we could be fetched in the yacht's little boat. Mr Johnson took me there in his car, then he sent the driver away with his car on his own. It was very dark by then. No one knew where I was, and Mr and Mrs Rufus wouldn't be able to kill me, which I think they would have done. I had already called my parents in Italy. That was to stop them looking for me."

He broke off and asked if he could have some water. The usher poured some into a fresh glass.

"Mr Johnson put me on his crew list and took me to the South of France, Monaco, and Northern Italy, because there are lots of Italian-looking people there. We didn't know how long I'd be on his yacht, but I felt safe there because his crew protected me, and Deborah had said she'd do what she could to move things along in England. Then Mr Johnson was arrested by the English police, and I was taken back with him. Mr Johnson is being held by the police – I think in London, but I'm not sure – and I've been put into a house in London that belongs to the London police. They brought me here this morning."

"And this lady you saw on the footpath – was she using a laptop?"

"Yes, Ma'am. She was working the keyboard and watching the Maserati, just as I would have done. It was a grey-white one, an Apple."

Tait said this was all very important information. Had Pachini spoken to Essex Police about it?

"I think so, it was while we were still in Monaco. Someone phoned one of the policemen who arrested Mr Johnson, and he passed his phone to me. This person said he was helping Essex Police, and he asked me lots of questions. I told him what I'm saying now."

She thanked him and allowed him to stand down. Did Rufus want to question him or return to the witness stand himself? Rufus, who had been staring in horror at Pachini, turned to his legal adviser, and they whispered agitatedly across Rufus's escort. Finally, the legal adviser stood up and said his client would like to remain silent at this time. His client also wished to point out he'd said nothing that was factually incorrect.

Tait called Snape back to the stand.

"In the course of your enquiries, have you found a grey-white Apple laptop?" she asked.

He said he had, and a specialist had examined it. It had been programmed to capture the signals from the tracker on Mr Slade's Maserati, but it had also been programmed to access the Maserati's controls in the way Mr Daniel Chilvers had described in his report, a copy of which she had seen. The same laptop could perform both functions at the same time.

"In other words, someone could know where the Maserati was from the moving map and control it like a toy. Would that person have to be near the Roman road to do that?"

"No, Ma'am. They'd take a chance no one else was on the road at the time, but it was a reasonable chance to take, and a crash with another vehicle would likely have killed Mr Slade anyway. If not, there could always be another attempt on his life, perhaps not involving a motor vehicle. We can't rule that out."

She asked whether he accepted Pachini's identification of the lady on the footpath. And the laptop the police had found, did he know who it belonged to?

"We're making good progress on both points, Ma'am. We expect to lay a charge of murder shortly."

"Do you know who tampered with the Maserati's firmware?"

"We're hopeful for testimony to clarify that."

Tait asked him to stand down and addressed the court.

"Under Rule 25, Sub-section 4, of the Coroners' Inquest Rules 2013, I have to adjourn my court and notify the Director of Public Prosecutions if it appears that the death of the deceased is likely to have been due to a homicide offence and that a person may be charged in relation to the offence. I rule that both conditions have been fulfilled, and I adjourn this court at this time."

The court lost its formality once Tait had withdrawn to her office. The public started to talk, Verity and Rufus broke into discussion with their legal advisers, and the media tried for personal interviews. As Snape was standing up, Verity's legal adviser caught his eye. Mrs Slade would like to speak to him in private, he said. And to Mr van Piet, if he wished to be present. Mrs Slade had seen him sitting at the back.

Snape used his authority to get the use of a side room and to have Verity's handcuffs removed. He'd take responsibility for her, he told her police escort, and they waited outside with Verity's legal adviser, since she didn't want him in the room with her. For all her exhaustion, Verity did her best to look self-possessed as she prepared herself to speak. She'd worked out in advance what she was going to say and how she was going to say it.

"As long as I did not know what suffering was," she began, "I was happy for others to suffer for my beliefs. That changed when my husband died. It changed further after my daughter's death, in part thanks to you and Mr van Piet. And now I have had to relive my husband's death at length and under questioning, it has changed completely.

"I have always acted with integrity, and because of that, I can see now that I am obliged to make amends. I shall inform the Coroner some of things I said in her court were misleading, and I shall co-operate fully with the police. I should prefer to

379

wait till Friday for that, since tomorrow I shall bid my husband a final farewell, and that will try me hard. I shall be the only person present when his last journey begins, apart from the officiating clergyman and my police escort." She allowed herself a thin smile. "I have to accept the police are part of my life these days."

She looked from Snape to van Piet. They were happy for her to keep talking, so she did.

"I suspect you saw from an early stage that my love for my husband, even more than my love for my daughter, was the chink in my armour. Certainly one of you did."

Van Piet said they'd never doubted her grief. She nodded knowingly and turned back to Snape.

"I still hold to my beliefs, Mr Snape, because they're right, but I didn't see until it was too late that the price to be paid for them should have an upper limit. I wish I had, and I'm sorry. That's all I wish to say for the moment. I shall add more later."

In the coroner's court light refreshments room, van Piet and Snape ordered a coffee each and sat down to pick over the inquest. Van Piet wondered where Verity had got her clothes and shoes from with The Lodge burned down.

"She's got more shopping accounts than I've got grey hairs, so we let her ring round. And we arranged for her bank to release the money, since we've impounded all her cards."

Snape went back to his coffee. A little later, he said,

"Rufus pretty much told us the truth about Pachini, didn't he? Davis too. It was a good way to hide the fact they intended to murder him. What put you onto Charles Johnson?"

"I thought, if someone wanted Pachini dead because he knew too much, someone else might want him alive for the same reason. He'd make a handy weapon, if he was managed right."

"So Johnson or Watkins as manager, then. Or both of them together."

"That's how it turned out. Watkins used the football to get to know Pachini, and she seemed to have got on well with Charles Johnson, who, so she told us, focused on his son after his wife upped and left him. Anyway, I had Johnson's yacht located. Sure enough, Pachini was on it, and the word was, the whole crew was armed to the teeth except for him. Davis and Verity likely also worked out where he was, and presumably they also worked out he wouldn't be talking to the law in a hurry, since there was a very obvious reason why he wouldn't. That bought them time, but it wouldn't last forever, so maybe they were waiting for him to go back to his parents, where he'd be less protected. Then they could shut him up for good.

"I wanted to talk to him myself, but not while we were feeling our way forward in case he leaked we'd been in contact. But then Watkins was killed, and that blew things wide open, so I had Johnson arrested, and Pachini was told he'd be safer coming back with him than staying where he was without the guv'nor on board. Did you make him late for the inquest, by the way?"

"No, the traffic saw to that. I have to say it did us a favour for once."

They heard the sound of heels tapping briskly on the easy-clean floor and glanced round. Tait had seen them and was coming over to talk to them. She had a slot of time before her next inquest.

"Did it work?" she asked as she sat herself down. She'd brought a cup of tea with her. "I heard Mrs Slade wanted to speak to you both in private."

She was looking at van Piet as she spoke, but he deferred to Snape, who said,

"She made a speech like someone going to the block on Tower Hill, but she also promised to tell all, and I think that's what she'll do. I hope so, anyway, she's the jewel in the crown. Thanks for nagging away at her," he added. "It could all have gone wrong if you hadn't."

Tait gave him her Gorgon look.

"I went by the book, Eddie, no more, no less. I call my witnesses, explain their rights and options, and take it from there. If that's worked to your advantage, that's good news, but that's all there was to it, as you know very well. Will Mr Pachini be charged? He kept quiet for a very long while."

"Unlikely, we're saying he acted under duress. We want him on our side when we prosecute."

"What about Mr Johnson?"

"His lawyers are claiming he acted on humanitarian grounds, and the CPS is doing its best to agree. We don't want him queering Pachini's pitch, so we'll agree as well. The Monégasques might do something about his mooring rights, since all his crew except Pachini carried guns, but I can't see too much else happening. What about you, Willem?"

Van Piet put his coffee down.

"If Watkins was alive, we could ask her how involved he was in her plans and see what answer we got. But she isn't, so yes, he'll get away with it."

"What if she's left something dire in her solicitor's safe? She might have, for all we know."

The NCA's enquiries had got nowhere, and no one had responded to two media appeals. The solicitor was probably on holiday. No shoes, no news – it happened every August.

"Whatever it is, it won't stick, Eddie, his lawyers will see to that. Justice can't be bought in this country, but a good defence can, and as Pachini said, Charles Johnson is a very rich man. You might as well accept it and let him go right now. It will save you a lot of trouble, and the tax-payer a lot of money. Prisons are expensive places to keep people in."

Chapter 34

All passion spent

The following Friday, van Piet took an early-morning underground to Canary Wharf. It was a golden day, the forecast was good for the weekend, and he was looking forward to a wake-up coffee with an old friend, Harry Brennon, who'd worked for Barclays Bank when Verity and Geoffrey Slade had been there. Barclays had its headquarters in One Churchill Place, a 512′ steel and glass tower with thirty-two floors. But van Piet preferred a Colombia coffee shop near the underground station. It was an environment he could control.

The coffee shop's through-put was non-stop at that time of day, and as van Piet was putting his change in his wallet, a small table on what passed for a forecourt emptied, so he moved out smartly and claimed it before anyone else could. Three minutes later, Brennon showed up and took the other chair. Brennon had been with Barclays all his working life. Like Taylor at the *Standard*, he suspected there was more to van Piet than banking, but unlike Taylor, he'd never tried to find out what it was. He'd always assumed if he knew, he'd never be able to speak freely to him again.

Brennon was just back from a month-long furlough in New York with Barclays Bank USA, so there was lots to gossip about, and then van Piet steered things round to the Slades. He gave his usual roundabout reason for asking about them.

"Geoffrey Slade was murdered I gather," Brennon mused, sitting back to make the most of the sunshine. "I picked up some of the inquest reports online. And Verity's accused of shooting her own daughter. I have to say, Willem, they're not the Slades I knew."

So how were they when he knew them?

"Young, sparky, keen as mustard. Geoffrey joined us first, and everyone liked him, then Verity came along, and everyone liked her too. They were in back offices from the start, and they couldn't learn enough. They stayed with us till just after they got married, then Verity founded Esklivia, and off they went. She used a bequest from her father to get it started, or so she said. I knew he'd been killed skiing off-piste in Austria, so it figured, but being curious by nature, I checked his will when it was published, and sure enough, he left her just enough to make it happen, provided things picked up fast. Which they did."

Van Piet suggested they'd have access to customers' accounts if they were in back offices.

"Come off it, Willem, you know they would – deposit, current, credit card, you name it. You could move around in those days, and that's what they did."

"What were they like socially? Were they easy to get along with?"

"As easy as you like, but you could tell Verity was the tough one. I guess that's why they fell for each other. She knew where she was going, and he liked being steered."

A taxi to Ashell House came next. The operations room had moved down a gear, and after a quick look in to say he was on site, van Piet went down the stairs to his office, where Garry and Snape were waiting for him. The info Watkins had posted to Taylor had been intercepted, van Piet had seen a copy, and he wanted to discuss it with Snape before they talked to Verity. Chiefly, however, he wanted to take Snape through the Capricorn data GCHQ had been feeding through.

As Garry screened through the accounts, Snape took in the usual big money being shunted out of the reach of the Revenue, but he also kept seeing one small account after another with equally small commission and management charges. There were plenty of small loans at favourable rates as well. Van Piet could see Snape was surprised. He'd have been surprised himself if he hadn't been expecting it.

"Did you ever wonder why the Slades should be interested in a country vet with no money?" he asked Snape as he was making some tea. "You'd think they'd stick to the big guys."

"Ashley Johnson, you mean? Five Willows was a good bet, Willem. Given time, he'd have done all right there."

"He'd never have been really rich, though, so there might be another answer. Can you sort the data by profession, Tom? Stay in the middle income range."

Garry obliged, and there they were: Vets, teachers, doctors, lawyers, air traffic controllers, scientists, officers in the forces, Members of Parliament – it was a long list.

"When the Slades were at Barclays," van Piet commented, "they had access to the accounts of any number of people like these. They were spread out through society, they were respectable, and a lot of them were key personnel. Most of their accounts would be solid, but some would show signs of struggle, and some would show a fondness for the good life. From a Russian point of view, the last two sorts would be the ones that mattered, and my guess is, the Slades made sure they got told about them.

"But the data we're looking at now aren't from a bank, they're from a company that exists to evade taxes, and most of its customers are either cheating the Revenue or they've got cheap loans they don't want to see cancelled. So as I see it, Esklivia's a honey trap without the sex. The Russians can put the bite on these people any time they like, and a fair number of them must have found that out already. That's one reason every account on Esklivia's books is being taken apart. The scope for subversion is major."

Snape could see all that, but where did Davis and the rest fit in? And why was Ashley Johnson murdered? He turned the Slades away, didn't he?

Van Piet tilted back in his chair.

"Verity can tell you all that better than I can. Is she still willing to see us?"

"She was when I phoned her earlier this morning."

"Then I suggest we go and hear what she's got to say. We don't want her to have second thoughts."

He asked Garry to book a car and driver for them, since the car that had brought Snape to London had gone back to Essex. Garry was staying behind in Ashell House. He was on an ad hoc committee to remove all traces of the SRO from any data that might end up in court. He had Davis's and Kett's travel patterns to finalise as well.

"Send me a text when you've sorted the travel patterns out," van Piet told him. "But don't do it before the tea's brought in for Mrs Slade. You can find out when that is from the desk."

He unfolded his copy of Watkins's info.

"You can see why she was so excited," he said to Snape, tapping it with his forefinger. "She dropped Clive Taylor in it very nicely as well. It's a shame about her, really. She was quite bright in her way – just not bright enough, and that cost her."

There are twelve women's prisons in England, and all of them were either full or unsuitable for prisoners accused of murder, so Verity, Anita Rufus and Cottrell were all being held in individual cells in Chelmsford Police Station. Snape didn't like it, but there was nothing he could do about it. To make things go smoothly he'd booked a Confidential Room to talk to Verity in - it would be less intimidating than one of the Interview Rooms. When she was brought in, she was wearing dark clothes again, with no jewellery or a wristwatch, and her absence of make-up made her look even more like an actress in street clothes than she had in Tait's court. The room's furniture was sparse, the ceiling light was on because it had to be, and the high window in the outer wall was barred, but the easy chairs were soft, and the walls had recently been painted a calming eggshell blue. Van Piet and Snape stood up as she came in. She held her hands out so her handcuffs could be removed, and Snape asked her escort to wait outside. A Confidential Room was for private conversations between prisoners and their legal advisers, he explained, so would Verity mind a stenographer writing down what they said in shorthand, since there was no recording apparatus installed? Verity said she wouldn't, so Snape put his head round the door and asked for someone to find Peggy Dougal. Mr van Piet would do most of the talking, he told Verity. He wasn't police, as she knew. That should make things easier for her.

They sat down in a rough circle, and a gentle knock on the door announced Dougal's arrival. She was a well-rounded, middle-aged lady with a big warm smile and a taste for floral dresses. She sat down in an easy chair nearer one of the walls, opened her first note pad and held her pencil poised to say she was ready. Snape gave the date and the time, said who was present and asked Verity to confirm she was waiving her right to have a legal adviser present, which she did. Then he handed over to van Piet, who began by saying the police were aware of a connection between Esklivia Investments and Russia. Was Mrs Slade already Russia-friendly when she joined Barclays? She said she was, although the phrase was Soviet-friendly in those days. She'd deliberately chosen to work at Barclays. She'd wanted to fight capitalism because it was wrong, so she needed to know what its weak points were. Slade wasn't politicised then, but she'd soon made him see things as she did.

So how did she make her first contact with the Russians? Or was it the other way round?

"I was in Lausanne on a Young Bankers' conference. The Russians were there – being in Switzerland, it was easy for them to get there - and I made contact for both of us. A whole host of Barclays' customers were blackmailed or bribed after that, and Barclays never found out. You can see why the Russians liked us."

Van Piet thought Barclays was Phase One in her career, and Esklivia was Phase Two.

"Esklivia looked like a conventional way for you to earn large sums of money," he suggested, "but it was really a data-harvester for your Russian friends. You made it look clean by starting it with a bequest, but I'll bet the Russians put enough trade your way to make sure it didn't fold."

"Of course they did. They were involved all along."

Van Piet recalled what Kossler had said about running computers offline. If personnel managers could do it, so could tax-evaders. It was worth a try.

"By the time you and Mr Slade bought The Lodge, you must have acquired some customers who were so obviously criminal, it was dangerous to keep them on Esklivia's in-house computers. Was that why the boulting house was built? To house computers you could run offline?"

Verity said it was. It protected Laura as well, since she had no access to them, and it was built to be super-secure.

Phase Three – the phase that concluded with Kett's arrest - must have evolved over time, van Piet thought, and he went on to detail how he believed Kett's money had been raised.

"It was a logical development, Mr van Piet. After Esklivia had become a success, we wanted to run our own agent, and our Russian friends were in favour. I increased Geoffrey's and my income from Esklivia, and when Millie Cottrell joined us, I made sure her salary would stay high, even if she made regular withdrawals. It was all dry land swimming at first. We had no way of knowing who our agent would be or how we'd recruit him or her, we just had this good idea and the means to make it work."

"But you finished up with a cell funding Dr Kett."

"That's how it was. Millie told us she'd studied with Jesse – we'd never heard of him till she mentioned him - and she'd stayed in touch with him since. She said he liked casual sex if he didn't have to put himself out for it, so I asked her to make herself available to him, which she did. She hated it, it was against her nature, and she stopped as soon as she could, but she did it for me until Jesse was one of us. It was a pilot project to begin with, but it worked so well, it took on a life of its own."

Van Piet asked whether Kett used the computers that were already in the boulting house.

"No, he needed much higher performance ones, and our Russian friends supplied them to keep them out of my accounts. Jesse used them to build a Command-and-Control unit that could paralyse large sections of British infra-structure. They were a tight fit in there, but we managed."

"And Dr Kett stayed offline. It must have been like setting up an ambush."

Thanks for the phrase, Ian.

"That's a good comparison. He did his tests on his computers at work and saved mine for setting things up. That was one of the pluses of living in the country. If I switched the cctv off, he could come and go as he pleased, and no one was any the wiser. The same applied to my office in London. He came there when he didn't need a computer. It meant he wasn't always coming to the same place."

"So things were rolling along nicely, but there were two flies in the ointment, weren't there. One was Deborah Watkins, and the other was Mr Slade."

Verity's face clouded, but she didn't disagree. Van Piet told her how he'd come to hear Watkins's name in Five Willows.

"As it happened, I already knew who she was. Before she moved to Five Willows, she was a financial journalist, and she hacked into the computers of Van Piet Banking looking for a story. There was, in fact, no story to find, but we discovered what she was doing, because she was still learning how to hack, and we sent her on her way. Shortly after Mr Slade was killed, she told Mr Snape and myself that you and your husband had visited her and her fiancé in Five Willows. She also told us she'd gone into Esklivia's computers to find out more about you, but she hadn't found anything suspicious, so she hadn't taken things further.

"However, we now believe that wasn't true. I don't know what she discovered about Esklivia, but I think it was big enough for her to keep looking, even though she was no longer a front-line journalist. I also think you found out about it, because her hacking still wasn't perfect. As a precaution, she was keeping her discoveries in a safe place, and when you tackled her, she said, if anything happened to her, everything would go to the police. That was her protection, and worse yet from your point of view, she continued to find out everything she could about you and your organisation. Have I got that right?"

Verity nodded, but she didn't say anything. She could guess what was coming next.

"The police couldn't discover anything to account for Ashley Johnson's murder because there wasn't anything to discover, and that raised the possibility the attack wasn't against him, it was against Miss Watkins. You couldn't afford to kill her, so you did the next best thing – you killed her fiancé in the hope it would hit her so hard, she'd leave your affairs alone. Was killing him your idea? And have I got the motive right?"

"It was Geoffrey's idea, but he wouldn't follow it up." She looked straight at van Piet, and he saw her swell in self-esteem. "I did it, Mr van Piet, I took it upon myself. And yes, you've got the motive right. I congratulate you."

So Geoffrey Slade hadn't been so nice after all. Just soft.

A knock at the door startled all four of them. Snape opened it fractionally, then further, to allow in a canteen assistant with a trolley of tea things. Verity had been looking weary, but after the tea and the break that went with it, she was eager to start talking again. Van Piet had seen it before, and so had Snape. Once the barriers fall, telling tales becomes a pleasure. But she was definitely flagging.

"Ashley Johnson's murder didn't go as planned, did it, Mrs Slade?" van Piet recommenced, and Dougal began a new note pad. "Miss Watkins

393

recognised you, and from that moment on she wanted revenge by having your daughter killed. An eye for an eye, so to speak, and you could do nothing about it. It took her a long while - her patience must have been monstrous – and it meant going back to her old job so she could really find things out about you, but finally she got the breaks she needed. One of them could have been Mr Slade's political sympathies. Did they change to the point where he was supporting Ukrainian nationalists?"

Verity looked downright annoyed.

"Geoffrey had a thing about patriotism I could never get out of him, and I must ask you to believe I tried hard enough. Land of Hope and Glory brought tears to his eyes, so did Americans singing The Star-spangled Banner or French people singing the Marseillaise. So when President Putin reclaimed the Crimea for Russia, as he had every right to do, it upset Geoffrey enormously. I thought it would pass in time, I'd seen these outbreaks before, but early last January, after he'd come back from a business trip to Prague, he defected. I expect he'd been talking to someone as usual. Anyway, Millie Cottrell had been hacking into his computers since she joined Esklivia because I'd asked her to. She found a secret e-mail he'd sent and, of course, she told me all about it. Geoffrey wanted to contribute to some kind of Ukrainian fighting fund, that was how much it had got to him."

Van Piet leaned forward.

"Did Miss Watkins find that out as well?"

"It's perfectly possible. Likely even, knowing her. Why do you ask?"

"It seems she was also hacking into at least one of Mr Slade's computers, because last February she

394

made contact with him in a place some way away from here, and we're sure it wasn't coincidence. He didn't seem to like it at first. Then we think he did."

Verity said it was news to her, but it didn't surprise her, Watkins had simply taken advantage of him. Geoffrey was sociable by nature, it was a weakness he had.

"I know what you're going to say," she went on, "so I'll say it for you. Once we knew Geoffrey had defected, he had to die. The problem was, how to kill him without putting our organisation at risk. There was no easy answer to that, so the worry dragged on and on."

"Until he decided to buy a Maserati," van Piet supplied. "Was it Miss Cottrell who told you how you could kill him with it?"

Verity said it was, she'd never have thought of it herself. Rufus and Cottrell set it all up, just as Pachini described in court, and Cottrell did the hacking with the grey-white Apple laptop. Neville Thurston was meant to destroy it, but clearly he didn't.

"Who tampered with the car's firmware? Was it Mr Pachini?"

"Pachini? Good heavens, no! He was only a mechanic, even if Derek called him an engineer. It was Millie and Derek, they did it between them one evening. And they expected the crash to destroy the evidence. It all seemed foolproof at the time."

"So Mr Slade never knew you'd found him out. Or that your reluctance to see him buy the Maserati was a well-organised charade."

"No, and I'm glad he didn't." She was earnestly clenching her fingers. "By letting him believe I knew nothing, I created a space in which we could go on loving each other. I even suggested he install the control on my smartphone that would detonate the explosives in the boulting house. I'd asked Neville Thurston to put them in as a culpably belated response to Geoffrey's defection – belated because I hadn't thought of it sooner - and there was Geoffrey making sure they'd go off properly."

So Verity killed Thurston with his own explosives, did she?

"Certainly. I had my reasons for wanting him dead. I have no regrets at all."

"He helped you kill Ashley Johnson, the police have strong evidence for that. Did Miss Watkins recognise him as well as you?"

Verity gave a cynical laugh. Her contempt for Thurston was total.

"No, he was far too eager to get away. I should have been as fast, but I wasn't. I'm sure Deborah came to suspect him, but that's not the same as knowing, is it, and I was happy to leave her in doubt. It sounds small-minded, but it made me feel I was getting some of my own back."

Van Piet's mobile buzzed. He frowned and apologised for checking, but it might be important. It was the text from Garry. He read it quickly, then he returned his attention to Verity. He could see she was tired, he said, but could they clear up one small point about Watkins's murder? He must have signalled something unpleasant was coming, because Verity looked suddenly wary. But she told him to go ahead.

He took her back to the inquest.

"Miss Watkins found out Mr Pachini knew more than he should have about your husband's Maserati, so she and Charles Johnson whisked him away just as you were poised to have him killed. But

396

she didn't use him against you, Mrs Slade, although she could have done, she just sort of kept him in reserve, and Mr Pachini was happy with that, because he felt he was in good hands. The point was, telling the police wouldn't put Laura in Miss Watkins's clutches, and that was what she was really after. Am I right about that?"

"We think alike, Mr van Piet. Once we found out where Pachini was, we thought we could wait till Deborah showed her hand, then we could trick her somehow, so we could kill her without putting ourselves at risk. Pachini as well, once he was back in Parma, since threatening to damage his parents might not be enough to keep him quiet. But you've got something else on your mind, haven't you. Something quite different."

It was if she had to make him say what she absolutely didn't want to hear.

Van Piet nodded.

"Laura wanted her father's death cleared up," he said, hoping she wouldn't break off before he was done, "and it's my belief she gathered from Miss Watkins that if she murdered her, the truth would emerge from Miss Watkins's cache of notes."

"She could always have asked her. It would have been much easier."

"Not if she was afraid she'd be hoodwinked, and she'd have more than one reason for that, including what you say in your blacklist. We've been reading smartphones, you see. But actually to commit that murder, well, that must have taken some doing. What do you think the tipping point was?"

Too fatigued to control herself, Verity blushed, and because she wasn't wearing make-up, it showed.

397

"I'm afraid I don't have that knowledge," she said, dry-mouthed and abruptly evasive. She took a deep breath and sat rigidly upright. "I've kept my word and helped you as much as I can, but now I've reached my limit. I'd like to go back to my cell, please."

The handcuffs went on, and as she was escorted out, she avoided eye contact with van Piet. The shame she thought had died with Laura had sprung back to life. Snape dictated the time of Verity's exit to Dougal, who closed her note pad and followed him out. Van Piet left last and shut the door.

"So what was in Tom's text?" Snape asked.

They were in the canteen of Chelmsford Police Station. The SRO car had gone back to London, so they were waiting for local transport.

"Information. He'd worked out how Davis, Verity Slade and Kett must have run their little trade in secrets. Look, I'll show you."

He took out a biro, smoothed a serviette, and listed the points one by one.

"First, Kett gets his briefing in Bonn. It could be from Uncle Friedrich, or from a Russian agent visiting Schaabstrasse 21, or from the safe outside Barbara Winckler's flat, it was always a choice of three. He then gets the data the Russians want, plus any he thinks they might want, Verity puts the money together, and they meet in Esklivia House, where the attaché cases get swapped. Kett fades away till the next time, Verity gets the data to Davis, and Davis takes them to her parents in Brighton, who hand them on to an entirely different Russian agent. Neat, isn't it?"

398

Snape put the serviette in his pocket. He'd copy it into his notebook later.

"It wasn't an urgent message. Why did you ask Tom to buzz it in when you did?"

"I wanted an unguarded reaction from Verity. The tea break interrupted her self-control, Tom's message interrupted it some more, and by that time she was always going to be struggling anyway." He paused. "I got what I wanted and I'm glad about it. It was a personal thing for me."

"How so?"

"Verity will answer for all the times she's broken the law, the courts will see to that, but they won't make her answer for what she did to Laura, and I think she should. She destabilised Laura badly when she had her father murdered, but to my mind, what sent Laura completely off the rails was what she saw or heard in Esklivia House when she was spying on her mother. That was just a week after her father's death, don't forget. Verity said Cottrell stopped servicing Kett as soon as she could, but she didn't say whether anyone else took over, and I think Verity did. I also think Laura witnessed her at it, and Watkins's photos told Verity what had happened. That's why Verity blushed and broke the session off just now – with Laura dead, it was all part of the past, but then I came along, and she realised I had her secret. I deliberately re-opened a wound this afternoon. I hope it stays open."

One of the canteen assistants came over: Mr Snape's car was waiting outside. Snape was going back to Police HQ. He'd got his key witness in Verity Slade, now he had to explain to Parnaby why he'd kept information back from him. He also wanted to sort out what to do about Oliver Rufus.

"He's been told what's happened, and his uncle and aunt are bringing him back next Wednesday. No one knows what will happen after that. He's fifteen, poor kid, and his aunt says he's all over the place. I'll get Social Services onto it."

He was truly angry now.

"These people," he went on. "These Rufuses, Slades and the rest. They think they're lords of the universe, but all they do is foul up their own lives, and everyone else's as well."

Van Piet agreed. There was the damage the Slades and their cell had done over time, and the damage Kett had set himself up to do as soon as his Russian friends asked him to. It wouldn't be easy to sort that lot out, and it wouldn't be cheap either. But it had to be done.

Van Piet walked down to the lobby with him.

"We never did find out what that book code was based on," Snape said as he signed out for both of them.

"It'll be in Davis's house, all you have to do is make a list of her books and let me have it. I'll ask Ian Kossler to do the rest. Any news about Watkins's solicitor?"

"Yes, at long last. He's a one-man law firm in Norfolk. His wife is his secretary and clerk, and they'll be back next Tuesday - from Nepal of all places. Needless to say, he didn't have a clue what was going on when the NCA finally contacted him."

"How did they get onto him?"

"Watkins used to drive up to see him, and that wasn't so clever."

"Why not?"

"There's been a lot of roadbuilding in Norfolk over the years, and she's on all the roadworks cameras. The rest was police work for beginners."

"So it's all coming good, is it?"

"That's what it looks like, especially now Verity's crossed the line. You were right, she was the one to break. She and her friends are a nasty lot. It'll be good to nail them."

"You won't really need Watkins's notes to do that, will you? Not with Verity chirping away."

"I suppose not." He managed a tired laugh. "Verity and her friends were scared stiff of them, Laura Slade seems to have murdered for them, and now we're saying they don't really matter that much. There must be a logic in there somewhere. You can explain it to me when I've got a free hour."

Snape disappeared to Police HQ, and van Piet called a taxi on his smartphone. When it arrived, he told the driver to take him to the Haywards' toy shop on Clacton front. He wasn't the least sure he was doing the right thing, but he felt, if he could talk to the Haywards face to face, he might be able to help them till they could sort themselves out. After that, he'd go back to the Hall. There was his Lisbon report to get out of the way, Célestine and Jackie were coming home Sunday, and Monday was August bank holiday. It was time to move on.

Acknowledgements

A well-penned article by Richard Lloyd Parry, Asia Editor for *The Times*, recalled the existence of book codes for me. And when I wrote about Kensington Palace Gardens, I drew on an equally well-penned article first published in *The Guardian* and titled 'What is it like to live on Britain's most expensive street?' It was written by Amelia Gentleman. My thanks to both these journalists.

My thanks, too, to Terence R. Onions, HM Senior Coroner's Officer to HM Coroner for Gloucestershire, who was kind enough to answer several questions about coroner's court procedure for me. I should say straight away that I've adapted that procedure to my own purposes, so any departures from orthodoxy are mine. And Hettie Tait, like all the other characters in this book, is an entirely fictional creation.

Colin Butler.

Printed in Great Britain
by Amazon